W9-BXL-219

THE LEGEND OF
Holly Claus

"'The Book of Forever,'" she read, "'Being the
Immortal Deeds of the Inhabitants of Our Land from
the Beginning of Time.'"

THE LEGEND OF
Holly Claus

BRITTNEY RYAN

with illustrations by Laurel Long

The Julie Andrews Collection

HarperCollins*Publishers*

MCLEAN MERCER
REGIONAL LIBRARY
BOX 505
RIVERDALE, ND 58565

The Legend of Holly Claus
Text and illustrations copyright © 2004
by Brittney Ryan
All rights reserved. No part of this book may be used or repro-
duced in any manner whatsoever without written permission
except in the case of brief quotations embodied in critical arti-
cles and reviews. For information address HarperCollins
Children's Books, a division of HarperCollins Publishers, 1350
Avenue of the Americas, New York, NY 10019.
www.harperchildrens.com

Library of Congress Cataloging-in-Publication Data
Ryan, Brittney.
   The legend of Holly Claus / Brittney Ryan ; with illustrations by Laurel Long.— 1st ed.
      p.   cm. — (The Julie Andrews collection)
   Summary: Santa Claus's daughter, Holly, comes to Earth
seeking an end to the curse cast upon her and the Land of
the Immortals by an evil wizard whose own punishment will
end only if Holly willingly gives him her pure heart.
   ISBN 0-06-058511-0 — ISBN 0-06-058514-5 (lib. bdg.)
   [1. Princesses—Fiction. 2. Magic—Fiction. 3. Santa
Claus—Fiction. 4. Wizards—Fiction. 5. Kings, queens, rulers,
etc.—Fiction. 6. Fairy tales.] I. Long, Laurel, ill. II. Title. III.
Series.
PZ8.R899Le 2004   2003025578
[Fic]—dc22   CIP
                                                                      AC

Typography by Larissa Lawrynenko
2 4 6 8 10 9 7 5 3 1
❖
First Edition

To all the children of the world—
may this book awaken the dream inside.

—B.R.

List of full-page
ILLUSTRATIONS

GRATITUDE

Holly Claus has Forever been in my heart, from the earliest days when my Grandmother Gaga told me stories of lands far away. Holly's legend became a book because of the support of many special people. My heart will Forever be grateful to Annie Barrows and Paddy Calistro, who guided me through this process. My thanks and love go to Laurel Long, whose artistry is as magical as Forever. I will Forever be grateful to Julie Andrews and Blake Edwards and the wise and wonderful Dr. John Hertz for their amazing belief in Holly and me. No words can express my thanks to Dusty Deyoe for her network of love and her incredible heart. And thanks to Chaplain Johnny Probst for his loving prayers.

The Legend of Holly Claus has inspired many people. Each of them believed in my dream and I will remember them Forever: Peter Koral, Maureen Horn, Emma Walton Hamilton, Tony Adamson, and Richard Tyler. Vivien Kooper, Katherine Tegen, and all the other talented people at HarperCollins; Randy Fields, Ed Abraham, Jonathan Arno, Rhett Butler, Dr. Lew Graham, Robert

Seidenglanz, Lee Winkler, and Norby Zuckerman. My heartfelt thanks go to our friends at Highline Entertainment—Bruce Wisner, Brad Spitzer, and Steven Aaronoff.

I am grateful to my mother, Sally Ryan Ashley, and my son, Ryan, for their love and belief in me. Sister Ignatia Anne and Sister Beverly Miles inspired me to follow my dreams as an artist, and I have never forgotten their words.

And most of all I thank God for the gift of this story. And the little Angel who whispered in my ear.

—B.R.

Prologue

New York City, 1878

I**T HAD ONCE BEEN** *a grand house, but not now. The ballroom, where ladies in pink and blue satin dresses had whirled on the arms of musta-chioed gentlemen, was gone, and in its place there were three apartments. The rooms had been divided, and then divided again, until the whole of that grand house was filled with tiny slots overflowing with children who didn't quite get enough to eat, mothers who scrimped and made do, and fathers who left before dawn and came back long after dark.*

Ten-year-old Christopher, alone in a sliver of an apartment near the top of the house, was wholly absorbed in the smooth wood in his hands, his eyes fixed on the creature he saw trapped inside the block. Steadily, precisely, he carved it out. Outside, the afternoon grew darker, and the icy rain began to fall. Inside, the sound of wailing babies and the sour smell of thin soup wafted through the flimsy walls. Absorbed in the magic of making, Christopher noticed none of it. He began to see pointed wings and ridiculous, triangular feet. A curving pull of the blade revealed a long, narrow beak. Sitting back in his chair, Christopher looked at his creation and laughed. It was the most peculiar bird he had ever seen.

Just then the sitting room door opened, and Christopher's mother stepped in quietly. Her shoulders hunched against the cold, but her face held the remnants of great beauty, chiefly in her enormous gray eyes. Now, unwinding the shawls that served her as a coat, she glanced at her son's intent face and, as if to ward away danger, she rested her hand upon his head for a moment. Then she rustled away to make supper in the dim corner they called the kitchen. She caught sight of a laboriously written letter and envelope lying near the chair and smiled at Christopher's familiar, awkward handwriting. Stooping to pick up the letter, she began to read.

Christopher's eyes were on his bird as he spoke. "Mother? What do you suppose I saw today over at

Stuyves—" He broke off when he saw the tears glistening on her face. "What's happened?" he asked anxiously.
"What is it?"

His mother shook her head. "Your letter, love. It's
your letter that makes me cry, but they aren't sad tears."
Her son looked at her doubtfully.

"The letter? But didn't you tell me that all children
write a letter to Santa Claus at Christmastime?" asked
Christopher. "Why would it make you cry?"

His mother dropped to her knees and looked searchingly in his eyes. "Tell me what you see in this room,"
she said.

Christopher looked around the sitting room. "A
wooden table. Your chair. A lamp, with a beautiful glass.
My books. Lots of books." He smiled. "You." He leaned
into his mother's arms.

"And it's enough, darling?" asked his mother in a
whisper.

Christopher looked at her questioningly. "Enough? I
don't understand," he answered slowly. "This is home.
This is where you are. It's more than just enough."

Without replying, his mother tightened her arms
around him and held him for a long time. Then she rose
to her feet, folding the letter carefully into its envelope
and slipping it into his pocket. "Mrs. Broder at the

bakeshop, my dear boy, has been kind enough to extend our account for another week," she said cheerfully. "Will you take the carriage to get a loaf of bread, or shall I send the butler?"

Christopher frowned judiciously. "The horses are getting fat and lazy, Mother. But so is the butler. He's an awful lazy fellow. So I suppose I had better go myself."

"And where's your scarf, then?" his mother said, catching him by the arm. "It's dreadfully cold." She could keep her voice cheerful, but her eyes betrayed her.

Christopher wound the woolen muffler around his neck. "I'll be fine. It's a very warm scarf. I'll put it over my head if I get cold," he said, watching his mother's face. "I promise."

"Don't forget to post your letter," called his mother, as the door closed behind him.

He stood at the door, bracing himself for the cold. As he always did when he was trying to make himself feel brave, he reached into his coat pocket to touch his father's watch. It didn't matter that the watch hadn't worked in almost a year. It had stopped right after his father had died, and there was no money for repairs. His father could have done it; he had loved intricate mechanisms. Christopher stared into space, remembering

"But didn't you tell me that all children write a letter to Santa
Claus at Christmastime?" asked Christopher.

his father bent over a tiny, broken toy. Christopher wrapped his hand tightly around the watch; it was fine the way it was.

Oh, the cold. On the dark sidewalk, Christopher leaned into the wind, for he had learned that fearing the cold made it worse. You had to act as though you weren't cold. You had to step lively instead of huddling near the walls—

Christopher stopped, ignoring his own rules.

He wasn't cold.

He looked around him; there were all the people pushing past him, freezing. But he wasn't. Christopher looked up toward the Bowery, where the gaslights were gleaming, and then down at the teeming darkness of Second Avenue. By rights, his feet should have been turning numb, but no. Luxuriating in his comfort, Christopher walked to the postal box and dropped his letter in. All grew still for a moment. Suddenly, a great, golden wave of warmth rolled through him, a velvety liquid warmth that coursed from the top of his head to the tips of his toes. It had no source and no end, and, standing there in the dark, slushy street, Christopher knew that something extraordinary had just happened to him.

Chapter One

IN **FOREVER, THE LAND** of the Immortals, the first snowflake was always silver. Father Christmas watched it swirl and twist from the heavens. It lay, shimmering, on the great crystal stairs that led to the palace. And then the rest came, just a few at first, before dozens and hundreds and thousands spiraled through the air in a lacy ballet. Soon the stairs, the terrace, and the vast gardens beyond were cloaked in snow. The stone nymphs that lolled in the reflecting pool reached up their graceful stone arms and caught the feathery crystals in their palms. The bronze horses at the top of the clock tower touched noses and whinnied, shaking snow from their manes. And the trees on the avenue, usually so stiff and dignified, forgot themselves and swayed back and forth, their branches rippling in the white air.

Father Christmas—who is known to some as Nicholas Claus and to many as Santa Claus—flung open the window with a shout of exhilaration. Like new, every year. The jolt, the wide, brilliant burst of light that started the season each year. Yes, it was here! Impulsively, he leaned as far out of the window as he could and caught a handful of snowflakes. He spun around and hurled them wildly into the room.

"Ahem!" A sorrowful-looking goblin brushed the snow from his immaculate jacket.

"Oh! Melchior! Sorry, old friend, sorry!" called Nicholas jubilantly. "It's the first snow, Melchior, the first snow! And do you know what this means?" He clapped the goblin on the back, causing him to wince. "It means that the Christmas season has begun!"

"It means," said Melchior primly, "that there are letters to read and lists to make, and—"

"The letters? Are they here? Ah, Melchior, you know how much I love the letters." Nicholas's face softened. "That's where the magic really begins, isn't it? That's belief. When they write their letters, they're

*In Forever, the Land of the Immortals, the first
snowflake was always silver.*

believing in something they can't see, can't touch, can't hear. Even if it's just for a few minutes, they move beyond themselves, beyond their houses and food and finery. Don't you agree?" he said, turning toward the goblin.

"I'm sure I don't know," sniffed Melchior. "The dragons have delivered four hundred pounds of letters, and the bags are spilling all over the floor of the study."

"Melchior!" shouted Nicholas, thrusting his rosy face in front of the goblin's pale blue one.

"Yes-s-s, Your Majesty?" said Melchior.

"CHEER UP!"

"If you say so, Your Majesty," said Melchior mournfully, and limped out of the room.

"Goblins, goblins. What shall I do with the goblins?" muttered Nicholas to himself. "Weeping in corners all day long. But," he went on, brightening, "what would I do without the goblins? Good-hearted creatures, organized and efficient. Never been known to use their magic in the service of evil. Handy in the forest. Tidy. But glum. Every last one of them. Glum." Nicholas hitched his heavy velvet robe over his arm and strode down the long hallway to his study. On one side a row of windows showed him the whirling snowstorm outdoors; on the other a row of bright mirrors should have shown him the same. However, the twelve Boucane sisters had been up to their usual tricks and had transformed the mirror into a silvery sea for their own amusement. Nicholas didn't mind; he loved the Boucane sisters. Unlike the goblins, fairies were untidy and hopeless at household management. But they fluttered about on their tiny pink wings and made delicious mixtures of flower nectar and fruit juice, even though they never could remember how to make the same drink twice. Nicholas hurried on.

Melchior was right. The study was awash in letters. They were strewn over the thick rugs, piled in towering stacks upon the massive desk, tucked in the bookshelves, and heaped upon the soft chairs. There were elegant epistles in thick, creamy envelopes and raggedy scrawls on torn scraps of newspaper; there were letters from Lapland and La Paz, Ankara and Aachen, Copenhagen and Cooperstown. There was one particularly muddy bundle from California and a two-hundred-page missive from a large family of children in Edinburgh.

Nicholas sighed with satisfaction. He was ready: a lively fire crackled in the grate, and plump pillows beckoned him to his favorite chair. He settled back into cushions, noting that someone had thoughtfully filled his inkwell and arranged a vast scroll within easy reach. He stretched out his arm and plucked a letter at random from the nearest pile. Stiff, proper handwriting on the envelope, no extra rolls or flourishes. When he opened it, he found the staggering letters of a very small child. "Der ClaZ, Clarens has a hors. I want Won to. I Lov you. Miles." Smiling, Nicholas scribbled a note on the scroll.

"Dear Mr. Claus, I am taking up my pen in good health and hoping you are the same. Stella says you aren't real, but Mama says you are. Stella says I should ask you for a planet as a test, but that wouldn't be fair, I don't think, because no matter how good I am I can't have a planet all for my own self not even a little one. I would like a velocipede, but if I haven't been good enough for that, I would like another doll. Mary Blue, my other doll, drowned last summer, but I gave her a beautiful funeral and cried real tears. Stella says why would Santa Claus bring you a new doll when you threw the old one down the well, but I didn't. She fell. Hoping to hear of your continued prosperity and recovery of health, I am Your Very Sincere Friend, Molly. Stella says that's not the right way to end a letter, but it's in my book. If it isn't right, scratch it out." Nicholas shook with laughter as he turned to his scroll.

"Of course, she *did* throw that doll down the well, Your Highness," said a calm voice from the corner.

Nicholas glanced over to the speaker, a pure white wolf who lay, apparently asleep, on the thick, soft rug. "Of course she did," he agreed. "Banged her on the head first and then tossed her in."

"And the funeral, sire. She made the neighbor children pay to come."

Nicholas laughed harder. "Did she? That's my little Molly! Bless her soul." He thought for a moment. "It sounds as though we've lost Stella, though, Terra."

"Yes, Your Majesty," said the wolf quietly. She knew that it always hurt him when they stopped believing.

"But Molly, now; she'll be with us a long time," said Nicholas brightly. "Maybe she's one of the ones who will last forever." He reached for the next letter, but his mind lingered on Molly. How he would mourn the day she stopped writing to him. But no, he scolded himself, he would have the pleasure of watching her story unfold. And besides, that's how it had to be.

The carved clock ticked on through the afternoon. The snow whirled against the windows in
feathery plumes. The fire crackled and popped. Terra,
now truly asleep, sighed comfortably. Nicholas, bur-
rowed in his chair, read letter after letter. Many of
them made him smile; a few made him laugh out
loud; but each one was precious to him, for it told
him the story of a child he knew and loved. Kostya
was trying to be considerate of others and a new butterfly net would help; Astrid was certain she could be
good if only she had a set of paints; Santiago admitted that he had behaved terribly about the cat, but
regretted it and wanted some soldiers, please; Elena
and Concetta were bent on becoming pirates, so they
needed some books on the subject; Silas planned to
go west as soon as possible and would require a small
wagon. On and on it went, thousands of children,
each alive to possibility and dreams.

The door opened, and two bright blue eyes
peeked around the edge. "Tea?"

Nicholas looked up, pleased at the interruption.
"Viviana! Yes, of course, tea! Come in! Sit down!"
He waved his arms to indicate that she could have
any chair she pleased and then noticed that every
seat was covered with letters. "We'll find a spot,

my love! Come in!"

Viviana cleared a little place for herself near the desk. After deftly sweeping a pile of letters into an empty basket marked Correspondence, she placed a tray of tea and sandwiches on the desk and poured two steaming cups. Perched on the edge of her chair, she surveyed the letter-strewn study in silence. She removed one hairpin from her coil of auburn braids and jabbed it firmly back in place. Then she stood. "I'll just see if I can organize things a bit."

This was a ritual. Every year Viviana came into the study and brought order to the chaos, all the while tactfully pretending that Nicholas didn't really need her help in the least. Nicholas pretended not to notice as she bustled about the room. He bent his head over his letters, reading absorbedly, while she gathered up envelopes, retrieved letters from odd corners, and made neat stacks out of untidy heaps.

The dragons must have just *thrown* the bags into the room, Viviana thought, pulling a bundle of letters from under the sofa cushions. They always got over-excited by the first snow. She gazed around the room. She even spied a ragged envelope up on the picture frame. She pulled over a worn stool and climbed up to get it. From Sarajevo, she noted, glancing at the postmark. And what's that on the top of the clock? Good gracious. A very wet letter. Poor little thing must have written it in the rain. I'll just look under the carpet. I do hope none of these are left from last year—

A sudden hoarse sound interrupted her thoughts. She looked up, startled, and saw something she had not seen since her mortal life ended centuries before: her husband's tears. Tears were falling down Nicholas's cheeks. In his hands he held a thin sheet of paper, and as Viviana wrapped her arms around his shoulders, he silently held it up for her.

"Dear Santa Claus," it began. "You know I have never written. I could never think of anything I needed or wanted for Christmas. But this year I had a different idea. What do *you* wish for Christmas, Santa? You always answer children's wishes, but what about your own? Isn't there one thing in the world that you wish for but do not have? If you will post a letter back to me, I will do all that I can to bring your dream to life. Respectfully, Your friend, Christopher C."

"Well," said Viviana softly. "Well."

"No one—" Nicholas cleared his throat. "No one has ever asked me what I wish for."

"He's a very special boy, that's clear," said Viviana.

Then, gently, "Do you have a wish?"

"Me?" He looked at her in confusion. "Me?"

"Yes, you. You who give children their dreams. Do you remember your dreams?"

"Sometimes," said Nicholas slowly, his thoughts reaching back into lost time.

"Do you dream of a child?" Viviana whispered.

"A child?" Nicholas went still. Isn't there one thing in the world that you wish for but do not have? *That you wish for?* Yes, of course, of course! Like a great, golden wave of sunshine, a wish burst upon him in a shower of light. A child. He wanted a child, a child who would make their life complete, who would share the love that streamed between his heart and Viviana's. He looked with wonder at the letter that his wife held. How could he not have known? Astonishing, astonishing that this flimsy piece of paper with a child's scrawl had the power to change everything. Entwining his fingers with Viviana's, he looked across the cozy room to the snow-covered world outside and realized that this was a letter that would change the Land of the Immortals for all time.

Astonishing, astonishing that this flimsy piece of paper with a child's scrawl had the power to change everything.

Chapter Two

WHERE, YOU MIGHT ask yourself, is the Land of the Immortals? Don't bother to get up, for you won't find it in your atlas or spinning about on the globe. It's true that there are a few—a very few— maps that show this land. There was one in Amsterdam in 1459. And another in Madrid in 1622. But as soon as their existence is rumored, the maps seem to disappear. Only one person has ever claimed that he saw such a map. His name was Helvetius Erst, and because of him, one of the great legends of Christmas was born.

It all began on a cold March day in 1792, when Helvetius was seven. An old bookseller who lived nearby called the boy into his shop. With great ceremony he locked the door, closed the curtains, and swore the child to secrecy. Then he opened a massive wardrobe and pulled forth a glowing sheet of paper. Helvetius recalled later that it depicted a vast plain of ice: frozen seas encircling empty snowbound lands and towering glaciers. But there, in the middle of the white expanse, was a brilliant circle of green labeled *Terra Immortalium,* the Land of the Immortals. Helvetius asked many questions, but the old bookseller seemed to regret his impulse and quickly whisked the map away. Several days later he disappeared, taken, according to local gossips, by trolls. When the boy next returned to the shop, he found that the very bricks of the building had melted away into nothingness.

Helvetius Erst spent the next eighteen years trying to find the Land of the Immortals. Tantalizing rumors came his way: it was in the Himalayas, on the steppes of Siberia, sunk beneath the Caspian Sea, at the end of a bridge that appeared once each century on the northernmost crag of the Faeroe Islands. At long last he ventured into the Arctic Circle, pushing across hundreds of miles of ice in the hopes that one day he would see a thin slash of green breaking through the white. On and on he went, and though Helvetius Erst was still a young man, he began to appear as though he were sixty. Day after day he pressed on, until he was nearly blind from the dazzling glare of the sun on snow. He was nearly starving, because his food rations had dwindled to a bit more than nothing, and nearly crippled from the gnawing cold that deadened his feet until he could not walk. Finally, after weeks of trudging across a seemingly endless plain, Helvetius saw in the distance a shimmering purple mountain. He thought he had lost his mind. He fell facedown in the snow and began to weep, certain that he was doomed to wander, insane, until he died of starvation or cold. He covered his swollen eyes with his hands and howled. This is why he didn't hear the whisper of the sleigh running across the ice, nor the soft tinkle of the silver bells that hung from the reindeer's bridles. Helvetius knew nothing until he heard a gentle, reedy voice nearby.

"I told you, sire. A human."

"And you were right, Tundra. I don't know why I bother to doubt you," replied a rich, deep voice. Somehow hearing this voice made Helvetius Erst feel a bit less cold. "Poor fellow. Look at him. We shall have to revive him. Can you sit up, friend?"

Helvetius rolled over and looked up, overcome with wonder. Staring at him with kindly concern were a man with dark hair and a luxuriant beard and, even more astonishing, a large white wolf. "Who are you?" croaked Helvetius.

The man threw his long velvet cloak over his arm with a casual gesture. "We might ask the same of you, young man," he replied, "but, since you have inquired first, I'll begin. My name is Nicholas Claus, and I am the king of the land called Forever. This" —he waved grandly toward the wolf—"is Tundra, my guard, advisor, and friend."

"Thank you, Your Majesty," murmured the wolf.

"And now, my dear chap, you must tell us how you came here."

Helvetius had felt an unaccountable warmth spreading through his body. It seemed to be emanating from his stomach, or possibly his heart, but no matter where it was coming from, Helvetius was grateful. He leaned forward. "My name is Helvetius Erst," he began. "I came north, many months ago, I think, in search of a place called the Land of the Immortals."

Nicholas Claus looked at him keenly. "And where did you learn of this land?"

Slowly, Helvetius told him the story of the old bookseller and his glowing map.

"De Lusus, sire," said Tundra softly.

"Yes, of course. De Lusus never could keep a secret," agreed Nicholas. Then he turned toward Helvetius confidingly. "You see that purple mountain there, about six miles hence? It is not truly a mountain, but a glacier, a mantle of ice wrapped around a core of amethyst crystals. And it is not truly one glacier, but the outermost link in a chain of glaciers that encircles my kingdom—Forever, the Land of the Immortals. That's *Terra Immortalium* on your map. Each glacier in the chain is lit by a crystal core within, and each sends the glow of emeralds, rubies, sapphires, golden topazes, or soft opals throughout my land. But these mountains are not simply beautiful; they hold magic within them. No mortal may cross them. That's what you must understand, my boy."

Nicholas looked sympathetically at Helvetius. "You cannot enter. Even if you lived to reach that purple mountain, your legs would be unable to carry you farther. My kingdom is for those who have achieved immortality, and for them alone. Not even I have the power to alter that."

"But," Helvetius said longingly, "I am about to die. I know I am. I shall starve within a few days. Might I then attain Forever?"

"Oh, my dear fellow, I haven't made myself clear. Immortality is not merely what happens after your mortal life is over. It is more important than that. Immortality is what happens when love conquers time—when a person's ability to love others and to act in pure love and goodness stretches beyond death to live forever in the heart of the human race. Mortals who gave something precious to human history, who made the dreams and hopes of others come true— these are the ones destined for immortality." He looked toward the wolf. "Tundra, which of our people might be known to this boy?"

"I believe Robin Hood is well known in the mortal world, sire."

"Yes, yes, of course! Robin was a splendid mortal! The people of Nottingham were starving to death, and de Faucemberg sat eating roast pheasant on a silver plate. Not a particle of charity. So Robin took matters into his own hands. All that leaping out of trees gave him some fun, but in the end he managed to redistribute quite a lot of wealth. Never kept it for himself; gave it all away. You see? And thus, when his human span was finished, he came to live with us."

Helvetius nearly wailed, "But I shall never be a Robin Hood! I am no warrior. I shall never see the land that I have dreamed of all these years! I shall never—"

He stopped, arrested by the piercing gaze that Nicholas had turned upon him. The kind brown eyes were no less kind, but they revealed their owner's power. "Think, Helvetius. Think what you are saying. It is a failure of courage, and worse yet, a failure of love to relinquish your dreams so easily. Each of us holds within his soul the ability to conquer sorrow, fear, and misery with charity, compassion, and wisdom. If you truly wish to enter the Land of the Immortals, you must find a way to use what your soul knows." The stern eyes softened. "And you don't have to leap out of trees. We have many citizens whose names are not famous, whose works were known only to those who were saved by them. And these, too, attain immortality. If I were you," Nicholas added carefully, "I would reflect seriously upon the benefits that my travels could bring to others, say, in the area of maps."

"Well, yes, I suppose I could chart these polar

territories," said Helvetius, "but how could that help humankind?"

"It would save many lives that would otherwise be lost in the futile search for a shipping route over the top of the world. Just for example."

"I see, yes, that makes sense," said Helvetius, brightening. "There is no such passage, but they persist in looking for it."

"And the sailors perish for the merchants' greed," said Nicholas. "Now, dear chap, it's time I was getting back. Tundra, will you call the sled for this young man?"

The wolf raised his head and let out an echoing howl that seemed to shatter the chilled air into shards. A ripple of ancient fear stirred within Helvetius, and though he tried to hide it, he trembled.

"What's happening to this mortal, sire?" Tundra asked, looking at Helvetius's quivering hands.

Nicholas glanced at the young man. "He's frightened, Tundra. That's what it looks like to be frightened."

"Odd," murmured the wolf.

"We have no fear in Forever," Nicholas explained to Helvetius. "Oh, here's the sled! Right here, Vobis!" He waved an arm at a white sled that came dashing toward them, drawn by a single black horse. "Vobis will take you home now," he said, lifting Helvetius to his feet and leading him toward the sled.

Helvetius gazed with longing at the comfortable seat piled with soft, thick rugs. "But the horse," he protested. "The poor beast cannot draw me even a fraction of the distance I must go before she freezes."

Nicholas smiled. "You need not worry," he said. "You will be home in an hour's time." He guided Helvetius into the sled and settled the rugs snugly around him. "There. I know you will keep our secret well, for you have the rare gift of determination. I hope that I will see you again." He waved, and the black horse reared up. For a second the horse, sled, and driver were frozen in midair, and then they disappeared, leaving only a ghostly hole in the frozen air.

"She is fast, our Vobis," said Nicholas thoughtfully, climbing into his curving sleigh. Tundra jumped in by his side, and the reindeer began his graceful loping stride toward the distant purple mountain.

"This fear," began Tundra, after a few moments, "did you experience it yourself during your mortal life, sire?"

"Yes," said Nicholas. "Frequently. All mortals do. It's unavoidable. Some refuse to let it control their lives, but for others, fear becomes a prison. It turns them inside out, makes their hearts dry, and causes them to hate one another."

"What are they frightened of, sire?"

"Lots of things. Hunger. Sickness. Death. Shame. Disappointing one another."

"You see these things when you visit their world?"

"Yes, oh dear yes. That's why I go. That's why there is Christmas. It eases their hearts a bit; for a few hours, they are not so frightened and they can love one another a little more. When the elders created Forever and called me to be its king, they ordained that the great gate must be opened once a year at Christmas to let new immortals join us, but also—and just as important—to let me travel to the mortal world to deliver a balm of peace and goodwill to all the mortals while I deliver playthings to the children. We have so much of these resources, you see, and the human world is so sadly lacking in them." The sleigh passed over the glacier and, for a few moments, they were bathed in the brilliance of amethysts, violets, orchids, and lavender.

"May I ask another question, Your Majesty?"

"Yes, of course, Tundra."

"How did that human come to us?"

"How? Oh, I see what you are asking. Geography is a very complicated problem, Tundra. Human beings are addicted to geography. They make maps and charts, they plot and survey, and they think they can find anything. Now, you and I know that Forever doesn't exactly sit on Earth in quite the same way that a mortal country does, correct?"

"Correct, but he was there, on Earth, and . . ."

"And he could see the glaciers from his position, which is not, well, true, is it?"

"No, sire."

"So your question, then, is this: Was he here or were we there?"

"Exactly, sire."

"Ridiculous question," said Nicholas, smiling sideways at the wolf.

Tundra's ears twitched. There was a silence. "You did it, sire."

"Yes."

"Why, sire?"

"Because he needed help."

"You brought him here."

"Yes."

The wolf sighed. "Sire, you—how can I say this?—you love these people so much, I know, but—but—I wonder if you are too generous. Now here is another one who knows about our country, and perhaps he will tell others. Look at de Lusus. Look at Mylius. They reveal our secrets."

Nicholas stared at the sky. "Secrets are worthless until you give them away," he said softly. "If this one tells, and I think he won't, the story will only bring more hope into the world, and that is what I desire. And besides, he gave me an idea."

"An idea for what?"

"An idea that will provide an explanation for my appearances. The mortals are sure to find it highly satisfactory." He began to chuckle. "I will build a little villa in the Arctic—perhaps right upon the North Pole—and set up a toy manufactory. I shall be Santa Claus, a kindly old saint who delivers toys to children on Christmas Eve, which, of course, I do anyway, but this will keep them from wondering and guessing about Forever and the immortals."

"They will wonder how you manage to produce enough toys for the world's children," said Tundra.

"I've already thought of that. I'll dress up the goblins in little suits, little red suits, and call them my workmen."

"The goblins will hate that," said Tundra. "Imagine

Melchior in a red suit."

"I'll say that they're elves," Nicholas said blithely.

"They'll hate that even more."

"I know, I know," Nicholas said, laughing.

"And, sire, to whom do you plan to reveal this?"

"That, Tundra, is the most ingenious part of my plan! I will make a selection of poets from many lands, and then I will approach each one with a highly confidential, private invitation to my workshop, enjoining each to utter secrecy. They will come and see the elves working away; they will see me, perhaps in a red suit myself; and then they will go home and spread the word! You know poets—they love to talk."

"How will you explain Christmas Eve?"

"Traveling the globe in one night? I'll tell them the truth."

"They'll never believe you."

"Yes, they will, Tundra. Humans need magic sleighs and reindeer. They need them more than you can possibly imagine."

And that was how, many years ago, the story of Santa Claus took shape. Nicholas's North Pole workshop was a resounding success. Grumbling, the goblins dressed themselves in red suits and covered their blue cheeks with rouge. They arrayed mountains of toys upon tables and hammered at dolls and rocking horses, while Nicholas greeted a small, enthusiastic band of poets with chuckles and enormous platters of food. The poets gulped and nodded, chewed and took a few notes. Some months later, by a strange coincidence, a number of books about Santa Claus appeared, each declaring that he was a jolly, rotund old fellow in a red suit who lived at the North Pole in a workshop full of elves who made toys for good little boys and girls.

When Nicholas read those books, he laughed and blessed the day that Helvetius Erst had seen his fateful map. It seemed as though the Land of the Immortals would be safe for all time.

Chapter Three

NICHOLAS HAD come to think of the letter he had received so many months ago as The Golden Letter, for somehow the generous heart that had penned the words had met and mingled with his own wish for a child, and a strange spiritual alchemy had occurred. The elders of the universe, seeing the wish of one and the love of the other, had wrought an uncommon wonder, and Nicholas and Viviana were presented, at last, with their own child.

Now summer was quickening into fall. On a cloudless day when the leaves were just beginning to flame into gold, a vast crowd gathered silently on the Terrace of the Swans before the Crystal Castle of Forever. Mermaids, naiads, and even quarrelsome water sprites shared the cool waters of the reflecting pool. A pink cloud of fairies hovered above the heads of the poets, artists, princes, heroes, magicians, gnomes, goblins, centaurs, and fauns who waited patiently for a sign from the castle. Behind them, the gardens of the palace unfurled their splendor, and beyond that, the Veridian River curled like a blue-green snake through the field where herbs and fruits grew. This plain, which had no name, stretched on as far as the eye could see and glowed with a pulsing light. Sometimes the sky above was dreamy, soft, silvery; sometimes the air was bathed in the colors of sunset. Far beneath the plain were the caves of the ancient wizards, whose spells and potions caused the magical light.

Suddenly there was a stir in the crowd. A wave of excited whispers rippled through the assembly as Nicholas stepped out upon the palace steps. "He's here!" "But look at his face!" "Look at his eyes! They're glowing!" "I told you!" "Everything must be all right!"

Everything was more than all right. Beaming,

Nicholas bowed to the fairies. He bowed to the dragons, who were still looking sleepy from their summer nap. There was Melisande—he waved. And Beatrice—he waved again. There were poets, bunched around a tree, arguing about anapests. There were the goblins, fussing and fretting next to the pool, probably driving the water sprites mad. Gawaine, always useful, was urging the centaurs to step back and allow the gnomes to see. Nicholas looked up. The phoenix nodded with slow dignity from his perch on the old oak. The roc offered his usual terrifying smile.

Nicholas felt as though his heart would burst with joy. He opened up his arms wide and called, "My people! This is a great day in our land, for a child has been born to us—the first child ever to be born in the Land of the Immortals! You have a princess, my friends, and Viviana and I have a daughter!"

An enormous shout went up from the multitudes, punctuated by excited cries of "I told you so!" "Just as we thought!" and "I could tell the minute I saw his face!"

"What's her name, Your Highness?" called out one of the naiads in a voice like a bell.

Nicholas grinned. "We have named her after the bright flora of Christmas: she is to be called Holly!

And I assure you, the universe has never beheld such perfection."

Even the goblins had to smile at their king's delight. The Boucane sisters were so excited that they flew about in a frenzy, bumping into one another and into the roc, who looked at them disdainfully. The mermaids thwacked their tails enthusiastically in the water, and several poets, momentarily distracted from anapests, decided to compose odes to the new princess of Forever and then hold a contest to see which was the best. The unicorns and lamellicorns gamboled upon the great lawn.

Throwing his head back, Nicholas laughed heartily. Never had the universe contained such an abundance of delight.

Can the sound of laughter waft along with a breeze? Curl and twist on clouds? Travel through frozen gray fog? Tumble through empty caverns, slip down slippery rock precipices, ooze into sucking mud, and seep up through the cracks of an iron fortress? Perhaps. Perhaps laughter is so powerful that it penetrates rock and metal. Or perhaps the thin, silvery ears that heard the sounds of joy in the Land of the Immortals were especially keen.

Herrikhan twitched and sat up. A mouse, whose frantic attempts at escape had been amusing the warlock the evening before, was attached by a thin silver collar to Herrikhan's iron bedstead. Now he snapped the collar open, and the little beast dropped into his waiting palm. It lay there, stiff with terror, its heaving sides the only sign that it was still alive. Herrikhan stroked the quivering rodent with a long, dirty fingernail. "A child has been born in Forever," he remarked conversationally to the mouse, "and Nicholas is a proud papa. How darling. Not only a beloved king, but a happy family man. Nicholas was always lucky." Cautiously the mouse opened one eye. Except for an unnatural whistling in his *s*'s, Herrikhan's voice sounded quite normal. "Awake, are we?" cooed Herrikhan, stroking rapidly. "Wee little mousie would be happy in the Immortal Palace, wouldn't he? Little mousies love cozy warm rooms with deep velvet sofas and soft woolen rugs, don't they? And Nicholas the family man with his lovely Viviana and his baby princess would drop nice toasty crumbs for you, wouldn't he? Then little mousie and all the other fools would sing jolly songs to their beloved king, wouldn't they? Oh yes, little mousie, you would be happy in Forever, wouldn't you?"

Herrikhan fell silent, but his finger did not cease its stroking. Suddenly he hurled the mouse against the opposite wall with all his strength. The squeal, the soft thud seemed to satisfy him. He leaned over the edge of the bed to watch the roaches descend upon the body. Though Herrikhan's eyes rested on the pile of insects, his thoughts were elsewhere. "A baby princess," he mused. "Holly. Very festive, I'm sure. That's the trouble with our most sovereign state," he added, raising his voice a bit. "Not enough festivities. Don't you agree, Beyschlag?"

"Yes, my lord." A thick, yellowing white head came into the room. It was enormous, nearly as large as an eight-year-old child; its eyes were gaping pink holes and its mouth was a lipless crumble. Two rubbery arms hung from the yogurty folds of his sagging neck and, though these limbs appeared useless, Beyschlag used them to propel himself forward, as he had no others. "Not enough festivities," he repeated with a grin.

Herrikhan grinned back, his silvery skin pulling against his cheekbones. "Kindly Santa wouldn't begrudge me a little fun, would he? Jolly old Saint Nick brings joy to all—isn't that right?—and would hardly turn away his old chum Herrikhan from

"Oh yes, little mousie, you would be happy in Forever,
wouldn't you?"

the christening. After all, I'm an immortal too." He giggled.

"Immortal too, my lord."

Herrikhan picked up a mirror and gazed at his reflection. "I've aged terribly in the last century. I must spruce up for the party, my dear." Hardly were the words out of his mouth when the seams of his silver skin tightened into smoothness, and his narrow, glinting eyes appeared to widen and lighten. His robe, splattered with strange yellow stains, ballooned into the air and resettled itself into a graceful purple velvet tunic. The iron band that had encircled his head so tightly ever since the first terrible day he had come to Odyl could not be removed, but Herrikhan did have enough power to enrich it with jewels and filigree until it almost looked like a crown. "Much better," he purred to himself.

"Much better, my lord," repeated Beyschlag.

As long as you didn't catch a glimpse inside his mouth, Herrikhan looked similar to a human. The mouth betrayed him. No warlock could alter the color of his mouth; they could always be identified by their telltale tongues. The best warlocks, the ones who meant no evil and who used their enchantments for the benefit of others, had mouths colored a pleasant shade of aqua. The variable warlocks betrayed their weakness with mossy green gums and throats. Warlocks who stirred up trouble had mouths the color of pine trees. Herrikhan's mouth was black. His tongue was mottled gray and black, and his gums were the color of tar. His teeth, long and yellow, were sharply pointed.

It had not always been this way. Thousands of years before, Herrikhan had walked out of the stars, a fair young man, and stepped down into the mortal world to play the games of its mortals. The elders of the universe, who had set him in the sky at the beginning of time, had so admired his strength, his courage, and his ability that they did not send him back to his celestial home. As a result of their indulgence, Herrikhan grew infatuated with life among the mortals. In return, all the world grew infatuated with Herrikhan. As he stepped through the forests, animals and birds followed behind, as if drawn by a magnet. In the towns, mortals bowed before his wisdom and heroic skill. As time passed, Herrikhan swelled with the importance of his own power. He became a king, ruler over a vast and populous domain. He grew greedy and commanded his people to wage war upon their neighbors. Hordes of Herrikhan's soldiers laid waste to the nearby regions, and slaughter and famine followed his victories. Upon their leader's orders, the victors enslaved their former enemies, and Herrikhan's territories became infamous for the cruelty of the powerful and for the poverty and despair of the weak. Herrikhan grew fat and indolent; his desires were constantly satisfied, and his pleasure was law. Larger than his bloated body was his monstrous pride; as the years wore on, he grew discontent with the monuments and palaces that had been erected in his honor. None of them, he felt, did justice to his grandeur, his might. Lying on a golden couch, his massive belly supported by two great golden pillows, he reflected sourly on the structures devoted to his admiration.

The problem, he realized, was that admiration itself was insufficient.

An idea grew in his inflamed heart. Admiration must give way to worship. The mortals must be taught that he was a god. After all, he reasoned, he was immortal and nearly a god already. As the mortals were easily persuaded, he merely needed to inspire them with awe and terror. Hardly a demanding task. He yawned. Accordingly, in the following months and years, Herrikhan summoned up from the pits and bogs of the subterranean world all the sorcerers, witches, and alchemists he could beguile to his cause. They taught him their secret arts, their powers of conjuring, until, in the end, he could transform himself into any creature, lay spells of any sort, and create any object he desired. Far from being a god, Herrikhan was now a warlock of monstrous proficiency, and his former teachers cowered before him.

As he laughingly practiced his new skills—an alchemist was miniaturized and put inside his flacon to boil; a witch's hands were petrified and fell off—Herrikhan was unaware of the elders who watched him from afar. Finally the time for his first performance approached. Herrikhan issued a proclamation, calling all citizens of the many cities within his empire to gather before their temples at a certain day and certain hour. At precisely the moment designated, a figure clothed in flashing silver emerged from each temple roof and hovered in the air over the screaming populace. It was Herrikhan, multiplied into many figures. He gestured for silence and began his announcement. "You will be pleased, my people, to hear of my elevation to divinity. The elders of the universe visited me in the night and begged me to take upon my shoulders the yoke of omnipotence. After much persuasion, I agreed. In my beneficence, I have come to tell you of my transformation before I undertake my sacred tasks, allowing you, my people, to worship me before all others and earn precedence in heaven." Herrikhan stepped back, dropping his eyes earthward in a pretense of modesty.

To his astonishment, his subjects did not instantly comply. Rebellious murmurs reached Herrikhan's ears: "Blasphemer!" "Deceiver!" "Godless jackal!"

Fury rose in Herrikhan's throat. "You dare to hesitate?" he howled. "You will feel the wrath of God!" He pointed his finger toward the ground, and a slender rod of metal hurtled toward his populace. When it touched the ground, the staff exploded like a bomb and thousands of slivers flew into the eyes of the people, blinding them.

Suddenly, from the clouds scudding across the sky above Herrikhan's head came a tremendous roar, and he was flung from his perch. He fell, screaming, into a cavernous tear that appeared in the land. Down and down he plummeted, and as he fell, the voices of the elders revealed his punishment to him.

"You, Herrikhan, once our favored princeling, have become a deadly disease in the universe, a spreading decay of cruelty and disbelief. You have time and again chosen evil over good, and you have

dared to use the gifts we bequeathed to you to feed
your hunger for power. Far from a god, you are now
a force of destruction. In the normal course of events,
we would simply annihilate you. However, some in
our membership have pleaded for a different arrangement, reflecting both the enormity of your offense
against the universal harmony and our own responsibility for your vile deeds. Thus we give you notice,
Herrikhan, that you are now our prisoner, shackled
for eternity by the curse of the elders. You are con-
demned to Odyl, the fortress that sweats beneath the
earth in its bed of molten fire. The air of that realm
will be as necessary to you as oxygen once was to
your mortal body. In Odyl, you will remain, crippled
by your own wickedness. Because no being in our
universe may be deprived of the freedom to choose
the good, we cannot forbid you to practice your wiz-
ardry in Odyl. Know that you will have few subjects
in that infernal realm, for though you are permitted
to travel to the mortal world and beyond, you will not
long survive outside Odyl and each exercise of your
enchantments will further weaken you. To protect the
innocent of the universe, we also decree that when
you leave the fortress, bitter storms will accompany
you to signal your arrival to your victims. Moreover,

you will be powerless except in the presence of fear. But where love overwhelms fear, you will have no dominion."

Herrikhan fell heavily onto the ground, his bloated body slapping against the warm layer of scum that coated the ground. Groaning, he rolled over, conscious of a driving pain in his head.

"Your new status," continued the echoing voice around him, "will be shown by an iron band around your brow. We are lodging it in your skull now— there—and it will never come away as long as the curse remains unbroken."

Herrikhan lay still. For days and days, he lay on the ground where he had dropped. Every once in a while, a soft, yellowing arm poured water down his throat. Slowly, his bones began to reappear under his graying flesh; later, as he wasted, his joints jutted up, almost cracking the skin.

Then, one day, Herrikhan's eyes clicked open. His eyes saw a long, pale expanse of featureless metal. He blinked. "*As long as* the curse remains unbroken?"

He was answered with silence.

"I know you can hear me!" Herrikhan called, raising himself a bit. "Tell me how the curse can be broken."

The lights went out in Odyl, and a long sigh reverberated through the halls. "To free yourself from the curse, you must possess the purest and most compassionate heart ever born. This heart must be free from stain and must be freely given to you in the fullness of love. If you can attain this, you will once more be free. These are the laws of the universe, and they cannot be altered."

Herrikhan rolled over and looked up at the glowing orange sky of his new home. He smiled up in the direction of the world. "You shall see me again," he hissed.

Chapter Four

MELCHIOR HAD agonized over the christening. How was the queen to walk from the palace to the Square of the Sybils, where the cathedral stood? Who would lead the processional? What if the queen grew tired? What if she tripped and—horror!—dropped the princess? Where would the immortals gather? How would they all fit? What if they made too much noise and—horror!— the princess cried? Melchior had not slept for days. At three o'clock in the morning before the christening, he and his trustiest goblin assistants had risen from their pallets to set to work. Under his feverish super-vision, a red velvet carpet had been laid out from the palace doors to the cathedral steps with exquisite care. Not a wrinkle, not the slightest curve was to impede the royal path, he insisted. Velvet cordons were put up to keep the eager crowds from hovering too close to the baby. Goblin underlings were given strict orders to eject any immortal who spoke above a whisper. At nine thirty, with a sigh of relief and self-congratulation, Melchior declared that everything was in order for the great day. He and his fellow goblins retired to wash and dress for the great occasion.

Unfortunately, when Melchior left, the Boucane sisters came fluttering into the Square of the Sybils with their arms full of flowers. The carpet, they decided, was boring. And the velvet cordons were ugly. They covered the red velvet with petals in every hue of the rainbow. And, since they were fairies, stringing garlands of yellow roses along the facades of the palaces around the square was only a moment's work. They convinced Zenwyler the centaur that it was a centaur's job to knock over the cordons, which he did with crashing enthusiasm. The immortals arriving on the scene cheered loudly, and the Boucane sisters curtseyed.

Then, above the cacophony, rang the single, pure note of a silver pipe, and a sudden silence fell over the square. This was the call of Pan's flute, and it could mean only one thing: the Amaranthine Gates, the portals to Forever, were opening. The citizens of the Land of the Immortals looked at one another with growing excitement. A swelling parade of immortals came streaming into the square, led by Gaia and her handmaidens. These were the magical beings who lived below, assisting—or in some cases, thwarting—the other beings in the mortal world. First, in flowing gowns strewn with spring flowers, were Persephone and Demeter, followed by the nymphs who guarded the world's streams and rivers; then the sileni, dancing and whistling; the gnomes, on their best behavior; the leprechauns, also on their best behavior (though that wasn't saying much); the fairies who worked in the tooth bureau; Berchta, the ugliest woman in the world, clutching the arm of Sendivogius; then the magic foxes and owls; the guardian wizards, hoping their charges could manage their kingdoms alone for a day; the Chaldean witches, looking grave; the hearth spirits; the rusalki; and hundreds of others. The square had to swell to accommodate them all. The beings with wings took their seats aloft, and the stronger ones held up the little folks so they could see.

Last of all the winged horse, Pegasus, appeared in the sky. White as snow, he glided slowly to the ground, and a woman clothed in cloud-colored robes slipped off his back. This was Sofya, and she stood for a moment, surveying the crowded square, her serene eyes resting on each of the nearby faces. She was thousands of years old, and the long braid that swung against her knees was silvery, but her face was unlined. Gracefully she made her way along the flowery carpet toward the cathedral's sapphire doors and disappeared within.

A moment later Tundra and Terra appeared at the top of the promenade. A gnarled wizard spotted them first and squealed, "They're *here!*"

Tundra, looking dignified, and Terra, unable to quench a curling wolvish smile, padded forward. Then came Nicholas, Viviana and, most important of all, the froth of lace that was their new princess. The crowd sucked in a collective breath.

Nicholas reached out to touch the hands extended toward him until he and his family reached the steps of the cathedral and, like Sofya, disappeared behind the sapphire doors.

Time passed. The chorus of angels within the

cathedral could be heard outside, and the immortals nodded their satisfaction to one another, imagining the scene within.

"Oh, look, here they come!" cried a wood nymph. The griffin, who had been circling lazily in the sky above the square, called down that Fortinbras the bell ringer was climbing into the tower. Sure enough, just as Nicholas pushed open the doors, an ecstatic arpeggio pealed from the giant bells. The new father smiled and stepped aside to let his wife pass. They both turned to watch their daughter emerge into the glorious sunlight in the arms of her godmother.

Sofya paused and looked out upon the assembly of immortals below. A radiant smile flashed across her face, and she held the baby up for all to see.

Low ooohs of admiration rippled through the crowd. Holly Claus was an extraordinarily pretty baby. Her cheeks were soft and touched with rose, and her round green eyes were the color of the shade in a grove of trees. Her hands, like tiny stars, clutched at nothing. Without a whimper, she looked in calm wonder at the population of Forever. And then she laughed.

There was something so contagiously silly in her chuckle that the fairies couldn't contain themselves.

And neither could the fauns, nor the witches—not even Befana—nor the sprites. In a matter of moments, the immortals were all giggling and cackling like children.

Holly was laughing at something the rest of them couldn't see. Only Emmalylis, the youngest and smallest of the Boucane sisters, knew what was happening. The will-o'-the-wisps had come. These are the tiniest of fairies, and because mortals simply dismiss them as dust motes and leave them alone, they are the only fairies that willingly show themselves to humans. Babies know what they are, though, and the will-o'-the-wisps love them for it. For a baby, these little golden fairies will wiggle and dance and somersault through the air for hours. And that is what they were doing for Holly on the bright fall afternoon when the first child born in the Land of the Immortals met her magical kingdom.

✳ ✳ ✳

The feasting went on for hours. Tables had been set around the Terrace of the Swans, and every citizen of Forever, as well as every magical visitor from the mortal world, was invited to the celebration. Eternal life gives a certain edge to the appetite, and the immortals feasted as they had never feasted before: towering glacé castles, roast meats, puddings both sweet and savory, glogg (in honor of the trolls), a magnificent macédoine of fresh fruit, and flower nectar concoctions of numerous kinds. For the duke of Savoy, notoriously touchy, a monstrous *maccherone* had been constructed. For the roc, broiled snakes. For the pixies, piles of pineapple, which they loved and rarely got. Every appetite was satisfied until the guests moaned with joy and remorse, and the dancing began. Nicholas led the fairies in a hornpipe, and the rest of the guests soon joined in. A roundelay upon the lawns, a caper along the edge of the reflecting pool, a waltz on the lower terrace—the dancing went on until the sun grazed the tops of the trees.

Holly, who had slept soundly through the jolting carriage ride to the castle and through the riotous festivities that ensued, awoke as the crowd grew quiet. Guests drew around as Sofya lifted the baby from her soft nest and gently cuddled her against her neck, stroking the small, downy head with one finger. Nicholas and Viviana looked on tenderly as Sofya began to whisper into their daughter's tiny ear in Russian. After a few moments, Sofya lifted her eyes and looked toward Nicholas. "It is as you wished, my dear friend. To your daughter I have given the gifts of wisdom and strength. And, as certainly as I am Sofya, goddess of Russia and keeper of Holly's spirit, these will serve her well for all the days of her life. However, there is a greater gift than those I have given, and that is love. This is not for me to give, but only to foresee, and I tell you, my friends, that your daughter will not only light your way with love but will illuminate the path of each person she meets. Nicholas and Viviana, immortal beings, you are in the presence of the purest and most compassionate heart that has ever been born."

Hardly had the words left her mouth when a shriek of ripping metal tore the quiet evening. It echoed throughout the kingdom and, bewildered, the guests looked at one another, the sky, the ground, for an explanation. Nicholas jumped to his feet in alarm, but the torturing scream ceased—and nothing followed. There was a minute of confused silence, then

agitated voices called out suggestions and the smaller
beings began to buzz nervously about. The roc, startled out of his usual nonchalance, flew into the air to
investigate from above. Viviana, pale with fright,
rushed to retrieve her baby from Sofya. The goddess
relinquished the child and stood, stone-still, listening
intently as though she could hear something that the
others could not.

The anxious guests did not notice a thin chill
creeping along the soft lawns until it wove its way
among them. They shivered, and the clammy damp-
ness rose around their legs. They looked wildly
around—what had happened? The fog seemed to
bring with it a sour smell, a rotting odor with a faint
whiff of metal. Some of the sprites began to choke.
Others gathered their belongings hastily, preparing to
flee.

"Stop." Sofya's voice, usually so tranquil, had a ring
of command. "We must stay together. Herrikhan has
arrived in Forever."

Chapter Five

HERRIKHAN! The guests looked uneasily behind them. What was he doing in the Land of the Immortals? Hadn't he been banished for all time?

Nicholas and Sofya exchanged glances, for they alone knew the conditions of the curse: Herrikhan would be freed if he could possess the purest and most compassionate heart ever born.

But she's only a baby, thought Nicholas.

You know him, Sofya replied silently. You know that he will take any chance to attain his freedom.

He can't come here, fumed Nicholas.

He can try, cautioned Sofya.

Sofya turned her black eyes to the anxious crowd. "Come!" she cried. "Come and listen, immortals. Herrikhan can only enter your presence if you feel fear. When you trust in the power of love and are brave and resolute, he has no purchase on your souls, and he falls back to his tomb in Odyl. Remember, Forever is not a land of fear." She stepped down from the dais and walked among the immortals, touching a hand here, a shoulder there. There was something in her face that soothed them. "Make no mistake," she assured them, "love will prevail."

The naiads shook themselves, the fairies and goblins took deep breaths. The knights and princes squared their shoulders, the queens lifted their heads majestically. All of the immortals braced themselves and pushed fear away.

It worked. The damp air thinned and faded. The wind-lashed trees calmed, and the night grew still. The stench lifted, and the soft scent of evening primrose floated about. The Land of the Immortals sighed and returned to itself.

Meanwhile, Terra and Tundra loped through the quiet, darkening streets of Forever and out into the forests beyond. Even the woods were eerily empty, for all the witches, sprites, and pixies were at the palace. The two wolves ran, not speaking, toward the gates mounted in the farthest crystal glacier on the outskirts of the land. These, the Amaranthine Gates, were wrought from thousands of jewels—a diamond for each immortal who had passed through—set in a hundred-foot arc of gold, and the light they cast stretched like a bridge from the mortal to the immortal worlds. On the gates were graven the words that served as the legend of the land, Love Conquers Time, and it was beneath these ancient letters that the newly made immortal souls entered Forever, that magical visitors from Earth were admitted, and that Santa Claus made his ceremonious departure on Christmas Eve.

When the jagged sound of metal had torn through Nicholas's gardens, Terra and Tundra had turned to each other with a look of foreboding. There was only one way such a sound could be made: someone or something was attempting to break down the gates. With a silent, scarcely perceptible nod, the two wolves slipped away at a casual pace until they were beyond sight of the palace and then ran with ever-increasing speed toward the boundary of Forever. Finally the gates came into view.

"They're still holding," affirmed Terra, with a breath of relief.

The arc of gold glittered in the falling rays of the sun, but there, on one side, the jeweled post had been torn from the ground. It hung, shattered, a good two feet above the ground where it had been lodged.

The wolves contemplated the wreckage. "How did he do it?" Tundra muttered.

"*Why* did he do it?" Terra said sadly. She padded closer to the twisted shards of gold. "The gates will open for any immortal. Why did he need to destroy them?"

A chill wind gusted through the gash in the gate. Terra hesitated, then leaned forward to sniff. With a wild howl, the wind ripped through the hole and buffeted the wolf against the rungs of metal.

"Terra!" called Tundra, panic in his throat.

That was enough for Herrikhan. He seized Tundra's fear and dragged Terra toward the breach in the gates. Frenziedly she fought, snapping at the wind and digging in her legs, but her defenses were useless against her invisible enemy. Tundra leaped forward to intervene, but he was thrust aside by the gale and lay, pinned and helpless, against the glacier's edge, while his beloved Terra was pulled, howling,

through the rent in the metal.

One instant she was in the Land of the Immortals; the next she had fallen forward, onto mortal soil. The tearing wind took its vengeance on her and, now subject to mortal wounds, Terra was soon beaten. Her legs collapsed under the battering of the storm, and though she made a last, desperate effort to regain Forever, she was blinded by the choking dust that whirled around her head. Tundra called her name frantically. She dragged herself farther and farther in the opposite direction, away from the gates and then slumped hopelessly to one side and lay down, panting, unable to continue.

Cloaked in clouds, Herrikhan looked down contemptuously at Terra's still-breathing frame and, with a flick of his wrist, sent out his birds. In a swarm they descended on Terra, pecking one another viciously in order to reach the food they were ravenous for.

Tundra screamed once and then hid his head.

Utterly unaware of the carnage that was occurring at the gates, Sofya continued the ceremony that had been interrupted. Composed and graceful, she approached little Holly, burbling and gurgling in her mother's lap. Leaning down, Sofya fastened a small, intricately designed locket around the child's neck. Then she kissed her soft cheeks. "I did not know that you would need this so soon, my Holly. Stored within this locket is a secret that belongs to the elders. You must never open it but wear it always. It will keep you safe and guard you all your days. Never forget that the power of love is within you, and it will be your shield. Now you may rest easy, my child, for the strength and wisdom I have given you can never be stolen away. Wear this locket in peace and safety, and let it remind you that you are not alone."

Sofya straightened and turned to the guests. "I have also brought you, Holly, the gift of laughter—in the form of"—Sofya struggled briefly with her cloud-colored robes—"of"— the robes appeared to be leaping up and down—"of—oh, for heaven's sake, sit still a minute! In the form, I say, of—oh, bother!

Here she is, and her name is Alexia, and she's not much older than you are, and she has terrible manners."

"Don't!" insisted a little gray fox, jumping out of the cloak. Momentarily abashed by the sight of the crowd, Alexia sat down with a thump. Her shyness lasted only a few seconds before it was overcome by her curiosity. She approached Viviana's chair, tail high, and put her forepaws upon the seat. Her golden eyes looked into the baby's soft green ones with unblinking interest, then she scrambled up into Viviana's lap to join her new friend.

"Down, down, Lexy!" scolded Sofya and, reluctantly, the fox obeyed.

Now the other guests brought forth their gifts for the baby. Gaia approached, bearing a quilt made of rose petals. Shy fairies came in groups, offering fairy lights and magic straws. The fearsome Sphinx gave the baby a small silver capsule that contained the answer to a terrible riddle. The water nymphs had worked for days to make a swan-shaped boat from abalone shells. The dwarves and trolls presented caskets of jewels, as they always did. Unlike the magical beings, whose presents tended to be rather impractical, those who had lived a mortal span presented toys, books, and soft swaddling blankets. Soon the stacks of boxes, chests, and barrels threatened to overwhelm the terrace and, noticing that Holly was fast asleep and Viviana was shaking with exhaustion, Nicholas brought the celebration to an end.

The last good-byes were over. Melchior and his assistants were clearing off tables and tsking over wasted food while Viviana was resting inside the palace and Holly was nestled in her lacy cloud of a cradle. Out in the cool evening, Nicholas dropped onto a bench and sank into thought.

Some time later he straightened. "Terra!" he called. "Tundra! We must make a tour of the periphery." Silence answered him. "Terra! Tundra!" he called again. Nothing. This was most unlike them. Nicholas felt a chill of dread run down his spine. "Tundra. Terra," he said, almost inaudibly.

Trying to ignore the dread that clawed in his throat, Nicholas turned on his heel and headed for the stables. Alarmed by his grave face, the stable goblins hastily saddled Vobis, and Nicholas swung onto the horse's back. "The glaciers, Vobis," he commanded briefly. "Begin with the amethyst."

Vobis did not have to be urged. With one startling leap they were on their way, and moments later the purple glacier, glowing eerily in the starlight, came into view. Silently Nicholas took stock and moved on. The moon arose and shed its heartless light on the mountainsides, but all was quiet. There was no sign of damage, no evidence of invasion. To overcome the whisper of fear that had followed him for hours, Nicholas assured himself it was likely that Herrikhan, defeated, had simply turned around and gone back to his prison. But where, then, were Terra and Tundra?

On he rode, to the farthest-flung outskirts of his kingdom. The crystal glacier came into view, and then the Amaranthine Gates. Peering through the gloom, Nicholas saw that the soaring gold gates were still standing, and a worry that he hadn't even realized he was harboring faded. Then, coming closer, he made out the hole blasted in the gatepost.

"Faster," he said hoarsely to Vobis. Seconds later he was striding toward the shattered metal when a dark shape thrown across the ground caught his eye. "Tundra?"

There was no answer.

Nicholas knelt beside the wolf, stroking his thick, white fur. "What's happened here? Are you wounded? Oh, Tundra, come back."

A long shudder shook the wolf's frame. "I cannot, Your Majesty," Tundra said in a low voice.

"You must, my friend," said Nicholas, "for I cannot manage without you."

There was a silence. "She's dead."

"Terra?"

"Yes."

Nicholas was quiet. "How?" he asked finally.

"The wind." Tundra's voice shook. "There was a terrible storm. I don't know how—but the wind pulled her against the gates, and then out—and Terra . . . Terra got confused. I tried to go after her, but I was held back, sire. I was pinned against the ice. It was evil—it was as though the storm wanted me to watch her die. And then," Tundra choked, "then, birds swarmed over her." The wolf stopped speaking.

Nicholas rose to his feet and walked toward the

jeweled bars, then burst through them as though they had been made of nothing more substantial than spider-webs. He glared into the darkness outside the gates and saw, not far off, Terra's battered body. He approached and knelt down, closing the lids over her eyeless sockets and offering a prayer that her soul would soon forget its suffering. Then he lifted her into his arms and walked swiftly back to his own land, setting her next to Tundra. "Come back to me when you can, Tundra, I beg of you," he said.

Slowly he walked toward Vobis. As he climbed into the saddle and turned away, he heard the first of Tundra's howls, and his skin crawled. Herrikhan has had his triumph, hasn't he? thought Nicholas. But why Terra? Terra is nothing to him. It's the pure heart he must have.

As he rode he noticed that the dark trees and sil-very glades lining the valley floor seemed curiously empty, as though everyone was hiding. As though *something* was hiding. A slight rustle of leaves caught his attention. What if he's here? thought Nicholas suddenly. What if somehow he's made his way in? He pulled at the reins, and Vobis strained forward. What if he's inside the palace? Who would know, except for Sofya and me? Not even Viviana would be able to recognize him. What if he's crept up the steps, what if he's walking toward the baby's cradle, his hands out, reaching down to touch her—

Terror caught at him. His heart was thundering in his chest. "Home," he said urgently. "Home *now*."

Chapter Six

NICHOLAS RAN **up** the palace stairs, the clatter of his boots echoing across the empty gardens. "Lotho," he gasped to the house goblin who stood at the door, "where's the queen?"

Shocked by the sight of his master's flushed face and gleaming eyes, Lotho stammered, "Her Maj-Maj-Maj is in the nurs-nursery, Your Maj-Maj—"

Nicholas raced toward the staircase, calling back over his shoulder, "Get the dragons up. I want the dragons flying over the palace. Tell Melchior."

"Wait, Nicholas! We must get Holly now—this

instant!" It was Sofya, her hair streaming behind her like silver water. As she skimmed toward him, her feet scarcely touching the smooth floor, Nicholas saw, for the first time in his thousand-year memory, an expression of alarm on her face. The sight of it was enough to set his heart thumping.

He nodded and dashed up the stairs. The Hall of Mirrors was dark and silent now, and the glowing candles that emerged from the walls to light their way could hardly keep up with the two figures racing toward the nursery.

They burst through the doors, their ragged breath sounding harsh in the quiet, moonlit room. A small fire crackled in the fireplace, but it took a moment before they perceived Viviana's figure standing still, as though she had just jumped up in surprise. Her wide eyes were staring into a dark corner of the room.

Dreading what he was to see, Nicholas followed her gaze.

In the first seconds, it was only a thin outline, a few sharp dashes in the gloom. But then it began to take shape. The edges of the robe, the glint of dull iron, and the gaunt, ridged face seemed to assemble themselves from a cloud of flea-colored particles. Herrikhan stepped forward, his narrow eyes clicking

from one horrified face to the next. "How charming
to find you here, Sofya," he said, his tongue jutting
rhythmically from his mouth. "I have so been looking
forward to our reunion."

Sofya's eyes slid away from his, down to the fleecy
bundle that lay in the cradle. With a quick movement,
she lunged toward the baby, encircling her arms
around the soft blankets. She drew back, preparing to
flee.

"Sssss." Herrikhan hissed his laughter. "Oh, my
dear, have you forgotten that love and fear can go
hand in hand?" He flicked his hand toward her, and
she froze into a living statue, with Holly in her
arms. "I always knew when you were frightened.
Particularly when you were frightened of me." He
loomed over her with a gloating smile. "You too,
fool," he whispered, paralyzing Nicholas with a wave
of a finger. "How entrancing to find you all so terrified. It makes everything much simpler than I
expected, I must say. And now, little what's-your-
name," he muttered, drawing a small, hide-covered
box from the folds of his robe. "I brought you a present. Daddy's not the only one who brings presents to
good little girls," he cooed, flipping open the box to
reveal a small, strange object. It was transparent, gelid,

cunningly made. It was a heart of hardened snow.

"I suppose," said Herrikhan, looking with distaste at the squirming bundle, "that I shall have to handle you myself." Gingerly, he lifted Holly from Sofya's frozen arms, laid her upon the floor, and began to unwrap her blankets. The baby lay in her nightgown, looking curiously up at the hollow eyes fixed upon her. Herrikhan shook himself. All that was left to do was frighten her thoroughly. His gray lips flattened as he watched Holly's light eyes dance over him. Then he opened his black mouth wide and screamed, high and shrill, his rotting breath hot on her cheeks, his jaws distended, and his narrow eyes bulging.

Holly's face crumpled. She gave a little mew of fear and pressed back against the cold floor, her tiny arms flailing weakly through the air.

Nicholas, imprisoned in his frozen shell, felt part of his soul turn dark with rage.

"Perfect, my dear," purred Herrikhan, busily extracting the snow heart from its container. "Splendid." Holding the mass between his thumb and forefinger, he reached toward her. Somehow her soft gown seemed to dissolve around his fingers and, before her parents' horrified, helpless gazes, he pressed the ice-cold heart deep into her chest, his fingers disappearing into her flesh and then emerging clean, holding nothing.

The weak cries stopped. Surprised into silence by the cold new center of herself, Holly lay still. Herrikhan watched her searchingly for a moment and then stood, a twisted smile cracking across his face. "That should suffice. Your heart is encased—all its *purity* and *compassion* will be preserved," he spat, "until you are fully grown and ready to be married—to me." He cast a contemptuous glance at Holly. "But don't get above yourself, miss, for you are nothing but a vessel, a squirming vessel, that will eventually become useful to me. I regret to inform you that I am unmoved by our engagement"—he bowed—"and if I could throw you from that window to the stone terrace below without losing my chance at freedom, I would do so immediately, just for the sake of the expression on your daddy's face, my future bride." Herrikhan laughed, thinking of it, and prodded the baby with his scaly toe. "However, self-control is my watchword now, isn't it, my dear? And I shall simply make do with the expression on your father's face right now." He flicked his fingers—one, two, three—toward Nicholas, Viviana, and Sofya.

Freed, the three flew to Holly and lifted her from

Holding the mass between his thumb and forefinger,
he reached toward her.

the cold floor, cuddling her and comforting her. Viviana covered the little face with kisses and tears, pressing gently on her small limbs to reassure herself that her daughter was still whole. Nicholas bent over the tiny figure in his wife's arms, his eyes filled with tears.

Sofya was the first to recover. She rose slowly to her feet and fixed her wide black eyes on Herrikhan's icy gray ones. So filled with disgust was her look that the warlock took an uncertain step backward.

"You can't do anything to me," he said shrilly. "I'm immortal!"

"You think I wish to kill you?" she said, smiling. "I will let you do that yourself." She took a step toward him.

"A fine godmother you are," Herrikhan said, licking his dry lips nervously. "You didn't offer much in the way of protection tonight, did you? I cursed her and you just stood there."

"I did not know which curse you would choose until it was too late," Sofya said, stepping closer, her eyes still on his. "Does that make you feel powerful?"

"I am powerful!" he protested, his voice rising. "I got here, didn't I? I brought fear to the Land of the Immortals, didn't I? And you just froze, you and that fool they call king!" Nicholas looked sharply up from Holly, his mouth curling in contempt. "Oh yes, give me your regal look," screamed Herrikhan, "but you didn't act much like a king tonight, did you, Nickie? I shut your whole country down, and if you think it's over, you're even more of a fool than I thought! Because I will win!" He pointed a clawlike finger at Holly, held close in Viviana's arms. "I'll have her heart, and then I'll be free, and then—then—I'll grind this place to dust under my heel!"

"Wisdom is never without power," Sofya replied. "You know that the child must choose to go with you of her own free will."

"I'll crush her will," he retorted quickly. "In due time I'll crush her will completely, and then she'll be mine without a murmur."

Sofya shook her head. "Love will prevail, Herrikhan, just as it always has."

"I remember one time that it didn't," the warlock snapped. "Now, I'd love to stay and relive our past, my dear, but I must be on my way. My birds need feeding," he snickered with a glance toward Nicholas.

Nicholas rose slowly. "Get out," he said in a low voice. "Get out before I'm tempted—" He raised one arm.

With a little bark of terror, Herrikhan spun himself frantically and dissolved into a cloud of flea-
colored particles that swirled into nothingness.
Nicholas stood staring at the faint, greenish ring of
mucilage that the warlock had left behind.

"Nicholas! There's something wrong with Holly!"
cried Viviana. "She's pale and gasping, or—or—"

"Take off those blankets," ordered Sofya, flying to
her side. Quickly they stripped off the cozy blankets
that Viviana had just finished wrapping around the
baby. With each layer they removed, Holly seemed to
breathe more easily, and when she lay once again clad
only in her thin gown, the glow returned to her
cheeks. In a few moments, she was gurgling compan-
ionably to the ceiling above her head.

"What happened?" Viviana asked Sofya.

The goddess looked suddenly tired. She sat down
rather heavily on a soft chair. "Her heart is made of
snow now," she began. "You saw it happen. It will beat
like our hearts, keeping Holly alive, provided it
remains cold—frozen, as a matter of fact. It is impera-
tive that the snow remains frozen, for if it melts, Holly
will die." Nicholas and Viviana stared at her in horror.
"I'm sorry, my friends. There is no other way to tell
you. What happened just now is an example of what

will happen if Holly is too warm. Her heart will soften and skip; she will grow weak and faint and gasp for air. Rest easy," she comforted them, "Holly does not feel the cold upon her skin. To her, it is now comfortable—and comforting—to live in a frozen world. But you must take care. No blankets, no fires, no heat should touch her. It is probably"—Sofya surveyed the room—"too warm for her still, but I can change that." She searched in her robes and found a thin gold rod. With it, she gestured in a broad arc across the ceiling, and snow suddenly swirled from all sides, cloaking the floor in sparkling crystals. Viviana shivered. "Yes, it's cold. But you will grow used to it and, as you see, Holly finds it delightful."

The baby was kicking her hands and feet in an ecstatic tattoo, her eyes dancing at the shower of rainbows that fluttered around her. Under her parents' anxious eyes, Holly grew rosier as the temperature dropped, until finally, covered only in her light gown and a gauze of snowflakes, she fell asleep.

Nicholas, Viviana, and Sofya talked far into the night, laying plans for the frozen world that was necessary for Holly's survival. After Viviana fell asleep, exhausted by a day that had begun in rejoicing and ended in

THE LEGEND OF HOLLY CLAUS

sorrow, Sofya and Nicholas talked on.

"How could I have let it happen?" he groaned remorsefully. "If only I hadn't let myself fear him, he would have been powerless."

Sofya's keen eyes rested on his face. "The day that Holly was born, you changed. You are a father first and an immortal second. Tonight you feared as a father fears, for the safety of his child."

"But oh, the damage that has been done! The Land of the Immortals has never before known fear."

"And now it does, and yet it will survive," Sofya said. "Perhaps that is the lesson that the elders wish us to learn."

"Us? You, too, Sofya?"

"Yes, Nicholas, I will be learning alongside you."

"What do you mean?"

"I cannot go home now. . . ." She paused, searching for a way to soften her words. "I cannot go home until this darkness lifts."

Then Nicholas understood. "Oh no. No. Not a curse. Not here," he said, and dropped his face into his hands.

The Square of the Sybils looked very different than it had twenty-four hours earlier. It was still thronged with immortals, the same immortals who had cheerfully crowded together to see the little princess emerge from the cathedral, but now their eyes were fixed in consternation on Nicholas, who stood in the center of their cluster. His golden crown was the only touch of warmth under a sky filled with harsh gray clouds. The crystal buildings that lined the square seemed different, too, their luster gone, a dark outline of shadow etched around each wall and sloping roof, as though something were pressing against each surface. The immortals shivered, not only because of the frigid wind that scoured the square, but also under the burden of Nicholas's words: "... decreed that if any of our citizens should come under the curse of an immortal, our country must thenceforward be closed until the curse be lifted." Nicholas cleared his throat. "What that means, friends, is that we cannot leave and, I'm sorry to say, our visitors cannot leave either." Anxious whispers broke out. "And I won't keep the worst of it from you, immortals," Nicholas continued. "The very worst part is this: no new souls may enter our land until the curse is lifted." He looked at the ground.

"What?" "What about the souls that deserve immortality?" "Where will they go?" "Why?" several called.

"I don't know. It's never happened before, and I don't know where the new souls will go. And as for why, I can only say that it is the law of the elders, that's all."

"But how can the curse be lifted?" shouted Zenwyler the centaur, ready for combat.

"I don't know," Nicholas repeated helplessly. "We will learn that together."

Sofya stepped forward. "Holly, and Holly alone, can lift the curse that rests on her head. I have faith that she will."

Nicholas glanced gratefully at his old friend. "Yes, of course. She is a remarkable child—she has wisdom and strength. This is only temporary, I'm certain of it."

"What about Christmas?" called one of the goblins who had worked in Nicholas's North Pole performance.

"I believe that I will be allowed to make my usual journey around the world on Christmas Eve," Nicholas explained. "The mortals must not be deprived of their happiness."

"But some of them are being deprived of their trusted helpers," said a wizard who advised a young, rather flighty mortal king. The immortals nodded glumly, and several fairies folded their wings.

"Just for a short time. I'm certain of it," Nicholas said again.

Silently the immortals stared back at him. In their eyes he saw devotion, sympathy, loyalty, pity, and something he had never seen before—reproach.

Chapter Seven

THERE WAS A special feeling about
the Christmas preparations that year.
The immortals were determined to
fight the gloom that had gathered over
the kingdom with Herrikhan's curse, and often they
succeeded. The narrow, climbing streets of the village
seethed with activity as the Yuletide was honored in
manifold and marvelous ways. The air grew rich with
the smell of puddings, candies, and other treats; the
houses rang with songs and carols; and the gardens
and walls were lined with garlands and wreaths. In
every corner, the great task of manufacturing gifts for

the world's children surged forward. All day and deep into the night, immortals wielded and welded, hammered and harnessed, carved and curled. The fauns galloped around with little baskets of doll parts, which they delivered to the gylfyns, who had six hands apiece and could assemble them with dizzying speed. The Trojan heroes spent hours by their firesides, crafting perfect toy soldiers for small boy soldiers. The pixies were in charge of joke toys, as usual, and one of their Earth-dwelling cousins came up with a splendid new invention: shiny bubbles that floated right into your mouth and came out your nose.

The fairies, who had been put in charge of packaging, produced the most exquisite presents that the Land of the Immortals had ever seen, each wrapped in luminous fairy paper with pink and silver bows.

Gaia and her maidens coaxed the largest fir tree in the kingdom to come to the Square of the Sybils for a few weeks. The tree was quite vain, and when the goddess promised her the most elegant decorations in the universe, she couldn't refuse. And Gaia was as good as her word: pulling stars from the heavens, she hung the tree with their winking lights and with prisms made from the obliging jewel glaciers. The fairies came to perch upon its branches too, and with their wings unfurled, they looked for all the world like a flock of small, gilded butterflies.

In the afternoon of December 24, when Nicholas and his reindeer made their traditional procession through the village to collect the toys from the various workshops, he stopped to admire the tree. "It's the most beautiful one we have ever had," he said to Gaia, who inclined her head graciously. He looked around the square, which was lighted with torches against the early dusk and garlanded with holly in honor of the new princess. "Perhaps," he said hopefully to the immortals who gathered round to wish him well, "this Christmas will be the most beautiful ever." The assembled goblins, fairies, fauns, and sprites nodded in agreement, and the centaurs, who had rich baritone voices, joined together to sing him along his way.

Nicholas leaned back against the bulging sacks that stuffed his sleigh and hoped that Christmas would bring comfort to his sorrowful kingdom. "Peace on Earth, goodwill to humankind," he murmured, lightly touching the reins to urge the reindeer forward. Catching the spirit of their master, the reindeer dashed jubilantly along the snow, pulling the sleigh as if it weighed no more than a feather.

"What's the trouble, Donner?" called Nicholas as

they slowed near the gates.

"There's a crowd gathered, sire," the reindeer replied in a low voice. "I'm afraid I'll hurt them if I jump."

There was a small, wistful group of immortals huddled near the shimmering gates. They bowed to Nicholas as his sleigh drew up alongside them, and one of the wizards came forward. "Please, Father Christmas, I—I have a favor to beg of you," he began nervously, his old eyes fixed pleadingly on Nicholas. "Wouldn't it—couldn't it be possible—permissible to take me with you tonight? I could just sit here, in the back, you see? Next to the sack? I don't weigh much, sire, and my little king, the one I'm guardian to, he's in a terrible way—"

"I don't think it would be allowed, Cadmus," Nicholas said sympathetically.

The old wizard was near tears. "He's going to get himself killed, sire! He's listening to the wrong people, and his uncle is plotting against him, and . . . and he's only a boy!"

Nicholas looked at the old man's face and then leaned out and grasped his wrinkled wrist. "Climb in, sir. We shall do our best." Faces brightened in the little knot, for if Cadmus could go back to the mortal world, then so could they, eventually.

The reindeer wheeled around and retraced their tracks to get a good running start. Eagerly they stretched forward and began their leap. Up, up—the sleigh was almost airborne. But then something happened. Or rather, didn't happen. The reindeer crashed to the ground, their hooves scrambling against the ice. A horrible suspicion jumped unbidden into Nicholas's mind—perhaps he had been mistaken; perhaps his Christmas journey was now forbidden. He tried to push the thought away. "One more time," he murmured to Donner.

"It's him." Donner gestured to the wizard, who pretended not to hear.

"We'll try it one more time," repeated Nicholas.

So they did. The same crash and scramble occurred. Gloomily Nicholas and the reindeer backed up yet again, this time without a passenger. For the third time, he gave the command, and the reindeer leaped forward. Their hooves pounded on the hard-packed ice, and now— Yes! They were up, the sleigh rushing through the air behind them. It was going to be all right. Nicholas shouted jubilantly to the whole universe, "Merry Christmas!"

Far below Cadmus screamed in a quavering voice,

"Tell him to ignore General Vanderschott! Ignore Vanderschott!"

"Yes, of course!" Nicholas cried, waving.

Of all the citizens in the Land of the Immortals, Holly was the least troubled by the curse that had befallen Forever. She lay in her lacy cradle or in her mother's arms, making gentle baby sounds of delight at the snow that whisked around her. After the first few nightmarish weeks, Viviana had woken from her trance of dread, determined that her child would flourish in her frozen surroundings.

"I won't have her treated like an invalid," she said to Nicholas. "She must have a childhood like any other."

Gently Nicholas reminded her that Holly was not like any other child.

"Still. She has to have a wonderful childhood," said Viviana firmly.

"She will," said Nicholas. They gazed down at the smiling Holly, cradled in Viviana's arms. "Isn't she the most beautiful thing?" asked Viviana.

Nicholas touched a tiny pink finger. "The most beautiful thing," he agreed. "You know what I think?" he said suddenly. "I think the will-o'-the-wisps are here, and that's what's making her smile."

"Really? They're here?"

"I'm not certain, but that's my guess."

"You could find out easily enough."

"I could. But the wisps like to be let alone. I'll ask them at the next convocation."

"But that's not for a hundred years!" protested Viviana.

"I can wait," Nicholas said calmly.

Viviana smiled down at Holly. "Your father is a very patient man. Your mother, on the other hand, is—"

"Still living with the mortal clock," interrupted Nicholas, smiling.

"I wonder which of us she'll take after. You, I hope."

"She does seem even tempered. Never cries," Nicholas said.

"Not since that—that night." Viviana's voice trembled.

"Hush, hush. It's over now," counseled Nicholas.

"It's not over," cried Viviana. "Our child lives in a snowstorm!"

"Yes. I have been thinking about that very thing, my dear. We need to make a few improvements in Holly's nursery."

* * *

Holly's room was soon transformed from a typical, if lavish, nursery to a frozen wonderland. The floor was laid out in large tiles of mother-of-pearl, a soft rainbow glowing in each square of milky white. The tapestries that lined the walls were removed and replaced with rows of delicate shells. Holly's cradle, too, was fashioned from a giant shell and draped with a canopy of the thinnest gossamer silk. The rose petal quilt that Gaia had given Holly was all the cover she needed now, and on the coldest winter nights she slept under the flowers, breathing their soft, eternal scent.

When the thick velvet curtains had been removed from the high windows that stretched across one side of the room, Viviana had a sudden inspiration. She called in the Valkonyd gnomes, famous for their silence and their superb metalwork, and asked them to make the princess a grove of silver trees. "A grove of trees," she repeated. "In silver. Don't you think that would be nice?" she babbled, sounding ridiculous even to herself.

"Yes," said Samander, the leader of the Valkonyds.

"Can you make such a thing?"

"Yes," he said simply. At that, the entire group bowed quickly and took their leave.

A few days later, they returned, nearly a hundred

of them, carrying the trees. They were exquisite. Tall silver birches, oaks, and maples climbed from the floor and branched out over Holly's ceiling, their limbs tapering to delicate sprays of leaves, each paper thin and veined in a flawless replica of nature's own miracle. In Holly's room a forest grew, a crystal forest that offered cool shade for the summer months and a glittering lace of branches in the winter. The gnomes had used their magic well, and the silver trees followed the seasons like all others.

"It's—it's magnificent!" Viviana had said, staring in amazement at what they had wrought.

"You have made a marvel," agreed Nicholas, looking gratefully at Samander.

The Valkonyds bowed. There was a silence. A few gnomes nudged Samander with their elbows. Sighing, he took off his hat and stepped forward. "Hmm," he said.

"Yes?" said Viviana. "Ask for anything, Samander."

"Hmm," he began again. Then, clearing his throat loudly, he said, "Can we see her?"

"Holly?" asked Viviana.

The gnomes nodded.

"Certainly, of course. I didn't know you hadn't, at the christening. . . ." stammered Viviana.

"Too short."

So Viviana brought Holly from the next room. The gnomes crowded around, gravely observing the baby's sleep-flushed cheeks and drowsy eyes. Finally Samander put out a stubby brown hand to touch the little reddish gold curl that had recently sprouted atop her head. "Good," he said, with finality. Bowing quickly, the Valkonyds turned and left.

Exactly one year and one day after Herrikhan's assault on the Land of the Immortals, Tundra returned. On a crisp fall afternoon Nicholas was deeply immersed in a particularly murky human dispute, his spectacles resting atop his head, his desk covered with testimonies and counter-testimonies, when the door of his study opened quietly, and Tundra limped in.

The two friends stared at each other in silence. The wolf looked thin and worn, his fur ragged and his eyes tired. Nicholas saw that he had a long, raised scar on his right forepaw, but he knew that Tundra would not willingly tell him how he had acquired it, nor anything else of the long year he had spent on the edges of the country as a solitary animal. "Welcome home, friend," Nicholas greeted him quietly. "I have missed you more than I can say."

"Thank you, sire. I am glad to be home." Tundra limped toward the rug that lay in front of the crackling fire. He turned once, preparing to lay himself down, but stopped suddenly and leaned his head forward to smell the rug. He stiffened, and then walked on his tired legs to another part of the room, beside Nicholas's desk, where he lay down without a word. In less than a minute, he was asleep. Nicholas stared down at the familiar face and waited. Five minutes, ten minutes. When he was finally certain that Tundra would not wake, he pushed back his chair and tiptoed out to tell Viviana the news. And to find a soft rug to lay next to his desk.

Tundra slept for three days, waking only to consume enormous quantities of meat and drink copious draughts of water. On the fourth day, Nicholas was again at his desk, still hard at work when Holly toppled in the door. "Bump," she said.

Holly had been a determined but not very dignified walker for the last three weeks. Each day she tried to escape from the nursery suite, causing her mother and the nursery goblins no end of alarm, for the crackling fires and stoves that heated the rest of the palace posed a risk to Holly's snow heart. Ignorant of the danger, Holly scooted out the nursery door at every opportunity, eager to explore the fascinating territory beyond her rooms. She never cried when she was picked up and removed to where she was supposed to be; she just hummed and tried to wrap the goblins' hair around their noses. Twice she had succeeded in escaping. The first time she had been found in the attic room where old magic wands were kept. This garret was quite cold, but "Who knows what kind of a wish a one-year-old baby might make?" Viviana had moaned. The second time Holly had made her way to Nicholas's study, a place she immediately concluded was paradise, for it contained not only her daddy, but also a variety of interesting objects like globes and books and ink and a letter opener that were all too dangerous to be within her reach. Forgetting her fugitive status, in his delight Nicholas had tossed her in the air, showed her interesting pictures in *Animals of the Planet Earth,* and held her up to the open window to see the trees tossing in the wind. By the time a wild-eyed goblin burst into the room in a desperate search for the baby, Holly and Nicholas had become allies for all time.

Now she had once again escaped and headed straight for Nicholas's study. She picked herself up and chortled at her father. He chortled back. Her eyes scanned the room in search of the nice, dangerous letter opener and she caught sight of Tundra, sleeping on his side. When she encountered anything truly compelling, Holly abandoned walking in favor of the speedier crawl. In an instant she was breathing heavily in Tundra's face, her nose pressed up against his. She inspected him closely. "Dog," she said.

Tundra didn't even open his eyes. "I am not a dog," he said.

"Dog," she repeated, reaching for an ear.

Tundra lifted his head and looked at Nicholas. "There's a small person in your study, sire," he said.

"I know it, Tundra. That's Holly," said Nicholas distractedly, waving one hand to put out the fire and the other to open the windows.

"Ah. Holly." Tundra squinted as she pulled more firmly on his ear. "Pleased to make your acquaintance, Your Highness."

"Dog."

"I am *not* a dog."

"Woof."

"Exactly," said Tundra, and there was something in his voice that made Nicholas turn. Holly was patting the wolf's soft neck gently, and Tundra was smiling.

The next morning Nicholas observed, peeking

over his spectacles, that the wolf raised his head expectantly each time footsteps passed in the hallway outside the door. He said nothing, and Nicholas, too, kept a discreet silence. But after lunch Nicholas returned to his desk to find Tundra's rug empty. The afternoon ticked quietly away—one hour, two hours, and still he did not return. At four o'clock, consumed by curiosity, Nicholas slammed his books shut and walked, ever so casually, toward the nursery.

He heard them before he saw them. Holly was shrieking, "Go, go, go!" between gales of laughter, and Alexia, sounding determined, was calling, "Hold still! Hold still!"

Nicholas opened the door. Holly, dressed in a blue nightgown which revealed that she was supposed to be napping, sat astride Tundra's back, her hands clasped around his neck. The little fox, who couldn't bear to miss out on any fun, was trying to take her seat behind Holly. This she hoped to accomplish by leaping wildly in the air at Tundra, who stepped neatly aside each time. Alexia couldn't understand why she was having no success, and Holly thought it was the funniest thing she had ever seen. But they did not astonish Nicholas; Tundra did. Here was Tundra the majestic, the calm, the solemn, Tundra whom

Nicholas had always declared should have been king in his stead, dancing across the floor with a baby on his back and a silly fox under his feet. To Nicholas's profound relief, he looked vastly amused.

From that day on, Tundra divided his time between his old duties and his new. He was Nicholas's most trusted advisor, a conscientious voice of reason, and an astute and ready guardian. But he was Holly's companion, protector, and confidant, who watched over her with pride and tenderness. Sometimes Nicholas would come upon the two of them fast asleep, Holly's arm curled around her faithful friend, worn out from their day's play, and he would say to himself that it made perfect sense. Holly was the one person who could never remind the wolf of his lost Terra. Nicholas was grateful that his daughter had the loyalty and love of the being he most admired.

Chapter Eight

BUT WHY?" Holly said, glancing worriedly from her mother to her father. For the sixteenth day in a row, as the Land of the Immortals sweltered under the summer sun, a blizzard fell from the silver branches of the trees in her room. The mother-of-pearl floor was frigid under her bare feet, and Viviana shivered within the velvet coat she kept in Holly's rooms to wear during her hours there. "Why do I have to be cold?"

"Because your heart has to be cold to do its job," Nicholas said.

Holly thought, her four-year-old imagination struggling to picture her heart's job. "You said other boys and girls," she said after a moment. "You said other boys and girls had illness, just like me. Can they come to play?"

"Oh, sweetheart," said Nicholas, gathering her up in his arms. "Sweetheart, I'm sorry. In the mortal world, there are other girls and boys, but there are no other children in the Land of the Immortals. You are very special here."

Holly's troubled green eyes rested on his. "All right," she said finally, and slipped out of his lap. Her feet padded lightly across the floor to her hideaway. This was a little nook that Samander's gnomes had carved into the largest silver tree. Holly had covered the opening with a scarf embroidered with green leaves. When she wanted to think, work out a problem, or be alone, Holly would crawl into her cavern and close the curtain. Now she waved to her parents and disappeared behind the scarf. Nicholas and Viviana heard her rustling about, making herself comfortable. There was a long silence. Then, very softly, Holly began to whisper. "Yes," she was saying, "here. And you can have this one too. Would you like my dolly? Her name is Kasana. She has two dresses. Kasana has illness too. Do you want a cream bun? Mmm. Yes. Do you want another? You can have them all. . . ."

Though Holly was permitted to wander freely through the palace on very cold days, she spent much of her time in her suite of rooms. The silver trees now arched over a glass bed with a canopy of lace instead of the shell cradle, and in Holly's playroom the baby's rattles and rockers had been replaced with dolls and books and puzzles. Tiny glass and wood animals paraded through a miniature town at one end of the room, and at the other stood Holly's easel and paints. Music boxes from the workshops of Forever lined one of the long, low shelves that ran under the windows, and in the dusk Holly often stood watching the sunset as their tunes spun daintily along. A cushioned window seat in one corner faced a plush sofa and a small armchair grouped around a tea table. She dined with her mother and father in the palace dining room, wearing a gown spun of snow, the work of Mr. Guillée, whose creations twinkled like diamonds in the candlelight. On particularly warm nights, Nicholas assisted her snow gowns by calling up a small flurry of the enchanted snow, which kept her heart the proper temperature without inconveniently melting into the soup.

Outdoors was a more complex matter. True, on a

crisp winter day the gardens were even colder than the palace and therefore more suitable for Holly. But the problem was variability; who could predict when the sun would grow strong and heat the chill air to a dangerous degree? And what, exactly, was that degree? Not even the immortal Dr. Gaston Lavalier of the St. Amboise Institute could answer that question with any certainty. There had been several frightening incidents since the fateful night of Herrikhan's visit, but nothing approached that first experience. And, in her toddler days, Holly had managed to place herself in several warm rooms without ill effects. But, as Viviana insisted, perhaps she had been rescued in the nick of time. It was a mystery, a puzzle, and to Holly, a baffling punishment that she was just beginning to wonder what she had done to deserve.

Late that night, long after her bedtime, Holly crept out of her glistening bed and stole across her room to look out the window. She climbed upon the cushioned seat beneath the glass and pressed her face against the pane. The sky was still pink in the west, and far beyond the palace gardens she could make out a few of the colored lanterns strung along the village streets. Shadows passed back and forth across the distant lights; maybe someone was dancing; maybe there was a party. Holly pushed her ear to the glass, straining to hear a few fleeting notes of music. Nothing. Only the soft whisper of snow brushing against the floor. Cautiously Holly put both of her hands to the sash and pushed. A shrill creak broke the silence of the room. Holly froze, expecting a harried goblin face to peek round the door. Nothing. She pushed again, lifting the window above her head. A wave of soft, warm air greeted her. The night was sweet scented and rich with sounds. Little rustles and chirps emerged from the dark branches below her, and the swelling anthem of cicadas rose from the lawn beyond. From far away snatches of laughter and stray notes of music danced through the air. Holly leaned forward, drinking in the languid, summery air like a potion. She tilted her chin up and scanned the stars, the moon, the enchanted dust of the nighttime sky. She dreamed.

"Holly." She jumped guiltily. It was Tundra, his white fur shimmering in the dark room. "You know that window should be closed. It's too warm outside for you to have your window open."

Holly was too little to argue, too little to explain that she wanted to be part of the party, that she wanted to see the creatures who laughed together in the warm night, that she was tired of the shushing snow and silvery breezes. All she could do was cry. She put her head down on the window seat and sobbed. Tundra watched her for a while without interrupting, but then he rested his head near hers on the cushion and gently licked her ear. His sandpapery tongue tickled, and Holly stopped crying and gave a little hiccup.

"Your ear is filled with tears," Tundra observed.

"My nose is filled with tears too."

"Are you too hot?"

"No," Holly said listlessly. "I'm fine. I was watching the shadows. They're having a party down in the village."

"Would you like that? A party?" asked Tundra hopefully.

Holly glanced up, her face bright with hope. "What do you mean? A real party? With children?"

"No—no," Tundra stammered, regretting his words. "No—you know that there are no other children here. With grown-ups. In the ballroom."

Holly drooped again. "No. No, thank you."

The wolf watched her, aching with sympathy, and then said, "I'm sorry. That's not what you want at all, is it?"

Holly seemed to have grown older as she looked at

her friend. She said, "It's all right; you wanted to make me happy, because you love me." She wrapped her arms around Tundra's neck and buried her face in his fur.

"Time for bed," he said.

"Time for bed," she repeated obediently, dropping off the window seat onto his back without warning. Tundra was used to this maneuver and patiently carried her to her bed, where he dumped her unceremoniously onto her soft mattress. Silently they touched noses, and Holly rolled into a little ball and fell asleep.

Time went on, and Holly made some discoveries that changed her life. The first of these came on a gloomy, bitterly cold evening in February. Always enlivened by brisk, frosty weather, Holly was trotting around her room busily, creating a circus with her dolls. Holly's circuses were exciting events that featured death-defying feats of courage, such as jumping over sleeping wolves. At the moment one of her dolls was preparing to stick her head into the mouth of a lion. Holly was looking around for a lion. Then, she remembered that she had one, a toy lion, on wheels, too, which would be ideal.

But where was it? She looked around thoughtfully. She had made a zoo recently. In the closet. She pattered off to the closet, looking like a busy angel in her snowflake nightgown. It was nearly a room unto itself, and it held no clothes—those were kept in an icy cold wardrobe—but only old toys, odds and ends and bits of things that nobody could bear to throw out. Holly peered into its shadowy depths. The lion was there, lying on his side, but her attention was caught by a strange object. A long cylinder, covered in smooth black leather, was balanced atop a stand. Holly stared. What was it? She had never seen it before. She pulled the stand out into the light, observing the brass fittings around the cylinder's case and the thick glass at one end. The other end sported a small peephole. Inspired by a vague idea, or perhaps a recollection, Holly pushed the stand to a window.

Some minutes later, when Nicholas and Viviana came in to read Holly her good-night story, they found their daughter perched on a precarious stack of books, gazing raptly through a telescope that neither of them could remember seeing before. Holly turned to her parents, her cheeks flushed with excitement. "What is it?" she asked her father breathlessly.

Nicholas leaned down to the glass, fully expecting to see the lights of the village brought a bit closer by the telescope. Instead a living vision of a tropical island greeted him. Brilliant red and blue macaws clung to swaying palm trees, greedily snatching palm fruits from one another. Beyond the thick foliage, clear blue water glinted under a balmy sun. Nicholas gazed at this picture of warmth for a moment, but Holly's insistent tug on his robe returned him to her questioning face. "It's an island, sweetheart," he said.

"But the blue. What's the blue?" Holly persisted, and her father realized, with a wave of sadness, that his daughter had never before seen a large body of water moving. To Holly, water was a frozen substance, white and still, not the splashing elixir of oceans and lakes, streams and waterfalls. Once again Nicholas was reminded that his daughter was imprisoned in half of a life, and he was overcome by a sudden urge to smash the telescope. The telescope would only show her what she could not have. Swallowing hard, Nicholas explained water to Holly, watching her eyes go round with astonishment. When he was finished, she silently turned back to the telescope and looked for a long time at the dancing sea and the quarreling birds.

Later that night Nicholas and Viviana tried to remember where the telescope had come from. It was perfectly likely, of course, that it had been in that crowded closet for years without anyone noticing.

The telescope would only show her what she could not have.

Viviana was almost certain that she had seen it among the great pile of christening gifts; Nicholas was almost certain that it had not been there the day before, but the truth was that they simply did not remember. What did not occur to either of them was that they *could* not remember because the enchanted telescope had spread a spell, like the thinnest of cobwebs, over the whole household. It was a mild spell, nothing dangerous or obvious, nothing that would give away its author or his intentions—just a little spell that made them all accept the telescope without too many questions. After a few days, Nicholas and Viviana stopped wondering about the origins of the mysterious spyglass and smiled at the sight of Holly gazing through the lens at the vast seas, bustling cities, and exotic landscapes far beyond her frozen room.

For Holly, the spyglass was a window into a thousand stories and lives she had never before imagined. Peering into the small lens, she saw children playing tag in a dusty Dakota side yard on a summer afternoon; a proud father boastfully displaying his new son in Zanzibar; a beautiful woman in a violet silk gown swirling across a London ballroom in the arms of a prince. She watched, intrigued, as a resolute cluster of men struggled up an icy gorge in the Himalayas. In

Paris a lady demonstrated the workings of the wondrous new elevator to a crowd of awed bankers. One
particularly fat banker refused to climb aboard the dangerous contraption. Three thousand people dropped to
their knees before the dowager empress of China,
whose stiff silken robes glowed like flames above the
sea of bowed backs. When Holly was finally pulled
away by a scolding goblin, her green eyes still saw a
lone figure, free and untamed, tearing across the empty
plains for the pure fun of it.

There was a peculiar feature of the telescope. It
seemed only to show the world in its happiest, most
alluring guise. Whether Holly trained the glass on a
hectic metropolis or a sunbaked Bantu village, she saw
only its best possible face: no hunger, no enslavement,
no poverty, no greed, no evil, no violence. Through
the lens, the mortal world was a place of joy and
adventure, where good deeds always met with just
deserts, bravery was rewarded with triumph, industry
resulted in success, laughter bubbled forth from all,
and children were free to gallop wildly across the
plains without any goblins to stop them. Lying in her
glass bed at night, with the shadows of branches
bending above her, Holly put herself to sleep by
imagining her life in the mortal world.

Chapter Nine

HARD-BOILED EGGS," Holly was saying. "And lemonade and fried chicken and cake."

Tundra shivered. "*Fried chicken? Who would eat that? I'll have something before we go.*"

Holly sighed. "Tundra. Will you at least pretend to eat with us? It's a picnic. I read about them, and you're supposed to have fried chicken. Please?"

"Oh, all right," Tundra grumbled.

"And besides, you like cake," Holly reminded him.

"You like cake," Alexia said. "But I love cake.

Especially frosting. Do you remember Holly's eighth birthday?"

"Vividly," said Tundra.

"Remember how I woke up in the middle of the night and told you that if anyone said the word *frosting* I was going to be sick, and then you did say the word *frosting* and then—"

"I remember," interrupted Tundra.

"Why did you say it, I wonder?" Alexia looked at him questioningly.

"I've often wondered the same thing," Tundra replied.

Holly was in the closet, searching for a basket. "You always take food in a basket on a picnic. Oh, here's one." She looked around. "And we need a blanket, to sit on. They always sit on a blanket."

"You don't have any blankets, remember?" said Alexia.

"Maybe Mama does," said Holly, and went off to look for Viviana.

After much assembling of goods and pleading with the kitchen goblins, who saw no reason why plates and cups and forks should be taken out of doors, the three friends ventured out into the palace gardens. Holly led the way, for it was her idea, after all. She had read about picnics in her storybooks—how children liked eating outside even if there were bugs in the food sometimes, and how they played games afterward—and even though she knew that most picnics didn't take place in the snow, she was determined that hers would meet the standards in every other way. It was a brilliant, icy day, and their feet made crisp prints in the new snow as they trudged through a small meadow to Parian Pond. Surrounded by fir trees, the pond was now frozen to a glassy sheen, and there, on its banks, Holly spread the bright red blanket she had borrowed from her mother. Carefully she set out the plates and cups (she had brought one for each of them despite the fact that she was the only member of the party with hands) and laid the food out on each. Tundra and Alexia looked confusedly at the lemonade and chicken and, after a few polite nudges, left them alone, but Alexia gobbled down egg after egg, and Tundra consumed a monumental slice of chocolate cake. Too happy to eat much, Holly grinned at her companions between nibbles. "I see what they mean," she said. "It *is* more fun to eat outside. And we don't have to worry about bugs in our food."

After a while Holly lay back, pillowing her head in her arms, and looked at the light blue sky. Alexia began to explore the edges of the pond in the hopes of finding a duck to annoy.

Holly glanced up at Tundra. He was staring fixedly into the distance beyond the pond. "What do you see?" she asked.

"I'm not sure," he said. "Something strange."

"Let's go find out."

"All right," he agreed. "But I go first. Just to be safe."

Holly smiled. He always said that. "All right. Your Lordship." Tundra was officially Lord High Chamberlain of the King's Household, but his title made him twitch.

"Let us proceed, Your Royal Highness, princess of the Aubade and of Sherenhalle," Tundra replied smoothly.

Holly stuck her tongue out at him, and they walked amiably along the side of the pond toward the black trees beyond. The trees tended to hibernate in the winter, but there were a few whispers and rustles as the wolf and Holly stepped between their branches. "Greetings, Your Royal Highness. Greetings, Your Lordship," said an old pine tree in dignified tones.

Holly almost snorted with laughter, and she felt Tundra's ribs shaking next to her, but they managed to nod their heads regally and walk on. Now Holly, too, began to discern a peculiar happening in the snow-covered field beyond the woods. A small white reindeer, about the size of a regular deer, was repeatedly climbing atop a small mound and hurling himself to the ground below. Despite his repetition of this activity, there was apparently something about it that the reindeer found deeply distressing, for he was crying.

Forgetting caution at the sight of the reindeer's distress, Holly ran forward. "What's the matter, reindeer?" she called just as the deer leaped from his perch. Her call startled him, and he landed more awkwardly than ever. This, evidently, was the last straw, for he broke into resounding howls.

"I c-c-can't do it!" he wailed. "I caaaaan't!"

"Can't what, little reindeer?" asked Holly, patting his back softly.

"Can't flyyyyyyy!" he squalled.

Tundra's eyes smiled, but he said gravely, "You don't have to learn on your own. Very few of you are born knowing how to fly; that's why there are lessons. You'll learn how to fly there."

"But Don-Don-Donner won't let me take the lessons," sniffed the reindeer.

Holly was indignant. "Why? Why won't he?"

This set the little reindeer off into a new vale of tears. "Just look at me! Look at my eyes!"

"We can't see your eyes while you are crying so," Holly said gently.

The reindeer tried to conquer his tears. He lifted his head and looked into Holly's face. She saw that he was cockeyed: one brown eye looked straight ahead, while the other veered east. "You see?" he said sadly.

Holly rubbed the rough fur underneath the reindeer's chin. "What's your name?"

"Meteor."

"Can you see? With your eye, I mean?" asked Holly.

"Yes," answered Meteor defensively. "Well, mostly. Maybe not things in the distance. But the others could do that, and I could just pull. I'm very strong," he added.

"But Meteor, you have to be able to see into the distance to pull the Christmas Eve sleigh," began Holly. "Because there are so many stops to make, you know."

Meteor hung his head. "I know," he said miserably. "I know. And there are lots of other reindeer who would get a chance before me anyway. I guess I just want to fly. I don't have to pull the Christmas Eve sleigh. I just want to fly. And Donner says I can't."

Holly glanced toward Tundra. He nodded. "Listen, Meteor," she began, kneeling to look into his face, "we can help you learn to fly. Tundra and I can go to the flying classes, and then we'll tell you what we learn. We'll repeat every word Donner and Comet and the other teachers say!"

Meteor sat down on his haunches with a thump. "You're Princess Holly," he announced, looking very pleased with his discovery.

She nodded.

"Well!" Meteor looked her up and down. "Not at all what I expected."

"What did you expect?" she asked curiously.

"I thought you—you . . ." the reindeer trailed off guiltily.

"What? I what?" Holly asked.

"I heard, um, that you—well—you were an, um, invalid," Meteor stammered, trying to find what he considered to be a tactful word.

Holly stared at him. "Invalid? Do you mean my heart? My heart has to stay cold all the time, so I can't go out much. Except when it's like this outside. What do the immortals think is the matter with me?"

"Lots of people say that—that it's your heart, just like you said," Meteor assured her hastily. "But—but—nobody sees you, you know, so they imagine things."

"What things?" Holly persisted.

"Oh, just silly things."

"What things?" Holly repeated.

"Well." Meteor looked at the ground. "I heard that you were tiny, the size of a fairy or a pixie. Some folks say that you can't walk, and some folks say that you were stolen away by a wicked witch years ago and that's why—" He concluded abruptly.

"And that's why what?" Holly pressed. It had never occurred to her that the citizens of Forever thought about her at all, much less that they could have fabricated such strange tales about her.

"That's why the king doesn't come among us the way he used to—because he's busy trying to win you back with dark enchantments," mumbled Meteor.

"That," snapped Tundra, "is the most ridiculous thing I've ever heard."

"I know. But you asked."

Holly was quiet. She looked up to the smooth, white sky. It would begin to snow again soon. Finally she dropped her green eyes to Meteor. They were filled with tears. "Will you tell them?" she begged. "Tell the people that you saw me, and that I'm not tiny or stolen or any of those things. It's only my heart, because it has to be cold, that's why they don't see me. And my father isn't learning dark enchantments; he's just taking care of me." Tundra butted his nose against her head in sympathy. Holly blinked her eyes very hard. "Now," she said in a stronger voice. "Let's talk about these flying lessons."

The next day Holly slipped casually into the stable where Donner was teaching an excited group of young reindeer the basics of flying. She climbed atop a swinging gate and perched there, looking innocent, as the deer were lectured on the importance of the running start and the correct alignment of the back. She lay upon a bale of hay with a straw in her mouth while Comet led the practice leaps.

"He says it's all about believing in yourself," she told Meteor later that afternoon. "Donner talked on and on about wind speeds and the force of gravity near Earth's surface and how fast you have to be running before you can get airborne, but Comet just said that you have to believe that you can fly. And I think he's right. The ones who were muttering to themselves about wind speed and gravity kept falling, but the ones who were confident made long, beautiful jumps into the sky."

So the practice sessions began and, as long as the weather held, Holly and Tundra met Meteor in the little field behind the pond each afternoon. There Holly would repeat the day's lesson and coach Meteor in his practice leaps. Day after day he jumped doggedly through the snow, sometimes achieving a graceful arch, more often producing only a spray of ice and a tangle of kicking hooves. Many times in a single afternoon, Meteor would pick himself up out of the snow, his fur damp with effort, stumble to his feet, and croak, "I think I'm getting it." Holly and Tundra, looking on, frequently doubted that Meteor would ever attain his goal, but they never doubted his dedication.

One freezing day Alexia accompanied them to the practice field. She had set out with them many times before, but, having a distractible nature, had been diverted time and again by ducks, squirrels, and, once, a badger. She had, therefore, never met Meteor nor assisted in his lessons. Now she threw herself into the project, shouting out inspirational words and useless suggestions as the reindeer dashed up and down the runway that Holly had smoothed out of the snow for him. But when Meteor returned from his eighteenth attempt, Alexia curled her tail haughtily around her feet and regarded him with narrowed eyes. "You're not trying," she said.

Meteor looked at her, shocked. "Of course I'm trying, you silly goose! I've been working my legs off for weeks!"

"You might be more encouraging, Lexy," said Holly.

Alexia lifted her nose obstinately in the air. "But he *isn't* trying. He's hoping, but that's not the same thing. He's running down the whatchoocallit saying to himself, 'It would be wonderful if I flew this time,' but what he really needs to be saying is 'I'm flying, I'm lifting up, I'm in the air!'"

Holly looked at her in amazement. "Why, Lexy, I think that perhaps you might be right!" She turned to Meteor, whose face was sulky. "Meteor, let's try Alexia's idea. Say to yourself that you're flying and do your best to believe it. Think about lifting off the ground, how it will feel to have the air rushing by all around you. Don't think about anything else!"

"It won't work," he muttered.

"See," sneered Alexia. "He doesn't really want to fly."

"I do too!" Meteor burst out. "I want it more than anything!"

"Not more than you're scared of failing," she retorted. "You don't want to really, really try and fail, so you don't really try."

Tundra shook his head at her lack of tact, but his eyes held new respect for the fox. Holly, too, realized that somehow Alexia had seen to the heart of Meteor's problem. But now she stroked Meteor's hanging head. "Meteor, dear," she whispered, "we're all afraid to fail. I am too. But it's only us here, and we love you whether you fly or not. So go ahead, go ahead and try with your whole soul."

Meteor lifted his head. "All right," he said. "I'll do my best."

He wheeled around and trotted briskly to the top of the runway. He rubbed his nose in the snow—that was one of Donner's tips—and squinted down the length of the field. He paused for a moment, thinking, and began to run.

They all knew even before he lifted his forelegs that he was going to get it this time. There was something new in his gallop, in the determined posture of his head, in his charge forward. When he finally made the leap, it looked as though he wasn't even aware of

it. All he was thinking about was flight itself, the dazzling swirl of air beneath him and the lightness as his
body overcame gravity—and then, suddenly, it was
happening. He grazed the straggling bare branches of
the bushes that clustered at one end of the field and
simply kept on running, up and up, higher and higher,
until the trees that ringed the pond were little black
brushes behind him. He wheeled in the sky, and the
sun glared full in his face. For one exhilarating
moment, he believed that he could fly to the sun
itself. Then he looked down. Holly and Tundra and
Alexia were far below, cheering and yowling encour-
agement, their upturned faces glowing. Meteor
smiled back at them—and plummeted to the ground
in a matter of seconds. Fortunately he landed in a soft
bed of powdery snow. While he was shaking himself
off, his three friends clambered to his side through the
thick drifts.

"Good work, fine work, my lad!" Tundra congrat-
ulated him.

Alexia bounced at the wolf's heels. "See? See?
Wasn't I right? See?"

Holly, at a disadvantage with regard to number
of feet, came last, flapping her arms wildly as she
struggled through the powder. "That was splendid!

Marvelous!" she cried, falling into a snow bank. She popped up, still grinning. "Tremendous! Anyone would think you'd been flying for years!"

Meteor walked lightly over the snow and knelt so that she might steady herself upon his back.

"Thank you," she said, grateful for his assistance.

"No. Thank you," Meteor replied earnestly. "I could never have done this without you. I am yours to command—forever."

"Then I command you to lift me up," said Holly, laughing. She twined her arms around his neck, and, as he pulled her out of the little hollow, she whispered, "I am so proud of you."

"Even if I can't do it again?"

"Even if you can't do it again. But I think you will."

And he did. Meteor took several more flights that afternoon, as much to escape Alexia's endless self-congratulation as anything. By the next day, he had overcome his gnawing fear that he would lose his new ability just as quickly as he had gained it, and by the day after that, he was capable of lolling in the air like a bird and landing wherever he pleased. The next week, at Holly's suggestion, Meteor drew Comet aside and confided that he could fly. Comet of course demanded that he prove it, which Meteor happily did. Then Comet dragged Donner away from his appetizing dinner to behold the unusual phenomenon of a self-taught flyer.

"Humpf," said Donner, still chewing. "How'd he figure that out?" His eyes followed Meteor as he landed.

"Don't know," said Comet.

"How'd you figure that out, boy?" he called to Meteor.

"Some friends helped me, sir," replied the cock-eyed reindeer.

"What friends?" asked Donner suspiciously. "Was it Toller?" The students were instructed not to reveal the mysteries of flying to outsiders.

"No, sir, not Toller. It was Princess Holly and Tundra. And Alexia, the little fox," Meteor added, a bit unwillingly.

"Princess Holly? How do you know her?"

"Well, she saw me trying to fly one day. I guess I made a pretty sorry sight, so she decided to help me. Sir."

"Mmm," said Donner, thinking, I wondered what she was about, lying around the stable, looking like a cherub. "What about your eye? Can you see?"

"Haven't run into anything yet, sir."

"Mmm. Well, I suppose you'd better join us, then. Your landing could use a little work."

"Yes, sir," said Meteor obediently.

Comet smiled kindly at him. "I congratulate you on your determination. It is a valuable trait."

It was Comet who told Nicholas. That evening at the dinner table, Nicholas watched Holly closely. She was chattering away to Viviana and Sofya about the puzzling question of why little mortal girls sometimes had to wear gloves and sometimes had to take them off. She had watched several glove donnings and doffings through the telescope and found the whole thing baffling. Neither Viviana nor Sofya, whose mortal lives had ended long before anyone ever thought of gloves, could answer.

Nicholas broke in abruptly. "I hear you're learning to fly."

"It's harder than it looks," Holly replied.

"By all reports, you have done very well by young Meteor."

"Who's Meteor?" asked Viviana, bewildered.

"He's a reindeer I was helping to fly—" began Holly, but Nicholas interrupted again.

"And that was very kind, my love, but in the future you must leave the task to Donner and Comet. I do not wish them to feel as though we do not appreciate their authority."

Holly eyed Nicholas thoughtfully, reading what lay beneath his words. "You think you're protecting me, but they think you're hiding me because there's something wrong with me," she said finally.

"What do you mean?" asked Nicholas, laying both hands upon the table. Sofya sent him a penetrating look.

Holly retold fantastic rumors that Meteor had imparted to her. "Really, Papa, I think it would be a good idea if I came to the village once in a while. Especially when it's cold, as it is now, nothing will happen amiss, and it will put a stop to these silly ideas."

"But how can you teach a reindeer to fly when you don't know how to fly?" Viviana said, unable to worry about the larger problem until the smaller was resolved.

Holly explained while Nicholas sat in silent thought. This was the cause of the new distance he had felt between his subjects and himself. He felt an insistent current of dread that trickled underneath every thought, hope, and plan for the future. Each time he left the palace, he stopped upon the staircase to look back one more time. As he checked in on the workshops where the toys were being made or listened quietly to the reports of the Committee for the Aid and Comfort of Earthly Creatures, his attention was distracted by a tiny whisper of fear: is Holly safe? Perhaps Herrikhan was even now at her door. Perhaps I have seen her for the last time. Nonsense, he would scold himself, utter foolishness. Cowardly foolishness.

His people knew. They saw that his eyes, which once revealed his thoughts, were now veiled, but they could not guess the secret that was behind the divide. They knew he did not show them his soul as he had before. They watched the new shadows that hovered on the edges of their land, and they drew their own conclusions. Nicholas glanced at Holly, who was describing Meteor's inaugural flight; her face was glowing, and her hands flew about in an animated if not very accurate imitation of the reindeer's flight pattern. It's not right, he thought. We can't keep the immortals from learning to love her as we do just because we are frightened of her future.

"Holly, I believe you are right," he declared suddenly. "You should visit the village, become acquainted with the immortals, learn about their lives. We must not keep you all to ourselves."

Holly and Viviana looked at him in surprise. "Really?" Holly squeaked.

"Really?" echoed Viviana.

"Yes. Really. We must plan an excursion as soon as possible." Nicholas smiled happily and stroked his beard. "How would you like to attend a pelote game?"

Sofya sat in silence, looking absently at the plate before her. Her eyes narrowed, as if she was trying to remember something, and then it was gone. She looked around at her friends and smiled. "Pelote. What a splendid idea."

Chapter Ten

IT WAS A BRIGHT winter afternoon, brilliant with sun and ice. Red berries glistened under little cloaks of frozen water on the holly trees. Holly, who usually stopped to admire her namesake, ran past with only a wave, her black boots crunching patterns in the snow. Tundra strode easily beside her, his footsteps crackling as they broke through the icy crust. "I do think"—Holly gasped as she struggled to keep up with her friend—"I do think that Sofya might have ended my lesson a little bit early."

"Save your breath for running," advised Tundra.

"Still," said Holly.

Some of the immortals had fretted about their enforced stay in Forever, and some had viewed it as a well-deserved holiday from their daily cares, but Sofya had found a vocation. From the very beginning, she had been Viviana's most trusted friend and comfort, but as Viviana grew beyond her first, paralyzing fears about Holly, Sofya had turned her attention from mother to daughter. Holly, she knew, must be pre- . pared for the part that Herrikhan had forced her to play, the struggle that would, inevitably, take place between them. She watched as Nicholas attempted to protect his child from every danger and decided that she must teach Holly what her father could not bear to have her learn. Prudently she said nothing to Nicholas and Viviana; she simply offered to become Holly's teacher. And they gratefully accepted, for who would not wish their child to be taught by the wisest of wise women.

To the casual observer, Sofya's lessons might pass for straightforward, intelligent education. She taught Holly her letters and numbers, as any good governess would do. But she also taught the art of imagination, the calculus of the heart, and the science of courage. Holly was thoroughly convinced that her teacher was the most brilliant creature in the world, and she drank in all that she was taught. Sofya, too, was satisfied, for her student was learning the secret lessons underneath the daily ones—and unlike most students, Holly was never bored and always wanted to go to school.

But not today. Today Holly had just wanted to go to the pelote game. Sofya had been firm. School ended at three o'clock and not a minute before. Holly wiggled. Holly bounced her pencil. Holly pulled at her curls. Holly wrote 456 when she meant 645. Then the clock struck three with a golden chime, and Holly whirled out of her chair and leaped into the hall, where Tundra waited.

They were running now, faster and faster, and as they rounded a small grove of trees the Parian Field spread out before them. Holly gasped in surprise. There, on the open, frosty turf, a pelote game was in full sail. Immortal pelote bore some resemblance to its mortal counterpart, but it was a much rowdier affair. The players wore long, curved baskets on their arms, which they used to scoop and hurl a small red ball into their nets, thereby scoring a point. However, the baskets were also used to parry and thrust and make mayhem in order to keep the ball holder from approaching his net. To add to the unruliness, there were not two teams, but three, and not three nets, but four. The extra net was called the spider's web, and any time the ball landed there, a point was subtracted from the team whose member had launched it in. Aside from this refinement, there were few rules, and all of those were broken continually, so the air was thick with shouts and accusations. The only keeper of order was an unusually lanky goblin called Fritz (his real name was Elitrion, but everyone called him Fritz because of his hair), who blew his whistle at each infraction and busily kept score at the same time.

Fauns, goblins, and satyrs played pelote, but the truly spectacular games were played by the centaurs, for these creatures boasted four legs *and* two arms. They were massive beings, capable of running at furious speeds, as befitted their horse nature, and they were wily strategists, generous collaborators, and expert cheaters, as was to be expected of those with mortal minds. As a result, Centaurian pelote was rough, fast, and incredibly exciting. Holly watched open-mouthed as thirty-eight roaring centaurs pounded across the field in pursuit of a thirty-ninth, who was yipping with delight, his basket curved triumphantly above his head with the red ball nestled in its depths. Dashing toward his net, he lowered his arm to scoop his treasure in, and was knocked over by a massive thrust against his side. Two centaurs went grunting into the mud, and the ball went spinning out of reach, slipping across the icy grass in an uncertain path.

Now the screaming phalanx of equine men bore down upon the little red ball with thundering hooves. Holly saw Zenwyler at the front, yowling with excitement as he stretched his basket forward to scrape the ball up from the ground. Fritz was blowing his whistle wildly, screaming, "Time OUT! TIME OUT!" but nobody paid him any attention, because, truly, they didn't care about the points at all. They didn't care about anything but chasing and grabbing and roaring and throwing.

"Holly! Come over here and sit down," Nicholas called from his sleigh. He had been there since the beginning, and had, in fact, tossed out the ball that opened the game, an honor suitable for the king, but also one that nobody else wanted, because the centaurs had been known to trample the ball tosser. Their respect for Nicholas kept him relatively safe, but it was still a perilous moment, and he always had to remind himself of his immortality as the ball left his hand. Then he ran.

Holly hurried to her father's side. "Papa," she said,

slipping into the seat next to him, "this must be the most exciting game in the world."

"I think so too," Nicholas confided. "Especially the Centaurian games. Watch Lysinias. He's the one over on the left, the chestnut one. He's a sharp one; watch him, now, there he goes! He's going to slip in behind Leneth and apHoug—watch him!" The chestnut centaur had successfully divided his opponents, and now he knelt to retrieve the precious red ball.

"But my favorite is Zenwyler," Holly murmured, her eyes on the game. "He's so enormous, and he's having such a good time."

"Yes, there's nobody like Zenwyler," agreed Nicholas. "Not so strategic, perhaps, but the boldest of them all."

As if to prove his point, Zenwyler was at that moment leaping over the back of another player— not, of course, a player who was standing still, but a player who was running. Catching sight of the huge form hurtling through the air above him, the other centaur made a quick decision and veered directly into the path of his landing. Zenwyler crashed to the ground, somersaulted, and scrambled to his feet, bellowing in rage. In vain Fritz blew mightily on his whistle, but the furious Zenwyler took matters into his own hands. He quickly pulled off his basket, reached down with his strong arms, and lifted his adversary up by the neck. The other centaur struggled, but his strength was no match for Zenwyler's. The equine man hurled his foe over his own back and went thundering down the field toward his burden's own team. As they pounded toward him to rescue their teammate, Zenwyler reared up like an unbroken stallion and dumped his unwilling passenger into the path of the oncoming hordes. There was a wild shouting as the centaurs tried to halt themselves before they stomped on one of their own, and Zenwyler, roaring at his victory, went dashing off to retrieve his basket. Holly, along with the assembled fauns, satyrs, and goblins, leaped to her feet to cheer him on.

Holly was too excited to stay in the sleigh for long, and she soon left to join the throngs that paced and jumped on the sidelines. From the comfort of the sleigh, Nicholas looked on with benevolence as his Holly clapped and cheered with the others. This, thought Nicholas, is exactly what she should be doing—joining the other citizens of Forever, enjoying what they enjoy. He watched her slip her hand into the paw of a faun who was equally exalted by the antics on the field. An astonishing pass resulted in a

goal, and Holly and the small faun, whose name was
Macsu, exchanged grins of pleasure. Nicholas noted
that even the cautious goblins were exchanging words
with Holly now, pointing their long blue fingers
toward the field to indicate important developments.
Nicholas, shivering, wrapped his scarf more closely
about his neck. Dark clouds were scudding across the
sky and the temperature was dropping precipitously.
"Tundra," he began, "do you notice how Holly is—
Tundra?" Nicholas sat up and looked around. Tundra
was no longer there.

Nicholas stood, scanning the ring of beings around
the field. He caught sight of the wolf, perched on a
little rise, looking fixedly at the centaurs playing
below. Nicholas, who had felt a moment's reassurance
upon finding him, now felt puzzled. "What in heaven
is he staring at?" he murmured, following Tundra's
gaze. It seemed to be one of the centaurs, a smaller,
gray fellow trailing a bit behind the others. Well, and
what of it? Nicholas wondered. He looked again. A
sharp stab of uneasiness punctured his sense of well-
being. He knew for certain that he had never seen
that centaur before.

The next few seconds seemed to take place with
agonizing slowness. Tundra glanced quickly up at

Nicholas and then found Holly in the crowd. At the
same time, the gray centaur, now lagging conspicu-
ously, wheeled around on the frozen ground, turning
toward the sidelines in apparent bewilderment. The
crowd of fauns began to hoot at this display of confusion. Fritz, who had been silent for the last minute,
counting, began to blow his whistle furiously, for he
had just found that there were, in complete defiance
of the rules, forty players on the field. Holly looked
wonderingly at Macsu, hoping he would explain the
meaning of the whistle. The wind began to howl in
the black trees that surrounded the grass, and a putrid,
smell blew across the circle of spectators.

"Faugh! Phew!" cried the fauns and goblins,
shielding their faces from the stench. Holly, coughing,
hid her head against her new friend's shoulder, which
kept her from seeing the white flash of Tundra as he
raced past her toward the grass.

The gray centaur was cantering toward the edges
of the field now, and Nicholas, who was running
toward Holly, caught sight of his black mouth opened
in a triumphal shout as he hurled a glowing red orb
right to the spot where the girl stood. The ball did not
touch her, but landed nearby, where it instantly
melted the snow around it and exploded into flames.

"Papa! What's happened?" Holly was crying as Nicholas reached her side. Fleeing creatures pressed against her, and the fiery heat was growing, though it seemed to feed on nothing. Nicholas saw Holly grow pale. Quickly he picked her up in his arms and turned toward the sleigh, but he found himself surrounded in all directions by hissing fire. Desperately he spun around, seeking an opening, but there was none. By the time he sank to his knees and laid Holly in a cradle of snow, she had already fainted.

Tundra, meanwhile, had caught up with the gray centaur. With one pounce he had landed on the animal's back and plunged his teeth into his neck. It didn't occur to him in that moment that Herrikhan could not be killed, or that he himself could be in danger. In pure lupine fury, Tundra thought of nothing but hanging on, no matter what, for as long as he could. The centaur struggled, cursing and squealing, but he could not long endure the punishment of Tundra's teeth. He stumbled and fell.

It had taken the other centaurs a few moments to understand what had happened, and now they stood, shocked into stillness, watching the fight. Zenwyler shook himself. "Come, centaurs!" he roared. "To battle!" Mobilized by this cry, the centaurs charged toward the wolf and his enemy with thundering hooves. Zenwyler, the fastest and the angriest, reached the gray centaur first. Calculating swiftly, he aimed a powerful kick at the centaur's hindquarters, missing Tundra by a few inches.

The gray centaur gave a shrill scream and a final wrench. "You shall suffer!" he squealed. "I'll turn your hooves to lead, you donkey!" There was a whisper, and Zenwyler fell back, crippled. Tundra's jaws clenched more firmly on the centaur, but it was too late: the beast dissolved into a stinking cloud.

Holly leaned her head against the door. It was wooden, and she could hear quite easily what was being said in the room behind it. She was not supposed to be there; she was supposed to be lying down, recovering from the disaster of the previous day, but she had heard the voices of the delegation coming down the path toward the palace doors, and she had crept through the secret passage that led from her sitting room down to the great hall. (It was not, as a matter of fact, a very secret passage.)

She heard the quiet voices of the fauns, who had come, they said, at the behest of the Citizens' League. Of course, Holly had guessed that the centaurs would not come to the palace themselves, for they did not get along well with floors and ceilings and doors, but she also guessed that the fauns had been selected for the delegation because they were the most tactful creatures in the Land of the Immortals.

At the moment, however, the quiet faun voices were simply answering Nicholas's worried questions about Zenwyler's condition. Yes, they confirmed, Zenwyler's lead hooves appeared to be permanent and undetachable. Yes, Dr. Lavalier had inspected them, but saw no way to operate. Yes, the centaur could walk, but only slowly, and he would never play pelote again. Yes, he was feeling very low.

"But sire, we have come here to speak with you of another matter," began a bell-like voice. Holly recognized it as Romulus. He was one of the oldest fauns, known for his blue waistcoats and his famous class, the Flora of Forever, which had educated generations of newcomers on the landscape of the immortal world. Now that there were no more newcomers, the old faun wandered about a bit aimlessly, collecting specimens that were not needed for a book he would never write. Now, however, he sounded quite sure of himself. "The child, sire, the princess? We were all delighted to see her yesterday, sire. More than de-lighted," he amended quickly. "She is charming, and we have nothing, let me say, but the strongest feelings of devotion and admiration for her. We want nothing but the best for Princess Holly." He coughed deli-cately. "With that in mind, sire, I have been asked to represent to you the *anxiety* that exists in the minds of some of your citizens with regard to her presence at public events or—er—in the village." There was a pause while Romulus gathered his resolve. "Some of the immortals—not myself, of course, but some—feel that her presence is dangerous to us—them."

Sofya's silvery voice sounded now. "Remember, Romulus, that it is not Holly who brings danger to us, but our own fear. We do this to ourselves."

There was a shifting of hooves, and then a quaver-ing voice asked, "But how can we feel otherwise when she is with us?"

There was a moment's silence, and then Nicholas began to speak, his voice heavy. "Romulus, Silenux, and all you others, thank you for your honesty and bravery. I quite understand your concern, and, indeed, I share it myself. I had hoped that you would come to know and love my daughter as I do, but I know now that the risk is too great. Holly will no longer be permitted to come among you."

A small, angry voice suddenly interrupted the proceedings. "Well, I think it's a shameful thing to be a coward!" Holly pressed her ear against the door to catch every word. "I only met the princess yesterday, but she's a dear, dear child, and if she is willing to take the chance of coming to us, I think we ought be willing to receive her with pleasure. After all, it's much harder to be in her shoes than in ours, isn't it, Romulus?"

It was Macsu, the faun from the pelote game. Holly gasped and, without thinking, pushed open the wooden door that hid her and ran across the stone floor to Macsu's side. There was a ripple of worry when she appeared, but she didn't notice that; she knew only that she had a loyal friend.

"Dearest Macsu, thank you for speaking," she said softly, "but you mustn't worry yourself or get angry with your friends." She nodded her head toward Romulus. "He's right, you know. I don't want anything more to go wrong in the Land of the Immortals. I've already caused enough trouble, I know. Tell poor Zenwyler that I'm very, very sorry. Sorrier than I can say. And maybe you can come visit me sometimes. Here, in the castle." She tried to smile. "We can have a tea party. Someday."

The delegation turned to go, saluting her as they passed out the door. Holly watched their departing backs until the last one had disappeared. Then, without a word to Nicholas, who sat as though frozen in his chair, she walked back to the hidden passageway and returned to her room.

That night, Nicholas, Viviana, and Sofya gathered in Viviana's sitting room, just as they had in the long hours after Holly's heart was turned to ice.

"He won't come back," Sofya was saying firmly. "Not now."

"Why wouldn't he?" Nicholas said gloomily, pacing back and forth before the fire. "It seems he can do anything he has a mind to."

"Nicholas," Sofya said, staring straight into his eyes, "despair is unworthy of you. He won't come back because he got what he wanted."

"And what might that be?" asked Viviana, sitting tensely in her chair.

"He wants Holly to be lonely," Sofya said. "He wants her to long for companionship and purpose and to feel that she cannot find it here, in the Land of the Immortals. He has destroyed her chance to live happily here by instilling fear of Holly among the immortals and even in Holly herself."

"Why is he so cruel?" cried Viviana.

"He's not simply being cruel," answered Nicholas bitterly. "If she is lonely here, she will find the mortal world that much more tempting. That's what he's after, isn't it, Sofya?"

She nodded.

"But what could I do? I can't have her endangering the people here. Think of Zenwyler! Crippled, barely able to walk—and all because of us!"

"You did the right thing, Nicholas," said Sofya. "You had little choice. But it will make Holly's life very narrow. She is not meant for solitude."

Nicholas's mouth tightened. "She will have us, and that must be enough."

"But not forever," said Viviana.

"Yes. Forever," replied Nicholas.

"No!" cried Sofya and Viviana together. They exchanged glances. An eternity of captivity, no matter how loving, would break her heart. "Now, Nicholas," began Viviana, "you know that someday Holly must make her own choice—"

"If she makes the wrong choice, he will destroy her," Nicholas broke in. "I cannot allow that to happen."

"You cannot prevent it from happening," said Sofya.

"Yes, I can," Nicholas replied shortly. "She is safe here, in the palace, where we can watch her and protect her. And this is where she will stay."

The two women looked at each other. He is making a mistake, flickered Viviana's blue eyes.

Yes. But he will learn in time. Holly will teach him. And love will prevail, answered Sofya's black eyes.

Nicholas stared into the crackling fire, silent.

Chapter Eleven

HOLLY WAS TOO frightened and
miserable in the days and weeks that
followed the catastrophic pelote
game to ask why she had been the
target of the fiery orb. It appeared to her, from all that
followed, that the event was somehow her fault, and
she assumed the guilt without ever questioning
whether it truly belonged to her. As for Nicholas and
Viviana, they resolved to tell her of Herrikhan and his
scheme to free himself from the prison of Odyl. "She
must know," they would agree. "It's too dangerous to
let her remain in ignorance." But time and again, they

would approach the moment and fail. They could not bring themselves to say the words: You have been cursed. Far, far below us there lives a gray-skinned warlock who will perpetrate any evil to attain your heart, who will destroy us all if he succeeds, who is waiting for you.

Instead they would lovingly kiss Holly good night and smooth her hair, wishing her a long and restful sleep as they closed the door. And Holly, watching the moonlight glint on the silver leaves above her head, would pull her rose-petal blanket up to her chin and whisper her prayers, which always ended with a plea to the elders to spare her from bad dreams. Most nights her plea was answered, and she sank into a down-soft sleep. But sometimes the elders seemed not to hear her and, as she slept, a nightmare crept on spidery feet to fill her mind. In it, she was tall, much taller than she truly was, and all around her were children. They were small and helpless, and she was taking care of them. They rolled to and fro on the grass while she watched and laughed along with them. All the while, in the back of her mind, there was a pressing doubt, a fear that she couldn't quite locate. Then she saw that the gentle lawn where the children were playing was heaving itself up in horrible, grunting lurches. Violently, it spewed forth a creature unlike any other she had ever seen: shrunken, yellowing, a gelatinous white syrup oozing between the wrinkles of its flesh. The beast would quiver, its head swiveling as it searched the mild scenery for its prize, and Holly would know with shuddering certainty that she herself was the thing sought. Frantically she would lift her legs to flee, and then her eyes would fall upon the children. She couldn't leave them. But some flash of movement had caught the beast's eye, and it turned, aware now of her presence; lifting a long, yellow finger, it pointed at her and opened its mouth in a gaping black smile. Its arm uncoiled, stretching sinuously out to pull her—

Holly woke up, panting. Her hair was drenched with sweat. Tundra lifted his head. "Do you want me to get your mother?" he asked, his voice filled with sympathy.

It took a moment for Holly to unclench her jaws. "No."

"Why not?"

"It makes them worried."

"But why should you bear it alone?"

There was a short silence. "I'm not alone. I'm with you."

Tundra thought about that. "Do you want to go on the balcony and look at the moon?"

"No."

"Do you want me to tell you a story?"

"No."

"Are you sure you don't want me to get your mother?"

"Yes."

Tundra, dissatisfied, continued to look across the darkness toward Holly's bed. He heard her thumping her pillow lightly and rolling over. The room was quiet. Tundra put his head thoughtfully upon his crossed paws and closed his eyes.

A muffled sob sounded from the bed. Tundra got up and approached Holly. A beam of moonlight showed him that she wasn't asleep; her head was buried in her pillow and her shoulders were shaking. Gently, he nudged her and, in accordance with long tradition, she lifted her tear-stained face and touched her pink nose to his. "I wish I weren't immortal," she whispered.

"Why?"

"I'm afraid they will never stop."

"The nightmares?"

"Yes."

"They will, Holly. They are going to stop some-day. I wish I could tell you when."

"I wish you could too," said Holly. She pulled his ear, which caused him to sigh with contentment. "Tundra?" she asked.

"Mmm?"

"Can I sleep in your bed?"

Tundra opened his eyes. "It's not really a bed; it's just a mat. It'll be too hard for you."

"No, it won't. I'll bring the window-seat cushion down."

"Hmm. All right. No kicking."

Holly arranged the cushion next to the hollow that Tundra had worn in his mat, and the two friends settled down with a bit of thrashing and wiggling. "Stop that. Lie still," ordered Tundra.

Holly obediently lay still. A few moments passed. "Thank you," she whispered.

"For what?"

"I'm not scared anymore."

"That's good. Go to sleep."

Twelve hours later Tundra stood in the shadow of an ancient oak tree, looking up into its black branches with an uncharacteristic expression of pleading.

"Come, Callistus, please. Be a good fellow," he called toward the upper reaches of the tree.

"No," replied a wrathful voice from within.

"This is your king's daughter! This is your princess! Where's your loyalty?" cried Tundra, changing tactics.

"I told you before, I have nothing but sympathy for Princess Holly, but I see no reason why I should end up with lead wings to keep her from having bad dreams. Everyone has bad dreams," the voice rationalized.

"You won't get lead wings, you miserable, flea-bitten pigeon," Tundra growled.

"You can't promise me that," the owl replied snappishly.

Tundra sighed. "You're right, Callistus, I can't promise you that, but it's extremely unlikely. I spend nearly every minute with the girl, and I haven't been turned to lead yet—"

"Sheer luck!" crowed Callistus.

"You'll drive me mad, bird! All the witches say that owls alone know the spell to ward off nightmares, and yet none of you custard-hearted wretches will help us!"

"Go away!" replied the owl, his voice muffled as

he retreated farther into his nest.

"No!"

"Then go ask Euphemia. She's no custard heart," the voice suggested.

"Where is she?"

"Not far. About a mile north. Oak tree. Can't miss it. Sign outside her nest says E-U-P-H."

"Why?" asked Tundra suspiciously.

"You'll figure it out when you get there," said Callistus sweetly.

Tundra turned, ignoring a sound of snickering from above. A quick lope brought him to the tree he was seeking. The sign with its ragged letters did not inspire confidence, and Tundra's doubts increased upon the appearance of Euphemia. True, she was a snowy owl, resplendent in her milk-white feathers, but there was something unreliable in her tipping walk and, as she edged out upon a thick branch and peered down through the thick web of leaves, Tundra very nearly begged her pardon and left. He was, however, desperate.

"Yes, certainly, certainly," Euphemia assured him. "Dispelling nightmares—child's play. One of the very first spells we owls learn. Just a matter of a few words. But of course," she added hastily, "the words must be spoken in Strigigormese. So I can't teach them to you."

Tundra explained what he wanted—and was taken aback by Euphemia's immediate acceptance of his invitation. "Oooh, the poor dear princess! Of course, I'm terribly busy, busy, busy, but one must answer the call of duty, don't you agree? A matter of devotion to the royal family," she fluttered. "I'll just pack my bag. Don't go anywhere!" She hopped and flapped down the branch toward her nest.

Tundra eyed her sign. "Why does it say only E-U-P-H on your tree?" he called.

There was a longish silence. "I can't quite hear you, dear," said Euphemia, rustling sticks loudly.

"Why does your sign say E-U-P-H?" bellowed Tundra.

There was another silence. Then the owl poked her head out. "It was those dratted squirrels," she said. "They threw the sign on the ground during one of their games. And it broke. And I've simply been so, so, so busy I haven't had time to make another. All ready now!" she called blithely, surfacing from her hole with a dead mouse wrapped in a little pink kerchief.

They returned to the palace just in time to greet Holly as she emerged from her schoolroom. Tundra explained his plan. It was well known that owls, with their special wisdom of the night, had power over dreams. Witches in the mortal world were famous for sending owls to deliver hair-raising nightmares to unlucky recipients. Less commonly owls were used to dispel dreams, to send them packing when they visited too often or caused hopeless longings. If it worked for mortals, Tundra reasoned, there was no reason why it wouldn't work in the Land of the Immortals. Euphemia would simply perch above Holly's bed in one of the silver trees. When, with her owlish magic, she perceived that Holly was being assailed by a nightmare, she would utter her secret incantation, and presto! the nightmare would disappear.

Holly looked from Tundra to Euphemia with excitement. "You can do this?" she asked the owl breathlessly.

"Certainly," said Euphemia. "My family is renowned for its incanting. Think no more of it, Your Highness."

"How wonderful," exclaimed Holly. "No more nightmares. Forever."

Tundra and Holly spent the afternoon showing Euphemia the wonders of the palace. In a cloud of light snow, they scaled the highest turrets, where the owl admired the view, and explored the deepest dungeons, which were actually pantries. As usual, Holly had supper in her own sitting room, surrounded by her animal friends: Alexia, who had been told to behave herself until the owl got over her natural fear of foxes; Tundra; and now, Euphemia. Tundra noticed that as the night wore on, the owl became more and more silent. Alexia chattered on as usual, detailing each and every event of her day, and Holly interrupted now and then with questions, but Euphemia, who had gabbled ceaselessly during the afternoon, was now quiet.

Later still, as Holly put on her nightgown, Tundra kept watch on the owl and noticed with a sinking heart that she was apparently asleep in her tree, her head sunk deeply into her feathery breast, her eyes closed.

Soon enough, the room was quiet. Moonlight streamed in through the windows, painting the walls with light and black shadows. Tundra's eyes drooped. Holly slept.

An unknown number of hours or minutes later, the wolf was awakened by a tiny clicking sound. Following the discipline of instinct, he made no move but only opened one eye. As he scanned the layers of darkness, he saw the shadowy form of an owl perched on a thin window ledge, her beak caught in the latch. Helplessly she beat her wings against the glass, but she could not free herself.

Tundra watched her for a while. "Homesick?" he asked finally, his voice cold.

"Mft urk. Op," Euphemia replied in Strigigormese.

"Why should I? It doesn't seem as though you're going to be helping us."

"Udfcd. OP!"

"What?" said Holly sleepily from her bed. "Oh, look, poor little Euphemia!" Quickly she ran across the room to detach the owl's beak from the metal ring. "Does it hurt, dear? Are you all right?" she asked.

Euphemia said nothing.

"You should be ashamed of yourself!" Tundra burst out.

"I know," said the owl softly, her head sinking into her neck feathers.

Holly looked from one to the other, baffled. "What are you two talking about?" she asked.

"She was trying to run away," Tundra explained.

Euphemia sniffed. "I had to."

Holly laid a finger on the owl's head. "Why?"

"I can't make your nightmares disappear!" she cried suddenly. "I can't remember any of the incantations!"

"You never knew the incantations," stated Tundra, trying to contain his anger.

"You're right," wailed Euphemia. "I never knew them! I tried and tried, I studied for days, but I just couldn't learn them. I failed! I failed the test and now I've failed you, too!" she squawked. "Callistus will do a better job than I ever could, anyway."

"He won't come," Tundra said, shooting a worried glance at Holly. "He's afraid."

"Afraid?" asked Holly. "Of what?"

"Afraid that his wings will get turned to lead," mumbled Tundra.

Just as he had dreaded, Holly's face crumpled. "Oh," she said softly. After a moment she turned to Euphemia with a small smile. "You see? You're braver than Callistus, no matter how much Strigigormese he knows."

Euphemia lifted her head a little way out of her chest. "Yes," she said wonderingly, "I guess I am braver than Callistus."

"Callistus the custard heart," said Tundra to

reinforce Euphemia.

Euphemia shuffled her tail feathers. "I'll stick by you through thick and thin!" she cried. "That is, if you want me to," she added shyly.

"Of course we do, Euphemia," said Holly. "Stay with us."

"This doesn't solve the nightmare problem, though," said Tundra. "What are we going to do about that?"

"You won't have any nightmares if you *never* go to sleep," cried Alexia irritably from her corner. "She doesn't care—she's an owl. But I'm a fox, and I need to sleep at *night*. And so do you, Holly, so *stop talking*."

The next morning Euphemia began her new life at the palace. Soon the sight of Holly walking about with a large snowy owl perched upon her shoulders was a common one, and though Tundra continued his search throughout the kingdom for a cure to Holly's nightmares, he never regretted his first attempt.

In Nicholas's study there was one book that fascinated Holly more than any other. It rested upon an intricately carved wooden pedestal, and one of Holly's earliest memories was of staring in wonder at its wooden birds and monkeys, which emerged from a forest of curling vines and lush flowers. Her fingers had traced the smooth curves and ridges for hours as she imagined the secret world of the carvings: how the animals would leap off the pedestal in the dark of night and swing themselves about on her father's bookshelves, skittering and scrambling in the monstrous, oversized world of people.

As Holly grew, she graduated from staring intently at the pedestal to staring intently at the book itself. It was a curious object, bearing the marks of many centuries of honor. Its covers were metal, a dully glowing ancient metal laid over with jewels. This book had never truly had an owner, but each of its caretakers had shown his or her reverence by adding an ornament to the binding, until the book shimmered with smooth rubies and emeralds, roughly cut sapphires and moonstones, finely faceted diamonds and, in the center of the cover, an enormous black opal. Nicholas, in whose hands the volume had rested for more than a thousand years, had called upon the finest painters of Forever to add a secret to the book. It was a painting on the edges of its pages, only visible when the closed book was tilted slightly into the light. Holly, for many years forbidden to touch the volume,

had squinted earnestly at the rims of the pages for
months before the picture was revealed by a stray sun-
beam. It was a portrait of the Land of the Immortals,
circled by jewel-colored glaciers, in the fading light of
a winter sunset. In the picture snow was falling, and
somehow, each tiny snowflake glimmered as though it
had caught the last rosy glow of the day. There, in
the center of the landscape, wound the Veridian
River, green as a snake, and upon the Great Prospect
a ring of magic trees stood, their bare branches climbing to the sky.

One summer evening when Holly was twelve
years old, she came wandering into her father's study,
accompanied, as usual, by a flurry of snow. Nicholas,
who was reading at his desk, quickly closed the
window, shutting out the soft twilight air before his
daughter could long for it. Without a word, Holly
flung herself down on the green velvet sofa and
buried her face in the cushions. Nicholas said nothing, but he observed his daughter's feet kicking aimlessly—bam, bam, *bam*, against the arm of the
sofa—and concluded that she was bored.

As if in response to his thought, Holly groaned,
"I'm booooooored." She propped her chin against the
pillow and sighed. "There's nothing to do."

"There's plenty to do. You could read. You could work on that doll I saw you making yesterday. You could write a letter to Mother Selting, who hasn't been feeling entirely well this week. You could study your Latin. You could organize my correspondence. You could practice the song that Miss Malibran gave you last week. Any number of things to do."

As an answer, Holly dropped her head off the side of the sofa and looked at her father upside down. "I wonder if the mortal children ever get bored," she mused. "I bet they don't."

"Of course they do. All children get bored."

"They don't look bored when I see them in my telescope."

"Mmm," said Nicholas, turning back to his book.

The only sound was the rhythmic pounding of Holly's feet.

"Papa?"

"Mmm?"

"Can I look at the book?"

"What? This book? I'm reading it."

"Not that one. The one up there." She pointed with her chin. *"The Book of Forever."*

Nicholas had known that this moment would come. He had been steeling himself for it for years,

but even so he could hardly keep from bellowing "NO! No, you may not!" Instead, exerting all his self-control, Nicholas said nothing for a moment, then looked into his daughter's wide green eyes and said, "Yes, my dear. Yes, you may. I think you will find a cure for boredom in its pages."

Feeling suddenly adult and responsible, Holly checked to make sure her hands were clean. Nicholas, watching, smiled indulgently. "Don't worry. Your hands cannot dirty this book."

"Still," Holly said. But she walked over to the wooden stand. She pulled a nearby stool to her aid, climbed upon it, and, ever so gently, lifted the front cover of the book. "'The Book of Forever,'" she read, "'Being the Immortal Deeds of the Inhabitants of Our Land from the Beginning of Time.'" She slowly turned the thick, creamy paper. On the first page a monumental *P*, entwined in flowers and flames, began the book: Prometheus. Then Deucalion. And there was Gaia, and there, the Muses. Holly began to read, slowly at first, then with growing speed. Each of the immortals of the universe was recorded in its pages, together with the deeds that had endowed him or her with eternal life. Magical creatures and gods, who had been immortal for all time, were included in the catalogue, with an account of their accomplishments and gifts to humankind. Each of the thousands of pages was illuminated with a portrait of the subject, and Holly was astonished when she encountered Thucydides, whom she had once seen drinking mead at a cafe, to realize how lifelike and vigorous the portraits were. "How did they—?" she began, and fell silent, for she had stumbled upon Nicholas's page. There he was, his kind, powerful eyes and luxuriant brown beard. Her eyes skipped over to his biography, and she learned with growing amazement of his life, centuries before, in the bustling little town of Myra, and of the children he had helped there. A few pages farther on, she found Viviana's picture, looking as though she was suppressing a laugh, and read of her mother's work in Cappadocia.

Selflessness, generosity, kindness in the face of evil, faith, charity, justice, strength, bravery, modesty, serenity, devotion, and, above all, love—Holly read on and on of those who had used these gifts in the service of others, and the stories entered her heart. There was Galen, trying to bring order to the chaos of superstition that was medicine. And here was Merlin, who had done his best for Arthur though he knew full well that it was out of his hands. Erasmus, the great reconciler, rubbed elbows with Erasmus Darwin, who

"Holly Claus," read the elaborate letters at the top.

reconciled little. Holly's eyes rested on Mozart's tired face, and the exuberant Bachs, all of them. And look, Tintoretto, wild eyed. Mother Selting and her protégé, Finta, who had saved countless innocents from the inquisitors before dying in prison them-selves. Holly giggled to read of Mrs. Nicholls, who always appeared rather dull as she walked meekly through the village, and her mouth dropped open as she learned of the exploits of Miss Malibran, who seemed so strict during music lessons. On and on she read, oblivious to the time, oblivious to her arms and legs shaking with weariness, oblivious to Nicholas's searching glances in her direction.

Holly lifted her head, and then turned to face her father. He knew what she was thinking. Bending over the book, she began to turn pages, faster and faster, her long fingers stumbling against the thick paper.

And there it was. She looked as though she had been painted yesterday; indeed, the dress was the one that she had worn the day before. Holly looked closely at the curling smile and green eyes; she studied her own reddish golden hair as if she had never seen it before. Almost unwillingly, she moved her eyes to the accompanying page. "Holly Claus," read the elaborate letters at the top. The rest of the page was blank.

Chapter Twelve

ISTEN—THE BIRDS are beginning. And the sky is turning pink, see? Holly, darling, you simply must get some sleep." Viviana stroked her daughter's forehead.

Holly leaned her head against her mother's shoulder but did not answer. Dark blue shadows encircled her eyes, and she stared blindly at the intricate pattern of the carpet. "I don't belong here," she said again.

Nicholas, who had been explaining for hours, replied patiently. "Of course you do. You are our child. You belong with us."

"But I've done nothing—nothing except bring a curse to the Land of the Immortals. No wonder they're frightened of me."

Nicholas replied, "You didn't lay the curse. Herrikhan did. They're not frightened of you; they're frightened of him."

"I've done nothing to help the humans, nothing for the world, nothing!" her hoarse voice continued. "I'm not an immortal—I'm some sort of trick! I'm a freak of nature, or—or—a natural disaster. I've done nothing but cause trouble from the moment I was born."

"Oh, Holly, that isn't so. You've filled *our* hearts with more love than we ever believed possible," Viviana said.

"There was a boy," Nicholas began, and Holly recognized the first words of a story she had been hearing all her life. "A boy named Christopher, who lived in the Empire City and sent me a letter. In that letter he asked me a question that I had never been asked before. He asked me if there was anything I wished for, anything I wanted and did not have. And do you remember what happened next, Holly?"

"Yes, Papa," said Holly, the darkness in her lifting. "You wished for me."

"We knew, as we read his words, that the only thing we wished for was you," Nicholas continued, watching as the old tale smoothed the lines of worry from his daughter's face. "It was as though his letter was filled with sunshine and gold. All of a sudden, we knew the dearest wish of our hearts, and we knew that you would come into being. We have felt that joy, Holly, every day of your life."

"In spite of the curse? In spite of what I have done?" asked Holly unbelievingly.

"I do not think I would change anything unless I could know that you would be exactly as you are in this very moment," Viviana said.

Holly rested in the circle of her mother's arms. "Sunshine and gold," she murmured, her head drooping. There was a long silence, and then Nicholas nodded. She was asleep. Outside, the indeterminate pink of the dawn was crisping into brilliant blue.

It is odd, Holly thought as she climbed the winding stairs in the fullness of the afternoon, that in a land where most of the population does its best to avoid me, I should be running away to the attic to hide from the few friends I have.

The attic was not really an attic. It was actually a

tiny room at the very pinnacle of the castle's tallest turret, accessible only by a narrow spiral staircase that made everyone else in the household queasy. Nicholas claimed he was too fat to squeeze himself around the last bend in the stairs, and Tundra announced that it was against wolf nature to be so far away from the ground. Even the housekeeping goblins, normally so diligent, refused to ascend the heights to clean the turret or replace the banner that waved from its steeple. Holly, as the only enthusiastic turret visitor, was therefore responsible for these tasks (Viviana refused to watch when Holly leaned out the slip window to pull the banner in). Today she was escaping, not cleaning.

She rested on the stone window ledge, her face open to the gentle summer air while her back was cooled by light swirls of snow. The palace sat upon a small hill above the valley of Forever and, from her dizzying perch, Holly could view a great swath of her country laid out like an expanse of fabric. She saw the village, the Veridian River twisting through farms and gardens, and beyond them the vast plain that had no name. Today it pulsed with a purple light, and Holly could just see a scrap of a wizard, his hands on his hips, who was watching the results of his spell with pride. Perhaps, she thought, he is one of the ones who can't go home. Perhaps he wakes every morning thinking for just a second that he is in his own bed, in the mortal world, and then his eyes open and he knows that he is still a prisoner. Does he think of me? Does he say to himself, If only that baby had never been born, I would be able to live the life I want? And then he must take up his ball and scry his king or whomever he guides, and he probably watches as the king makes the wrong decisions over and over again, and he sits here, helpless to change anything.

"Ohhh," groaned Holly, burying her face in her arms. But it was no use, for even in the shield of darkness she could not defeat the pictures that had crowded her mind since the night before: the immortal souls waiting patiently for admittance to Forever, the frozen misery on the faces of the visitors as they learned that they could never return to their homes, the horror that Tundra had endured near the Amaranthine Gates, the plunging drop forward as Zenwyler's feet turned to lead, and the shrieking panic that followed.

And there was something else, too. Something that hovered on the edges of earliest time, swaying and shivering in the oldest part of her memory. She was falling down and could not save herself. Below her was nothing, and above her loomed a dark, slick cavern that screamed and screamed and screamed.

Holly jerked her head up and steadied her hand against the edges of the window. For the first time, the turret seemed precarious. She looked toward the sky, and the blue seemed to shudder slightly. She looked down to see the cheerful landscape below, but her vision was impeded by sharp little explosions, like fireworks, that rained through the air before her eyes. The sky is falling, she thought crazily. Farms, fields, grass, river, plain with no name, name with no plain, millage, village, spillage.

"No," she said out loud. "No. I will not be frightened. I will not hide. You. Herrikhan." She had not said his name before, and it made her feel a bit sick, but she took a deep breath and continued, "Herrikhan, I know what you want. I know what you expect—I don't know how I know, but I do—you think that I'm going to crawl to you and beg you to take my heart and release the others. You think that I'm going to make a bargain—me for them—but I tell you now that you're wrong. I know what you'll be if you're freed, and I won't help you. I'll fight you. I'm going to make myself an immortal, a real immortal, somehow, and I'm not going to give in. I'm going to do it by myself. I'm not frightened of you!"

Without warning, Sofya was at her side. Her cloud-colored robes rustled slightly as she encircled Holly's tense figure in her arms. "Yes, my love," she whispered, "that's right. You fight. You have the heart of a lioness."

Holly bowed her head gratefully against her godmother's cool linen shoulder. "Did he hear me?" she asked in a low voice.

Sofya's black eyes flicked around the tiny stone room. "He's not here, I can tell you that. But I expect that he heard you."

"Oh, Sofya, what am I going to do? How am I going to become a real immortal?"

Sofya held her tighter. "You're a real immortal, Holly, I promise you."

"But the book."

"Your story will be written there in the fullness of time."

"How?" Holly cried despairingly. "How can I do anything worthy of my birthplace if my birth has turned the Land of the Immortals into a prison that no one may leave? What am I to do?"

"That," said Sofya, "would be telling."

Holly stared at her. "You know what's going to happen."

Sofya shook her head. "No, I don't, for which I thank the elders of the universe every day of my life. I can see a number of possible futures, and any one of them could happen. There is not one certain future, that much I know. Each of our lives creates what is to come. The universe is not a clock that has been set to run in one direction. It is a maze, a giant puzzle that changes and grows each time a player takes one path over another. Every time you make a choice, you make the future. I don't know how your story will end; I have to wait and see like everybody else." She smiled. "Including Herrikhan."

"But you do know what I'm supposed to do next," insisted Holly.

"No, really, I don't. What I meant was this: nobody can tell you what to do. You must decide for yourself because that's part of your path."

"Should I go to the mortal world?"

Sofya shook her head. "You must follow what you know—I cannot tell you." She laughed softly. "I do know that your father would throw me out of this ridiculous tower if he found out that I had encouraged you to make such a journey. And, by the way, I do not know a secret means of evading the curse and traveling to the mortal world. If I did, I would have used it myself," she said.

"Oh," said Holly, disappointed.

Sofya brushed her cheek. "But such a means may very well exist." Holly looked up, but her godmother was glancing around the tower room with distaste. "Why do you insist on holding your conferences in a pigeon coop, my dear?"

"Did you climb up all those stairs?" asked Holly, thinking of it for the first time.

"Are you mad, child? What's the point of magical powers if you don't use them to avoid overexertion?"

"It's worse going down," Holly said.

"I have no intention of clomping down four hundred stairs like a goat. I shall go the way I came."

"Some of us don't have any other option," said Holly with a smile.

"Pooh. Your father is a dear, dear man, but he's an absolute stick-in-the-mud about magic. He thinks it develops character to do such things the mortal way."

"You mean I have powers?" cried Holly.

"Hardly," said Sofya witheringly, "but you could."

"*Really?* Can I fly?"

Sofya rolled her eyes. "Just like a child—wants to

do the most difficult thing first of all, now, this minute. Certainly not. If I were to teach you, and I am by no means saying that I will, you'd start where everyone starts, in the kitchen."

"The kitchen?"

"Taking the lids off jam pots."

"Oh," said Holly, disappointed.

"There, you see? If you don't find jam pots intriguing, it shows that you lack the proper moral fiber for more advanced instruction."

"I'm sure jam pots would be lovely," said Holly hastily. "Though flying sounds a bit more exciting."

"Excitement is overrated. However, if you want, I'll buzz you down from this disgusting hovel."

"Yes, please."

In reply, Sofya laid her white fingers upon Holly's hair and whispered a few words in Russian. There was a whistling sound, and in the next instant, Holly found herself lodged in the arms of one of the stone nymphs in the middle of the reflecting pool.

"Good gracious!" shrieked the nymph, trembling.

"I'm terribly sorry," apologized Holly. "There was a little flying mix-up. I'm awfully sorry. I do hope I haven't nicked you."

There was no sign of Sofya anywhere, so after a

few more moments of begging the nymph's pardon, Holly clambered down her stone tunic and waded through the murky water toward the palace. Her shoes were ruined, and the whole episode took twice as much time as walking down the stairs would have.

It was only much later that Holly realized that her search began on that day. If she had been asked at the time what she felt about the discovery of the curse that her birth had brought to Forever, she would have replied that she felt sorrow, confusion, alarm, and remorse. She would have said that she felt helpless. But something was working slowly inside her, a growing sense of longing that she felt almost like physical hunger. It didn't seem to Holly like bravery, because most of the time, the dread of her inevitable encounter with Herrikhan lay like a seam of lead at the back of her mind, but it was bravery. Instead of resigning herself to a life of caution, protection, and hiding, Holly began to search for a way to deserve the immortality she had been born to.

She spent more and more time at her telescope, transfixed by the patterns of mortal existence. Hours would click by as she gazed, enthralled, at a family or a neighborhood or even a single child pursuing his or her daily activities. Though she still visited the humid jungles and wind-torn mountaintops around the world, she was increasingly drawn to the Empire City—known to the mortals as New York City—spellbound by the electric vitality of the place. The people had a look there, she decided, that was like no other place. Jaunty men in bowler hats stepped, pigeon proud, along Wall Street, their prosperous stomachs pushed out before them. Ladies in open carriages lifted their gloved hands to greet one another on the Ladies' Mile while gangs of ragged children swooped between the horses' hooves. Pushcart vendors, policemen, peddlers, and pickpockets vied for the same spots on the sidewalks. Servants stepped out of the swollen mansions of Fifth Avenue, looked at the sky, and withdrew to make their reports. From the top floor of one rattlebang apartment house, a vigorous old lady shouted the news of the day to her friend, an equally old, vigorous lady in another rattlebang apartment across the street. Trolleys clanged, horses clopped, children shrieked.

The spyglass was a subtle enchanter. In the beginning it had beguiled Holly with only scenes of jollity and joy, but now shadows were permitted to gather around the edges of the mortal world, and Holly sometimes saw a lonely face, a lost soul, or one of the small, sad stories that filled the lands. The telescope cleverly filtered out the great cruelties and desperate injustices, leaving only the tiny tragedies, the ones that could have easily been remedied, to make her want to help. Watching a haggard woman bend her head under the bitter wind, with a thin shawl pulled tightly around her shoulders, Holly would sigh and shift restlessly from foot to foot. One day she caught sight of a collier's boy beating the weary horse that pulled his cart, and she cried out in anguish and ran from the room. Tundra found her hours later in the closet, carrying on an imaginary argument with the villain. "I would have stopped him, Tundra," she said sadly. "If only I had been there."

Holly and Sofya neglected to mention to Nicholas that magic had become part of Holly's curriculum, and after a few weeks, Holly could remove the lids from jam pots with only the slightest lift of her eyebrow. It was not a particularly interesting thing to do.

One cold afternoon Tundra padded through the castle in search of Holly. She wasn't in her sitting room. She wasn't in the schoolroom. She wasn't in the kitchen coaxing a snack from the goblins. Tundra proceeded down to the reflecting pool, where the stone nymphs twittered and giggled and finally told him that the princess had not passed by. Tundra padded on. She wasn't in the topiary. She wasn't in the herb garden. She wasn't skating on Parian Pond.

Tundra sat on his haunches and sighed. Then he squinted at a grove of trees near the water. A pair of legs was dangling from one of the pine trees. Tundra came closer. The legs belonged to Holly. She was sitting on a pine branch with her eyes closed. She was also whispering.

"What are you doing?" Tundra asked mildly, after a few minutes.

"Shhh. Flying," Holly replied, without opening her eyes.

Tundra waited a few minutes longer. Then he cleared his throat and remarked, "You're flying very unnoticeably."

"I'm trying to use magic," said Holly through clenched teeth.

There was a sudden eruption of honks, shouts, and yips from the pond, and Alexia tore from a thicket of reeds. "And stay out!" called an outraged duck. Catching sight of Tundra, Alexia ran to join him under the pine tree.

"I don't know what's the matter with those ducks," she panted. "They're so touchy."

Holly laughed and the fox looked up. "Oh, Holly! What are you doing?"

"She's trying to fly," Tundra said.

Alexia stared at Holly sitting on the branch. "Didn't we already do this?" she asked. "With Meteor?"

"I'm trying to use magic," Holly said again. "And it would be helpful if you would stop talking."

So they sat in silence, watching Holly whisper to herself.

"She's not getting anywhere," Alexia commented to Tundra.

"Shhh."

There was a flurry of white wings, and Euphemia glided to a branch above Holly. "What are you doing, dear?" she inquired.

"She's trying to fly," said Tundra, unable to keep laughter out of his voice.

Euphemia looked smug. "Child's play, dear." She ruffled her feathers and smoothed them down. "I'll teach you."

"I'm trying to use magic," Holly said for the third time.

Euphemia shook her head. "No, my dear, magic is not necessary. You simply need to concentrate. Now, grasp the branch with your talons, or, well, your feet will have to do. Now lift your behind and straighten your back."

"But Euphemia—" Holly tried to interrupt.

The owl ignored her. "Then, *spread* your wings. That is the central point, my dear, you must spread them before you push off. This is the error made most often by fledglings. They do not *spread* their wings—"

"Euphemia, I don't have any—"

Holly's words ended abruptly as a small black object hurtled past her and thudded to the ground.

It was a penguin. A small, bedraggled penguin. He lay at Tundra's feet without moving, his eyes screwed shut.

Holly, abandoning magic, climbed quickly down the tree. "Are you all right?" she asked. "Can we help you?" The penguin opened one eye and quickly shut it again. "We won't hurt you," Holly reassured him. "I promise."

The penguin opened both eyes and found again a wolf, a fox, an owl, and a human girl staring at him. He stared back at them with obvious terror. Then, with a sudden lurch, he began to scramble away as fast as his feet would carry him, which, given penguin construction, wasn't very fast. Alexia was soon in front of him, barking explanations and exhortations, which only terrified him more. The penguin swung his head desperately from side to side in search of an escape route and finally chose one: up.

Unfortunately penguins can't fly. He flopped again to the muddy ground and lay there, shaking.

"Look, Holly," said Euphemia, "he can't fly any better than you can."

Holly looked sympathetically at the little bird. "Were you trying to fly, little one?"

He nodded.

"Is that why you fell out of the tree?"

He nodded again.

"How'd you get up there, anyway?" Alexia yelled. Alexia believed that shyness was the same as being deaf.

A look of fear came over the penguin's face. He shivered.

"He's too frightened to tell us," observed Euphemia.

"I think somebody scared him," Alexia concluded.

Tundra had an idea. "Was it the roc?"

At the sound of the roc's name, the penguin began to tremble violently.

"It was the roc," said Tundra. The penguin nodded.

It was a penguin. A small, bedraggled penguin.

"The roc put you in the tree?" exclaimed Holly indignantly. "Why?"

Quivering, the penguin shook his head. He didn't know.

"The roc has a somewhat peculiar sense of humor," Tundra said.

Alexia snorted, but Holly was outraged. "That miserable roc! Just because he's big, he thinks he can do anything. You poor thing!" She looked tenderly at the bird. "Would you like to come home with us?"

The penguin looked at her nervously, but he nodded. Holly lifted him from the snow and cuddled him close. She carried the still-shaking penguin back toward the palace with Tundra, Alexia, and Euphemia following. She tiptoed discreetly through the halls, hoping to avoid a conversation with the goblins about her rather dirty new guest, and reached her sitting room with a sigh of relief. "The first thing you need is a nice bath," she said, setting the penguin on the floor and walking briskly toward the bathroom. A tiny gasp arrested her steps. She turned to see the penguin, frozen with wonder, catching his first sight of the snow that accompanied Holly within the castle walls. The newcomer stared in silence, and then his curving beak opened and, despite himself, he stuck out his tongue to catch a few flakes in his mouth. A squawk of joy erupted from him, and he spun a circle on the frigid floor.

Holly looked at him with dawning realization. "You need the cold too, don't you?" she asked. The penguin nodded, and Holly smiled down at him, glad that her icy world had some benefit for another. "Me too, and if you would like to stay here, you are welcome to share it with me." The penguin nodded even more vigorously and gave a little hop. Holly laughed. "Of course, of course. Consider it yours." She curtseyed elegantly.

The penguin bowed back so deeply that he almost toppled over.

Happy to find a companion to share her chilly existence, Holly danced to the bathroom to draw an icy bath. Moments later the penguin was hurling himself ecstatically down the sloping rim of Holly's crystal bathtub while Holly perched on the side, her feet dabbling in the freezing water.

It was a long time before Holly learned the penguin's history. She never did learn his name because it turned out that he did not have one. When he finally began to speak, she discovered that he had lived alone in a cave under the emerald glacier for as long as he could remember and, until his unfortunate encounter with the roc, had never known that other beings existed. Since he had never been spoken to, he had to learn how to speak, which he slowly did, but he often stuttered when he was nervous.

To Holly, whom he loved in the way a baby penguin loves the first face that hovers over him as he pecks his way free from the shell, he offered the responsibility of naming him, which she was delighted to accept. After much considering and comparing, she christened him Empire, in honor of the Empire City. After a few days Holly began to call him Empy, which seemed to suit him so much better as he waddled along in the shadow of Holly's skirts. Unlike Alexia and Euphemia, who regarded the palace as their own private property and all the other inhabitants as slightly annoying relatives, Empy never felt entirely comfortable moving through the great chambers and vast halls. He preferred to stay in Holly's suite, cooled by the charmed snow, waiting patiently for her return or watching anxiously for her next departure. Very rarely Empy joined the other friends in an outdoor adventure and, even then, he never seemed to enjoy any part of it as much as the return to the silver glade in Holly's room.

Chapter Thirteen

THE FAIRIES WERE in the midst of a hide-and-seek extravaganza. No one, not even the fairies themselves, knew how these things got started. Every few years a little game snowballed into a giant fairy melee, and for a few weeks the sky above Forever seethed with fairy flocks whirling from one spot to another in search of their hidden cousins. The other immortals had mixed feelings about this. Some loved the sight of the great cloud of fairies hovering and humming over the land; others thought that the game was further evidence of the irresponsible nature of fairies. It's true that the fairies had no regard for others when they were in the midst of a game, and they would torpedo into bystanders without even an apology.

Once Lysinias the centaur had been tormented nearly to madness by a fairy who insisted that there was a will-o'-the-wisp hidden on his back. She had run up and down and up and down his spine, prying with her tiny fingers under each hair until he began to shriek. He caught her by her wings and held her hostage, demanding that the game come to an end. But he paid dearly for it; a vast swarm of fairies descended upon him with their wings flapping, and each fairy bit off one of his hairs until he was bald and shivering. Then they pelted him with cherries and laughed at him and, finally, when he gave up and released his hostage, they put a spell on him so that his coat grew back purple. This, of course, had made him furious, and Nicholas had been forced to intervene before there was an all-out war between centaurs and fairies.

This particular hide-and-seek extravaganza was different from previous games, because it was taking place inside the palace. Usually the whole of Forever was the field, but this time the revels had erupted during the icy winter months, and fairies have a horror of cold. Instead of calling the game, the Boucane sisters had hospitably invited the extended fairy family to continue the fun at the palace, which, they assured their cousins, was plenty large enough for a rousing revel. With fairy blitheness, they neglected to inform Nicholas of their intentions, and the first hint to the household came when Melchior was knocked down the stairs by a sudden blow to the back. A team of fairies, in violent pursuit of another, swung out over his prone body while Nicholas, who had been discussing palace drainage a moment before, looked on in bewilderment. Fourteen fairies slipped down the banister, whooping and singing, and a third contingent swung happily on the chandelier that illuminated the Great Hall.

Nicholas, with typical indulgence, permitted the game to continue, once Makena, the eldest Boucane and mistress of the revels, had begged Melchior's pardon with sincere remorse. Nicholas soon regretted his benevolence, though, for the game had been going on for two weeks and showed no signs of coming to an end. He himself had been knocked over twice— and, as Holly observed, that took some doing—four of Viviana's five sitting room lamps had been broken, the glass case containing Nicholas's scepter was shattered, and all the house goblins were threatening to quit. They sidled through the halls, looking nervously over their shoulders and murmuring mutinously. The angrier they got, the bluer their skins grew. Melchior, his arm in a sling, was the color of a morning glory.

Holly, however, loved the fairies. She ran after the humming flocks, following them down hallways, up stairs, into crevices. When one of the larger fairies got stuck in a keyhole, Holly tactfully prodded her out with a stick and told no one. When, in the midst of a two-day heat, she caught sight of the hiding fairy in the shade of an orange tree in the conservatory, she kept quiet. While Tundra sat next to her with a blanket over his head, the picture of aggrieved dignity, Holly dangled her feet through the stair posts and jeered and cheered at the tumultuous scoring sessions that took place on the chandelier. "Isn't it wonderful?" she cried to the wolf. Tundra grunted.

Even Holly found the revels a bit unnerving on occasion. While fairies have tiny voices—four or five fairies together can barely be heard by human ears—put seven hundred fairies together and they make a sound like a herd of elk stampeding over glass. Sofya had put her foot down on the second day and refused to allow any of them into the schoolroom, so when

Holly felt the need for a little peace and quiet, she went there. In the silent room she sat, the snow swirling and swishing around her, casting a lacy veil over the hard edges of the desks and chairs. Holly worked on her clay models, pulling and smoothing faces out of the malleable stuff. Something strange seemed to happen to her when she took the soft clay in hand; her mind drifted as her fingers moved nimbly, and when she emerged from her reverie, in five or ten or twenty minutes, she looked with amazement at the figure she had created. It was almost always someone she knew and it was almost always an apt likeness. She looked at the face in her hands; how had she done it? Her mysterious talent certainly did not extend to drawing or painting: her portrait of Tundra had made Sofya laugh so hard she cried.

"Perhaps I'm a sculptor," she said to herself late one afternoon, admiring a clay replica of Makena she had just completed. She could hear the fairies' thin screams somewhere in the palace. It sounded as though they had broken into Viviana's sitting room again.

"Everyall," said a soft voice in her hair. Involuntarily Holly reached for her curls and felt the delicate brush of wings against her fingers. Little feet, no heavier than the lightest touch of a falling leaf, pattered along her hand. Holly tried to breathe softly; she had never been so close to a fairy. "Cloud not," the little fairy said. "Worn wire of me." She glanced in the direction of the shrill shrieks.

"But you're one of them," rejoined Holly, taking a guess as to the fairy's meaning. She remembered what Nicholas had once told her about fairy talk—it was not exactly another language, he had said, but a way of talking in pictures. Holly smiled at the tiny, scowling face. It was Emmalylis, the youngest and tiniest Boucane. She perched upon Holly's wrist, her sea-green wings wrapped tightly around her as if to protect her from the noise.

"Don't you like hide-and-seek?" asked Holly.

"Lost and sought overmuch to a stream," said Emmalylis crossly. "Sharp-edge, honed knife tongues, too." She pulled on her green hair and looked approvingly around the room. "Pale world, empty bucket."

"Yes," Holly agreed. "I came here to get away from the fairies, but before I knew it, I had made this. See, it's Makena."

"A long way to look down," Emmalylis observed.

Holly stared at the little figure. Emmalylis was right; Makena's face was proud. "Yes, I suppose so. But she is a grand fairy. I keep trying to make dolls. You know, pretty dolls for the little girls in the mortal world, but I can't seem to do it. Every time the face turns into someone I know. It shows too much, too. I don't think Makena would like this face, do you?"

"She looks in the mirror and her blood sings love."

Holly had to think about that one for a moment. "You mean she would just see this and love herself?"

"A golden balance."

"You mean yes?"

Emmalylis nodded. "Your father all clasped in warmth? Bags sag with petticoats stiff, heads, and lace, too. Under your hand?"

Holly could feel her brain twisting and straining to transform this idea into words. "Oh! Yes! Dolls for my father to deliver on Christmas. Dolls for the children—in lace, like you said."

Emmalylis peered into her face and asked lucidly, "Why?"

Holly's shoulders drooped. "Because I have to do something," she said quietly. "Because you and all your cousins are trapped in the Land of the Immortals, and it's all my fault. Because I don't deserve to be an immortal. I've never done anything important for the people in the mortal world."

"Under your hand swirling like paper on their towers, then hard to your shoes."

"But I can't!" Holly burst out. "I can't get there! Remember? My father's the only one who can leave. The rest of us just stay here, locked in, until . . . until"—she couldn't bring herself to say his name— "he comes to get me."

Emmalylis regarded Holly with bright, searching eyes. "Half round in a long night," she said finally, seeming to select her words carefully, "dazzled with whiteness up, your heart goes."

"How does it go?" asked Holly intently.

"Sign in a long night," said Emmalylis, clearly exhausted by the effort to make Holly understand. "From snow to snow." Then she shook her head. She could speak no more.

Holly pulled her soft handkerchief from her pocket and made a little bed for Emmalylis. The fairy crawled toward it, rolled the fabric over her head like a tent, and fell asleep instantly. Holly watched over her until the room grew dark.

Holly settled herself more deeply into the nest of cushions she had arranged in her sitting room. "Half round," she muttered. She had been wracking her brain for hours to find a meaning for the fairy's words.

"Say the whole thing again," demanded Alexia for the twentieth time.

"She said 'Half round in a long night, dazzled with whiteness up, your heart goes,'" recited Holly.

"That makes no sense at all," sniffed the fox.

"I think it does," Holly said earnestly. "That part about my heart—I think she was trying to tell me that there's a way for me to go to the mortal world and do something important there. I really think that's what she was trying to say."

"Then she's wrong." Alexia scowled. "What about the curse?"

Tundra looked at Holly sympathetically. "Maybe she was making it up. Fairies are terrible liars, you know."

"She wasn't making it up. She was trying to help me."

"I don't know why you don't just ask your father," said Alexia.

"I told you," said Holly patiently. "If I tell him, he'll try to stop me. He doesn't want me to go to the mortal world."

"I don't want you to either," said Tundra.

Holly rubbed between his ears. "Hush." She threw back her head and stared at the branches above her head. "'Half round.' That's the best clue. What's half round?"

There was a long silence.

"All right, what about 'dazzled with whiteness up'?" she said. "What could that be?"

"Maybe there's half a hole in the bottom of one of the glaciers and if you fall into it, you'll end up in the mortal world," suggested Empy.

Holly hid a grin that would have hurt his feelings. "Maybe you're right."

Alexia was not so tactful. "The glaciers aren't white, silly. They're colored."

Empy stared at the floor.

"Now Lexy, don't be such a crab," said Holly peaceably.

"Why can't you find Emmalylis and ask her to explain?" suggested Euphemia.

"Fairies can't explain," replied Tundra. "She already did her best."

"Besides," said Holly, "it would take me months to find her again."

"What about Sofya?" whispered Empy. "Won't she help you?"

Holly sat up straight. "Sofya! Of course! She knows everything!"

"Good thinking," said Tundra.

"For a penguin," said Alexia.

Though Holly knew that Sofya lived in the castle and where her apartments lay in the old wing under Uther's Tower, she had never visited her godmother's rooms before. As she stood the next morning before the carved wooden doors with their brass fittings, she hesitated at the prospect of entering these private chambers. Not that she would be unwelcome; she just wasn't quite sure what she would see.

Holly raised her hand to knock, but the wood itself seemed to melt away, and she found herself inside a large, shadowy room, hung with rich tapestries and lit only with flickering candles in brass lamps. On the walls, pictures of princesses, firebirds, and golden horses had been painted in enamel, and from behind a lacy screen a thick curl of steam spread the scent of tea through the cavernous space.

"Come in, goddaughter," said Sofya, emerging from behind the screen with her usual serene expression. "Would you care for some tea?"

"Um. No, thank you," said Holly, unable to take

her eyes from the jewel-bright paintings.

There was a silence.

"Are you paying a social call, Holly?" asked Sofya finally. "Isn't it rather late in the evening? Shouldn't you be asleep?"

Holly smiled. "It's morning, Sofya!"

"Really," Sofya said, unperturbed.

"Really. You would be able to tell if you opened the curtains."

Sofya looked at the velvet hangings over the windows. "I prefer to make my own time, dear. Now do tell me what I can do for you." She sipped her tea.

Holly explained the events of the previous day. When she repeated Emmalylis's words, Sofya shook her head disapprovingly and exclaimed, "Fairies! Such a naughty lot. I shall have to speak to Makena."

"No, don't do that," pleaded Holly. "Emmalylis was trying to help me."

"But Holly, she has not helped you in the least!" cried Sofya. "She has only made you want something you cannot yet have. Emmalylis has given you a riddle that you are not ready to solve."

Holly was near tears. "Sofya, you know that the only thing I want is a chance to deserve the immortality I was born with. Please, Sofya! I'm an outsider

here, and I can never be anything else until I journey
to the mortal world and make my way. Help me!" She
knelt beside her godmother's sofa.

At the sight of Holly's misery, Sofya's face softened. "Oh, my dear. Let us try again. What you are
truly asking me to do is grant your wish, are you
not?"

"Yes," said Holly, looking up, hope flashing across
her face. "Send me to the mortal world," she begged.

Sofya sighed. "And what will you do when you get
there?"

"I don't know," Holly confessed. "All I know is
that something is drawing me to the Empire City. I
know my destiny lies there. I know I will find my
heart's work there."

"That is the truth," Sofya said simply.

"Then send me! You have magic. You can grant
wishes."

"No. Holly, it is the law of the universe. I cannot
grant you a wish that is within your own power to
attain."

Holly stared at her godmother. "My own power?"

"Yes."

"You know this?"

"Yes."

"When?"

"Oh, child, soon! You can find the way, and you must seek it patiently. It will happen soon enough." Sofya stood up abruptly and paced toward one of the covered windows.

Holly sat in silence, and then lifted her head. "I'll be patient. But tell me one more thing. Please."

Her godmother smiled. "What is it?"

"Will I die there?"

The cloud-colored robes came to an abrupt halt, and Sofya stood as though frozen for a long minute. Then, to Holly's astonishment, her godmother's form was surrounded by a nimbus of electric blue, like that of a flame. Slowly the robes grew transparent, and Sofya disappeared before Holly's eyes.

Chapter Fourteen

S HE SAID *SOON*. She said it twice," Holly insisted.

"She's an immortal," said Alexia gloomily. "Who knows what *soon* means to someone who's lived five thousand years."

Empy snuggled against Holly's knees, and she stroked his head.

"Do you want to play the Empire City game?" Tundra asked.

Holly nodded listlessly. "All right. You ask."

Tundra sat up. "Who's the mayor of the Empire City?" he asked.

"Easy. Mr. William Strong."

"Easy, was it?" said Tundra, ruffled. "How about this? Who rules the department of street cleaning? You'll never get that one."

Holly stuck out her tongue at him. "Colonel George Edwin Waring."

"Junior."

Holly laughed. "Colonel George Edwin Waring, Junior, whatever that means."

"I'll give you the point anyway," said Tundra generously. "But here's a good one. You're at the corner of Tenth Street and Fifth Avenue. How many blocks must you walk to reach Washington Square?"

Holly closed her eyes and counted. "Four—no, five, if you count the alley."

"What's a block?" asked Empy.

"Mortals arrange their cities in squares, each divided by a street. They call each square a block," explained Holly.

Alexia regarded Holly with awe. "How do you know all this?"

"Tundra and I decided that I should get ready for my journey by finding out everything I could about the Empire City. I've been reading some of Papa's books."

"And she made a map of the city, using the tele-scope," said Tundra.

"Research," said Euphemia approvingly. "Very owlish."

"Just try it," urged Alexia.

Holly looked at the gigantic Amaranthine Gates. The golden posts had long since been restored, and there was no sign of the havoc that had once been wreaked upon them. The gems that lined the golden bars glittered in the afternoon sun. Holly's heart began to thump. What if the curse had just sort of faded, and nobody knew it? What if she walked right up to the gates and pulled them open? What if that was all it took to be free?

"You won't know until you try," said Alexia.

Holly glanced back at Vobis, calmly waiting in the snow. The horse offered no opinion.

"All right, Lexy," Holly said. What if? She took an unsteady breath and approached the shining metal. Maybe? She stared up toward the heavens and could barely see the tops of the gates. With a shaking hand, she reached for the loop that held the latch—and stopped. She could not lift the metal circle; it was immobile. Tentatively she shook one golden bar and then pushed with all her might. The enormous gate did not even register a shiver.

Then something caught her eye. On the other side, in the mortal realm, the snow was lined with shadows. Yet there was nothing that would cast a shadow. But the shadows existed, thin and patient, waiting. Her throat tightened, and she understood. These were the immortal souls, exiled from their destiny by the curse she had brought. Her eyes stung with tears.

"Maybe I could dig under it," Lexy was saying. She strolled toward the gate and began to paw at the snow near the post.

"No, Lexy, don't," Holly said urgently. "We shouldn't be here." But the fox had already stopped.

"It's as though there's a wall inside the ground," she said, looking at her paws. "I'm breaking my claws on it, even though I can't see it." She looked back at Holly. "We must go."

"Yes," said Holly with relief. "This is a sad place."

Time enfolded the five friends in its patient arms. Holly turned seventeen, and the expected journey still did not occur. She did her lessons and spent long hours molding her clay figures; she enjoyed her friends and loved her parents, but always and under each moment, she waited. There was something quiet and watchful in her face, a shadow of suspense on all her doings. Though Nicholas and Viviana did not know of Holly's unshakable belief that her destiny lay in the mortal world, they knew that their daughter was no longer content with childish things. They saw her gazing absently from the windows into the sea of trees below, and they recognized the longing in her eyes.

One bright October morning, as Holly and Viviana sat together in Holly's snow-charmed sitting room, they heard heavy footsteps thumping down the hall. Nicholas entered, looking exasperated, and threw himself into a chair. It shuddered under the impact.

"Goodness, Nicholas, be careful," Viviana said, eyeing the chair.

Nicholas sat in preoccupied silence. Finally he burst out, "There's nothing I can do about it! My hands are tied."

"Your hands are tied about what?" asked Viviana.

"The fairies," he said grimly. "I'm going to have to enchant them. They're completely out of hand."

"Enchant them? What do you mean?" cried Holly.

"Cast a spell. Maybe not on all of them, but on most. It's the only way to control them. Oh, not forever," he said, catching sight of Holly's stricken face, "but for a few months. They're absolutely mad. Do you know what they did last night?"

"Oh dear," said Viviana apprehensively.

"They broke into the doll shop and had a revel! And do you know what they did at that revel?"

Holly shook her head, wincing in advance.

"They ripped the head and limbs off every last doll in the shop and made a bonfire out by the lake! Didn't see anything wrong with it! 'We wanted to go skating by firelight,' Nemekele tells me! Our entire stock of Christmas dolls! Hundreds of dolls! Christmas is only two months away! Didn't see anything wrong with it!" Nicholas ranted.

"They probably didn't, love," said Viviana.

"I know! I'm sure they didn't, but that's just the problem. They've got absolutely no sense of responsibility. They've got no sense of proportion. They're complete savages!"

"Oh, Papa, they're not!" said Holly. "They're wonderful! Of course, they're careless and wild, but that's because they live by their own lights. You know that they don't understand the human world. It's not their fault—it's just the way they are."

"But what am I to do about the dolls?" demanded

Nicholas. "They're destroyed."

"Why don't you use your magic to make new dolls instead of locking up the fairies?" Holly replied.

Nicholas shook his head. "It's not as easy as that. You see, even if I use magic, I have to envision the face of each doll first, and right now I need hundreds and hundreds of dolls. That's not something I can do in a few weeks. But I suppose," he said unwillingly, "I suppose that there's no help for it now. The dolls will have to look alike. Maybe, if the goblins agree to take over the train shop, I can come up with three or four different dolls, but that's the extent of it. They'll be no better than the dolls in mortal shops and the trains will be dull, but what else can I do?"

"Let me help!" said Holly.

Nicholas turned doubtful eyes to her. "Have you ever made a doll?"

"Yes. Yes, I have. I'll show you." And Holly jumped up, scattering papers as she ran to her workroom to retrieve her little clay models.

She returned with her skirt held out before her, forming a basket for her work. "Look!" she said, dropping down before her father. He peered into the heap of figures and faces. He picked up a replica of Viviana, and one of Sofya, and studied them wonderingly.

"You made these?" he asked, astonished. "They're remarkable!"

Viviana regarded her clay portrait. Brushing the face with her hand, she murmured softly, "You've made me so lovely, Holly."

Nicholas smiled. "It's a perfect likeness, my dear."

"You see!" said Holly, turning to her father in triumph. "I can make the faces. I can make lots of them in two months, too."

"Can you do as well in porcelain?" inquired Nicholas.

"I don't see why not."

Nicholas looked down at the face he held in his hands. "Quite interesting. Miss Malibran. She would love it."

"Well? Can I?"asked Holly.

Her parents glanced at each other, wordlessly telegraphing their pleasure with their daughter. "Of course you may, darling," said Viviana.

"That will be most useful," said Nicholas, using an appropriately businesslike tone, and shook his daughter by the hand to seal the bargain.

Holly began to work in the doll workshop. Almost at once she made an important discovery. She had never been so happy in her life. Finally, after all her years of hoping, she was doing something for the mortals, and when she left the workshop in the evening, with Tundra walking quietly by her side, Holly looked around at the immortals stepping through the streets and did not feel ashamed. She lifted her head and grinned at a centaur who was galloping home with a basket on his hairy arm.

"Evening, Your Highness," he said politely and then flashed her an enormous, toothy smile.

He doesn't blame me, she thought. Her step became lighter.

Of course, it did not escape her notice that the workshop was nearly empty. Nicholas insisted it was the cold that accompanied Holly that kept the others away, but she knew better. Normally the place was humming with goblins, gylfyns, and fauns, who delighted in dolls and doll making. It was quiet now that she was there, for the old stories lived on, and most of the magical creatures believed that to be in her presence was to risk a visit from Herrikhan. Only three immortals were brave enough to take the chance: the old goblin Mraka, who spoke so little that no one knew if he understood that he was in danger; a lavender gylfyn named Thelejima, who declared loudly that he would protect Holly against every intruder with his six arms, which he then flexed for her, one by one; and Holly's old champion Macsu, who hugged her with all his strength and settled his chair at her side. "Tell me," he said cheerfully, "tell me everything that's happened since the last time I saw you."

So Holly chatted with her friend, but when it came time to work, she grew quiet. She closed her eyes and saw a face—where did it come from? Was it a child she had seen in her telescope? Or was it simply a mirage floating in her mind? Her hands, shaping the thick porcelain, followed the contours of her vision. Without opening her eyes, she stroked two round cheeks into existence, curled a chin like a wave, and coaxed a small nose into a point. Her eyes flew open, and she made the brows, the forehead, and a mouth open as if to talk. "Welcome," she breathed to her creation and laid it upon the table, for Mraka and Thelejima were in charge of limbs. Macsu watched speechlessly in the chair next to her.

"How did you do that? You made a perfect face— without a mold—in less than five minutes!" he spluttered.

"I don't know how I do it," said Holly, coming

back from the dreamy world she inhabited when she made dolls.

"You're magic!" he squealed.

Tundra, who had been snoozing in the corner, lifted his head and looked warily at Macsu. Holly just shook her head. "If you can't fly, you're not magic," she said.

Even after long hours at the workshop, Holly continued to long for the Empire City, and when the five friends gathered every evening for supper, their conversation usually turned to the puzzle of how and when Holly's journey was to be achieved. Again and again Tundra and Holly pondered the clue that Emmalylis had presented to Holly, and Sofya's strange response. Alexia proposed increasingly preposterous plans for escape, such as bribing the griffin or disguising Holly as her father on Christmas Eve. Empy racked his brains for a way to be of use; he had even gone so far as to leave Holly's rooms to search for Emmalylis himself. But two fairy sisters—Io and Pialana—had pounced on him in the Hall of Mirrors and chased him from one end to the other until he had fled back to Holly's lap in despair.

Euphemia was silent. The more that Holly and

Tundra discussed the problem, the quieter she became. Each night as they began to pursue the topic anew, Euphemia flew into the farthest branch, sank her snowy head deep into her chest, and slept. Or seemed to sleep. One dark November night, as the wind howled, Holly draped herself over a pile of pillows and said, for the thousandth time, "There must be *some* way out."

And for the thousandth time, Tundra asked, "But what?"

There was a squawk from the silver trees. "Stop it!" cried Euphemia. "Stop saying that! Do something!"

Holly sat up. "But what?"

"That's what he keeps saying," squalled Euphemia. "I can't bear it. I'm only a stupid owl who doesn't know anything, but I don't understand why you both sit here every night saying the same thing. Get up! Do something!"

"What would you advise us to do?" asked Tundra.

Euphemia looked nervously from one to the other. "Research."

Holly smiled. "What kind of research, dear?"

Euphemia turned her head away, so they couldn't see her face. "Well," she said, "studying. Reading. I mean to say, weren't there lots of ways to get into the

Land of the Immortals in the old days? I don't remember myself, but it stands to reason that there were, maybe. You could study the history books—find a secret passageway, maybe."

Holly sat up straight. "You're exactly right, Euphemia. We need to do some research! We've been terribly dense!" She jumped to her feet and shook out her skirts. "A secret passageway," she repeated thoughtfully. "I'm going to Papa's study!"

Euphemia seemed to grow several inches larger. "Research!" she said proudly.

Nonetheless, their first attempt was not successful. Holly pored over a book entitled *Forever and a Day*, and Tundra flipped through magical handbooks as quickly as was possible for a creature without hands. Euphemia, whose pride was greater than her reading skills, was found with numerous books upside down in her talons, and eventually announced that her job was to be lookout. When the three finally tottered back to Holly's suite at four in the morning, they had found nothing. But Holly refused to be discouraged. She brought books from her father's library into her sitting room and studied them, searching anew for a clue, an idea, a hope.

"It says here that a convoy of gnomes floated here

on a magical boat in 1521," said Tundra. "Oh. Never mind. The boat was blown up by Albigenes in 1523."

"The roc came by magic carpet, according to Dappertutto," Holly said several hours later.

"He did? Couldn't he fly?"

"Doesn't say. But the carpet returned to Persia afterward, so that won't work."

Silence hung over the room. For a long time, the only sound was the shushing of turning pages. Holly sighed.

"Holly?" It was Euphemia, high up in her silver branches.

"Yes, dear?" replied Holly absently, picking up a book called *Immortal Journeys.*

"Hum. Well. Why don't you look in that big book?"

"Which big book?"

"That big one. In your father's study. On the stand."

Holly stared at the owl. *"The Book of Forever."*

"Yes. That's the one," replied Euphemia.

Holly was already running toward the study.

How many pages were there in *The Book of Forever*? Thousands? Tens of thousands? More? Holly read every one, and as the days slipped into December, she read of heroes, magical epochs, and immortal history, but no secret passageways. Each time she thought she had found something, she was informed that it had disappeared, been transformed, or was now accursed. There was only one name that offered even a glimpse of a possibility. It was called the Boreal Rainbow.

She came to Tundra with the massive book in her arms. "What do you think of this?" she asked tiredly. "It's the Boreal Rainbow, a rainbow made of the light of the aurora borealis. Listen: 'Appearing only once every five hundred years, the Boreal Rainbow signals the opening of a passage between the mortal and immortal worlds. Its brief duration as well as its radiant colors make it an astonishing sight to the mortals, who often mistake it for a signal of a great empire's end.' What do you think?"

"Once every five hundred years," he reminded her. "When was the last one?"

"It doesn't say." Holly looked searchingly at the book. "But that could be it, couldn't it?"

Tundra looked at her with pity. "Yes. Maybe that's the one."

Chapter Fifteen

MEANWHILE, Christmas was coming. Holly and Macsu had no time for chatting now. They both worked feverishly to create enough dolls for the mortal children on Christmas Day. Thelejima's six hands were a blur as he assembled arms and legs with lightning speed. Only Mraka moved at a normal pace. Methodically he buttoned small cloaks and dresses, tied shoes, and arranged hats delicately on shining hair. The row of smiling dolls grew longer and longer. It was four days before Christmas and they only needed four hundred more.

Three hundred and ninety-nine more. Three hundred and ninety-eight more . . .

"Ten thousand five hundred and forty-four finished!" trumpeted Thelejima, "and *three hundred and eighty-two to go!*"

Holly and Macsu were applauding themselves when the door opened and Nicholas entered the workshop. He stopped in the doorway, surprised. Who is that woman? he wondered. It was Holly, stepping briskly across the shop to set a finished doll upon the shelf for firing and then swirling around to begin another at her little table. Her coppery hair was bundled back with a large, green silk scarf—it was really the makings of a doll dress—and her cheeks were flushed with excitement. Her long hands were covered with porcelain dust, and she did not so much walk across the room as dance. She's a grown-up, Nicholas thought. She's not a child anymore. How much longer can we keep her with us?

His thoughts were interrupted by Holly's cry of greeting. "Papa! Do you see? Look how many we have made!"

"And all of them unique!" said Nicholas with delight. "Every single one has a different expression, a different character. You've wrought marvels, you four!"

"She's wrought the marvels," a creaky voice said. It was Mraka. He pointed his chin at Holly. "I've not seen the like before."

"I'm pleased that she's won your good opinion, Mraka," said Nicholas, beaming.

Mraka nodded; that was enough of speaking.

"Thank you, Mraka," Holly leaned over and whispered in his ear. He smiled a thin smile and bent over his work again.

"Sire!" cried a voice outside the workshop.

"Yes! In here!" called Nicholas, opening the door. "Come in, my dear Farmer."

A tall, oddly dressed man bustled in, bearing a sheaf of papers, all covered with extensive calculations. "This just in," he said, his high voice somewhat muffled by, coincidentally, a muffler. Bright eyes peeped out from under a straw boater, which was kept from blowing off by a long velvet cord. This was Horatio Thaddeus Farmer, the uncannily accurate meteorologist of the Land of the Immortals, who felt that it was his duty to keep Nicholas apprised of all weather conditions anywhere on Earth at all times. "I must inform the king" was his favorite slogan, and he was continually bustling off to the castle for what he called "royal consultations." Most immortals edged away from Farmer when he began to talk cumulus and cirrus, but Nicholas found him deeply entertaining and welcomed him into the castle study with a look of serious consideration that brought joy to Farmer's heart. Now, quivering in excitement, he began to gesture wildly with his papers. "I thought you should know, sire: an unforeseen cold front will descend upon the North American mortals tomorrow, bringing snow and ice destined to last until Christmas Eve. *Most* unusual to see such a vast expanse of cloud cover. Really quite odd." A shadow of perplexity crossed Farmer's face, but he recovered himself with a dry cough. "The entire eastern portion of the United States, always excepting the state of Florida"—here Farmer sniffed—"can therefore expect a white Christmas. In the western territories"—he refused to call them states—"there will be—"

"It will be snowing in the Empire City?" Holly broke in.

Farmer glared in irritation over the top of his glasses at this intrusion, then recognized the speaker and bowed hurriedly. "Yes, Your Highness. Snowing copiously."

"How cold will it become?"

"Well below freezing every night, Your Highness," simpered Farmer.

"And during the days?"

"Quite cold. Not, perhaps, always freezing, but still quite cold. If it please Your Highness," he added with a flourish.

"Oh, it does, Mr. Farmer. It does," Holly said with shining eyes. She turned to her father. "Papa!" she said urgently. "Did you hear?"

Fighting the dread in his heart, Nicholas tried to maintain an even tone. "Yes, my dear. It will be a white Christmas in the Empire City. New York City."

"Papa?" Her entreaty could be read upon her face. "Couldn't I try?"

"Try what, my dear?" said Nicholas with false heartiness.

"You know, Papa," Holly said. "You know. Take me with you. On the Christmas Eve journey. Please. Please."

A swarm of contending fears chased one another through Nicholas's mind as he watched his daughter's eyes search his face for hope. It's impossible, thank God. We've tried it before. It can't work. So there's no harm in attempting it. But what if we succeed? Then what will I do? She can't come. She can't. Her heart couldn't stand it. But it will be cold. Perhaps not cold enough. Farmer's been wrong before. And Herrikhan. If he learns she's there, he will do everything in his power to find her. It would be so easy for him among the mortals. *He could kill her there.* "No!" he barked suddenly, surprising everyone. "Never!"

Like any weatherman, Thaddeus Farmer recognized an impending storm when he saw one. "I'll just take myself off," he called shrilly. "Your Royal Highnesses! My humblest respects to the queen! Good day!" He bolted for the door.

Thelejima, Macsu, and even Mraka looked at one another in consternation and invented emergencies in the storerooms that required their immediate attention. As the last gylfyn arm disappeared down the stairs, Holly turned to her father. Upon her cheeks burned two pink spots, and her eyes seemed to spark like fireworks. Still her voice was steady when she said, "Please explain your answer, Papa."

It's a strange truth that no matter how persuaded we might be of our own correctness, the discomfiting realization that others disagree with us causes a paralyzing inability to argue the case convincingly. "It won't work," Nicholas began, foolishly beginning with his weakest link. "We've tried it before."

"What's the harm in trying it again? Perhaps because I am your daughter, I might have a chance."

Nicholas saw that he had begun badly, but he couldn't seem to put it right. "No. It's too dangerous for you in the mortal world. Your heart—"

Holly interrupted eagerly, "But you heard Mr. Farmer. Below freezing. Snow. Papa, I go outside here in the winter. There's no reason why it should be any different there. Think—"

"No! What would we do if you fainted? How could I get you to safety? Do you expect me to endanger Christmas for the children? I say no. It's too dangerous!"

"Papa," said Holly, struggling to keep calm, "are you frightened that Herrikhan will—"

At the sound of the name he dreaded on her lips, Nicholas felt his composure crumble. His response was hasty and wrongheaded. "No! I forbid it!" he snapped.

Holly had never been angry in her life, but she was angry now. She caught her father by his sleeve. "Forbid it! How can you? How can you dismiss me and my dreams as if they were dust?" Her eyes were fierce. "You can't forbid it, and you can't stop me. Neither you nor Herrikhan will stop me from going to the Empire City if I can!" She turned on her heel and ran out of the workshop, leaving Nicholas fuming, not at his daughter, but at himself.

Two hours later Holly was wrapped in her mother's embrace. Several damp handkerchiefs lay crumpled among their skirts, but Holly had stopped crying now. She leaned back and looked lovingly at her mother's face. "It's Herrikhan. I know it." She sighed.

Viviana shuddered at the name. "Yes," she agreed. "Your father's frightened for you, that's all."

"But you're frightened about him too, and yet you're not so unreasonable."

Viviana smiled, a little sadly. "Only because I know it will do me no good. If I could stop you by being unreasonable, darling, I would do it. But I know that if you see a chance to journey to the mortal world, you will take it, regardless of the danger."

Holly was quiet; her mind was wandering back to the edges of that horrible night long ago, the blurry instants summoned from the darkest caverns of her memory—falling down, down, while the wind above her screamed. "No," she said, stopping herself. "I can't stay here for eternity because I'm frightened of him. That would make me a coward and a failure, not an immortal." Absently she pulled at the fringe of Viviana's silken shawl.

Viviana's arms tightened around her daughter. "If only I could just keep you right here, like this," she murmured.

"But you can't. I hope." Holly smiled at herself. "I keep reminding myself that this is just speculation. For all I know, I'll never get out of the Land of the Immortals."

Viviana gave her a penetrating look. "That's what you know, but what do you feel?"

"I feel certain that I'm going to make a journey to the Empire City," Holly confessed.

"Yes," said her mother, "so do I. Nobody else can leave the Land of the Immortals, but somehow it seems absolutely certain that you will." She sighed.

"I will come back, Mama. I promise I will," said Holly.

If you can, Viviana added silently. Aloud, she said, "Look at you. You're a woman now."

Holly shook her head. "Sort of. I still feel like a child most of the time."

"So do I. And I'm over a thousand years old."

"Do you?" Holly glanced up quickly. "I always think that when girls get married, that's when they start feeling grown up."

"No, darling. If anything, you feel more like a child than ever when you fall in love," answered Viviana.

"Really?" said Holly, frowning. "I wonder. . . ." Her voice trailed off.

"If you'll ever fall in love?" Viviana finished her sentence.

Holly blushed. "What does it feel like?" she asked hesitantly.

Viviana twirled a strand of Holly's hair around her finger while she thought. "It feels like time has stopped." She paused. "It feels like you're shaking with excitement. It feels like you're more alive than anything in the world. It feels like a secret."

Holly stared at the tips of her toes without seeing them. "A secret," she repeated dreamily. Then, suddenly shy, she pulled Viviana's shawl over her head.

"How do you know for certain?"

Viviana smiled compassionately at her hidden daughter and pulled the shawl from her head. "How do you know that you're in love? Ah—you know. It's a song that only the two of you will hear." She laughed softly. "Wait here."

Viviana rose from the chair and disappeared into the next room. When she returned, she was carrying a crystal box that held a thousand prisms dancing with flecks of color as a couple waltzed on crystal ice. She handed it to Holly, who gazed in wonder at the extraordinary object.

"What is it?" Holly asked breathlessly.

"A music box. Your father gave it to me. I was mortal then, and young, and I had many suitors. One day—at a harvest festival—I saw your father and thought I had never known such a wise face. He was standing next to an oak tree, and when he saw me looking at him, he reached into its branches and drew out this box. I came closer—though I was not supposed to talk to men my father did not know—and I heard the most wonderful, indescribable music. All I wanted was to listen to that music and look at your father, forever. The music wrapped us in magic, and we began to dance, and"—Viviana chuckled—"my friends thought I had gone mad, because they could hear nothing. Oh my, how they laughed at me. But I didn't care. I didn't care about anything but him after that." She sat with a gentle smile, lost in memories.

Holly reached out a long finger to touch the crystal gently, and her mother placed the box in her hands. "Keep it," said Viviana.

"But you and Papa—don't you want it?" stammered Holly.

"It has done its work for us. It must be passed on, as it was to your father."

Holly looked curious. "Who gave it to Papa?"

"Sofya. But that's a long story, which you will hear another time. Take the music box now and keep it for the day when you fall in love. On that day, it will play its music for you."

❈ ❊ ❈

That evening, Holly and Nicholas exchanged apologies and hugs. Holly, worn from her work and the unfamiliar experience of being angry, decided against her usual research excursion. She curled up in her crystal bed, the silver leaves above her whispering lightly, and gazed at the music box that rested on her pillow. Its colors were muted in the shadows of night; only a few shards of blue and purple glinted under the glassy surface of the box. Euphemia hooted softly in her sleep somewhere above Holly's head, and Alexia wheezed in a distant corner. Outside the palace, the dark sky was scattered with stars.

When Holly awoke hours later, the first thing she saw was the music box, radiant with color. Colorful prisms danced upon her pillow and across the bed. Holly looked in sleepy wonder at her own arm, now made exotic with spangles of pink, green, lavender, and golden light. Soon Holly's silent wonder transformed into a vague yet insistent curiosity. Her room was dark. It was still night. Why was the box glowing so? As the sea serpent of sleep pulled her back into its thick waters, Holly decided she was having a confusing dream. She rolled over—and was greeted by another, even more remarkable sight. Her windows, where the black of night had so recently reigned, now displayed a sky of pulsing light. Hundreds of shades of color were ranged across the night in a monumental arch. Holly blinked. She sat up and rubbed her eyes. With growing excitement, Holly tiptoed over to the window and regarded the scene before her: the great, glimmering rainbow seemed to emerge from the reflecting pool below and swung out over the Land of the Immortals in a great bridge of color that had no end. "The Boreal Rainbow," she breathed.

Tundra appeared at her side, his silver coat turned iridescent opal in the light. "The Boreal Rainbow," he repeated, awestruck.

They stared in silence until Holly murmured, "Half round in a long night." Tundra turned toward her questioningly. "Half round in a long night," she repeated. "It's exactly what Emmalylis said. The rainbow is a half circle, and this is December twenty-first, the longest night of the year. She knew it all along."

The two old friends looked at each other for a long moment, then Holly whispered, "I promise I'll come back."

Tundra looked away. "If the curse—" He stopped.

"What?"

"The curse, Holly. You can only come back if

the curse is broken."

"Shhh," she said, wrapping her arms around his neck. "I'll come back with Papa on Christmas Day. Somehow, I'll come back."

If you can, Tundra thought.

One by one the other friends awoke and learned what had happened. Euphemia was sent out with a message to Meteor to get the sleigh ready at once. Holly rushed about her dressing room assembling dresses and shoes under Alexia's critical eye.

"You can't bring that, dear. No mortal lady wears that color these days," the fox exclaimed.

"Lexy, you're not being very helpful," cried Holly distractedly, holding up a blue poplin skirt in one hand and a pair of black boots in the other. "I need three dresses that won't look out of place in the Empire City. That's all I care about. You pick them."

"And shoes, and gloves, and a hat, and petticoats, and a nightgown," chanted Alexia.

Holly stopped rushing around and stared at the little fox. "How do you know all this? You've never looked through the telescope, not once."

Alexia gave the fox's approximation of a shrug. "I just pick it up here and there. Foxes have a keen fashion sense."

"Splendid. You choose," Holly said with relief. "I've got to get some porcelain from the schoolroom, and I have to wrap the music box in a petticoat, and then I have to get portraits of Mama and Papa." Holly spun around the room with a growing stack of precious items in her arms. "And Sofya."

Tundra eyed Holly's satchel dubiously. "Not too much, Holly. We don't know how much weight the rainbow will bear."

"I know, I know. But Tundra, I have to take *The Book of Forever,* don't I? So that I'll know if I've earned my place here?"

They all turned to look at the monumental book, its glinting silver covers laden with jewels. Tundra shook his head. "It must weigh as much as you do, Holly."

"I have to take it," said Holly. She strode to the table where the book rested and stood before it. "Please, take this journey with me," she said, addressing the volume humbly.

There was a soft clap, a sort of reverberation. The massive book lay on its table still, apparently unmoved. But when Holly reached to pick it up, the book flew gracefully into her outstretched arms as though it had the weight and bulk of a silk scarf.

Which it now did.

"Thank you," Holly said, patting the book's covers as the animals goggled in awe.

Finally Lexy finished her selection, and Holly packed the satchel with all the required garments, the music box, the book, the portraits, and a fine porcelain mixture for doll making. Holly spent a long time bent over the clasp, and as she raised her head, her friends saw that her eyes were filled with tears. "Good-bye," she began haltingly. "I'll come back soon."

"*Good-bye?*" they chorused incredulously.

"What do you mean, Holly?" cried Alexia. "Aren't we going with you?"

"You can't go without us!" cried Euphemia.

Empy began to wail.

Tundra was silent, his face inscrutable. Holly looked at them all anxiously. "My darling friends. I wish I could take you with me—you know that I do. I shall be so lonely without you on this strange adventure—" Her voice shook, and she stopped for a moment, looking at them with tears in her eyes. "I don't know if I can get along without you, for I never have had to before. I will miss you every instant of every day. But—but, I have to look like a mortal, you know." She dipped her head to look pleadingly into

Tundra's eyes. "And mortals don't walk about the Empire City with an owl, a penguin, a fox, and a wolf. They simply don't."

Eight eyes looked at her with varying degrees of compliance; they understood, but they didn't like it. "I'll be back in a few days," Holly reassured them, wiping her damp eyes with her hands. Still they were silent. "I have to write to Mama and Papa," she said hurriedly.

While she was penning a note filled with love and apologies and a promise to meet Nicholas in the Empire City on Christmas Eve, she could hear the animals murmuring behind her. Once finished, she turned to find them ranged in a semicircle around her chair. Alexia, who had clearly been elected spokeswoman, stepped forward. "We have decided that we cannot let you go alone." Holly began to protest, but she was silenced by a severe look. "And we have also decided that Tundra must be the one to make the journey with you. Number one: he looks like a dog, and mortals are often accompanied by dogs. Number two: he is the fiercest, should you need protection. Number three: he refuses to stay behind."

Holly gave Tundra a lingering look. "I can see that it is no use arguing with you."

"None whatsoever," he said firmly.

"Then I won't." Holly smiled at Alexia, then at Empy and Euphemia. "Thank you for understanding." Empy waddled over and rubbed his head on her knees. "I'll be back soon," she said again.

Holly was packed cozily in the sleigh with Tundra at her side and her satchel at her feet. Eight young reindeer, led by Meteor, stamped in the snow, impatient to begin the most exciting journey of their lives. Holly glanced back to her window, where her friends, made invisible by the darkness, were certain to be waving good-bye. She gave a lingering look to the palace itself, its turrets, towers, and wandering walls, the setting of her childhood, the home of everything she knew and loved. Then, her face alight with excitement and hope, she turned forward and grasped the smooth leather reins with fierce strength. To freedom, she said to herself. Aloud, she called out, "To the Empire City."

The reindeer had been waiting for this moment for years. With a single concerted movement, the deer leaped forward, straining against the tug of gravity. Down the long, snow-covered field they ran, their hooves beating heavily against the ground. "Up!"

cried Meteor. "Up now!" And in perfect unison, they lifted. Their silvery shapes appeared like ghosts in the reflecting pool and on they rose, into the rainbow that arched over the silent sky. As they lunged through the radiance of the Boreal Rainbow, there was a quick moment of wondrous warmth, and they emerged resplendent, rainbow deer alive with the hues of the heavens, their hooves trailing glistening rainbow dust, their bridles alight with prisms and jewels. Tossing their color-gilded manes in the wind, they rode on.

Soon they approached the gates of Forever, locked and silent beneath them on the snow-covered ground. Holly, her eyes fixed on those golden frames, forgot to breathe. Suppose they couldn't get through. But the sleigh sailed smoothly over the boundary that separated the immortal from the mortal world without a shudder or a pause. As her homeland slipped quietly into the distance, Tundra watched the girl he loved assume the majesty of a woman. She did not, as she would have in the past, fling her arms around his neck and seek comfort in his presence. Instead, she sat straight and firm, the guardian of her own future. Holly, too, felt the transformation that was taking place in her being: with each passing minute, her dreams came closer to reality. She was hungry to

As her homeland slipped quietly into the distance, Tundra watched the girl he loved assume the majesty of a woman.

embrace the mortal world and begin her work there, to earn the immortality she had been born with and to free her country from the curse she had brought with her birth.

Far away, in a place that was neither now nor forever, but a rotting always, Herrikhan rose from his pallet. The cold front had been tiring, terribly tiring, but his work was just beginning. It was not in his nature to feel joy; what he felt was triumph. He crossed his iron floor and stood before his mirror, stroking his skin with a scabbed forefinger. Beyschlag, rocking in a corner, watched without interest, his limp hands mechanically feeding a softened pink something to his mouth.

"Ssssss," Herrikhan whispered, leaning toward his reflection and pulling his lips down over his long teeth. There was nothing he could do about that. "Delighted to make your acquaintance, Miss Claus," he said, his voice deepening, his lips scarcely moving. "Do you plan to stay long in our fair city?" His eyes narrowed critically. "Your presence supplies it with a beauty heretofore unknown to me." He lifted his chin and stared intently at his mouth. "What a charming locket you wear. It is very like one my grandmother wore, may God rest her soul. Bless me." Herrikhan paused. His tongue had slipped from between his lips; quickly, he pulled it back. "Bless me, the similarity is remarkable. Would you be so kind as to permit me to inspect it?" He fell silent, satisfied. The color of his mouth was nearly unnoticeable from most angles.

Herrikhan looked at his hands, his yellowed, horn-like fingernails. He raised them to his forehead, dug into his flesh, and pulled. Thick, meaty furrows of skin peeled away. Faster and faster he scraped—his neck, his ears, his scabbed arms and bony shoulders—ripping and tearing the silvery flesh.

Underneath all was smooth and glowing with warm, human color. A strong face looked back from the mirror, healthy and vigorous. The slits of eyes grew in their sockets until they were wide and clear. His bones melted into recognizable human form, high cheekbones, narrow lips—perhaps a shade too narrow—over a firm chin. The long fingernails retreated, to be replaced by meticulously groomed, strong hands. Wincing, Herrikhan shrunk the iron band imprisoning his head into a thin wire that bit deeply into his flesh and then camouflaged it with a wealth of hair, perhaps longer than was strictly fashionable. Thick brown locks, brushed with silver, cascaded

over his unlined forehead, and only the most discerning eye could detect the narrow band within.

Herrikhan smiled, keeping his lips closed. The handsome eyes flicked downward, and his tattered robe appeared to melt away, revealing the sober, well-cut jacket and waistcoat of a wealthy New Yorker of the 1890s. Upon his watch fob, the emblems of several distinguished clubs hung unobtrusively. He wore a handkerchief in his pocket, and his discreet silken tie lay on the snowy linen of his shirt. He rattled his penknife in his trouser pockets and took a few steps in the swinging stride of a man of affairs, roaches cracking beneath his shining shoes. He turned back to the mirror with a flourish. He bowed. He reached out a hand, and a black bowler appeared between his fingers. He placed it upon his head only to sweep it off. "Delighted to make your acquaintance, Miss Claus."

He grinned. "Beyschlag!" he barked. "Do you admire my human beauty?"

Beyschlag regarded him, his lipless mouth chewing rhythmically. "Your beauty is beyond compare, my lord."

Freedom. Holly threw back her head and laughed into the wild openness around her. The wind whirled, buffeting her cheeks and tugging at her hair. Her eyes gazed jubilantly at the mortal world that flashed beneath her. Over the dust of deserts and the jagged limbs of mountains, the reindeer ran. Finally the flowing rainbow pulled the sleigh above the gray Atlantic toward America, where the first dim sparks of light showed that the Empire City was drawing near. Holly held her breath.

Suddenly the great lady, her arm upflung, was visible in the harbor. Without thinking, Holly stood up in the sleigh.

The city of possibilities stretched out beneath her, glowing with light and its own spirit. Snowflakes turned in their gyre like white butterflies, floating into the great avenues and the tiny alleys, falling alike on tall edifices and the tumbledown tenements. The deer, drawing close to their destination, descended

Her eyes gazed jubilantly at the mortal world
that flashed beneath her.

from the sky, and before Holly's eyes the city unfolded in wave after wave of extravagance.

The Great White Way, glittering with new electric lights, greeted her first and loudest. She could hear the tinkle and clash of riotous music and stamping feet, the roar of laughter, and a badly played violin. The jolly confusion of Broadway changed to calls and whistles as they whirled over the shadowy, teeming streets of the Lower East Side. Now they followed the screech and rattle of the elevated railcar as it lurched uptown and into its station, disgorging passengers who looked to Holly's eyes like small brown bears, they were so heavily bundled and befurred. A dazzling gilded dome slid into view; it was Pulitzer's tower, the tallest building in the world. Before Holly could do more than gasp, the tower was gone, replaced by the transcendent spires of St. Patrick's. Farther on, the scene grew hushed and elegant; wide, well-kept avenues were lined with mansions, blooming with turrets and towers, pillars and porticoes. Over their solemn mansard roofs, Holly flew northward, toward the brick barracks of the new Metropolitan Museum, and then, abruptly, west, to where the snow lay thick upon the hills.

Gently, softly, the sleigh landed.

Chapter Sixteen

New York City, 1896

PERFECT SILENCE. She could hear her own breath, ragged with excitement, escape into the frozen air.

It was nearly dawn. The sky had been growing lighter for the last hour. Now she could see the thin black tree branches clustered in the distance and the lonely, looming palace that stood behind them. Between the trees and the brick terrace where she stood was a long, steely expanse of empty ice. And there, directly before her eyes, was an angel, perched on a marble pedestal. For a moment the world seemed to draw in its breath and wait, suspended. And then the first rays of the sun touched the city, and the icy roofs and branches glowed with light.

She could feel it before she heard it: the great city awoke. Suddenly the atmosphere began to crackle with the electricity of over a million lives. Sounds, isolated at first, grew and blended and formed the chorus of the day. Horses' hooves hammered against the granite streets, the early risers shouted greetings at one another, streetcars rattled, silvery sleigh bells jingled, children whooped, windows slammed shut against the cold, and machinery hummed to life once again. The first bundled and muffled pedestrians began to hurry through Central Park toward Fifth Avenue. Not one of them lifted his eyes to see the girl who stood, coatless, atop the Terrace, watching the scene before her as though she could never see enough.

Meteor, still saturated with the violet adornment of the Boreal Rainbow, was waiting patiently in the meadow below the Terrace. Holly smiled at the picture her rainbow deer made, their brilliant shades glowing against the white expanse of snow.

"Don't they look like magic?" She nodded her head in their direction.

Tundra, sitting at her feet in an imitation of doggy obedience, murmured, "They are beautiful. But magic shocks the mortals, you know."

Holly smiled. "I have a plan, Tundra. Wait and see." Lightly she ran to the meadow and whispered into Meteor's lavender ear. Tundra saw him nod and grin, and in a few moments, to his surprise, the rainbow deer had been reborn as a carousel, linked by silken ribbons. Holly came flying back to Tundra, her eyes shining. "There!" she exclaimed. "Isn't that the most spectacular carousel you've ever seen? Don't you think the children will love it?"

Tundra shook his head. "You thought of everything, didn't you?"

Holly laughed. "I had a long time to plan. But I never thought they would be all the colors of the rainbow."

An early riser, clad in a stiff black coat, strode by the Terrace, firmly on his way to some important business. The rainbow deer, turning in their carousel ribbons, were apparently beneath his notice. He strode along, his eyes fixed on his own concerns. Tundra had agreed, during the sleigh ride, never to speak in the presence of a mortal, but now he murmured, "I don't think mortals are very observant, Holly."

Captivated by the waking city, Holly didn't hear Tundra's words, but she turned to the sound of his voice and threw her arms around his neck. "Can you feel it? Can you feel how wonderful it is?" she said passionately. "This is everything! This is life!"

"I don't understand how dogs sit still for so long," he muttered.

"Let's walk, then!" She waved to the angel. "Good-bye, angel!"

The angel was silent.

"Remember—they don't talk here," said Tundra between his teeth. A mustachioed man in a fur-lined coat looked curiously at Holly as he walked by. "Is there something wrong with the way you're dressed, Holly?"

Holly looked down at her clothes. She was wearing a simple shirtwaist above a long, graceful skirt of forest green patterned with holly leaves. "I think I'm supposed to have a hat and coat," she admitted. She paused to peer into her satchel and drew out a fashionably upswept hat featuring a satin ribbon that matched her skirt precisely and a green cloak. "How did she . . ." Holly murmured in surprise, slipping the cloak over her shoulders. The light material fell in handsome folds around her, giving the impression of a much heavier wrap. "Clever Lexy." Next she fastened the hat upon her shining wreath of hair with an alarmingly long hatpin and tucked up a few flying curls. "There," she said. "Do I look respectable?"

Tundra eyed her. "I believe so. Humans would be better off with fur, in my opinion."

Holly ran up the Terrace steps and disappeared down the other side. Tundra hurried after her, and together they encountered the Mall. The long thoroughfare was covered in snow, and a curtain of tree branches shielded it on each side. It was here that the city's wealthiest citizens came to parade in their victorias and landaus in the summer and their sleighs in the winter. The first of those was now turning up the avenue. A stiff coachman drove a fine pair of black horses, pulling a large, solidly built cutter, shell shaped as fashion required, replete with red leather seats, furred rugs, and jingling bells. Holly marveled at the proud horses and the elegance of the cutter, yet there was something not especially cheering about the scene.

As she was pondering this, the expressionless coachman pulled tightly upon the reins and abruptly brought the cutter to a halt, disgorging a little band of children and a tightly wrapped lady with a large chin and a severe expression. Holly's heart lifted; here, finally, were the children. She had been waiting all her life to meet them. She stepped forward eagerly, but her greeting died on her lips.

"Charles, you will stand still," snapped the severe lady. "Alice, a young lady does not jump from one foot to the other. Jerome! Harrison! Walk forward this instant! Evelyn, if I see your finger approach your nose again today, you shall be most sincerely sorry. Lines, please." The five children struggled into two lines, with the oldest boy, Charles, at the lead. "Play!" cried the lady. "You may play for exactly thirty minutes, according to your father's instructions. Foolhardy as they are," she added in a mumble. With a sour face and a series of fussy flounces, she settled herself back into the carriage and began to read a book entitled *The Depravity of the Impoverished Classes.*

As Holly looked on with growing unease, the five children walked, still in formation, to the frozen lawn. There they stopped still and waited for the thirty minutes to pass. The littlest boy, Harrison, bent down and picked up a stick, but he did not seem to know what to do with it afterward.

Holly couldn't stand it. On an impulse, she went toward the silent cluster of children with her arms outstretched. "Come, children," she called, "shall we make snow angels?"

They looked at her suspiciously. Finally Charles

said, "What's a snow angel?"

Holly smiled. "Come. I'll show you."

The five children exchanged glances and, apparently concluding that anything was better than standing around, they followed her to a spot in the lawn where the snow lay untouched and thick. Holly threw off her cloak and hat. "Look! You hold out your arms and fall into the snow, as flat as you can without losing your breath." She fell backward like a monument toppling. "Then you wave your arms," she said, "so it will look like you have wings. And then," she said, carefully rising, "you have to get up without ruining your angel. That's the hardest part. See!" she concluded triumphantly, "a perfect angel!"

The children regarded her with round eyes. "You're a young lady," squeaked Alice after a moment. "And you fell in the snow on *purpose*."

"It was fun," said Holly. "Even young ladies have to have fun. Come on!"

They seemed paralyzed with surprise. Evelyn's finger rose cautiously to her nose. Then Harrison said in a clear voice, "I bet I could do that." He walked to a fresh patch of snow and flopped back in it. "Hey," he said after a moment. "This is fun." Slowly he extricated himself from the snow, mangling his angel a bit.

"I'm going to do it again," he said. "I've got to get up better."

"Me too," said Jerome.

"It would look nice if we all did it together," suggested Holly. "Then we could make a row of angels."

"Yes," said Evelyn unexpectedly. "Let's do that."

For the first time, the five children played instead of waiting silently in the snow for the exercise to be over. They ran and slid and threw themselves enthusiastically into the snow. Harrison got the idea of drawing pictures with his stick, and Alice built a snowman. Thoroughly involved in her book, Miss Bellows, their governess, noticed nothing, not even the time, and a glistening hour ticked by.

"Let's go over to the lake and go skating," said Holly. She sat down breathlessly after helping Alice complete her second snowman.

"Yes!" the children shouted in unison. Evelyn wrapped her hand in Holly's.

Holly jumped to her feet and donned her cloak and hat. Cheerfully the children swarmed after her as she turned northward. "Come along!" she cried.

"Charles!" shrilled a furious voice. "Alice! Evelyn! Jerome! Harrison! Come this instant!" Miss Bellows slammed her book shut and strode toward the little group. "How dare you!" she hissed. "How dare you exhibit such wicked behavior? Cavorting with a *stranger*!" Her voice whistled with rage.

The children, abashed, offered no defense. They dropped their eyes and fell into sullen silence. Holly looked on with horror. She stared at Miss Bellows's too-big chin and finally broke into her tirade. "Excuse me, Miss Bellows. It was my suggestion, going to the lake. The children are not to blame."

The grim face turned toward her. "And who, pray tell, are you?" snapped the governess.

"My name is Holly Claus."

The sharp eyes took in her disheveled appearance, and Holly hastily tucked her flyaway hair back under her hat. "And under whose authority have you invited the children in my care to go skating with ruffians?"

"Under my own," said Holly steadily.

"I am afraid, Miss Claus, or whoever you are, that is insufficient. The children of Dr. Louis Braunfels do not proceed in such a disordered fashion. And they most certainly do not skate in the kind of low company you obviously find attractive."

"What do you mean by 'low company'?" asked Holly, honestly curious.

Miss Bellows turned redder than ever. "The

common, squalid characters who frequent the lake, that's what I mean by low company, Miss Claus."

"Ah," said Holly, staring at Miss Bellows's face. "That's what you mean," she repeated absently.

"And now I bid you good day!" snapped Miss Bellows.

Holly tilted her head questioningly. She seemed to be thinking about something far different than the topic at hand. She looked into Miss Bellows's small blue eyes for a moment, until the governess dropped her gaze. The children watched, openmouthed, for Miss Bellows appeared, suddenly, not to know what to do. She was twisting her handkerchief in the strangest fashion.

"What are you afraid of?" said Holly softly.

"The children," gulped Miss Bellows.

"Why?" asked Holly.

"Because they hate me."

"No. They are frightened of you, but they don't hate you. They will love you if you love them." Holly looked intently into Miss Bellows's eyes and then transferred Evelyn's hand from her own to the governess's.

Miss Bellows swallowed visibly. Evelyn, staring at her governess's fearful face, suddenly felt a rush of compassion for Miss Bellows.

"It's all right, Miss Bellows," she said. "We'll go home now."

The governess looked uncertainly at the other children. Charles glanced at Holly, who nodded encouragingly at him. "Yes, Miss Bellows," he said, nodding. "We'll go home and have our lessons. Perhaps you can tell us more about the constellations. That was awfully interesting. Let's go home."

He took Miss Bellows by the arm. Hastily, Alice kissed Holly's cheek, and Harrison and Jerome followed suit. "Good-bye, Holly! Good-bye!" they called. Harrison, trailing behind, whacked the tree trunks with his stick.

"That's a bit better," said Holly, looking after them. "But, my heavens, what a tangle these mortals get themselves in."

"Your father says it's because they're afraid," said Tundra under his breath.

"Yes. Papa knows." She thought of her father, peering mildly over his spectacles, and felt a stab of homesickness. Holly picked up her satchel. "Let's go to the carousel. I want to tell Meteor and the others how beautiful they are. Perhaps we'll meet some low company. They must be happier than the high company."

❊ ❊ ❊

The Mall was thronged with sleighs and little cutters now. Horses paraded by, their bells jingling merrily, and even the pampered bundles in the seats behind seemed to have been energized by the irresistible morning. Ladies put back their veils and greeted one another. Young men lifted their smooth black hats at the passing ladies and called out jovially to one another, "Frozen yet, Taylor?" "Splendid morning, isn't it, Brace!" "Mind on the right, Bostwick!" More than one appreciative glance rested on Holly as she stood watching the surging traffic with a slight smile on her lips and a vibrant look of interest that was utterly unlike the cool composure prized by society ladies of the day. "Remarkably pretty girl, that," said one young man to his companion as their horse trotted past.

"Don't fancy the dog, though, Law," commented his friend, gazing at Tundra. "Looks like the sort with big teeth."

"Now, now," said Law, "bravery and chivalry, Knapp. Let's turn around here and drive by once more. Perhaps she'll take a bow." He turned his horse smoothly and retraced his path, but Holly was nowhere to be seen. "Where's she got herself to, then?" he muttered, then, "Whoa! Whoa! What's the trouble up there, Knapp!" He pulled violently on the reins to keep his horse from plunging off the path. "What the dickens!"

"It's a kid," said Knapp sourly. "Right in the middle of the way. Get off, you filthy brat!" he called.

A very small child was standing in the middle of the avenue, staring at the dozens of horses and vehicles around him. Drivers called out threats and issued harsh commands, but the child, frozen in confusion, stood rooted to the spot. Law, having regained control of his horse, spit out a curse, and when that failed to dislodge the boy, he reached for his whip.

Holly appeared at the child's side, her cheeks flushed with running. "What are you doing?" she cried furiously at Law. "What on Earth are you doing?" she repeated, catching sight of his hand upon the whip.

Law turned pink and dropped the whip as though it were on fire. "Child's a danger to the horses, running into the road like that," he muttered.

"A danger to the horses?" Holly repeated in such disbelief that Law blushed further. "He's a *child*." Turning to the urchin, who was staring at her in wonder, she said, "May I pick you up?"

The little boy nodded solemnly, and without a
glance at the two shamefaced drivers, Holly took him
up and walked to safety at the roadside. He was the
first child she had ever held in her arms, after a life-
time of waiting, and she breathed in his sweet, dirty
scent rapturously. After an extra hug, she set him
gently on his feet. "Now, where is your mama?" she
asked.

The boy was silent. "Got no mama," he said finally.

Holly looked at him anxiously. "Are you here with
your papa?"

"Got no papa."

"Who—who takes care of you?"

"Nobody. I takes care of myself," the ragged boy
said proudly.

"How old are you?" demanded Holly.

The boy rubbed his face. "Dunno."

"Where do you live?"

"Why, here!" he replied, waving his arm about.

Holly looked around at the bright snow and leaf-
less trees. "In the park?"

"Yeah! Look, I'll show you!"

"Lady don't want to see nothing like that," said a
rough voice. An older boy had slipped from between

the trees and now clasped the little one under the elbow. "I'll just take him, ma'am," he said to Holly. "You don't have to worry about him no more."

"Who are you?" asked Holly.

"This is Jemmy," said the little boy with the air of one presenting royalty.

"Jeremy," said the older boy instantly. "He can't say it."

"Pleased to meet you, Jeremy," said Holly with a smile. "I'm Holly. What's your name, dear?" she asked the small child.

"Bat," he answered promptly.

"Bat?" repeated Holly.

"Bat. 'Cause I can see in the dark, like a bat."

At this, Jeremy seemed to feel that the child had revealed too much, and he once again took Bat's elbow. "We'll be off now, ma'am," he said with a polite bow, and Holly was struck by his grace and innate good manners, which made his patched clothes and general grubbiness unnoticeable.

"Do you live in the park too?" she asked, to keep him from leaving.

"Sometimes," answered Jeremy.

"Sometimes Jemmy gets a *job*," said Bat.

"What he means is I get a room when I have a job.

But now—now I'm staying here."

Holly looked around at the snowy woods. "Where do you sleep?"

"I'll show you!" said Bat eagerly, but Jeremy tightened his hand.

"Lady don't want to see it," he said firmly.

"Oh, but I do, Jeremy," said Holly. "Really, I do."

"No. Ma'am."

"But why?" cried Holly in disappointment.

"Not for the likes of you to see," Jeremy said stiffly.

"Aw, Jemmy, she won't tell," interrupted Bat.

Holly turned to the older boy. "Is that what you're concerned about?" She smiled. "I won't tell a soul. And besides"—she laughed—"I wouldn't know who to tell."

Jeremy had long ago learned that faces told more truth than words, and in the warmth of Holly's smile, his doubts began to dissolve. He looked at her curiously. "Where're you from? You're not one of these ladies." He pointed his chin at the passing sleighs.

"That's right. I'm not. I'm from a country far away," replied Holly.

"Italy," said Bat, looking wise.

"All you know," said Jeremy scornfully. "She talks English, don't she? She has blue eyes and gold hair, don't she? She's not from Italy."

"Come on, Jemmy. Let's take her to the Place," pleaded Bat.

"Okay," conceded Jeremy. They began to walk toward a thickly wooded section of the park, Bat running ahead and Tundra padding behind.

"I got a dog too," said Jeremy, looking backward. "You'll see him at the Place. He ain't as big as yours, though. That one looks like a wolf."

Tundra choked, and Holly quickly began asking questions. She learned that Jeremy was eleven and Bat was thought to be about four. "Don't know for sure," said Jeremy. "Just came wandering along one day when he was a little tyke. Couldn't barely talk or nothing. But we took care of him."

"He said he has no mother or father," said Holly hesitantly.

"Yeah. Probably not."

"Do you?"

There was a pause. "I got 'em," said Jeremy grimly. "If they ain't dead yet."

"You don't know—where they are?" Holly asked. She did not want to hurt him with her questions.

"No. But I can bet you that wherever they are, they're drunk."

"Drunk?" asked Holly.

Jeremy grinned. "You really are from another country, ain't you?" They turned a corner, and, in a tiny clearing screened by rocks and thick bushes, Holly saw a ragged group of children huddled around the embers of a very small fire. There were perhaps fifteen or twenty, ranging from two Bat's age to several boys whom Holly took to be older than Jeremy. Though the majority were boys, Holly saw a good number of girls, too, dressed in layers of pinafores and dresses, their thin legs wrapped in rags. The children all stared intently at the fire, as though their watching could keep it from dying, and Holly, looking at their thin cheeks, thought she had never seen such wretched faces. One girl, who was supported by another, began to cough a thick, painful cough. After the attack was over, she lay down on a thin blanket next to the brightest part of the fire and closed her eyes.

Bat ran to the little cluster. "Jemmy's here!"

All of the children looked up quickly. The smallest children began to smile. They called out, "Hi there, Jeremy!" "What's the news!" "Got any food?" A small, rascally looking white dog appeared from behind a clump of bushes, wagging his tail wildly.

Jeremy strode energetically toward the group.

"Why so glum?" he demanded. "Hungry?" He began pulling knobby packages from his pockets and distributing bread around the little band. "Marty! Thought I told you to get some more wood." He tossed a stump of bread into the air, and the little dog caught it efficiently.

"I went a-looking," sniffed a big boy with black hair sticking out in tufts under his worn cap. "But there was cops everywhere."

"Well, go on, get some now. I didn't see any of 'em and I just come through the Mall." Reluctantly the boy rose and ambled off. "Hiya, Sidewalk," Jeremy said to the dog, who was now clamoring around his knees in a frenzy of welcome. "This here's my dog I told you about," he said to Holly proudly. "His name's Sidewalk 'cause I found him on one and 'cause he walks sideways."

Holly noticed that the little dog circling around Jeremy did have a peculiar sideways gait, like a circus horse. It was a cheering sight. "I've never seen a dog do that," she said and, forgetting that she was in mortal territory, dropped to her knees. "Why do you walk sideways?" she asked the dog curiously.

Assuming the question was directed to him, Jeremy said, "Aw, I guess he got his leg broke when he

*Holly saw a ragged group of children huddled around
the embers of a very small fire.*

was little and that's how he learned to walk with it. Come on, now, Sidewalk, leave the lady alone." The dog, recognizing Holly's sympathetic heart, if not her words, licked her cheek enthusiastically.

"It's all right," she said, rising. She glanced at Tundra and noticed with amusement the scandalized look on his face.

Jeremy's attention had shifted. He approached the sleeping girl and put his hand on her cheek. He whistled. "She's burning hot."

"Least someone is," said a shivering girl.

"Wake up now, Lissy. I brought you some chocolate," said Jeremy softly to the little figure on the ground. "I got a blanket, too."

The girl opened her eyes. "Chocolate?" she murmured. "For real?"

" 'Course for real. Come on, sit up." Jeremy lifted her up and gave her a small packet, which she eagerly opened to reveal a smooth, dark square of chocolate.

"Ohhh," said all the other children, their eyes fixed upon the morsel.

"That's for Lissy, now," said Jeremy sternly, and the others nodded.

"Who's the lady?" said a ragamuffin of unknown gender, looking at Holly.

Jeremy glanced up. "That's Holly," he said. "She wanted to see our Place." He rose to his feet and approached her. "What do you think? See, we sleep in there, except in the summer." He pointed proudly to a small shack constructed of thin wood gleaned from boxes and covered with a few flapping cloths. "See, we got hay to keep us warm." He paused, clearly waiting for her to admire his home.

But Holly was quiet. Her eyes moved from Lissy, who was licking the last bits of chocolate from her fingers, to Bat, who was shoving one of his pals off a log by the fireside so he could take his place. What kind of a world was this, where children lived in the cold, cared for one another, and stared at food with hungry eyes? Was this part of mortal life? How could it be? How could Earth have been arranged so that children were cold and hungry? For the briefest moment, she wished she were back in the Land of the Immortals, hidden away among the silver trees. But no, she thought in a flash of comprehension, for that is exactly how these children came to be here, by people hiding from the sight of their hunger and hopelessness. "No," she blurted out involuntarily. Jeremy looked at her curiously.

"No what?" he asked.

Holly collected herself. I must do something, she thought. I must help them if I can. She turned to Jeremy with a smile. "You've managed beautifully, Jeremy," she said. "And I can see that you take good care of the children."

"Yeah," said Jeremy roughly, trying to hide his pride, "we do all right here." His eyes darkened. "Except Lissy. She's not doing too good."

"Is there a doctor—" began Holly tentatively, but she was interrupted by Jeremy's bitter laugh.

"Tried to take her, didn't I? I had money, too, but they wouldn't let us in." His voice rose in an indignant imitation, "'Get out of here, you vermin!' That's what she said to me and Lissy. I wanted to—to smash the place, but I didn't, did I, 'cause it wouldn't do her no good anyhow." His fists clenched. "So I got her some warm food instead. Helped her more than a doctor, probably."

"Jeremy," said Holly urgently, "are they hungry right now?"

He looked at her. "'Course they're hungry. They're almost always hungry."

"Let's go get food for them," begged Holly.

"With what for money? I ain't worked in a couple days."

"Money?" Holly was near to tears. "You need money to get *food*?"

"Lord," said Jeremy, looking at her in awe. "Where in the world do you come from?"

"I come from a place called Forever, the Land of the Immortals. There is no money there," said Holly with dignity. Beside her, Tundra rustled uneasily.

"Sheesh. How can I get there?" asked Jeremy.

"You can't. At the moment I can't either. My father will come for me on Christmas Day and I will return with him. But Jeremy, I need to know—"

"Your dad's coming on Christmas Day?" interrupted the boy.

"Yes, but Jeremy—"

"How's he gonna get here? All the rails are closed because of the snow."

"He'll come by sleigh. But *Jeremy*!"

"What?"

"Where can I get some money? I want to buy some food."

The boy sighed at her innocence. "You can't just get it. You got to get a job. You got to work for it. Or you got to sell something. I guess that's another way to get money, but I never had nothing anyone wanted to buy."

"What do people want to buy?" demanded Holly.

"Oh, you know, houses," Jeremy said airily. Holly's face fell. "And smaller stuff," he added, "like jewelry and clothes and fancy things."

"Jewelry?" cried Holly. "Look! I've got a bracelet!" She held out a slim wrist, where a golden bangle glistened. "Can we sell it and buy some food for the children?"

"But what about you? If you spend it all on us kids, you ain't going to have nothing to eat."

"Then I'll get a job," said Holly. "Come on, let's go sell this and buy some food."

Jeremy laughed at her impatience. "Well, first you have to go to a jewelry store and then they have to write you an order for the bank and then you have to go there for the money, and after all that you can go to the store to buy food."

"But that will take too long!" cried Holly. "What can I do *now*?"

Jeremy stared at the snowy ground, thinking. When he looked up, his eyes were shining. "I know. I know what."

Half an hour later, the thing was accomplished. Jeremy led Holly, trailing Tundra, to a little pavilion where a bearded man named Henry McElhenny was serving sizzling sausages on toasted bread. His equally rosy wife poured generous cups of tea and cocoa at his side. Jeremy, an old friend of McElhenny's, opened negotiations with the confidence of a natural salesman, and within several minutes the deal was struck. In exchange for Holly's golden bracelet, McElhenny would feed all the hungry children who approached his stand until Christmas Day. Hands were clasped all around, and Holly, who realized that she was faint with hunger, asked if she might be the first customer. She was served two sausages with a flourish, and she and Jeremy settled down to the task of consuming their sandwiches immediately. Try as she might, Holly's tendency to wipe her mouth with her napkin slowed her down, and Jeremy finished long before she did. As he licked the last savory drops from his fingers, Holly suggested that he take the opportunity to tell the other children of their sausage windfall, and the next moment he was dashing back across the park.

Holly watched him go, waving to passing acquaintances as he ran.

"He's a fine boy," said a voice at her side. She looked up to see McElhenny standing by her.

"Yes," she agreed warmly. "He has a great spirit."

"They call him the King of the Park," McElhenny said, his eyes on the retreating figure. "He knows every nook and cranny of it and every child who comes here."

"I hope—" Holly began, but did not know how to continue.

"Yes," said McElhenny. "So do I. I hope that life does not break him. He sees too much misery."

"Woof," said Tundra flatly.

Forgetting herself, Holly asked, "What did you say?"

"Woof," he repeated, more pressingly. She bent down to look at him. He crossed his eyes ever so slightly.

"I think your dog is hungry," said McElhenny.

"Woof," Tundra said, nodding emphatically.

"Look at that!" crowed McElhenny. "Anyone would think he understood what I said! Good dog!"

Holly got Tundra a sausage, which he gobbled down at once. She was just getting him a second when Jeremy returned with a horde of children. The rumor had flown through the park: there were sausages to be had at McElhenny's—free for the asking. "Hi! Jeremy! Is it true?!" shouted a pair of twins, emerging from a nearby field.

"Yeah, it's true. Come and get it!" Jeremy called.

"Present from my friend Miss Holly here!"

Urchins straggled out of the bushes and scampered up from the lake, greeting Jeremy with waves and hollers. He in turn brought each child before Holly with the whispered information, "She's the one that done it. Gave up her own gold bracelet. Say thank you. Go on, say it!" until Holly begged him to stop.

Soon McElhenny's pavilion was filled to bursting with children chewing sausages. Holly had the pleasure of seeing Lissy eat two, her eyes screwed up tight as the warm food filled her empty stomach. Bat was spilling cocoa ecstatically down his shirt as he lapped at it with his small pink tongue like a cat.

Suddenly an unpleasant voice cut across the din of chattering children. "Good God! It's turned into a pesthouse! Disgusting. We shall not be lunching here, Louise."

Holly saw an elderly man, warmly wrapped in a fur-lined coat, staring at the children with an expression of revulsion. By his side stood a girl of about ten—his granddaughter, Holly presumed—looking at the scene with envy.

"Step away, Louise," snapped the man. "Don't allow them to soil you."

The girl, flushing with embarrassment at her

grandfather's words, turned to go, but Jeremy, eyes flashing, called out, "We ain't pigs, mister!"

Startled, the silver-haired man stopped in his tracks. "How dare you address me, you young tramp!" he bellowed.

The girl put her hand on his sleeve. "Come, Grandfather," she said, her face flushing still more as all eyes turned upon her.

"Leave go of me, Louise. Sir, I demand to know what you are about, harboring ruffians," shouted the old man toward McElhenny.

"I see no ruffians here," returned McElhenny calmly, "unless I take you into account, Mr. Sterling."

The old man gasped and drew himself up to his full height. "You will regret that, McElhenny," he said with icy dignity, and swept away.

Louise looked desperately from her retreating grandfather to the children who regarded her solemnly. "I'm sor-ry," she stuttered. "My grandfather shouldn't have said what he did—"

"Louise!" came the call.

"I'm sorry," the girl repeated, looking at Jeremy. He nodded, and she smiled gratefully and ran to catch up with her grandfather.

❄ ❄ ❄

"It's better than the poorhouse," Jeremy was saying some time later. "They keep you shut up there until you think you're losing your mind. Preaching and preaching at you, day and night."

The pavilion was empty now, except for Mr. McElhenny and his wife, who chopped and mixed in the kitchen. The children, warmed through and well fed for the first time in many weeks, were actually playing. They had begun by slipping and sliding down the little hills nearby, but then Bat, perched on the top of a rock, had caught sight of the miraculous rainbow carousel below. Lodged now inside a gazebo of ice, the deer pranced and capered. Bat stared. He rubbed his eyes. And then, with a whoop, he scrambled down from his precipice. "You ain't gonna believe it!" he hollered to Joan and Chick, who were rolling down a nearby hill. "Come on! You ain't gonna believe it!" In seconds the carousel was swarming with children. Each deer carried two or three wiggling riders, and when they began to turn in the glistening gyre, the frosty air was filled with shrieks of rapture. Oddly, the bundled grown-ups who scuttled along the nearby paths took no notice of the carousel and its delighted freight.

Back in the quiet pavilion, Tundra snoozed next to Holly's chair, and Holly, her head propped upon her hand, listened to Jeremy's tale with sympathy.

"So you came here."

"Yeah. Came in the summer, when I was near on eight. No nicer place I ever been than the park on a summer night. All the folks with houses lie sweltering and tossing, but out here in the cool air—why, we're the comfortablest people in New York City!"

"But Jeremy, you can't live here always," said Holly.

"Dunno why not," replied Jeremy.

"Don't you want a home someday?" asked Holly.

For a moment the boy kept his look of stubborn denial. Holly bent her head to see into his eyes, and something seemed to melt in his face. "Well, yeah, I'd like to have a home," he admitted. "Who wouldn't, I guess. But it ain't going to happen, so's there's no sense thinking on it."

"Why ain't it—isn't it—going to happen?" asked Holly.

Jeremy resumed his stubborn look. "It just ain't. I've got no schooling, no money, no nothing. If I'm lucky, I'll get to be a hodman or rail layer or something like that, and maybe I'll have a little room to myself somewhere, but that's all. That's all."

Holly kept her eyes on his. "What would you be if you could choose anything?"

Jeremy ran his fingers over the table between them. "I guess," he said after a moment, "I guess I'd be a doctor, wouldn't I? So's I could cure kids like Lissy." He spread his palms flat. "But it ain't going to happen," he said harshly. "So I can just forget about it."

Holly said nothing. I won't forget about it, she promised silently.

Jeremy looked at her with curiosity. "I never met anyone like you. You look like a fine young lady, but you don't act like one."

"Well, thank you very much. What do I act like?"

"Like no one I ever met. You act like you care about me and the other kids."

"I do," said Holly simply.

They smiled at each other. "We got to find you a job," Jeremy said suddenly. "*You* can't sleep in the park."

"No," said Holly with a trace of regret. "I don't suppose I can."

"What's your name, anyway. Your whole name."

"Holly Claus."

"What—like Santa Claus?" said Jeremy incredulously.

"Just exactly like Santa Claus. He's my father."

Jeremy laughed. "That's a good one. You said it so serious, too."

"I'm perfectly serious," said Holly.

"Yeah, right," said Jeremy comfortably. "I'm not so much of a kid that I believe in Santa Claus."

Now it was Holly's turn to stare. "You don't believe in Santa Claus? I've heard of such people, but I never thought I'd meet one."

Jeremy sat up, unsettled by her obvious surprise. "Come on now, no joking. Is your name really Claus?"

"Why would I joke? My name is Holly Claus. I am Santa Claus's daughter. I come from a world of immortals, and my father is their king."

"So now you're a princess?" said Jeremy warily.

"Silly. I've been a princess this whole time. It's not very important."

Jeremy folded his arms. "Prove it."

"I can't prove it. What does it matter who I actually am? I'm here now, and I'm your friend."

"She is Holly Claus, daughter to Nicholas, the king of Forever," said a low voice. "Also known as Santa Claus."

"Hush, Tundra," said Holly.

"Your dog talked," Jeremy stammered.

"He's not supposed to," said Holly with disapproval.

"Dogs don't talk," said Jeremy nervously.

"First of all, I'd like to make it clear that I'm not a

dog. I'm a wolf. Secondly, permit me to say that your disbelief in my king is most unmannerly, not to mention treasonous. Thirdly, perhaps your disbelief will be resolved by the simple realization that if I am not the average earthly wolf, then I must have come from somewhere else, namely, Forever, the Land of the Immortals, as Princess Holly has been kind enough to inform you," Tundra said with dignity. "I must insist that you keep all of this information to yourself," he added.

"He talks," said Jeremy.

"He's from the Land of the Immortals. All the animals talk there," said Holly patiently.

"And you're a princess. Santa Claus's daughter," Jeremy repeated.

"That's right."

Jeremy looked at Holly for a long time. It was a point of pride for Jeremy to never be surprised, but somehow this lady, or girl, or whatever she was, surprised him. She wasn't like anyone he had ever met before, and he had gotten used to the idea that he had met pretty much every kind of person that the world held. But he could tell she was different. Maybe it was her smile, which was sincere. Maybe it was that she listened to him even though he was only a kid. Maybe she really was what she said. Maybe, this one time, he could accept something on faith. Maybe— He grinned. "I believe you! I don't know why, but I do!"

"We're honored," said Tundra with a slight note of exasperation.

"Hush, Tundra," said Holly. "I'm glad you believe us, Jeremy. Of course you understand the importance of not telling anyone about—about Tundra talking. That's not what we're here for."

Jeremy nodded. "Won't tell no one. You can trust me." He looked wonderingly at the wolf. "Never thought I'd see anything like this. A talking dog."

"I'm not a dog." Tundra sighed.

A light was dawning over Jeremy's face. "Oh boy!" he said, looking at Holly. "Do I have a job for you!"

They made an odd little troupe, walking briskly— nearly running—as they hurried from Central Park down Fifth Avenue. If a passerby had stopped to take a second look, he would have been quite confounded: what on Earth would a delicate young lady be doing in the company of a ragged street urchin and an enormous dog? Luckily no one took a second look. So Holly, Jeremy, and Tundra ran through the throng- ing streets. At first Holly was too easily distracted by the grand houses that lined Fifth Avenue; the sight of the Vanderbilt chateau at Fifty-second Street stopped her abruptly. Jeremy was forced to retrace his steps to pull her from her trance. "Come on," he said impatiently. "We got to hurry."

She stared at the massive brick and marble mansion. "I thought you didn't have kings here."

"Ain't no king that lives there. Just a rich man. Come on, Holly. We can't be stopping now."

They turned left and then left again. Now the streets were smaller, narrower, dirtier. The houses here had no tracery, turrets, nor stained-glass windows. They were simple brownstones, old and a bit crumbly, with steep staircases. Then little shops began to replace the houses: a bakery with a tempting array of fragrant bread, a narrow shoemaker's shop, a dry goods store colored with bolt after bolt of fabric, a tiny bookshop with a sleeping owner. Jeremy came to a halt before a small storefront. Holly, hurrying behind, nearly ran into him.

"This is it," said Jeremy.

The windows were curtained, and she looked up at the sign above the door. It was oval, and in fluid, graceful script were carved the words CARROLL'S CURIOSITIES AND WONDERS.

Holly closed her eyes tightly and opened them

again. The shop was still there. She felt as though she had been traveling in an enormously long tunnel for days and days, and it had very suddenly ended, depositing her beneath this sign. Carroll's Curiosities and Wonders. Curiosities and Wonders. The words were familiar. They were more than familiar.

"What's the matter, Holly?" said Tundra in a low voice.

"I feel odd," she confessed. "I feel like I just dropped into a familiar but strange world from someplace far away."

"You have," Tundra reminded her.

"Yes. Yes, I know. But I feel like I've seen this sign before. Somewhere . . ." Her voice trailed off. Tundra was looking dissatisfied. "I'm sure it's nothing. Perhaps I saw it through the telescope. I'm sure that's all," she said quickly.

"Okay." Jeremy lowered his voice. "It'll be just like I said back there." He jerked his head in the direction of the park. "You're a young lady traveling to meet her granny in—in—well, it don't matter—just traveling to meet her granny, and you're stopped here for a few weeks"—Holly opened her mouth to protest, but Jeremy continued—"I know, I know, your pa is going to come for you on Christmas Day, but we don't have to tell Mr. Kleiner that. And seeing as you're short on money and how you've had a *position*"—Jeremy pronounced this word with great emphasis—"in a toy factory, and as how you run into me and I suggested it, we were thinking maybe you could find work here during the Christmas rush," he said, running out of breath. "Got it?"

Holly nodded seriously. "I think so. Where am I from?"

"Maine," said Jeremy.

"Main what?"

"Maine. It's a state. It snows all the time, and there's wild woods and lots of animals." A brief wistfulness crossed the boy's face.

"It sounds lovely," Holly said, noting his expression.

"Yeah," said Jeremy. "You ready?"

Holly nodded, and Jeremy pulled the door open. The familiar smell of wood, varnish, and paint wafted toward them, and Holly stepped into Carroll's Curiosities and Wonders.

Chapter Seventeen

THEIR FOOTSTEPS SEEMED to echo in the quiet shop. Holly, her eyes growing accustomed to the dimness, looked about and saw shelves stacked from floor to ceiling with toys of every imaginable description. There were painted blocks and stiff horses on wheels, spinning tops and elaborate castles well guarded by legions of tin soldiers. A gleaming metal carriage, child-sized, stood in a corner where it was overseen by a towering pair of stilts and a kite covered in silver stars. A splendid hot-air balloon embellished with scarlet swirls floated from the ceiling.

A row of nutcrackers, grinning diabolically, perched upon a glass case that contained a miniature country town. Holly drew in her breath with wonder and knelt to peer at the little stores and houses that lined the town's main street. Each tiny house was perfect in every detail, from its glowing windows edged with crisp white curtains to the umbrella, no larger than Holly's little finger, that waited conveniently on the front porch for its owner to take a bit of fresh air. A thick forest of trees—the largest no higher than a foot—sprouted behind the churchyard, and Holly could just see the flash of a silver stream running through the woods. A deer leaned down to drink from the cool water. Nearby in the snow-covered fields, two white rabbits paused to look over their shoulders. In the midst of the woods was a small clearing where a Christmas tree stood, garlanded in shimmering gold and silver, topped by an angel the size of a teardrop. Beneath its lowest branches was piled a stack of wee packages, wrapped in bright paper. Holly looked again at the splendid scene. She peeked into the tiny houses and squinted into the thick woods. All were empty. "Odd," she whispered. The little country had no citizens. There was not a single doll inhabitant in the whole land.

Holly rose. Her green eyes, accustomed to toys of every variety, skimmed over bears, brown and black and polar, over exotic Chinese lanterns and great flowery paper garlands, over a monumental mechanical railway well stocked with shiny trains in various degrees of authenticity. She glanced from a dazzling display of toy watches to the heavy cardboard pictures announcing that *A* was for *Acrobat* and *B* was for *Balloon*. Ships with masts at full sail. A piano complete with a secret mechanism that played lullabies. Puppets, both chilling and charming, and dozens of paper games, tricks, inventions, and diversions.

Where were the dolls? Holly looked again. And again. There was not a single doll in the whole store. Though it was bulging with toys—marvelous toys, Holly had to admit—in every possible cranny and corner, Carroll's Curiosities and Wonders contained not one doll. Not a tiny dollhouse doll, nor a homely rag doll, nor a dimpled baby doll, nor even an elegant porcelain doll too fancy to be touched. Curious indeed, Holly thought to herself.

The toy shop also appeared to be empty of humans. She and Jeremy and Tundra seemed to be the only living creatures there. Even the sounds of the street seemed distant and muffled within the well-stocked walls of Carroll's Curiosities and Wonders. The somber ticktock of an unseen clock was the only sound.

"Are you sure that your friend needs extra hands here?" asked Holly. "It doesn't seem very busy."

Jeremy looked around as if noticing the lack of clientele for the first time. "Oh, sure. It ain't so busy now, but you'll see—it gets bustling sometimes. Not that Mr. Kleiner wouldn't like more bustle. He's always groaning about not enough customers."

"Perhaps he would have more customers if he stocked dolls."

"Dolls?"

"Haven't you noticed? There are no dolls here," said Holly, amused at the uncomprehending look on his face.

Jeremy glanced around at the shelves. "Huh. You're right. Never saw it before."

"Don't you think it's odd?"

"Yeah, I guess. Girls like 'em," he said dismissively.

"Don't you?" asked Holly.

"Me?" he said with amazement. " 'Course not. Dolls are for girls."

"They're not just for girls," Holly said indignantly. "They're for everybody. A doll is a soul friend."

"Crikey!" Jeremy exclaimed. "Boys in your Forever place play with *dolls*?"

Holly was just opening her mouth to explain when their conversation was interrupted by the appearance of a small, thin man in a dark suit. Holly's first impression was that he was composed entirely of lines: his face was deeply and symmetrically lined, beginning with two vertical lines of worry between his eyebrows and proceeding down his face to a series of parentheses marking either side of his mouth. Despite these signs of anxiousness, he looked very kind, especially now, as he greeted Jeremy with a smile. "Good afternoon, my boy. How do you do today, with the cold?" Holly noted that he asked this question not casually, but searchingly, as if he truly cared how Jeremy did on this day. Her heart warmed to him at once.

"Aw, you know the cold doesn't get to me, Mr. Kleiner. And how're you coming along today? Don't seem too busy."

"Not at the moment," said Mr. Kleiner, frowning. "I should be thankful for the break, I suppose. This morning we had plenty of customers, and I was hard-pressed to attend them."

"Mrs. Bath still out, then?" asked Jeremy with

what Holly recognized as completely false sympathy.

"Yes. I do feel for her, and her toe, of course." Mr. Kleiner looked genuinely stricken by the thought of whatever ailed Mrs. Bath's toe. "But it is most inconvenient that she should go lame right in the midst of the Christmas season, most inconvenient indeed." He coughed guiltily.

"I don't reckon Mr. Carroll will be coming downstairs to help out," said Jeremy in a dry voice.

"I expect not," said Mr. Kleiner with equal dryness. Holly observed that they both looked somewhat amused by this idea and wondered why. But now Jeremy was moving smoothly ahead—

"That being the case, Mr. Kleiner, you maybe find yourself somewhat shorthanded."

"Yes, Jeremy, I rather think I am."

"Then," said Jeremy, grandly waving a hand toward Holly with the air of a magician, "I'd like to introduce you to my friend, Miss Holly Claus. She's worked in a toy manufactory before, so she knows the business. But she don't want to stay, sir," he added hastily. "No, she's just passing through on her way to meet up with her grandma, and finding herself a bit short on money, she's seeking a temporary position. And when we was introduced by our mutual acquaintance, I thought of you, Mr. Kleiner, and how maybe you might be needing some help just now." Jeremy concluded with a small bow and a hopeful smile.

Mr. Kleiner stretched out his hand to Holly and gave her an inquiring look. Those anxious eyes were wise, and she saw that though he did not entirely believe Jeremy's story, he was willing to pretend that he did. She looked back at him as she took his hand and said, "I'm pleased to meet you, Mr. Kleiner. Any friend of Jeremy's is a friend to the world, I'm sure."

Mr. Kleiner felt a slight stir of curiosity, though he tried to hide it decently. This was not simply a remarkably pretty shopgirl, but rather a young lady of education and refinement. He wondered what circumstances could have led her to seek employment. "So," he began, twitching his eyeglasses, "you've worked in a toy manufactory? Where was that?"

"In Maine," said Jeremy at once.

"Oh yes?" said Mr. Kleiner politely. "I did not know that that state harbored a toy factory."

"It was more like a workshop," said Holly, with her lips twitching. "I made dolls."

"Ah. Dolls," said Mr. Kleiner, and Holly noted that the two vertical lines of worry upon his brow grew deeper. "Dolls," he said sadly.

"I was just searching for dolls upon your shelves, when you came in," Holly said. "Perhaps I missed them."

"You did not miss them," Mr. Kleiner said. "We do not stock dolls."

"But why?" asked Holly in astonishment. "Surely they are very popular toys."

"Very popular. Very popular indeed," Mr. Kleiner added. "However, Mr. Carroll, the proprietor, does not care for dolls."

"Does not care for dolls?" repeated Holly.

"Is not fond of dolls," Mr. Kleiner said, as though that would clarify the matter.

"And so—" said Holly.

"And so we do not carry dolls," he said with ever-increasing gloom.

Holly could see that the failure to stock dolls was a painful point and sought to change the subject. "You have everything else a child could desire," she said warmly. "And this little town inside the case is a marvel."

"Mr. Carroll made it himself," Mr. Kleiner said, cheering up. "In every particular."

Holly looked at the scene, impressed. "He must be quite skilled, then," she said. "Those Christmas tree ornaments require a steady hand. I guessed they were of German manufacture."

Mr. Kleiner grinned. "You do know your toys, don't you, Miss Claus? German carving is as fine, but Mr. Carroll is of the opinion that their colors are not as delicate as they should be."

"I agree with his opinion. The Russians solve the problem nicely with their enameled ornaments, but I don't believe that they work on so small a scale."

"Quite so, quite so," said Mr. Kleiner. Jeremy looked from one speaker to the other with a smile of satisfaction.

"I would venture to say, sir, that if you moved the nutcrackers to the side, like this"—Holly pushed the diabolical nutcrackers away from the glass case's edge—"perhaps children would be more eager to visit your little town. Do you agree?"

Mr. Kleiner regarded the display and nodded. "Very true. Yes, I quite agree. Might I ask your opinion of this counter? Mr. Carroll believes that music boxes should be displayed together, but I believe that the children can scarcely see them here."

Holly tilted her head to one side. "Why not make a kind of treasure chest of the most beautiful, and put it here? You might leave the rest inside the case. You

see, just a few, like this." Holly quickly moved the stiff
row of boxes into an appealing array. "That way the
children will be drawn to them."

Mr. Kleiner looked positively elated. "Very good
indeed, Miss Claus. Very good indeed. I think that you
are precisely the individual we have been looking for.
How long can you stay?"

"Er—" Holly began, but Jeremy broke in.

"Coupla weeks," he said loudly.

"That will do," said Mr. Kleiner. "These last three
days before Christmas will be our busiest." He looked
around the empty store and sighed. "I hope. Well, Miss
Claus, I consider you ideal for the position, but I must
consult, of course, with Mr. Carroll." He licked his lips
nervously. "I'll just run upstairs right now." Absently,
he picked up a toy bunny and gave its ears a gentle
tug. "Yes, well. I'll just run upstairs right now," he
repeated. Squaring his shoulders, he marched to a
dark staircase that ascended from the back of the store
to a wooden gallery above. This gallery, which provided a view of the whole store, apparently led to an
upstairs apartment, but it was so dimly lit and thickly
swathed in velvet curtains that Holly could not tell
where in its shadows an apartment might be hidden.
Mr. Kleiner's soft footfalls soon stopped.

"I don't like it," said a low voice.

It was Tundra. "You don't like the store?" she asked.

"The store's all right, though it would benefit from a lamp. I don't like *that*." Tundra pointed his nose at the shadowy gallery. "What's up there, and why is this Mr. Kleiner uneasy about it?"

Holly looked questioningly at Jeremy. "Well," he began, "it's Mr. Carroll. He ain't exactly a friendly sort of fellow. It's funny. If I was the owner of a toy store, you could bet I'd be the happiest guy in the world, but not him. He never smiles, and he'll give you the shivers when he looks at you. He don't like anybody very much, but I guess he likes Mr. Kleiner better than anyone, 'cause he'll talk to him and he don't talk to no one else, hardly. Ain't much of a favor, I don't think, 'cause I've only ever heard him giving orders pretty sharp. Mr. Kleiner, please see to this; Mr. Kleiner this requires your immediate attendance, and such as that. Mr. Kleiner is the only one he lets upstairs, too, 'cept the maid, and he won't let her come into some of the rooms, even. But I got to say, he never done me no harm. When Mr. Kleiner asks him if I can deliver packages to folks, trying to get me a little work, Mr. Carroll says okay and pays me fine.

He just ain't very friendly."

Tundra's expression grew grimmer. "Holly," he said after a moment. "Let's leave this place. Something's not right here."

For a moment Holly teetered on the verge of obeying. Tundra was the voice of wisdom, certainty, authority; he had been all her life. And, she admitted to herself, she had the same feeling he did. There was something strange, even unsettling, about the shadows and doll-less shelves of Carroll's Curiosities and Wonders. Something unhappy. Another voice argued, haven't I come to the mortal world to help the unhappy? Hasn't that been the work of every human who became an immortal—who deserved immortality? Her mouth straightened into a stubborn line, and she stuck her small chin out. I will stay. I will stay right here, and if Mr. Carroll needs my help I will offer it with all my heart. I'll make this the best toy shop I can.

Tundra sighed. He recognized that look. He padded softly to a corner and sat down.

Holly glanced around. "Don't you think this room would look more cheerful if it had more light?"

Jeremy replied, "Yeah, but the electric lights are expensive."

"They are, are they?" said Holly. "Well, sunlight is cheap. Let's pull those curtains all the way back." She marched to the front windows, which were veiled in thick cloth. "Is there a ladder, Jeremy? If we take these down, the daylight will stream in. And why aren't there any toys in this window? How is anyone to know that this is a toy shop?" She looked around energetically. "Let's move those sweet bears into the window. We can give them a Christmas party." Throwing off her cloak, she reached for a particularly tempting brown bear.

Tundra, in his corner, watched the staircase steadily.

Meanwhile, Mr. Kleiner was knocking discreetly upon a heavy wooden door. "Mr. Carroll?" he called softly. "Mr. Carroll?"

Abruptly the door was pulled open from within. Mr. Kleiner stared as Mr. Carroll threw himself down in a chair before his worktable without a glance at his visitor and resumed his intent concentration on a small model of the planets. Though a close observer would discern that he was still a young man, Mr. Carroll's face was weary. His hooded eyes were joyless, and his mouth, set in a sharply defined jaw, was closed in a severe line. As his long fingers connected one delicate wire to another, a fleeting satisfaction crossed his face, but when he finally looked up, his expression was impatient. "Yes, Mr. Kleiner?"

"Hmm." Mr. Kleiner cleared his throat. "Excuse me, sir, there is a young lady downstairs seeking temporary employment. She strikes me as an exceedingly capable and trustworthy young lady, and since I am in need of assistance in the absence of Mrs. Bath, I should like to give her a place for a few weeks." Mr. Kleiner ran his finger between his stiff collar and his neck. "Provided you approve, of course."

"References?"

"Ahem. The young lady is from Maine and has not had employment in New York City before."

The hooded eyes gave Mr. Kleiner a steely glance. "You wish to employ a young lady who simply wandered in from the street?"

Mr. Kleiner drew himself up straighter. "Certainly not, Mr. Carroll. Young Jeremy brought her in and vouches for her."

"Ah. Recommendation indeed," said Mr. Carroll, his face empty of expression. There was a short silence as the thin, deft fingers connected another wire. Mr. Kleiner stood before the table, waiting. "I see you have made up your mind," said Mr. Carroll, without looking up. "Then do as you think fit. See to it that she minds her own business and not mine. I will be watching for any infraction of my rules. I trust you understand me, Mr. Kleiner?"

"Yes," said Mr. Kleiner shortly, and turned to go.

As he opened the door, Carroll spoke again. "What's her name?"

"Miss Claus," replied Mr. Kleiner. "Good afternoon, sir."

"Likewise," said Mr. Carroll.

Mr. Kleiner hurried down the stairs, but was halted midway by the sight that greeted him below. The toy shop was filled with unaccustomed light. A family of bears had encircled a small Christmas tree (which Holly had filched from another little scene in the back of the shop) laden with ornaments. They were clearly singing carols as they stood hand in hand— paw in paw—in some soft, cottony snow. And Holly had not stopped with the windows. She and Jeremy were stringing up a long, twisted garland of paper leaves and berries from one side of the store to another. Holly, atop the ladder, was just saying, "Don't you think one of those little gold medallions would look festive right here?" when Mr. Kleiner emitted a fearful squeak that betrayed his presence.

Holly turned to him and smiled. "Doesn't it look lovely?"

"My dear Miss Claus," began Mr. Kleiner. "My dear Miss Claus, loveliness is beside the point. Mr. Carroll is most exacting as to the arrangement of the store, and I'm afraid that your improvements will have to—"

The street door opened. A young woman heavily wrapped in a blue coat entered. "Good day," she said, lifting her veil and addressing Mr. Kleiner, who happened to be close to her. "I was walking by when I saw your delightful bears in the window. I had no idea this was a toy shop!" she said, laughing. "My boy absolutely must have that cunning brown bear with the little hat. Yes, that's the one. What a face! I had no idea you carried toy bears." Smiling radiantly at Mr. Kleiner as though he was giving her a gift instead of taking her money, she put the wrapped bear under her arm and swept from the store, the picture of satisfaction.

The small bell over the door jingled as it closed behind her. There was a strained silence, and then Mr. Kleiner began to laugh and laugh. After a moment

Holly began to giggle too, and then Jeremy. "Well, my dear," wheezed Mr. Kleiner, wiping his eyes, "I think you'd better continue with your decorating. Jeremy, please help Miss Claus. You may both consider your-selves employed."

"Thank you, Mr. Kleiner," said Holly. She reached out her hand, "Truly, thank you," she repeated, look-ing gratefully at the older man.

The lined face flushed a little as he took her soft hand in his. "I have a strange feeling, Miss Claus. I have a feeling that I shall be thanking you before many days have passed."

"Come on, Holly. Let's get them garlands up over the shelves," said Jeremy enthusiastically.

"Right, we'll fasten them up with these golden medallions. And Mr. Kleiner?" said Holly in a lightly wheedling tone, "don't you think it would be nice to have a Christmas tree? A real Christmas tree?"

Mr. Kleiner threw up his hands. "Of course, Miss Claus. It would be lovely. I will get one tomorrow."

Perhaps there is a secret world of toys. Perhaps they really do, as all children suspect, come to life after the doors close and dance and whirl the night hours away until the first grumbling human yawns and footsteps can be heard in the dawn. With the morning, they resume their frozen poses and trick us for another day, every so often catching one another's eye when we do something foolish. It almost seemed as if it were true, that afternoon at the toy store, as if the toys themselves knew that they were in the presence of Santa's daughter. For, under Mr. Kleiner's marveling eye, the store grew brighter, cheerier, livelier with each passing minute of Holly's stay. The gleaming engines seemed shinier, the stuffed animals more cuddly, and the wooden toys somehow brighter. Holly greeted each toy she touched like a long-lost friend; she straightened them and arranged them lovingly. She put old bear colleagues together; she created marvelous little chests bubbling over with treasures; she set tin soldiers into full battle array against a carved dragon who threatened their castle; she made a theater for the puppets out of a checkered silk parachute; she placed spinning angel candelabras in artful spots; she garnished and draped and devised until the room glowed, redolent with the spice and glory of Christmas.

"Now!" she was saying from the top of the stepping stool, her hands full of evergreen boughs (Mr. Kleiner had relented to the point of making a quick

trip to the flower shop). "Do you think that's enough?"

"Naw," said Jeremy, looking up at her with a smile. He couldn't remember a better day in his entire life: food and warmth and this lady who seemed to understand everything important. "Naw, you gotta have another one. Don't want to look skimpy."

Holly stepped up on the counter. "Never skimpy! Christmas comes but once a year!" She turned to look down at the boy. He seemed suddenly very far away. "But once a—" she said again, uncertainly. The bright lights above her were very bright. She blinked. "I'm afraid—" she began, and clutched at the shelf next to her.

Tundra made a flying leap from his corner. As Holly dropped limply from the counter, he landed in position directly below, breaking her fall. Jeremy, jerking out of momentary paralysis, reached forward to catch her, and Holly came to rest, unconscious but unharmed, on the wolf's fur back.

It took every ounce of Tundra's self-discipline to keep from shouting orders. He waited until Mr. Kleiner, shaking with distress, went to fetch some water, before he muttered urgently to Jeremy, "Open the door. She needs cold air."

Jeremy obeyed quickly, and, as the first gusts of freezing air eddied into the shop, the color returned to Holly's cheeks and she began to breathe normally. Mr. Kleiner came rushing back with a cup of water just as her eyes fluttered open. She and Tundra exchanged a long look; hers mutely grateful, his tender.

"That's a good dog you've got there, Miss Claus," Mr. Kleiner was saying excitedly. "I've never seen anything like it! As soon as you began to fall, he was beneath the shelf to save you. My word! What is he, a wolfhound? One of those Canadian dogs, I'll be bound. Good dog! Smart dog!" he bellowed to Tundra, and patted him heavily on the head. Tundra quelled an urge to bite him. "Now, Miss Claus," said the man, turning his attention to Holly. "You haven't had a morsel to eat for quite some time, am I correct?"

"Yes, sir," said Holly quietly. Anything was better than trying to explain the real cause of her faintness.

"Just as I thought! Young lady, you need some nourishing victuals." Mr. Kleiner gave her a keen glance. "Perhaps you are a little short of the needful, Miss Claus, but do not fear. I shall be happy to extend you credit against wages to be earned. And indeed!"

He gave a short laugh. "You've already earned enough this afternoon for a fine meal. You rest here, in this chair, and I'll run up the street. Meat pasty? Carrot soup? Most healthful, carrot soup. Lady cake? Tea, most certainly. I'll be back in no time. Stay seated."

"Thank you, sir," said Holly faintly.

The door banged behind him. Jeremy began talking at once. "But Holly, why didn't you tell him? You ate at McElhenny's. You ain't really hungry, are you?"

"No, I'm not hungry," said Holly. "I just wanted him to leave for a moment. Oh, Tundra, what am I to do?" she wailed.

"Whatsamatter?" goggled Jeremy. "What's going on?"

Holly buried her face in Tundra's fur. "I can't bear to fail like this," she said.

"I know, but you must remember, you're on mortal land. It won't help anyone if you die here," said Tundra softly.

"What!" yelled Jeremy. "Are you dying, Holly?"

His combined outrage and alarm made her smile a little. "No, no, of course not, dear. It's just that I have an illness. When I get warm, my heart doesn't work very well. In Forever I lived apart from everyone, in the cold, but I thought that here, because of the cold

weather, I could—" Her voice broke.

"Shhh," said the wolf soothingly. "You're all right now, aren't you?"

"But if I can't stay indoors, I can't stay here and then—then—" Two tears spilled from her swimming eyes and landed on Tundra's white coat.

"Hush, now. We'll find a way," he said.

"But how, Tundra? How can I possibly find a way to help the children in the park if—if—if—" She stopped. Her eyes were locked on the tears she had just shed. What was happening? They were quivering, ever so slightly, growing opaque and brittle. "Look," she said, awed. Her tears had turned to snowflakes.

A tiny crystal spiraled from the ceiling. It was followed by another and another and then another. Gently now, snowflakes wafted through the air as gracefully as flower petals in the breeze.

Jeremy's mouth hung open. "I never seen anything like it." He reached out and a tiny flake dropped into his palm. There it glittered brightly for a moment and then melted, not into water, but into a light breath of frosty air. "What is it?" he croaked.

Holly began to laugh, her coppery hair covered with spangles of snow. "It's magic, Jeremy. It's magical snow that keeps my heart at the right temperature

and never melts. I didn't believe it could happen here, but it can! Tundra!" She hugged the wolf so hard he coughed. "Tundra, you know what this means?"

"What does it mean?" asked Tundra.

"It means that the elders *want* me to be here." Unconsciously her fingers crept to the locket that hung around her neck. "Thank you," she whispered to the snow.

"This is some day," remarked Jeremy.

Holly jumped to her feet. "Now!" she said happily. "Back to business!"

"Perhaps it would be wiser," Tundra suggested, "to wait for Mr. Kleiner to return with his soup before you revive completely. It will avoid the necessity of explaining your condition."

"Oh!" Holly plopped back down on the floor. "You're right!"

"How're you planning to explain this?" said Jeremy, waving his hands at the snowflakes that were now lying lightly on the shelves and tables.

Holly and Tundra looked at each other in consternation, but before they could concoct a reasonable explanation for indoor snow, the shop door tinkled, and Mr. Kleiner stood at the front of the shop, staring at the snow that eddied lightly around him. The paper

packet in his hand slipped unnoticed to the floor. Silently he watched the snowy scene. He stuck out his gloved hand and caught a single snowflake. He inspected it, the two furrows on his brow deepening as it disappeared with a little puff, and gave Holly a long and searching look. Then his gaze shifted to Tundra, who tried to appear as innocent as possible. He turned back to Holly and said, "I trust there is an explanation for this."

"It's magic," replied Holly simply.

Mr. Kleiner nodded. He reached down to pick up the packet he had dropped, and when he stood again, his face was impassive. "That's what I thought." He handed the package to Holly. "Meat pasty?" She nodded hopefully, her eyes fixed on his face. "Carrot soup? It's most healthful, I assure you. I don't want to know how you did it, Miss Claus. Can you undo it?"

"I don't think so, sir," said Holly, dropping her eyes.

"Then I am afraid, Miss Claus, that you and—"

There was a particularly loud jingle from the bell. Two children, about eight years old, burst into the shop hand in hand. Their eyes were fixed on the twirling snow and their mouths were hanging open in awe. A vigorous lady carrying a variety of packages

bustled in after them, saying loudly, "Edward and Michael, how many times have I told you not to enter shops without me!" She grasped the two boys by the shoulders and gave them a healthy yank.

"But Ma!" cried the boys in unison. "Look!" They pointed at the snow-dusted toys and the crystals that danced in the air.

The vigorous lady glanced up and delivered another yank before the meaning of what she had seen settled upon her, and she looked again. "Well, I never!" she said softly. "How on Earth?" She stared. "How on Earth did you do it?" She turned to Mr. Kleiner, who turned to Holly.

"Magic, ma'am," said Holly. "Christmas magic."

The woman broke into a broad smile. "You don't say, miss. Edward and Michael, this is magic snow! It must have come from Santa Claus!" The two boys nodded. This was far more reasonable than most of the explanations grown-ups gave. "Look," said their mother cheerfully. "Look at those soldiers, boys! Aren't those exactly what you've been begging for?"

The shop door jingled again. A very thin boy in an elegant black coat stood inside, his eyes shining behind his spectacles. "Look, Mr. Carston. It *is* snow!"

"Impossible!" said a tall but gentle-faced man

entering behind him. "Good Lord!" he exclaimed in the next moment. "You're quite right, Martin! How do you suppose—?"

He was pushed aside by a gaggle of little girls— one, two, three, four, five—identically dressed in thick, warm coats and each as bossy as the last. Their teacher trundled up behind them, panting, "Girls, girls! Young ladies! Gracious! Your fathers shall hear of this behavior! Dashing down the street like a gaggle of geese! Gracious alive! Oh!" Then she took in the scene before her and was silenced. Not so the little girls, who shouted at the sight of the snow and then dispersed themselves around the store to inspect each and every snow-dusted toy.

An astonished gentleman in a brown coat. A bedazzled young lady in a bedraggled hat. Three children pulling their indulgent grandfather. A bundled baby on the shoulder of her nanny, gurgling with excitement. Four dirty boys in ragged clothes, who greeted Jeremy with shouts of admiration, asking him how he did it. Three fat, yellow-haired children who expressed their delight by falling on the floor. One very cold little girl, who looked up at the dancing crystals with starry eyes and then crept away with a good portion of the meat pasty, which Holly had

pressed into her hands.

Mr. Kleiner flew about, his grave doubts forgotten, pulling down bears and tops, trains and skates, for the children. Holly, too, was busy, bringing toys to children, and, in a few cases, children to toys. She seemed to have a special intuition for the precise toy that would fit each child. The thin, elegant boy left clutching a case of scientific instruments, and the gaggle of girls promised their miserable teacher that they would be well behaved for the rest of the afternoon only if they each received a tin dog that jumped up and down as it banged upon a drum. Holly doubted that they would ever be well behaved, but she found five tin dogs and smiled as she watched the girls leave. She wished that Nicholas was by her side; he loved little children who had the gumption to be naughty sometimes. The astonished gentleman bought a fire engine for his nephew. The bundled baby was rewarded with a new rabbit, which she drooled upon. The four ragged boys came away with a handful of candies apiece, courtesy of Mr. Kleiner, who had once been a ragged boy himself. The indulgent grandfather turned out to be a train enthusiast and bought an entire railway for his grandchildren. The fat yellow-haired trio disappeared for a few minutes and then returned with

their monumentally fat yellow-haired mother, who purchased three sleds, three pairs of skates, and three drums.

As these customers left, they were replaced by others, and the awestruck crowd continued to swell. The bell jingled so many times that Mr. Kleiner finally left the door open, since it made very little difference to the temperature anyway. More and more and more people stopped, peered, exclaimed, entered, smiled, and then found themselves leaving with a brand-new toy under their arms. Holly and Mr. Kleiner were now so busy that they could scarcely speak, and they resorted to brief, telegraphic communication as if they had been working together for years. Even Jeremy was quickly tying packages up in brown paper and red string and noting deliveries for the next morning.

It was only Tundra who saw the tall man in the black vest descending the staircase. Only Tundra watched the hooded eyes flicker and the man's lips narrow as he took in the snow, the light, and the festive, bubbling cheer of the place. Tundra saw his long hands in their gloves tighten around the newel post as his eyes darted around the shop as though he were seeking something and finally come to rest on Holly.

*It was only Tundra who saw the tall man in the black
vest descending the staircase.*

At that moment, Holly, unaware, was lifting a tiny child up to a shelf to choose between a giraffe and an elephant; but then she turned and found herself looking into a pair of gray eyes that seemed to have the power to shatter her soul. I know him, she thought instantly. I've known him forever. She felt her hold on the baby loosen and quickly set the child down. She could still feel the dark gaze upon her, burning against her hair and cheeks.

What is happening to me? she thought, noticing that her hands were shaking. She rose, attempting to summon a normal expression to her face. As waves of shoppers moved around her, Holly looked toward her oldest and dearest friend for reassurance. But Tundra was not, at this moment, a reassuring sight. He stood stiffly on taut legs, watching the newcomer fiercely, registering each movement of the figure on the stairs. Holly stared at him. She had never seen him this way before. Suddenly she realized what it was: he looked like a hunter.

Holly hurried to Tundra's side to reprove him. "Stop it," she whispered. "Why do you look like that? What's the matter? Don't answer," she said, glancing anxiously at the nearby customers. Obediently Tundra sat back on his haunches, but he never took his eyes off the stranger.

"Miss Claus!" Mr. Kleiner was calling. "Please come here. I'd like to introduce you to Mr. Carroll." Holly made her way through the store, conscious of the blood surging to her cheeks. As Mr. Kleiner babbled away about the events of that afternoon, Carroll remained silent, not even commenting on the mysterious snow that swirled about his shop. Mr. Kleiner grew more and more desperately animated until Holly at last reached his side. He turned to her with relief, saying brightly, "And here is the young lady who seems to be responsible for these remarkable happenings. Miss Claus, permit me to present to you Mr. Carroll. Mr. Carroll, Miss Claus."

Now Carroll turned his gray eyes full upon her again. And again, involuntarily, she thought: I know him. He looks at me as if he could never forgive me. But what have I done?

With something similar in form to a smile, yet utterly devoid of its content, Mr. Carroll bowed slightly and stretched out his gloved hand. "Delighted to make your acquaintance, Miss Claus."

Chapter Eighteen

HOLLY LOOKED AFTER the departing black coat with a twinge of disappointment. He had shown no sign, no tiny hesitation that revealed an awareness of her in any way out of the ordinary. And why should he? she asked herself. What nonsense. You don't know him and he doesn't know you. You're just a girl who works in his shop, no more noticeable than Mrs. Bath or her toe. The thought of Mrs. Bath's mysterious toe put Holly back in a good humor, and she turned to face the crowded aisles.

Two gangling boys in their teens, all legs and

awkwardness, were making their way through the
shop. Between them, with a thin hand in each of their
overgrown ones, was a frail little girl. She can't be
older than six, Holly thought, looking at her sickly
face with concern. The boys had to lean forward to
allow her hands to rest easily in theirs because she
was so tiny, but it was obvious that they did so
gladly. It was obvious that they would have stood on
their heads if she had expressed any desire for them
to do so.

"Promise me you're not too cold, Phoebe," the
larger of the two boys said.

"I promise. I'm not too cold," said the girl softly.

"Mother said we should bring you back in ten
minutes," the second boy said uneasily. "It's been
longer than that."

"I don't feel tired, Georgie, really."

"But Mothcr said, Pheeb," the boy pleaded.

The little girl's eyes filled with tears. Holly saw in
the tired face a reflection of her own childhood self,
blocked and baffled again and again by illness and by
those who wanted nothing more than her happiness
and comfort. She knew well the feeling of being a
prisoner in loving arms.

She approached the trio. The boys looked at her

helplessly. She smiled at them and knelt to Phoebe's height. "Isn't it lovely?" she said, pointing to the snow.

The little girl nodded.

"Look. Catch one." Holly held out a snowflake. "It doesn't melt. It just disappears—poof!" She dropped her voice to a whisper. "It's magic."

Phoebe's eyes grew larger. "I never saw anything magic before."

"But you believed in it anyway, didn't you?"

The little girl nodded again.

"Do you want to know a secret?" Another nod. "This snow helps me to get better from an illness I have. It stays with me to keep me cool."

Phoebe looked worried. "They're always telling me that I have to keep warm."

"Different illnesses have different cures. You have to be warm and I have to be cold, but we can visit each other. The snow will be here for as long as I am, and if you come back to see me tomorrow, you'll see the snow then."

"Are you better now?"

"Much better. Almost all better."

Phoebe looked up at her brothers and put her mouth to Holly's ear. "The doctor told my mother that I'm not going to get better. Don't tell them," she said, glancing upward. "They'll cry."

"Maybe you can trick the doctor," Holly said.

Phoebe smiled a little. "I'd like to trick him. He burnt all my dolls."

"He *burnt* them?" asked Holly, shocked.

Phoebe nodded seriously.

"Now, Pheeb, you know he had to," said the taller brother. "They were contagious. He had to."

Phoebe stuck out her pointed chin. "He didn't have to burn them all. He didn't have to burn Tempatsy."

"Aw, Pheeb. Any other doctor would have done it too."

"We can get you another doll, Pheeb," said the younger brother. "There's probably a good doll right here in this shop."

Holly hated to tell him that he was wrong. "I'm afraid," she began apologetically, "that we don't carry—carry—" She looked around the shop floor. Her satchel lay forgotten in a corner. "We only carry very special dolls," she said, standing up. "We don't keep them on the shelves. You'll understand when you see them. Can you give me just five minutes? I—I—I have to prepare it."

The two boys exchanged worried glances. "Our

mother said to bring her home in ten minutes, and we've been gone a good deal longer than that."

"Just five more minutes," Holly begged. "Please."

"Wel-l-l-l," they muttered indecisively.

"Yes," said Phoebe, her chin out again. "Yes. If you want, Frank, I'll put on your coat while we wait."

Holly was already flying to the storeroom, satchel in hand. Inside the quiet walls, she fumbled about in her bag for the porcelain that she had brought from the Land of the Immortals. Then, with a morsel of the clay in her hands, she closed her eyes and began to shape the soft substance with her fingers. With her eyes still tightly shut, Holly envisioned Phoebe's face, not worn and thin, but rosy and lively and stubborn. All the while her fingers stroked and smoothed, pulling a small figure from the formless stuff, giving it the vital essence that she had seen in Phoebe's eyes.

Holly opened her eyes and looked down. Yes, there she was, Phoebe herself, and Phoebe as she wished to be: healthy and strong. The doll's face was round and full, but the telltale chin was the same. Her legs, poor and bony no longer, looked like limbs that could run and jump and skip and even stomp. Holly smiled.

But what about clothes? A bare doll was not going to please Phoebe. Holly set the doll down and peered into her satchel. There Lexy had packed a scarf, a rich scarf of crimson silk embroidered with blue and green leaves. Not exactly what Phoebe would wear, but better than nothing. Holly glanced about the dim room for scissors; the scarf would need to be cut. She investigated a nearby drawer. No scissors. With increasing urgency, Holly scrabbled around searching for scissors, but it was useless. Maybe she could simply fold the scarf around the doll. The doll. Holly looked down upon the table and gasped with surprise. The doll was dressed in a frock of pink silk with a peacock blue sash. A cloud of dark hair floated around her face above her great brown eyes. Her cheeks were lightly tinted with pink, and her arms tapered into small, sturdy hands. The strong legs that Holly had fashioned were now clothed in white stockings and shining leather shoes, and all in all the little figure looked as though she had just blown in from some great adventure.

Holly stared, and, for the second time that day, her fingers crept unconsciously to the locket that hung around her neck. "Thank you," she said softly, looking at the doll in wonder. Then she understood. It was Phoebe's dream. The doll was not just a replacement for all the dolls the child had lost; it was

an embodiment of hope. This is what I am supposed
to do, Holly thought. This is what I have come for.

Quickly she caught the doll up in her arms and
ran out to the shop floor. There they were: the two
brothers were trying to convince Phoebe to come
away. The tiny girl looked from one to the other,
shaking her head. Holly walked swiftly toward the
group and knelt before the little girl. "Look," she said,
"I found your doll."

Phoebe stared down at the small, laughing face
and her eyes grew round with astonishment. "It's me,"
she whispered. "It's me!"

Her brothers leaned over curiously. "Great Scott!
Pheeb! It's you!" exclaimed Frank.

"But fatter and bigger," said Phoebe, patting the
doll's round cheeks.

"All better again."

"Yes," Holly suggested. "Perhaps it's you as you
will be soon."

The two boys exchanged cautious glances, but
Phoebe was enraptured. She smiled with quiet satisfaction and gripped the doll in her arms. "When I get
bigger, I'm going to have a dress just like this," she
said.

"We'll take this doll," said George to Holly. And

then, less certainly, "How much is it?"

Holly smiled at him. "There's no charge for this doll. She belongs to Phoebe."

Phoebe wrenched her eyes away from the doll and gave Holly a grateful smile. "Thank you, miss. Thank you for finding my doll."

"You're welcome, Phoebe dear."

Holly watched as the boys escorted their sister out of the store. At the window, they stopped, and Phoebe lifted the doll's hand to wave good-bye.

"How'd you do that?" said a low voice at her elbow. It was Jeremy. "There ain't no dolls back there."

Holly leaned toward him confidentially. "It's a secret, Jeremy. I couldn't possibly reveal it. Also, I don't know," said Holly with a giggle.

"That little thing—she didn't look so puny once she had her dolly," observed Jeremy thoughtfully. "Maybe you could make one for Lissy later. Might chirk her up some."

"I'll make one for all the children at the park, Jeremy. I promise. Lissy first of all."

But first the swelling crowds had to be attended to. Holly and Jeremy and Mr. Kleiner worked side by side as the afternoon wore on, until the streetlamps flickered on. Almost everyone had gone home now;

there were only two customers left, an elderly man and a young girl.

Holly was straightening up a disheveled display of stereopticons when she heard a familiar voice wafting across the store. "And you call this a toy shop? With not a single doll in stock, I wonder that you don't find yourself accused of false advertisement!"

"Grandfather," begged a young voice. "I don't need another doll anyway. I'd much rather have this little library. See? It has a cunning case. See how it all fits?"

"Louise," said the elderly man. "You do not want a library, and you needn't attempt to convince me that you do. You wanted a *doll*, and I see no reasonable explanation for a toy shop that does not carry dolls." He waved irritably at a passing snowflake.

"Crikey," whispered Jeremy, "it's that old belly-acher from McElhenny's."

Mr. Sterling was no less angry among Carroll's Curiosities and Wonders than he had been at the sausage pavilion in the park. His face was pursed into a knot of fury, and his cheeks were the color of a boiled lobster. His granddaughter, who still accompanied him, was also pink, but with shame. She hung her head as he continued to rant at Mr. Kleiner.

Though she was sympathetic to Mr. Kleiner's torment, it was Louise's plight that pulled at Holly. She skimmed across the floor to the girl's side. The child was dressed in a warm coat of dark blue wool edged with fur, but she was as piteous as any child Holly had yet seen on Earth. The girl's scrupulously arranged ringlets hid her burning face, but as Holly bent at her side she caught sight of her stricken eyes.

Holly straightened. "Actually, sir, we do carry dolls in our shop, but they are so very special that we are not able to put them on the shelves. However, I can bring one out for your granddaughter if you like."

Mr. Sterling stopped in mid-diatribe and attempted to rearrange his features into something other than outrage. "Hmph," he sniffed. "Yes, bring it out at once."

"If you please," added Louise softly.

Mr. Kleiner opened his mouth to contradict and then closed it again. "It will be just a moment," he said to Mr. Sterling.

Five minutes later—just as Mr. Sterling was beginning to sneer about the "unmitigated insolence of that irresponsible lackey"—Holly returned. Mr. Sterling finally fell quiet. For he saw that she carried in her arms a replica of his grandchild. There was Louise,

undeniably Louise, with her soft, dark curls and her light brown eyes and her generous mouth. But this Louise was a dancer. She was dressed in a trailing, diaphanous gown glistening with sequins, and on her feet were white satin pointe shoes. Her legs were long and slim, and her graceful arms were arranged in an attitude of rest. Her wide mouth was closed and serious, and the fearful expression in the child's eyes was replaced with a calm look of resolution in the doll's.

"What sort of hogwash is this?" cried Sterling, pointing a shaking finger at the doll, but his harangue was interrupted by his granddaughter's awed voice.

"How did you know?" she demanded, turning to Holly, surprise overcoming fear. "How did you know that I want to be a dancer? I've wanted to be a dancer all my life!"

"I could tell, dear," said Holly. "I could tell by the way you walk."

"Balderdash!" exploded Mr. Sterling. "Utter nonsense. You do *not* want to be a dancer, Louise. No granddaughter of mine will be a dancer. I don't know what you are about, young lady," he directed at Holly, "but I don't think much of it!"

"Don't speak to her that way!" Louise's voice surprised them all. Mr. Sterling looked flabbergasted. "I don't know how she knew, but she's right: I want to be a dancer. Every week when you think I'm at Miss Finkin's, learning how to waltz, I really slip across the hall and study ballet. And I'm good," she added decidedly. "I'm very good. And I will be a dancer. And," she said, holding out a hand to her grandfather, "I am your granddaughter, and I always will be."

If his nose had fallen off his face and walked out the front door, Mr. Sterling could be no more astounded than he was now. He seemed to be preparing for an almighty explosion; he gathered his voice, opened his mouth, and abruptly shut it again. All at once, he looked very proud. "Why, Louise, I do believe you've got the Sterling spirit." He whacked her lightly on the back. "Have you really been sneaking off to take ballet lessons?" he asked admiringly.

"Yes, Grandfather," said Louise, smiling a little now.

This seemed to put Mr. Sterling in the best of spirits. "Ha!" he shouted. "Chip off the old block! Ha! Never underestimate a Sterling! Ha!"

Holly smiled and drew away. The doll shows the way, and they follow it, she thought. A doll made of dreams. The idea caught and flamed within her. Oh yes, she thought, this is it. Oh, Papa, I wish I could tell you what I have learned. The dolls are their guides. They will lead the children to their dreams.

Cautiously she glanced at Mr. Kleiner. She had expected him to look appalled, but he did not. He looked quite merry. Their eyes met. He pointed up to the enchanted snow, then down to Louise's dream doll, and then, without a word, he pulled a key from his pocket and handed it to her. It was the key to the shop door.

"How much for this fine doll?" Mr. Sterling was saying.

Holly opened her mouth, but Mr. Kleiner cut smoothly in. "Four dollars."

"Very well." Mr. Sterling brought forth the notes. As he and Louise walked from the store, she turned back to say good-bye to Holly.

"Thank you. This doll makes me not so scared to

be a dancer," she said.

Now it was well and truly night. Mr. Kleiner closed the shop door, and they set about tidying the shop for the next day. As they worked, Holly sipped at her healthful carrot soup, and the lady cake was very nice. She and Jeremy shared it as they arranged a swarm of mechanical animals into a parade.

Mr. Kleiner counted the money in the till. "Easily our most successful day ever!" he announced, putting his spectacles on his head and counting once more. "Miss Claus, you and your abilities are a mystery to me, but I thank you from the bottom of my heart! And I promise to ask you no questions. That should please you."

"Thank you for your good opinion, Mr. Kleiner," said Holly demurely. She took a breath. "May I ask you a favor?"

"Certainly, Miss Claus," he said, adding again. The total hardly seemed possible.

"May I sleep here? In the storeroom?" she asked hesitantly. "I've nowhere else to stay."

Mr. Kleiner looked up. "Oh, my dear child," he said compassionately. "I would gladly give you shelter here, but Mr. Carroll would never allow such a thing. He's—he's an extremely private man, and he lives in the apartment abovestairs. Oh, no, no, he would never permit it. We'd both get the sack. But," he continued, brightening, "I believe that I have a room for you at my own place of residence. You see, my wife and I, we have a boarding house—a most respectable lodging— and there's a vacant room at the moment. It's quite convenient to the shop. Yes, indeed, just a few blocks away."

"Scratch," said Jeremy loudly.

"Beg your pardon?" said Mr. Kleiner.

"Scratch. She ain't got any. Money," he explained.

"Oh! That's easily remedied," said Mr. Kleiner. He pulled four dollars out of his pocket. "This is entirely yours, Miss Claus, since you somehow produced the doll that yielded it. This is more than enough for a week's room and board. I don't say it's anything fancy, but it should satisfy. Oh, and should you further require an advance upon wages earned, I would be happy to comply."

"This should be plenty," said Holly delightedly. She was a wage earner—just like a mortal!

"Now, you'll need to see Mrs. Kleiner at once," Mr. Kleiner continued. "I would, under most circum- stances, be delighted to guide you, but—ah—unfor- tunately, I am prevented from doing so this evening due to"—Mr. Kleiner smiled secretively—"a certain pressing errand. But Jeremy can take you, can't you, my boy? You know where it is, don't you?"

Jeremy did and, as he collected his own afternoon's wages, Holly disappeared into the storeroom and returned with her green hat firmly fixed to her coppery curls, and her bulging satchel over her arm. As they prepared to leave, a soft knock sounded at the door. Behind the counter, Mr. Kleiner started and looked nervously at the black shadow that loomed against the glass. "Mr. Carroll?" he called.

Silence. Then a knock once more.

Mr. Kleiner slipped off his stool and approached the door. "Is that you, Mr. Carroll?" he said warily, turning the key in the lock.

A smooth voice replied, "Hunter Hartman is the name. And you must be Mr. Kleiner. Very pleased to make your acquaintance. Your shop was recommended to me by Mr. Burns, Lucius Burns, of Pittsburgh." Mr. Hartman edged inside the door, his eyes fixed upon Mr. Kleiner with intense friendliness.

"Ah," said Mr. Kleiner uncomfortably. "And how is Mr. Burns?"

"Somewhat troubled by lumbago," said Hunter Hartman unconcernedly, glancing around the shop. "I see that he was correct in his description. This shop is indeed a wonderland." He smiled warmly, his soft eyes slipping around the little circle of observers, pausing ever so briefly on Tundra before moving on. "And precisely what I have been seeking. I am in need of a great number of toys for a certain project of my own." Again his glance seemed to include them all, and his smile grew warmer still. "I was told by Mr. Burns that Carroll's shop would see me through the task. And"— he opened his arms wide—"it is so!"

From the dark street outside, a sharp rhythm of footsteps could be heard. There was a pause, and Mr. Carroll stepped into the store. He too glanced around the little circle, but there was no warmth in his look. Unconsciously Holly stepped back, until her back met the cool glass case behind her. She watched, hypnotized, as his eyes raked across Hartman's friendly face. "What have we here?" he asked, his voice low and steady.

"This is Mr. Hart—Hartman," began Mr. Kleiner, but he was interrupted by Hartman himself.

"Mr. Hunter Hartman, at your service," said the visitor, extending his hand. After a slight hesitation, Mr. Carroll responded with his own. "I'm in need of toys, sir. A mutual acquaintance of mine and Mr.

Kleiner's, knowing of a certain project I have undertaken, suggested that I make my purchases here, at your shop."

"What leads you to believe that this shop is mine?" responded Mr. Carroll coolly.

Hartman's gray eyes flashed with anger, but it was soon subsumed in a jovial smile. "You are Mr. Carroll, are you not?"

Mr. Carroll nodded briefly.

"Aha! You see? I guessed correctly! And now, perhaps, might I embark upon my shopping? Time is of the essence. Perhaps this young lady"—the friendly eyes lingered on Holly, slipping from her wide green eyes down to her lips—"would be so kind as to assist me."

Tundra pressed himself hard against Holly's knees, and she heard a distant rumble in his throat. "I'd be glad—" she began slowly.

"My store is closed for the evening," Mr. Carroll said curtly, not looking in her direction.

"My dear sir!" said Mr. Hartman. "I assure you that you will be amply recompensed for your time!"

"My store is closed," Carroll repeated. "We open tomorrow at nine o'clock. I really must insist that you take your leave. Good night." He stood, arrow straight, blocking the way into the shop.

There was a short silence. Mr. Hartman nodded stiffly and left.

"G'night, Mr. Carroll," said Jeremy, oblivious to the tension.

Caught between regret for lost business and relief at his release from Mr. Hartman, Mr. Kleiner wished his employer a good evening and headed with a sigh into the frosty air.

Holly could not help stealing a final look at Mr. Carroll. He was staring fixedly at Tundra, who was gazing back at him. "That's my dog, Tundra," she blurted, for want of something to say.

Mr. Carroll looked up, and she saw that his eyes, empty now of anger, were tired. But her words brought a flash of amusement to his face. "Do you take me for a fool, Miss Claus?"

"Excuse me, sir?" she stammered.

"That's a wolf. Good night, Miss Claus." With a slight bow, he turned on his heel and walked toward the shadowy staircase.

Outside, Mr. Hartman waited. When Holly stepped out the door, she found him deep in conversation with Mr. Kleiner. He turned at her approach and smiled broadly. "And will you introduce me to your lovely assistant?" he said.

Mr. Kleiner nodded. "Miss Claus, Mr. Hartman. Mr. Hartman will return tomorrow to complete his purchases."

Taking Holly's hand, Mr. Hartman bowed deeply. "I am delighted to make your acquaintance, Miss Claus. Mr. Kleiner tells me that you have an intimate knowledge of the world of toys. I will place myself entirely in your hands. Though they are," he said, gazing down at her hand, which he still held in his gloved hand, "rather too lovely for such a burden."

His words hung in the air, and he smiled charmingly around the circle. Mr. Kleiner cleared his throat. "Do excuse me. I really must take my leave. Pressing engagement." He scurried away down the dark street.

"Perhaps you will let me see you home?" said Mr. Hartman. "It is dark for a young lady to travel alone."

Tundra sat down firmly on her feet, but Holly had already begun to refuse: "Oh, no thank you, Mr. Hartman. Jeremy will be seeing me home tonight." She grinned at the boy. "Because without him, I don't know where home is."

"Yeah, come on, Holly," said Jeremy suddenly. "We better get along. I bet it's after seven already."

Mr. Hartman pulled a glistening pocket watch from his waistcoat. "Quarter past, young man."

"All right, Jeremy. Good night, Mr. Hartman," said Holly.

"Miss Claus?" Hartman reached out a hand to detain her. She waited. "Miss Claus, may I be so bold as to say that finding you here is like stumbling upon a delicate flower in the midst of a parched desert? Royal courts, balls, society parties, and receptions I have been to, but never have I seen a lady who exceeds you in beauty. Forgive me for my audacity." He bowed his head humbly.

Holly smiled. "You are forgiven. And now, *good night.*" She, Tundra, and Jeremy stepped away and were soon lost in the darkness.

Hartman watched them go. "Till tomorrow."

Chapter Nineteen

THE CARRIAGE WAS old and rickety, and it swayed sideways upon the granite street, but the passengers paid no heed to this. A little door at the top of the cab snapped open, and a large blue eye appeared. "Snow ahead, miss. Pardoning the inconvenience."

"That's quite all right," said Holly graciously. The eye blinked, the little door clapped shut, and the driver heaved himself down from the seat with his shovel in hand. The horse stamped twice and was still. She turned to her friend. "Are you getting too cold, Jeremy?"

"Not me. I feel swell. I never rode in a cab before."

Jeremy yawned happily and wiggled into the worn leather padding that lined the carriage.

Holly turned back to Tundra and continued their conversation where it had been interrupted. "You never saw him before in your life. How can you be so certain that you dislike him?"

"I don't know how," conceded Tundra. "There's something about him—something that's not right."

"Maybe you just don't like mortals," suggested Holly.

"I like Mr. Kleiner," Tundra protested. "I even like Jeremy here, despite his disbelief in my existence."

"I believe in you now," objected Jeremy.

"But to get back to the point," Holly said. "You don't like Mr. Hartman or Mr. Carroll."

"Do you?"

"Well." Holly smiled in the darkness. "As for Mr. Hartman, it's nice to be treated like a young lady."

"What?" said Tundra incredulously. "You thought it was nice to be called a flower in the desert?"

"No one's ever called me a flower in the desert before," Holly said.

"He held your hand too long," said Tundra stubbornly. "It was indelicate."

"You ought to hear yourself. You sound like an old

hen. What do you think of Mr. Hartman, Jeremy?"

"Huh? Oh. I think he's a fellow with plenty of money, and he's going to spend it in Carroll's store. Don't see what else there is to think about him. He's friendlier than old Carroll, that's for sure."

"Ah, yes, Mr. Carroll," said Tundra. Holly was silent. "Well, Holly? Does he make you feel like a young lady too?"

"No," Holly replied hesitantly. "He makes me feel like something has happened, or is about to happen. And I want to get away, but I can't. As though my foot has fallen through the floor. I can't stop watching him. And I can't stop thinking that I know him. I know him." Her voice faded.

Tundra felt a sizzle of fear. *It's him,* he thought, his fur bristling along his back. It's Herrikhan, and I must stop him. Again, he pictured the glove gripping the banister as Carroll's eyes roved over the shop until they fell upon Holly's face. Then another glove gripped Holly's hand. It could be either of them, he thought despairingly. It could be anyone. His eyes fell on a short man who was thundering along the sidewalk with a tremendous scowl on his face. Perhaps that's Herrikhan. Or Jeremy—that would be clever, wouldn't it? The boy looked childish and innocent.

But still, thought Tundra. And then there was Mr.
Kleiner. Hadn't he suggested that Holly board under
the same roof as he? Wasn't that suspicious? Tundra's
muscles ached with the desire to lunge, to bring
something down, to seize and shake it until its head
flopped brokenly from side to side. No. He took a
breath. It could be anyone, but I mustn't frighten her,
he cautioned himself. Keep watch. Be ready. But be
certain first.

He shook his head to dispel his dark thoughts and
heard Holly asking, "Are you so tired, Jeremy? Would
you like my cloak for a pillow? I really don't need it."

Jeremy stretched. "Naw. I'm not so tired. When
you live like me, out and about, you catch yourself
some shut-eye whenever you can. This is nice and
cozy in here."

Holly glanced around the cab's tired interior. It
was neither nice nor cozy. "I have a present for you,
Jeremy," she said, reaching into her satchel.

Jeremy straightened. "For me?" he croaked as she
put a small figure into his hands. In the watery light
of the street lamps, he looked down. "Hey! It's one of
them dolls. Hey! Look at that! It's me!" With a rough
finger, he brushed the little face that bore his own
broad cheekbones and wide smile. "It's me," he

repeated. "But I have a nice suit on." The carriage rocked as the driver, having cleared the way, climbed back aboard. The horse resumed his tired tread.

"I know that boys on Earth don't play with dolls," began Holly anxiously. "But I thought maybe this could be a sort of memento." She looked at Jeremy, but his face was hidden in the shadows.

"What's a memento?" he asked after a moment.

"A—a thing that reminds you of someone or something that happened—" she began.

"I don't need no memento," he said, his voice hoarse. "I won't never forget you. I never got a present before, 'cept some food, and that's not the same. You give me this and I'll keep it forever."

"Don't you see?" Holly brought the figure up into the light. "It is you, all grown up into a doctor. It's you just exactly as wonderful and special as you are right now, but grown into the person you will be."

"A doctor?" A cautious smile lit Jeremy's face. "Yeah? Think I'll look like that? In my mind a doctor don't look like me."

"That's why I made this for you," Holly said, looking into his eyes. "A doctor can look just like you. Just precisely like you."

There was another silence inside the carriage.

Holly saw Jeremy rub his cheeks furtively. "Jeremy?"

"What you want to do that for?" he said. "I never did nothing to you!"

"Jeremy, dear, tell me, what have I done?" cried Holly.

"You go and make me want something I can't have! You give me this little doll thing, and I look at it, and it's like it's saying 'You can do it. You can become something good,' and you know I can't!"

"Jeremy," Holly said, and her voice was certain. "You already are something good. You're better than good. You've made a home for all those children, a real home. You've taken care of them and taught them that there's love in this world. You've done everything I ever wanted to do myself, and I admire you more than I can say. You have proven that you can change the world. You have to believe that you can make yourself what you want to be—I believe it already. And so does Mr. McElhenny. And Mr. Kleiner. And all the children in the park believe in you. You're the only one who doubts. Believe in yourself. Look! Look at what you can be!" She pulled the dream doll up before him, and his eyes rested on it thoughtfully.

"You think I changed the world?" he asked.

"Yes," said Holly definitely.

"You think I really could do it? Get some school-ing? Get to be a doctor someday?"

"Yes."

"I can't read nor write."

"You can learn," said Holly promptly. "What you need to know, you can learn. What you already know can't be taught."

There was another silence. "I heard of schools you don't have to pay nothing for. Mr. Kleiner told me."

"But Jeremy! That's wonderful! Are they nearby?"

"Dunno. Never asked no more about it."

"Why?"

"I got to thinking it'd be all little kids—babies—and me. Guess I felt stupid."

Now it was Holly's turn to be quiet. "I know what you mean," she said slowly. "I've felt sometimes like I'd be less trouble if I'd just sit back and be quiet. But dreams are too important. We can't just let our dreams dry up and die, because then our hearts would break."

Tundra, hidden in the dim corner of the carriage, bowed his head. Take her away now, and she will never smile again, he thought. He looked out the greasy window at the few passersby, bundled up against the fearsome cold, and wished hopelessly that Holly was safe at home.

❄ ❄ ❄

The door opened and before them stood a small, round lady. Her dark brown hair was brushed over her ears in an unfashionable bun. Her eyes were kind as she peered nearsightedly at the three faces before her. "Yes?"

"Good evening, Mrs. Kleiner, ma'am," Jeremy began. "This here is Miss Holly Claus, who is needing . . ." In a matter of moments, the arrangements were concluded to Jeremy and Mrs. Kleiner's satisfaction. As for Holly and Tundra, they were struck dumb by the mouthwatering aromas that were wafting into the front hall where they stood.

"Do come into the parlor, Miss Claus. Your dog is welcome too, of course. Come along, Jeremy. I am fond of animals, though I keep none myself. You see, we've scarcely enough room for humankind, let alone a pet." It was true. The parlor was stuffed with potted trees and flowers. There was even a vine growing from a brass bowl set near the door, and dangling flowers brushed Holly's face as she entered. The piano was lost in a jungle of orchids, and the dark horsehair sofa was embellished with the drooping fruit of a pomegranate tree that hung over its back. Making himself small, Tundra squeezed into a space between a curio cabinet and an aspidistra and waited for the source of the delicious smells to appear. "We're just waiting for Mr. Kleiner, for he will bring the candles," Mrs. Kleiner was saying. The front door shut with a muffled thud. "Yes, here he is now."

Mr. Kleiner appeared at the doorway, a little out of breath, as though he had been hurrying. His anxious face seemed to smooth as he caught sight of his wife. "Do excuse me, Sarah, for my lateness. Ah!" He clapped his hands together. "Miss Claus has preceded me! I am so glad."

"Come along then, all of you." Mrs. Kleiner beckoned them all through an archway.

"Me too?" asked Jeremy, looking down at his worn clothes.

"Especially you," Mrs. Kleiner assured him. "We must have a child." In the dining room, a table was set with flowered dishes. In the center a large platter held a steaming stack of potato pancakes, and silver bowls of applesauce guarded each end. Another platter, with roasted meat laid in tempting slices under a savory sauce, and yet another piled high with delicate fruit, completed the meal. Mr. Kleiner produced a brown paper packet from his coat and opened it, revealing nine candles. Carefully he placed them in the silver

menorah that stood on the table.

"It's Hanukkah," he explained to Holly and Jeremy. "The eighth and last night of Hanukkah. The Festival of Lights," he added, "commemorating a miracle that took place among our people." Holly nodded; the holidays and celebrations of all people were considered basic knowledge in Forever. Jeremy, however, looked blank. "Our people, the Jewish people," Mr. Kleiner continued. "We light the candles to remember the lamp that did not falter for eight long days. Then we say a prayer. And then—we eat!" He laughed at Jeremy's sudden change of expression. "Thank you, Sarah," he said, as Mrs. Kleiner handed him a flaming taper. "No, stay, you must help me." With a smile, she placed her small hand on his, and they lit the center candle. Holly looked on, her eyes soft, as their joined hands hovered over each candle and they spoke the prayer that invoked God's blessing. Quietly, her voice mingled with theirs as they completed the prayer. Mr. Kleiner smiled and released his wife's hand. "And now—"

"We eat!" cried Jeremy.

And they did. The crispy pancakes, loaded with applesauce, were consumed, resupplied, and consumed again in a matter of a half hour, and the savory meat disappeared at the same rate. After gaining Mrs. Kleiner's permission, Holly set out a plate for the grateful Tundra, and for a while they all enjoyed themselves without much conversation. At length Holly set down her fork, and then Mrs. Kleiner followed. Mr. Kleiner declared himself full and put down his napkin with a sigh of contentment. Jeremy, however, continued to eat with steady purpose.

As the minutes ticked by, Holly tried to ignore the familiar weakness that was creeping upon her in the close room.

"I never had such a tasty meal in my whole life," said Jeremy with his mouth full. "This might be the best day ever."

Mr. Kleiner laughed and glanced across the table. "Sarah," he said, "do we have a corner for young Jeremy tonight? It's bitter cold."

"I was thinking that very thing, Isaac. Jeremy, would you like to stay here tonight? Free of charge, of course."

"What's that?" Jeremy gulped. "Oh, thank you, ma'am, but I gotta be getting back to the kids. Now if you could spare some leftovers, ma'am, I wouldn't say no. For the kids. They never get victuals like this from one year to the next."

As Mrs. Kleiner bustled about, preparing a gigantic bundle of blankets and food, with a few coins tucked inside, Jeremy felt an insistent pressure against his leg. "What?" he said incautiously, looking down at Tundra.

Tundra glared at him, and then turned his head to Holly. She was very pale, and her hands were trembling. The warm, humid air of the Kleiners' over-stuffed parlor was sapping her strength with each passing minute. "Uh, Mrs. Kleiner, ma'am, Miss Holly here is pretty tired. Maybe you could show her the room you got for her?"

Mrs. Kleiner was all concern at the sight of Holly's pallor and conveniently attributed it to exhaustion. "You worked this poor child to the bone," she said, scolding her husband lightly as she guided Holly upstairs.

"I'll be all right," Holly said dully. Her pulse was

pounding in her ears, and she summoned all her strength to put one foot in front of the other. What was Mrs. Kleiner saying? Nothing fancy; do hope you're comfortable, oh dear, it's ice-cold in here, the girl comes to tidy at ten; breakfast at seven; poached eggs unless you prefer otherwise. "Poached eggs will be fine," stammered Holly, sitting down on the bed and feeling herself revive in the chilly air. Tundra trailed in behind them and hid himself in a dark corner, trying to be inconspicuous.

Plenty more blankets; the water closet is just down the hall here; oh, let me light the grate; there, you'll be warm in no time; is this little bag all you carried; well, it's not for me to question; always better to travel light; the other lodger, Mr. Hamerky, you should have seen his luggage when he came, my dear, and that reminds me, you'll hear his footsteps late this evening; poor boy is a printer, works day and night; I suppose it's better than no position at all. . . .

Still chattering, Mrs. Kleiner closed the door. The sound of her footfalls on the carpet died away. Quiet. Holly fell back on the bed, taking great mouthfuls of frigid air.

"Can you turn that thing off?" Tundra asked, staring at the gas fire.

"Yes." Holly rose and fiddled with the handle. The gas hissed away to nothing. Hungry for cold, she flung open the narrow window and found to her surprise a tiny balcony that hung over the street far below. "You are welcome to come in, snow," she called to the sky, and was rewarded with a scattering of flakes. She flopped down on the bed again. After a long silence, she said into the darkness, "Was it only last night we were at home?"

"Only last night."

"Oh." They were quiet, remembering. "I miss them all so much." Holly's voice shook a little. "Do you think Mama is worried?"

"I think she's worried, but not as much as your father."

"Mmm. But he'll pretend he's not, for her sake."

"And she will know that he's pretending and pretend herself that his calmness is the only thing that keeps her from a nervous attack," said Tundra with a chuckle.

"You know them so well," said Holly, laughing softly.

"I've known them so long. So many years." Tundra sighed.

There was a thoughtful pause. "Do you want to go home?" she asked.

"What, now?"

"Yes. Do you want to go home?"

"Not without you. Ever."

Holly looked at the cracks on the ceiling. "I don't deserve you, Tundra," she said humbly.

"Deserve." Tundra rolled the word around his mouth. "That's what I don't understand about humans. This deserving idea. If it's love, you don't have to deserve it." Holly lifted her head to stare at him. After a moment he smiled. "Doesn't that hurt your neck?"

"Yes," she admitted, and sat up. They looked at each other affectionately for a few moments, and then Holly stood. "I must hang up my clothes, or they'll be a mass of wrinkles tomorrow." She rustled through the satchel, pulling out a creased dress of gray wool. "Uh-oh," she said. "This looks terrible. What do you do with wrinkles, Tundra?"

"Grow fur," said Tundra indifferently. "You'll look fine."

"I wish Lexy were here," said Holly. "She'd know what to do."

The satchel snorted.

"What?" said Holly and Tundra to each other. Before their amazed eyes, the satchel snorted again.

And then clicked. And shivered.

Summoning her nerve, Holly quickly overturned the satchel onto the bed. Out tumbled a muslin nightgown, a tawny skirt, and an assortment of stockings and brushes and satin pouches. *Thump*—a great knob of porcelain fell out. Then *The Book of Forever*, still in a featherweight edition, floated to the top of the pile. A mysteriously bumpy roll of green silk appeared. It lay on the coverlet, giving no clue as to its contents. Holly and Tundra exchanged glances. "Should I bite it?" Tundra asked.

At this, the bundle erupted. "No! No!" it squeaked. "It's us, you hound!"

Holly began to laugh. Quickly she unrolled the silk and found three tiny creatures: Alexia, Euphemia, and Empy. They were no more than two inches tall, but they were themselves. Excitedly they began to jump up and down, their teeny voices raised to the highest pitch they could muster.

"About time!" cried Lexy. "I thought we'd never get out of that bag! So stuffy!"

"I did it!" screamed Euphemia. "I'm the one who thought of it, and Holly, *I'm* the one who remembered the magic words!"

All Empy could say was, "Holly, Holly, Holly!"

"I'm so glad to see you, my wonderful friends," Holly said. "I was just saying to Tundra that I missed you all horribly."

"We know! We heard!"

"I can barely hear you," Holly said, kneeling on the floor to see eye to eye with her friends. "Can you unshrink?"

Euphemia opened her wings proudly. "Yes, certainly," she said. "I'll take care of that in no time." She placed one wing around Lexy and one around little Empy. "Scadoddle, Scadaddle, Scadee!" At the last word, there was a quiet *pop*, and all three creatures disappeared for a fraction of a second, only to emerge from nothingness to their customary sizes.

Holly kissed them all. "Oh, my friends! My loyal friends!"

"*That* was Strigigormese?" Tundra asked.

Euphemia smiled proudly. "Yes. One of the more ancient incantations. And," she added, "*I* remembered it."

"Doesn't sound like I thought it would," said Tundra, considering. "I was expecting something more like Greek. Something noble."

"Tundra," said Holly warningly.

"Oh. Right. Very interesting, Strigigormese."

"Thank you," said Euphemia.

By this time Empy was in Holly's arms, but Alexia was peering critically at the clothes on the bed. "These look terrible. You should have hung them earlier."

"I was just saying the same thing," Holly replied.

"Luckily I brought a few odds and ends with me. Euphemia. Euphemia! Stop preening and unshrink that little bag there, will you?"

"Scadee, Scadaddle, Scadoddle!" quickly obliged Euphemia, and a tiny silk bag, suitable for housing a single ring, suddenly blossomed into a large valise.

"I can't believe that's Strigigormese," Tundra muttered as Holly opened the bag and exclaimed over the fresh and unwrinkled contents. She pulled out a silvery skirt embroidered with white snowflakes and a crisp white blouse. New boots, too, soft and white, and a gray hat with a soaring white feather. A silvery wool jacket lined in white velvet completed the outfit. A dress the color of sea foam, with a long, fitted coat of raspberry wool. Stockings, shoes, even hankies, all neat and tidy. Finally out came a shushing torrent of glinting, golden silk and a pair of satin dancing slippers of the same color.

"What in the world! Lexy! This is a ball gown!" Holly cried. "I don't think I'll be attending any balls, unless Jeremy holds one in the sausage pavilion."

"A lady is always prepared," said the fox sternly.

"Oh, it's lovely!" Holly assured her. "Perfectly stunning. I love the way the ribbons pull back here."

Under Alexia's watchful eye, Holly hung her new clothes carefully in the wardrobe and put the rest in neat stacks in the dresser drawers, all the while talking with her friends. Finally, as Mrs. Kleiner's mournful clock, far below in the hall, struck midnight, Tundra gave up suggesting that they go to sleep and commanded it. Exhausted, they all complied.

All except Holly, that is. She lay awake, her mind racing from one image to the next: tiny Bat next to the massive horses with their heavy hooves; Jeremy's hand on the little boy's arm; the dying light of the fire in the eyes of the children huddled around it; the little shack that barely kept the snow from their faces as they slept. "We got hay to keep us warm," Jeremy had said. But how warm could they be? Holly tried to imagine being cold, being freezing. Your skin must hurt, she thought, looking at her own shadowed hands. And your nose. And your eyes. She remembered Lissy's wracking cough and the way she had closed her eyes afterward.

Holly slipped from her bed and went to the little desk near the window. Pulling aside the curtain to admit the thin light of the moon, she broke off a morsel of the porcelain from her bag and began to smooth the warm lump in her hands. She had only seen Lissy for a few moments, so she had to close her eyes to remember the short chin and soft brow. Once well, the thin cheeks would fill out, yes, like that . . .

When her work was done, she peered into the darkness outside her window. On an impulse, she climbed out onto the tiny balcony and looked up at the indigo sky with its silvery crescent. From the clear night, a fluttering ring of snow crystals descended silently. "Magic?" she murmured as the glistening snow wove itself into a light mantle around her shoulders. It did not melt but grew, until she was wrapped in a cool shawl, spangled with the lacy patterns of the snow. Holly smiled and pulled the shawl close around her. She returned to the quiet room and slipped into the bed, wrapped in the gossamer shawl. Near her feet, she could hear Lexy's soft sighs and Empy's wuffles. A few snowflakes drifted in the open window. She was among friends. She was safe. She slept.

In a gray, stony house across the street, a lank curtain also dropped back into place. The inhabitant had had some trouble persuading the landlord to rent him every room on the floor. "But I got a good boarder there, in room three," the landlord had said, perspiring.

"I'll pay you four times his rate," the man said smoothly.

"For how long?" the landlord replied doubtfully.

"For a week."

"Well, I suppose Mr. Fairlee could come downstairs to the back parlor for a week. You say you'll only want it for a week?"

"A week," he said through clenched teeth.

"But you'll pay for a month?" The landlord still didn't believe it.

"Yesss."

"Well." The landlord sighed. "All right."

Oh, but it had been well worth it, he reflected now. Very well worth it. The girl was right there, within view. Nothing could happen without his knowing it. He looked down at his mortal clothes. Binding, scratching, chafing him throughout the day. He pulled off the black gloves and regarded the hands that had been imprisoned within them. Now the skin seemed to melt away, and the bones themselves squeezed and lengthened, until the familiar scaled silver skin slipped over the open flesh. Ripping off the black coat and stiff collar, he sighed. Oh, and the hat, the vile hat that seemed to rest just where the iron band bit most painfully into his flesh. He looked at himself in the long mirror. Much better. Ever so much better. Opening his mouth wide for the first time in hours, he smiled at his appearance and inspected his mottled tongue. The mirror began to spin on its stand. Around and around, madly. He started to laugh—wildly.

I am so very close, he thought.

Chapter Twenty

THUD. **T**HUD. The long-suffering satchel thumped rhythmically against Holly's knees as she walked through the pale, frosted city. It was early, and the bricks at the very tops of the houses were touched with the colors of the sunrise. Delighted with the crisp air, the slippery ice beneath her feet, and the exhilaration of freedom, Holly broke into a short run. Abruptly she stopped and slid along the frozen bricks, startling several pigeons and Tundra, who was still sleepy. "Excuse me!" Holly laughed at the birds, who replied with offended coos. "You should be up, anyway! It's a beautiful morning! Oops!" Holly neatly skirted a large, tired-looking man who was scattering sawdust on the ice.

"Hey!" he yelled, watching her go. "Ain't you kind of big to be sliding around?"

"You're never too old for sliding!" she called back to him, skidding along the sidewalk.

He guffawed but made a tiny slide himself. Putting down the bag of sawdust, he made a more determined run and slide. "Looney," he said, looking after Holly with a grin.

On she went. A trio of shopgirls, hurrying anxiously to one of the great department stores on the Ladies' Mile, caught sight of Holly's gliding figure and smiled at one another. Then one of the three, the youngest, gave a little push and slid herself. After an exchange of glances, the others followed, and three faces that had been stiff with worry and haste melted into something better.

Still sliding, Holly passed into the neighborhood of lofty mansions and graceful châteaux imported stone by stone from France. Now she could see the lacy treetops of the park, and she slowed and called over her shoulder, "Race you, Tundra! First one to McElhenny's gets a sausage!" Tundra snorted scornfully. Holly stuck out her tongue at him. "Scared you'll lose?" she teased.

In answer, Tundra leaped and bolted. Head down, he skimmed across the pavement and suddenly veered across the broad expanse of Fifth Avenue and into the park. He could hear Holly laughing and panting behind him, but in the ecstasy of running he flew faster, his paws scarcely touching the icy ground. He raced on madly, until he realized that the only sound he could hear was the light crunch of his own paws in the snow. He stopped dead, rolling into a crouch, and waited. Nothing. Only his own panting breath. Where was she? He cursed himself and leaped to his feet. If he had run fast before, it was nothing to his pace now. He streaked over a gentle incline and across the snowy lawn, retracing his steps until he reached the south tip of the Mall, where he saw her, a small figure flapping along the snow-covered walk with a bulging bag in her arms. Relief streamed through him, and, when he could breathe again, he loped to meet her.

"Show-off!" she cried when he came into hearing range.

"I'm sorry," he replied sincerely. "Are you all right?"

"Yes, of course. Why wouldn't I be?" she answered with surprise.

"Holly, doesn't it ever occur to you that this place could be dangerous?"

"What? The mortals?"

He hated to say it. "Not the mortals."

Comprehension dawned in her eyes. "I know. I mean, I know you are right when you say that there is danger here. Herrikhan is more likely to try to find me here than at home," she said slowly, as though learning a lesson. "But Tundra"—her voice dropped to a whisper—"I just can't feel it. I can't believe in it. I don't know why, exactly, but it seems impossible that I should be the center of this struggle. How could I be that important? I feel none of it."

That's because you have a heart untouched by pride or greed or self-interest. You're exactly what he wants. But Tundra didn't say any of that, because it would do no good. What he did say was "Come on, let's go deliver some dolls."

Holly's troubled face cleared, and her eyes, the color of the sea in a storm, lightened. "Yes, let's do that."

The snowy paths were beginning to fill with the day's pedestrians, wrapped to their eyes against the bite of the cold. Holly and Tundra walked sedately toward the Mall, trying to look like an average young lady with an extremely lumpy bag, no coat to speak of, and a large, snow-white dog. Yet several curious glances followed them. Soon enough Holly veered off the path, and they lost themselves in the scrubby forest that lay west of the great avenue. They had reached the Place. Again Holly saw the embers of the poor fire at the center of the encampment, but now, around its dying warmth, lay four heaps of blankets, each with a thin crust of snow on top.

Three of the mounds were still and sleeping, but the fourth wiggled as Holly and Tundra approached. A moist black nose poked out, withdrew, and poked out again. "Sidewalk!" Holly whispered, and the dog squirmed out from beneath the blankets and greeted her with a wagging tail. "Hello, friend," she whispered. "Is everybody still asleep? I've brought some bread for you." She reached into the bag and pulled out a lump of bread, which Sidewalk ate with gusto.

Abruptly one of the blanket rolls sat up. It was Jeremy. "Some watchdog," he said to Sidewalk. "Hi. G'morning," he said to Holly and Tundra. "Whatcha doing here?"

"I brought some breakfast," said Holly. "And some dolls."

"You bring one for Lissy?" asked Jeremy.

"Yes, of course," answered Holly. "How is she?"

"Not so good. When I come back last night, she was coughing something awful. She wouldn't take much to eat, neither. Said she wasn't hungry."

"She shouldn't be outside in this weather," said Holly.

"I know it. I told her she gotta go to the poorhouse or Children's Aid, but she says no. She says they'll lock her up, and she'd rather die out here with us." Jeremy passed his hand across his eyes. "I dunno what to do."

From inside the little shack came the sound of a wracking, gluey cough that seemed to go on and on. It was followed by small rustles and groans as the layers of children within awoke to a new day. The first to emerge was Bat, in dire need of a handkerchief but still a cheering sight to Holly, for he looked rested and reasonably well fed.

"Hot in there," he said. "Oh, Holly's here. Hi, Holly." He bounced over to her and looked up, confident of his welcome.

He got it. She kissed his dirty cheek, wiped his nose, and offered him some bread and milk. The smell of fresh bread invaded the sleepers' dreams, and soon more children straggled out of the hay-filled shack to greet Holly and enjoy the rare experience of having a full belly in the morning. Bruno and Marty, the two biggest boys, built the fire up, careful not to make it large enough to attract notice, and the children lounged around on the few dry patches of ground or on logs.

Finally Lissy, too, emerged from the wooden shack, holding Joan's hand. Holly saw the dark smudges around her eyes and the feverish color in her cheeks; she and Jeremy exchanged glances. "Good morning, dear," she said to the girl. "Come sit here, by the fire."

Slowly, slowly, Lissy walked to the spot Holly had indicated, her eyes fixed intently on the place. She dropped down with a sigh of exhaustion when she reached it, and Holly quickly swung two blankets around the thin shoulders and leaned the girl back against the log. "Are you cold?" she asked, handing Lissy a cracked cup of milk.

"Cold?" Lissy repeated vaguely. "I don't think so. No. I'm warm." She drank the milk.

"I brought you something."

Lissy turned her head. "For me? That's funny." She lapsed into silence.

"Do you want it?" asked Holly, puzzled.

"What? Oh. I forgot. Yes."

Holly reached into her satchel and brought forth

the doll. She laid it in Lissy's lap.

"What is it?" said Lissy. Slowly her vague gaze seemed to focus on the little figure that lay in her lap. She stared for a long time at the face, with its coiled brown hair and smooth pink cheeks. "It's my ma," she said hoarsely. "How'd you know what she looked like?"

"I didn't—it's not—" Holly broke off, unsure of the right way to answer. "I didn't know I was making your mother," she said finally. "I thought I was making you."

"You made it?"

"Yes."

Lissy's eyes traveled down to Holly's long fingers and rested there. "*You* made it?"

Holly smiled. "Yes. I thought I was making you, all grown up, well and happy—I thought that would be your dream."

For the first time, she saw Lissy smile. "I'm not gonna grow up and be well and happy. But if you was making my dreams, you made it right. I dream about my ma all the time."

"Is your mama dead?"

"Yeah. Long time ago, when I was six or something. But I remember how she looked before she got sick, and it was like this." Lissy drew a rattling breath and continued, "After she was dead, I kept looking and looking for her, 'cause nobody told me what dead was. I thought she had just gone away. Thought she was mad at me for something. Then I found out, and I stopped looking. But now I catch myself watching for her again. Yesterday, at McElhenny's, I saw a lady in a brown coat, walking kind of brisk, and I thought, That's her, that's Ma." Lissy lifted the doll's little arms. "Stupid, wasn't it? But now here she is." She cradled the doll against her neck.

Holly reached out and held the little girl. "Oh, this world is so hard," she whispered. "How can you bear it?"

"There's some good parts," Lissy answered. "This morning is good. This milk is good. Seeing my ma here in this doll is good. She loved me."

Holly didn't reply. Instead she drew forth the rest of the dream dolls from her satchel. "Look, Bat," she called to the little boy, who was even dirtier now than he had been ten minutes before. "Look, it's you." She held up the figure dressed in the bright silk shirt.

"Hey!" Bat shouted. "It's me! But bigger and fancier. Look at me!" He grabbed the little figure and danced it around in the air.

The other children crowded around him curiously.

"I'll be jiggered." "It even has that scar on your head!" "Whatcha got on there, Bat, silk underwear?"

"Naw," said Marty authoritatively, "that's horse-racing clothes, that is. You gonna be a horse racer, Bat?"

Bat's face lit with joy. "A horse racer? You mean you get to sit on the horses while they run?"

"Sure," said Marty, enjoying himself. "It's even a job. You can get paid for it. People bet money on the horses, and whoever wins gets a big pile of scratch. I seen it."

Bat's eyes grew round, and he stared at the doll version of himself reverently. "A horse racer," he breathed. "It's a *job*."

Jeremy grinned. "If you don't get squished on the Mall first. That's why he was out there yesterday morning," he explained to Holly. "He's crazy for horses."

Now the other children crowded around Holly, demanding and receiving their dream dolls. If their manners lacked some finesse, their appreciation of their gifts made up for it in Holly's eyes. They understood intuitively that these figures were not portraits, but somehow models of their inner selves and their hopes. They seemed to take strength from the sight of them, staring thoughtfully at the small faces as if storing them in their memories. Holly saw more than one child tuck the figure carefully into a worn inner pocket, then pull it back out for one more look. The younger children—Johnny, Jim, Sue, and Mel—began to play house with their new toys, which Holly found touching, given the probability that not one of them had ever lived in a real house.

"We'd better go, Holly," said Jeremy, after a while. He walked over to a fresh patch of snow and cleaned his face with a handful. "I'm ready."

As Holly gathered her bundles, she felt a small tug on her skirt. It was Bat. "You coming back?" he asked.

"I'll see you before I leave," she replied.

"You're leaving? When?" cried two or three startled children.

"Christmas Eve. Tomorrow night," she said. Jeremy turned away, suddenly very busy with his shoes.

From her nest of blankets, Lissy said, "Promise you'll come back one more time."

"I promise," Holly said.

There was another tug on her skirt. "Gimme a kiss," commanded Bat. Holly knelt to obey, wrapping her arms around his little boy sturdiness. "You can go," he said, not looking at her.

"Oh, Bat, I love you," said Holly, giving him an extra squeeze. He grunted in reply, but his neck turned red.

"Come on, Holly, we're gonna be late," urged Jeremy.

They flew through the streets, sliding and laughing, with Tundra trotting behind, and reached the toy shop as Mr. Kleiner did. His worried frown eased at the sight of them. "There you are!" he called happily. "I was beginning to think yesterday was only a dream!"

As they entered the door, the snow began to fall lightly, adding a dazzle to the Christmas marvels that filled the shop. Tundra took up his corner, which offered the advantage of overseeing both the shadowy staircase to the upper floor and the front door, through which he expected Hunter Hartman to arrive any minute.

Mr. Hartman, however, seemed to be less than punctual, and Tundra closed his eyes, trying to convince himself that he was ready for a nap. But when the store bell jingled for the first time that day, he leaped to his feet in an instant. To his disappointment, a middle-aged man, darkly bearded, entered the store with three boys trailing behind him.

"Now!" said the man with expectant pleasure. He looked around and rubbed his hands together. "We'll surely find what we seek here. By jove! They've rigged up some stage snow! How ingenious! What's it made of? Charles, what's it made of?"

Holly, eager to distract from this line of questioning, rustled forward and then came to a sudden halt. "Charles!" she cried. "Jerome and Harrison, too! How glad I am to see you again!" She held out her hands and the three boys ran into her arms.

"You never told us you had a toy store!" Jerome said enviously.

"It's not mine," she said, laughing. "I work here. Don't you wish you did?"

"Yes!" the three shouted.

"I could work here," Harrison announced. "I could climb the shelves and put the toys on."

"So you could," said Holly, giving him a squeeze. "I'd hire you in a minute, too, except that it isn't my store."

"Charles, a gentleman must introduce his acquaintances," his father prodded.

"Father," said Charles proudly, "I'd like to introduce you—" He stopped, warned by his father's waggling eyebrows that something was wrong. "What?"

"Ask the lady's permission," advised his father in a stage whisper. He smiled at Holly, who smiled back.

Charles appeared flummoxed by this hint. "Oh!" he said finally. "Holly, will you permit me to introduce you to my father?"

"Certainly," said Holly.

"Holly, this is my father, Dr. Braunfels. Father, this is Miss Holly Claus."

"Most pleased to meet you, Miss Claus," said Dr. Braunfels with a bow.

"And I, you, Dr. Braunfels."

Charles, with some assistance from Jerome and Harrison, was explaining to his father just how he knew Holly. "She fell over in the snow, bang!, not like a young lady at all," Harrison said admiringly.

"An excellent quality, to be sure," said Dr. Braunfels with a friendly smile. "Most young ladies are far too particular about their clothes to take the exercise that is so necessary for their health."

"You believe in fresh air and exercise, sir?" asked Holly. An idea was beginning to take shape in her mind.

"Yes, particularly for young people. Exercise, no

less than nourishing food and restful sleep, is vital for growth and health. Our children are nervous and debilitated due to—"

"Father!" whispered Harrison loudly. "Father! Don't start talking about corsets. Please!"

Dr. Braunfels ruffled his son's hair. "All right, Harrison. I'll stop. Aren't we here to find Christmas presents for your sisters, boys?" He clapped his hands together. "What shall it be?"

Jerome, who had been poking about in a low shelf, held up a lifelike rubber frog with a sagging rubber tongue. "Alice would love this," he said.

Dr. Braunfels shouted with laughter. "They'd hear her scream in Brooklyn, Jerome. Come now, think of the girls. What do they wish for?"

"Dolls," said Harrison. He looked glum.

"Dolls in silk dresses." Jerome sneered.

"Look at that sled with the steering wheel." Charles sighed.

"Evie likes to sled," said Harrison hopefully.

"No, she doesn't."

They all sighed. "Dolls." They looked at their father with tragic faces. "Dolls," they repeated.

Dr. Braunfels patted them on the back. "That's the way, boys. That's thinking of others before yourselves, which is also called the Christmas spirit. Very good. Dolls, then!" He turned to Holly.

This being precisely what she had hoped for, she was prepared. "Sir," said Holly, "our dolls are so very special that we don't put them on the shelves, but keep them safe in our storeroom for favored customers. I'd be happy to bring out two dolls for Alice and Evelyn, if you can wait for just five minutes."

Dr. Braunfels shrugged. "I'm sure the boys will manage to while away five minutes without much trouble," he said, but Holly was already flying toward the storeroom.

Hastily she removed the porcelain from her satchel and began to work, with Evelyn's face and then Alice's floating through her mind. Once the dolls were finished, she wove them magical silk dresses in her mind. But to her surprise, when she turned to the dolls after her reverie, she found that only Alice was dressed in the swishing blue ball gown of her imagination. The small figure that held Evelyn's dream was clothed in a simple white jacket over a plain skirt. Her eyes were clear, even serene, but her mouth was firm. She was, without a doubt, a doctor. Holly brought the dolls out to the front of the shop.

"Hey! It's Alice and Evie!" bellowed Jerome.

"Look at that!"

Charles whistled.

"Look at Evie," said Harrison. "What's she got on?"

Dr. Braunfels looked long and thoughtfully at the dolls he held, and when he lifted his eyes to Holly's, she saw that he was both troubled and intrigued. "It does no good to ask how you managed to—to—make these replicas of my daughters, I expect."

"That's correct, sir," said Holly. "I couldn't explain it even if I tried to."

"This is Alice as she will be, I see. Grown to a graceful woman. I am not surprised, for she is graceful now. But Evelyn? In a doctor's coat? I cannot imagine such a future for her. She cries when she sees someone hurt."

Holly interrupted. "Surely compassion should be the first qualification of a doctor."

Dr. Braunfels gazed at her. "True, and yet a woman's heart is too tender for the sights a doctor must endure."

"I disagree, sir. A tender heart is no liability, provided that its owner also possesses a steady mind and hand. You would not destroy a dream that has been modeled on your own—you could not"—Holly looked earnestly at the doctor—"simply because she's not a boy."

The boys turned from one speaker to the other, their mouths agape. "But the schools, the associations," Dr. Braunfels said, "every possible obstruction will be thrown in her way because she is female. The road is long and nearly impassable."

"But it is her road, not yours! If, knowing its difficulty, she chooses it anyway, you have no right to stop her," cried Holly.

The doctor smiled. "I must say, you are a very argumentative young lady, Miss Claus. Why do you care so much about my Evie?"

"Dreams are precious," said Holly.

"Yes," he said in a low voice. "You're right." He stared at the figure for another moment, and it seemed to stare straight back at him. "Well. Boys, I believe we have found the gifts we need. What is the price for these extremely unusual dolls, Miss Claus?"

This was what Holly had been waiting for. She cleared her throat and plunged in. "Sir, I will give you these dolls as a gift. But," she added, seeing Dr. Braunfels ready to protest, "I want you to give me a gift in return."

"What would that be?" he asked cautiously.

"I have a friend, a little girl, who coughs terribly. She has no money, so she hasn't seen a doctor. I think—I think she might die soon unless she gets some help. Will you go see her?"

Dr. Braunfels patted her shoulder sympathetically. "Of course, my dear. Tell me where the child lives." He pulled a memorandum book from his pocket.

Holly glanced at Jeremy. He nodded. "She lives in Central Park," began Holly.

"She what?"

"She lives with some other children in Central Park—"

"Now? In this weather?"

"Yes, sir."

"But there are homes! The Children's Aid Home is supposed to provide shelter—"

"She won't go, sir. She doesn't want to be locked up. None of them do. They say it's like jail. If I tell you where she is, you must promise not to reveal her secret. Do you promise?" Holly looked at him intently.

Dr. Braunfels put away his memorandum book. "Yes. I promise," he said, and Holly knew he would keep his word.

Jeremy appeared at her side like magic, with his cap on his head. "I'll take you," he said. "I'll take you there right now."

"We'll need to stop at home for my bag, but it's not far. Near St. Bartholomew's."

"That's along the way," said Jeremy.

"Take Evelyn, too," said Holly suddenly.

"Pardon?" said Dr. Braunfels.

"Take Evelyn with you. She should meet these children."

"I'll go too," said Charles. "Maybe there's something I can do."

"I shall be glad of your company," Dr. Braunfels said to his son, and then clapped his hat on his head. "Very well, young man." He turned to Jeremy. "Let's go!" He charged briskly through the door with a doll under each arm. Charles and Jeremy followed, and Jerome, with one final longing look at the rubber frog, grabbed Harrison by the hand and pulled him after.

Holly watched through the window as they disappeared into the swirl of carriages and snow and coats, and then turned back to the quiet store with a small sigh.

"That was a very kind thing you did," said Mr. Kleiner.

Holly said nothing. She did not seem to hear him.

The bell jingled, and they jumped. A pale woman with a cloud of black hair entered the shop and looked inquiringly at the shelves. "I heard that wonderful dolls are made here," she began, and before long Holly was back in the storeroom, quickly manufacturing a winsome doll for a solemn little girl of ten. Then another mother came in with twins peeking out from behind her skirt. She too had heard tales of marvelous dolls, and so Holly made twin dolls with shy smiles and devilish hearts. By now the store was humming with customers, as passersby were lured in by the sight of snow and held by the array of treasures on the shelves. Holly, coming from the storeroom with an armful of dolls, and Mr. Kleiner, winding up a music box for a curious toddler, exchanged looks of satisfaction: a bevy of little girls knelt before the little town in the glass case, each selecting the house she hoped to live in; a contented baby rocked her new teddy bear while her mother turned the shiny pages of a Mother Goose book.

Between, around, and among the crowds of children were adults, taking respite from the cold and crowded streets in the enchanted aisles of the toy shop. Here and there, Holly saw grown-ups who had discovered an old friend, a toy from childhood, and she watched as their eyes grew full of memories.

One old man with a face like a hatchet had been caught up in a bright Chinese puzzle for nearly an hour; he simply could not figure out how to unfold the intricate layers of wood that enclosed the tiny paper butterfly within, and each time he thought he was near the prize, he entrapped himself anew. Finally he stomped over to the counter and slammed the little box down. "Guess I'll take it," he snarled. Smilingly Mr. Kleiner collected his money, and the grim man turned on his heel. Then he paused. "Got any others?" he asked. Mr. Kleiner showed him six or seven equally maddening puzzles. "Guess I'll take 'em all."

Two hours passed in a matter of moments, and then, in an instant, the flurry was over. The store, which had been thick with people and loud with the clang and rattle of toys, was now empty and silent, except for the ticking of the great grandfather clock far away in the gloom upstairs.

"Praise be. I'll rest my weary bones for a minute or two," said Mr. Kleiner, easing himself onto a stool.

"And then you'll get us a Christmas tree, won't you?" teased Holly.

"Miss Claus, you are a tyrant."

"Pooh. You have no holiday spirit."

"You have enough for both of us." Mr. Kleiner laughed.

They both became aware of a presence on the gallery above. They looked up uneasily, but the only evidence of Mr. Carroll was the swaying motion of the velvet curtain that shielded the hallway from view.

Mr. Kleiner jumped to his feet. "Yes, yes, I'll be off for your Christmas tree. Back in a jiffy." Wrapping himself in an assortment of bright striped scarves that were undoubtedly the work of Mrs. Kleiner's knitting needles, he darted out the door.

Holly glanced around the empty store, unexpectedly alone and acutely aware of Mr. Carroll breathing, pacing, working, and frowning somewhere above her head. Unconsciously she tightened the snowflake shawl around her shoulders, as if it would bolster her. Don't be silly, she told herself. This is no time to act childish. I have responsibilities. And Tundra is here to protect me, even if he is asleep. She straightened her shoulders and looked around her for something to do. Yes, those masks and crowns could certainly use some tidying.

Just as Holly was striding purposefully toward the jumble of feathers and pasteboard, the shop bell tinkled and a timid-looking girl of about sixteen edged inside. Her eyes grew large at the spectacle of the dancing snow and the array of toys, and she pressed herself against the refuge of the nearest wall to stare in silence until Holly approached. Then she jumped. "Oh, I'm sorry, miss!" She gulped.

"Sorry?" Holly said. "What for?"

The girl twisted her hands. "Just—just—sorry, I guess."

Holly smiled into the anxious face before her. "You are welcome here. Can I help you find a toy?"

The girl offered a tiny smile in return. "Oh, not for me, miss. I'm just a housemaid. I come to pick up a train set for Mrs. August Inchbald."

"Mrs. August Inchbald likes to play with trains, then?" asked Holly seriously, hoping to coax another smile from the shy face.

The girl broke into a surprised grin. "Mrs. August

Inchbald don't play with trains, miss! She's a grown lady! The train is for her boy, for Christmas!"

Holly leaned toward the girl and whispered, "Perhaps Mrs. August Inchbald plays with trains secretly. In her ballroom."

To Holly's satisfaction, the girl began to giggle. "I'd like to see it, miss! Maybe next time I dust the chandelier, I'll catch her."

The two girls exchanged looks. They were both thinking the same thing: we could be friends. Then the housemaid sighed. "I got to be getting on, miss. Mrs. Inchbald don't like to wait. She ordered that train last week, and she was mad as hops when Mr. Kleiner said it won't come till now."

Holly glanced around the shop. A train, specially ordered. Where on Earth would such a thing be kept? "Of course. A train," she said, considering. "Hmm. Oh! It's sure to be in the storeroom." She ducked away to the little room, where she stared hopefully at the rows of shelves that lined the walls. Boxes upon boxes sat there, arranged according to some Kleinerian system that could neither be disturbed nor discerned, but Holly's quick scan told her that nothing on the shelves could possibly contain the length of a toy train. She returned to the waiting housemaid and said apologetically, "I'm sorry. I can't find it just now."

The girl's eyes grew wide. "You can't find it?"

"Well, no, but if you could come back this afternoon, Mr. Kleiner will surely have your package ready."

"She's gonna fire me," said the maid gloomily. "She said she would, if I come home without that train. She says I never do nothing right."

"But it's not your fault. It's mine," cried Holly.

"She won't believe me."

"Oh, my dear!" Holly turned in a rapid circle, hoping to spot the package lying unnoticed in a dim corner, but the corners held only their usual boxes. What can I do? she thought desperately. I can't allow this poor girl to come to trouble through me. Once more, she spun about but the train remained stubbornly absent.

The housemaid looked miserable.

Holly couldn't bear it. She had been left in charge of the shop, and now she was failing at her duty. She pictured Mr. Kleiner's disappointed face. She pictured Mrs. August Inchbald's haughty one. Suddenly she had an idea. "I'll go ask Mr. Carroll," she announced, a thrill of fear prickling along her back. "He should know where such things are kept." She stood still, gathering her courage. Holly was honest enough to admit to herself that she felt a kind of dread fascination in the possibility that she would see Mr. Carroll in his private chambers, but she was equally aware that she needed to do it quickly, before she lost her nerve.

Holly marched smartly across the shop, but at the stairs she paused. They looked darker and more forbidding than ever before. "I'll be back in a moment. You wait right here," she ordered. The housemaid nodded vigorously, but Holly was not addressing her. She was talking to Tundra, who had awakened. He flattened his ears and watched her through slitted eyes as she ascended the staircase.

The ticking of the clock was louder at the top. Holly looked around. The balcony that overhung the shop was empty of furniture or ornament and was lit only by the windows far below. Opposite her was the thick green-velvet curtain that cloaked the entrance to Mr. Carroll's apartments. Holly stared apprehensively at the lush folds; there was no apparent break in the fabric. It seemed to be a wall of velvet. After a moment she stepped forward, and her fingers brushed against the yielding softness. She pushed, certain that somewhere in the curtain's recesses there lay a way in, and found herself enveloped in velvet. She whirled about, feeling the first sharp touches of panic, and the choking velvet whirled with her, wrapping around her skirts like a crawling vine and blinding her in its green shadows. She threw out her hands, fighting to find space, because there had to be something beyond this thickness, this darkness—

Strong fingers grasped hers and pulled her from the stifling sea of cloth into a hallway lined with dark wood. Holly drew a deep breath, not daring to look up. Abruptly the strong hand holding hers let go. He said nothing. The silence grew, more suffocating even than the dark folds of velvet.

With dread, she lifted her eyes. He was staring at her, in astonishment or fury she could not tell. His hooded gaze was unreadable, his lips curled in a sharp half smile that might have meant anything. The impulse to run away was almost overpowering. There it was again—the feeling, so strong that it was a taste in her mouth, that she had known him forever. "Why do you keep coming back?" she murmured helplessly.

Even in the dim light, she could see his face stiffen as though he had been hit. He looked young now, and defenseless. "But it's you who seems determined to torment me," he burst out. In an instant tenderness washed away her fear, and, without thinking, she reached out her hand to his. Their fingers met and wove together.

He stepped back, dropping her hand. Once again his expression was impassive, his eyes cold. The last few moments seemed to subtract themselves from existence, like water disappearing in the sand, and Holly felt herself grow uncertain of what had just passed. "Miss Claus," he was saying, "please be so good as to explain your intrusion into my private apartment."

"I—I—was looking for a particular item that was ordered for Mrs. Inchbald," stammered Holly, trying to compose herself. "Her maid is here, and Mr. Kleiner is out, and I thought perhaps you would know where I might find their order, so I came upstairs to ask, and I got caught in your curtain and—"

"I do not concern myself with the operations of the shop," he snapped, "and I see no reason why you should forget the first rule of conduct impressed upon you by Mr. Kleiner—that my privacy should under no circumstances be disturbed."

Rebellion rose within her. He wanted to baffle her, but he would not succeed. "You don't know where deliveries are kept?" Holly asked shortly.

"I do not."

"Then I shall not detain you any further, Mr. Carroll." Holly turned to sweep away, but her eye was caught by something at the end of the hallway. It was a double door of rich, dark wood, and on its surface had been carved the face of a clock, a half belonging to each door. Exquisite care had been taken with every detail—the numbers twined with sinuous curls, and the wood shone with the luster of polish. The clock's hands pointed to ten minutes before four o'clock. Holly's gaze moved to Carroll's face. He had made it, she knew.

"Please leave," he growled.

Holly's eyes flashed. "I'd be delighted to, if you would show me the way through your ridiculous curtain."

In reply, he stalked to the velvet wall and drew aside the cloth with a little rod. Refusing to glance his way, Holly stepped through the aperture and returned to the gallery. She felt as though she had been gone for years.

Downstairs in the shop, Tundra felt the same way. As Holly descended the staircase, he watched her carefully and saw her confusion and hurt pride, and though he toyed with a pleasant vision of biting Mr. Carroll's ankle when he appeared next, his worst fears seemed to be unfounded, and he sat back, mollified. Mr. Kleiner had returned during Holly's absence, dragging a large Christmas tree behind him, and had, of course, efficiently located the troublesome train. Holly reached the shop floor just as the young housemaid was departing. She waved, endangering the bulky package under her arm, and Holly waved weakly back before she dropped onto a stool and drew a long breath.

Mr. Kleiner approached and laid a sympathetic hand on her shoulder. "I don't know what possessed you, Miss Claus. Was he dreadfully angry?"

"Well. Yes."

Mr. Kleiner sighed. "One time he threatened to throw a young sales clerk down the stairs. I don't believe he would have done it, but he threatened, nonetheless. The poor lad's nerves were quite shaken. Never really got over it, to tell the truth. First he hid in the storeroom every time Mr. Carroll walked through the shop, and then he began to hide there all the time, because he said he never knew when Mr. Carroll would appear. I had to dismiss him." He shook his head regretfully. "I believe he moved west."

✳ ✳
✳

Jeremy handed her a bright garland of golden stars.
"Reach it around here, and I'll get it."

Holly twisted it up over a branch. "There. That's
lovely. Here it is."

"Thank you." He unwound it further. "So then
he's looking down all their throats and thumping
them on the back. He says Grub and Chick got the
beginnings of it, but he can fix 'em. And all the other
kids are strong as horses, he says. He was jawing on
about how we're an example of the benefits of fresh
air and how he's gonna bring Marty and me to a
meeting for showing to this doctor who don't believe
in it or something. And he told me where my lungs
are stored and all about what interesting stuff is in
'em."

"Did Lissy mind leaving?"

"She cried a little, but I said I'd come see her
every day, and bring the other kids around some.
I guess she was glad enough to not be going to a
hospital after what the doctor said. I thought for sure
he was going to make her."

"What changed his mind?"

"That little girl of his. Whew! She's a bossy one.
'No, sir,' she says, 'Lissy's coming home with us. Not

going to no hospital.' She was stomping all over, but her pa didn't punish her or nothing. He just said she had to look after Lissy herself if she felt so strong. And she says she will. Then he picks up Lissy like she ain't no heavier than a loaf of bread and carries her off to his house." He shook his head, remembering. "She took that doll you made her," he added. "Hey, toss me that little beady thing."

"That's a wreath. Here. I'm glad about Lissy. I hope that Dr. Braunfels can help her— Jeremy, dear, will you hand me the glass bird? The one with the tail?"

"Perhaps I can assist you, Miss Claus," a smooth voice interrupted. Hunter Hartman had returned. He looked up at her, perched upon the ladder, and smiled charmingly. "You look like the princess in the tower. But I suppose it's no use my asking you to let down your hair." His eyes probed her upswept curls.

"No use at all," said Holly. "This tower is only large enough for one."

"Here's that bird, Holly," Jeremy said loudly. He scowled at Mr. Hartman, who looked blandly back.

"Thank you, dear. What do you think? Is it enough? The trees don't like it when their limbs are overburdened," said Holly without thinking.

Jeremy snickered, but Mr. Hartman seemed

unaware that she had said anything unusual. "Yes, quite beautifully balanced," he said, squinting judiciously at the tree. It was a beautiful tree too, glinting with glass icicles and rings of golden stars.

Holly, stepping down from the ladder, reached gratefully for Mr. Hartman's proffered hand and found herself lifted to the floor. She looked up, startled; his face was very close, and his large gray eyes rested thoughtfully on hers. A second too late, as though he had just remembered to, he smiled, the corners of his wide mouth crinkling. She stepped back.

"Miss Claus?" he said softly. Behind him, Tundra rose to his feet.

"Yes, Mr. Hartman?"

"Perhaps you would—would"—he paused for a moment, his words lost, then took a deep breath— "be so kind as to assist me in my purchases now?"

Tundra sat down again.

"Of course. What do you need?"

Mr. Hartman thumped his pockets lightly and pulled forth a list. "Modeling clay, charcoal, and paints," he read.

Holly was conscious of a slight surprise. Who was to receive these gifts? Dutifully, however, she made her way to the art materials. "Modeling clay, charcoal, and paints," she said. "Watercolors, I suppose."

"Yes. Watercolors."

"Paper?"

"Pardon?"

"Do you need paper—for the charcoal and paint?"

"Oh." He seemed confused. "Yes. Paper. To be sure. Now. What's this?" He squinted. "Ah. A weaving set."

Holly turned to a nearby shelf. "We have two. One has a sweet little loom, you see? But it's rather complicated to work. The other is a hand loom, and it's much simpler. How old is your daughter?"

He stared and then barked with laughter. "A daughter! I have no daughter, child! Nor a son, nor a wife. No," he said, leaning toward her, "nor a wife. And I confess that I am rather glad of it at the moment."

Holly blushed. She didn't know what to say.

Mr. Hartman spoke more softly still. "I don't mean to embarrass you, my dear. It's just that you take my breath away." He smiled down anxiously, as if to ask her pardon.

Holly granted him a smile and held out the two weaving kits. "Which shall it be, Mr. Hartman?"

He looked at them briefly. "Both," he said, returning to his list.

Resolving not to inquire again about his purposes, Holly waited for his next instruction.

"Now, bears."

"We have a lovely selection of bears, right over here."

And so it continued. The pile of toys grew until it toppled over, and still Mr. Hartman consulted his list and asked for more. He wanted everything, it seemed: boats and trains and silly tin toys; drums and pipes and a horrible kazoo that made deafening squawks; a wooden farm; tin soldiers and a giant castle to put them all in; soft lambs and ducks and rabbits to cuddle; party crowns and mysterious packages that exploded into showers of candy and enough ornaments to cover three Christmas trees.

In one corner Tundra watched with fierce concentration. In another sat Jeremy, suffering from a vague discomfort he couldn't define. In between and around scuttled Mr. Kleiner who, when he was not helping other customers, looked on in disbelief at the growing mound of purchases and reproved himself for harboring suspicious thoughts of such a fine customer. And above, unseen by all, stood Mr. Carroll, his eyes fixed on the tall figure that stood over the slender one, noting the friendly smile that made Mr.

Hartman's face handsome and the answering smile on Holly's lips.

"All of them," Mr. Hartman was saying.

Holly laughed. "You're mad. Nobody needs five rubber ducks."

"I need five rubber ducks."

"But that will leave only one, and he'll be lonely."

"Make it six, then, if you wish."

"If *I* wish? Mr. Hartman, you must decide for yourself."

"I've never wanted a duck so much in my life as I want that duck," he said, his eyes resting on hers.

"I see, Mr. Hartman. Whatever you ask."

"I hope you know what I am really saying, Miss Claus."

"I really don't know, Mr. Hartman," said Holly.

"That's because you're an innocent."

"Not entirely," she protested. "It's just that I didn't grow up here and—and—I'm not accustomed to your ways."

He took the opening eagerly. "Have you been here long?"

"No, only a few days. I'm here on a—a—visit."

"But you'll be staying," he said, moving closer to her.

She edged away. "No. No, I'm leaving tomorrow."

There was a slight stir in the gallery, but neither of them heard it.

"But then you will have seen nothing of our city! It's the most exciting place on Earth, in my opinion. We live in a great era of progress, Miss Claus, and New York is the center of it. Before long we will lead the world in our invention and industry. And yet we don't forget the arts in New York—our music, fine pictures, and great literature are the equal of any! Let me show you!" he said impulsively, laying his hand on her arm. "Come out with me this evening! Have a taste of something other than this shop," he urged her, looking around the store with a touch of contempt. "See the world."

He could not have said anything more calculated to entice her. The world—how glorious it sounded! Something unknown and exciting and utterly unlike what she knew. Holly wavered—and then nodded. "Yes. I would like to. Thank you."

"How marvelous, Miss Claus! We'll go to the opera—I think you'll be quite impressed, not at all like the old Academy backwater—and supper afterward at Delmonico's. Will that suit you, Miss Claus?" He looked at her with glowing eyes.

"Yes," she said uncertainly. Was it proper? She simply did not know. She would have to rely upon her own sense. "Yes," she said more firmly. "Yes, it sounds delightful."

"Shall I call for you? At eight?"

Some sort of cautious bell seemed to sound within her, and she shook her head. "No, Mr. Hartman. I will meet you at the opera house."

"But I couldn't think of such a thing! A young lady alone! It would never do."

"I will meet you at the opera house or not at all," she said.

There was a quick adjustment in his face, a flicker of frustration. "Oh no, Miss Claus, don't think of it! I will meet you at the opera house. Eight o'clock. Does that suit?"

"That suits excellently."

"Then I'll just hop over to Broadway and get our tickets," he said, twitching his hat as if he longed to clap it on his head and be off.

Holly stared at him in amazement. "But what about your toys?"

"Oh. Yes." He looked over to the heap of toys without interest. "I'm done now. Just total it all up." He pulled a thick roll of bills from his pocket.

As this was Mr. Kleiner's task, Holly retired to the storeroom after repeated promises to Mr. Hartman that she would not forget their engagement. Tundra rose with extreme casualness and followed her.

She was waiting for him. "I know you don't like it," she began.

"On the contrary, I'm sure I'll enjoy it immensely," he said.

"Tundra, darling, you can't. They won't let you. You know they won't."

"Then, Holly, I have to ask you—why are you venturing with a stranger into a place where I can't follow you?"

"It's my last night in the mortal world, Tundra," said Holly pleadingly. Out in the shop, the bell jingled. He was gone. "I'll never have another chance to enjoy the things that other girls enjoy. Please. Just this once."

Tundra was silent. He was remembering a summer night years before, when she had cried because she could not join the party in the village. He could refuse her nothing. "I'll wait outside the doors for you, Holly. I'll follow the carriage. You'll know where I am."

Holly knelt and embraced him gratefully.

When they emerged from the storeroom, Jeremy was alone in the store. He jerked his head up, toward the gallery. "He's up there. Mr. Carroll wanted him." He shook his head grimly. "He didn't look none too jolly, either."

"I repeat, I want her dismissed."

"And I repeat that I shall not do it," said Mr. Kleiner nervously.

"Am I not the owner of this shop? Have I not the right to make decisions about the management of the place?" said Mr. Carroll, his face rigid with anger.

"Yes. You have that right. But I shall not be party to it," said Mr. Kleiner with growing vehemence. "The poor child does not deserve such treatment. She has labored more devotedly than any other employee in this shop's history. She has worked wonders with the arrangement of the store. She has charmed every customer she has encountered. And, if you want hard business facts, we have made more money in the last two days than we earned in the month previous! She has the heart of an angel, and if you knew even a part of the generosity she has displayed in these past days, you would be ashamed of your request!" Surprised at his own fervor, he snapped his mouth shut and scowled at his employer.

"She cannot stay," said Mr. Carroll through clenched jaws.

"Then you will have to dismiss her yourself, for I won't," replied Mr. Kleiner, and he turned on his heel to quit the room. But when he reached the door, he stopped and looked back at the man who sat staring at his own hands. He looked infinitely lonely. "It would be wrong, and you know it," Mr. Kleiner said. "No matter what has happened, you would never knowingly do wrong."

"I might. It's as though I'm compelled to—" He broke off and shook his head.

"I don't understand you, and I don't pretend to, but I have known you nearly all your life, and I am certain—yes, absolutely certain—that you will not betray the child you once were by choosing the path of cruelty. I am certain of it."

Mr. Carroll drew a long breath. "Then, Isaac, you are much more certain than I."

"That's because I am older and wiser," said Mr. Kleiner. "And now I will return to business."

Mr. Carroll nodded. When the door closed, he sat at his imposing desk for a few moments, resting his head in his hands. Sighing, he arose and approached his workroom. He picked up a thin piece of silver wire, looked at it idly, and put it down again. Then, with decisiveness, he turned and walked briskly out the door to resume his hidden observation post on the gallery overlooking the shop.

Chapter Twenty-one

HOLLY STARED AT the empty folds
of green silk.

"Miss Claus, please do come
along! It's nearly seven o'clock!" Mr.
Kleiner's voice called from the shop floor.

She turned the cloth over as if expecting to find
some overlooked pocket within. It remained green
and empty. "Where could they be?" she whispered.

"Wherever they are, it was undoubtedly Lexy's
idea," murmured Tundra. "I expect that she got bored
and persuaded the other two to go exploring with
her. It's just like her."

"But I can't leave without them."

"I don't see why not. Serves them right."

"Miss Claus!"

"Yes. Yes, I'm coming," said Holly, giving in. She gathered her things. "I'm sorry, Mr. Kleiner."

Tundra glanced at her shrewdly. She was up to something.

"That's quite all right, my dear. Now, you have your doll money?"

"Yes, sir."

"She give it all to me, Mr. Kleiner," contradicted Jeremy, "for the kids' dinner."

Mr. Kleiner turned to Holly with a frown. "Miss Claus, forgive me for interfering in your personal affairs, but you must keep some for yourself. I have also given Jeremy some compensation for his hard work."

"I kept a bit for myself, Mr. Kleiner. You needn't worry," said Holly, smiling at his anxiety. "Shall we be off?"

In a matter of minutes, Holly, Tundra, and Mr. Kleiner had waved good-bye to Jeremy, who was going to visit Lissy, and settled into the hansom cab with sighs of contentment. They sat back, absorbed in their own reflections. Mr. Kleiner, totaling and retotaling the day's astonishing profits in his head, soon fell into a light doze. Holly was imagining Lissy in the splendor of Dr. Braunfels's house. Perhaps she has a canopy bed, Holly mused. And a ruffled nightgown—

Her aimless gaze fell upon a tall figure striding along the sidewalk next to the cab. She could see only the back of his black overcoat, just one of the thousands of black overcoats that darkened the streets of New York City on a winter's day, but the stride was singular—and familiar. She leaned forward to see the face, but he had slipped around a little cluster of pedestrians into the shadow of a building. He was tall, that much was clear; he wore a smooth black bowler, and he had a large bundle under one arm. Was it Mr. Hartman? And if so, why was he walking so determinedly through the slush of Third Avenue?

Holly pressed her face against the smudged glass, but the cab was pulling ahead of the figure in the black coat, despite his swift pace. There was something terribly familiar about that walk, the swing of it. Was it Mr. Carroll? Suddenly Holly felt an intense wish for the pedestrian to be Mr. Carroll. She wanted to see him, to watch the shadows in his eyes without him knowing that she did so. She pulled down the little glass window and leaned out, hoping that one more glimpse would reveal the stranger to be her employer. But she was thwarted; the black coat her eyes were seeking halted before a granite staircase that led to a large, official edifice. Now he was climbing the stairs. The cab jerked to a stop at a corner, and Holly peered back toward the building. There were letters inscribed on it, which Holly read sideways: SAINT CECILIA'S HOME FOR FOUNDLINGS. And now the tall figure was descending the stairs at a great pace. She squinted, but all she could see was that the bundle was missing. Whoever it was—Mr. Hartman or Mr. Carroll—he had delivered something to the home for foundlings.

"What's a foundling?" she asked.

"What's that, my dear?" asked Mr. Kleiner, starting from his nap. "Foundlings? Orphans, you know. Children found without parents. Foundlings." He subsided back into his snooze, and Holly closed the window. The cab rumbled on.

Tundra nudged her inquiringly, but he couldn't ask what she had seen, and she was glad. She didn't want to talk. She was thinking of the door at the end of the hallway, of the great, dark clock face. She was thinking of his hands brushing away shavings of wood as he worked, and then his hands outstretched to hers for one electric moment in the shadowy corridor.

Her heart was beating rather rapidly.

Tundra observed her with a frown. Something was happening to her, he knew that much. But he could not guess what it might be. Her cheeks were pale, and her green eyes, which were fundamentally incapable of disguising their owner's soul, showed only that she had received some sort of shock. As he stared, confounded, she suddenly smiled. The color came flooding back into her cheeks. She had never looked more beautiful.

"My dear child, you must make haste. Have you anything to wear?" cried Mrs. Kleiner when they arrived.

Holly, flying up the stairs, halted. "What does one wear to the opera?"

"Why, your best, Miss Claus, your best!"

"Thank goodness for Lexy," Holly murmured, and ran up the steps with Tundra at her heels. A moment later she was clad in waves of golden silk. She rustled to and fro, inspecting the minute slivers of herself that she could see in the tiny mirror above the bureau. "Tundra," she asked plaintively, "do I look all right? Or do I look foolish?"

Tundra lifted his head and regarded her judiciously. "You don't look foolish," he said slowly. "You look like a queen."

Holly laughed at that, but then her face fell. "Oh no! I forgot about the opera house! How will my heart bear it?" She stared at him in dismay. "I'm already almost warm." She went to her window balcony and flung open the door. A shushing sigh of snow fluttered into her hair and, beckoned by the cool air, she stepped outside. She closed her eyes, raising her face to the eddies of gentle snow, and then, just as certainly as the snow shawl had circled her the night before, she felt herself enveloped in a light web of coolness. She opened her eyes and beheld the magic crystals, now embedded like jewels in the fabric of her dress, making a pattern of enchanted golden lace on the cascading silk. She peered into the night sky for the giver of this gift, and murmured, "Once again—always—thank you."

Ten minutes later she descended. When she entered the parlor, Mrs. Kleiner let out an involuntary gasp of admiration and Mr. Kleiner leaped to his feet as though pulled on puppet's strings. "My word!" he muttered, taking off his glasses.

"You're perfectly lovely. I've never seen such a color," said Mrs. Kleiner. "Where on Earth did you find it?"

"A friend gave it to me," said Holly honestly. "Good night, dear Mrs. Kleiner. Good night, Mr. Kleiner. Good night!"

"Where's your coat?" cried the lady of the house, scandalized, but Holly pretended not to hear, and, slipping out the door, she and Tundra found themselves out in the great city at night.

"I'll be right here," Tundra was saying. "Holly, are you paying attention? Right here, by this pillar."

"By this pillar," repeated Holly obediently. She nodded, but her eyes followed a monumental dowager in peacock-blue satin who was borne from her carriage on the arm of a smiling young man in a collar so stiff it seemed on the verge of slitting his throat. Holly looked on, enthralled. Tundra sighed and waited.

The dowager and her escort were absorbed into the gilded lobby of the Metropolitan Opera House. Exquisitely dressed ladies and gentlemen streamed toward the lustrous theater, and Holly's eyes were full of black broadcloth and dazzling white linen paired with explosions of brilliantly colored silk and velvet.

"Holly!" Tundra hissed through clenched teeth. He wasn't supposed to be talking, but the cream of society that flowed by him was so hypnotized by its own elegance that it could not be bothered to take note of a talking wolf. "I'll be here if you need me!"

Finally Holly pulled her eyes away from the crowd. He had her attention. "I know you will," she said.

Tundra was relieved. She had heard him. "Well," he said. "Go on, then. Have a good time." In the falling snow, he watched as she climbed the marble steps, her back straight and her steps light. He could not see her face, but he could see her effect on the crowd around her. Several dozen women looked once and then twice, their faces sharp with interest and curiosity. The men accompanying them looked once and then kept looking, furtively. A tall man, his smile boastful, stepped forward to claim her arm. Jealous eyes followed the slim figure clad in what seemed to be a cascade of liquid gold and her companion as they ascended the great staircase.

"Every man in the Metropolitan Opera House wishes he were in my shoes," Hunter Hartman said, glancing about. "You are magnificent." He lifted the hand that rested on his arm to his lips. "Look around you," he murmured. "Look at them watching you."

Holly looked; there were indeed a number of faces

turned toward her, but Hartman seemed to gloat excessively. It gave Holly a peculiar feeling, as though she was his possession to parade before the spectators. She lifted her chin defiantly and changed the subject. "What are we hearing tonight?"

"*Otello.*" He shrugged. "Not quite as cheerful an evening as I had hoped, though de Reszke is sure to be good."

Holly turned to him, delighted. "But this is wonderful!" she exclaimed. "I have always longed to hear one of Maestro Verdi's operas! And they say this is among his greatest!"

He looked at her alertly. "Where do you come from, child? How is it that you know of Verdi, but have never heard even one of his operas? The old man's written such a pile of them; they would seem unavoidable."

"Where I come from—" stammered Holly, blushing a little as she tried to find words. "It's very— very—forested, and there aren't any opera houses." She lifted her eyes to his and realized with surprise that he didn't believe her and he didn't care. His mouth was stretched into an odd smile.

He turned his head away and said, very softly, "Oh, how I am going to enjoy this evening."

"And so am I," said Holly.

He did not answer, but lifted her hand again, expertly turning the palm upward and pressing his warm lips against her wrist. A faint shudder of revulsion buzzed through her.

Their box, swathed in velvet of midnight blue and encrusted with gilt in every possible location, afforded Holly and Mr. Hartman an unobstructed view of the stage. It also afforded them a view of the Diamond Horseshoe, the semicircle of boxes that belonged to the aristocracy of New York, which were handed down from one generation to the next. Holly's eyes danced as she watched the Morgans and the Vanderbilts, resplendent in diamonds and icy in manners, nod to one another from their thrones. Down in the orchestra prowled what appeared to be an army of penguins; young men with plenty of money and perfectly cut evening clothes roved through the theater, stopping to flirt with any lady, young or old, of sufficient social standing to capture their interest. Holly's presence was having a rather strong effect upon this portion of the opera-going population; more than a dozen young men who had been cultivating their taste for ladies less decorative than wealthy found their inner economy upset by Holly's glowing smile and capricious curls. One Mr. Law peered through his opera glass and fumed, "Know the girl from somewhere. Can't quite put my finger on it. Who's that fellow she's with?"

"Never saw him before. Doesn't deserve her," grumbled young Mr. Knapp.

Holly, oblivious to the opera glasses trained upon her, was enjoying herself immensely. It was all so grand. The humming crowd, the ladies like gauzy butterflies, the lavish golden ceiling where muses wafted on gilded clouds, the whole bubbling world of it entered her blood like champagne. Catching sight of the most majestic of all the society queens, she leaned forward to touch Mr. Hartman's arm. "Look at her! Is that a belt of diamonds?" she whispered. "She can't possibly breathe!"

"That's Mrs. Astor," he replied. He looked down at Holly. "Do you know who she is?"

"No. Is she someone important?"

Mr. Hartman laughed and laid his hand casually over the rail of their box, pointing a finger in the direction of Mrs. Astor. As if pulled by an invisible rope, the regal head turned, and Mrs. Astor, appearing vaguely surprised, nodded toward their box. Mr. Hartman nodded coolly back. Mechanically the grand dame turned her eyes away.

"Do you *know* her?" asked Holly, impressed.

"I've met her once or twice," said Hunter Hartman.

And then the curtain began to rise. The lights dimmed, and the crowd hushed. Holly leaned forward, eager for every note, and as she did so, a slight disturbance several boxes away caught her attention. She glanced over—and instantly dropped her eyes, for there, not more than twenty feet from her, was Mr. Carroll, taking a solitary seat in a box. Secretively she looked in his direction, distracted by the sight of him removing a pair of opera glasses from the pocket of his evening jacket. He sat back in his seat, obviously prepared to enjoy the opera. She realized with relief and regret that he had not seen her. After a short internal struggle, she lifted her head. Let him see that she was not just a plain little shopgirl, but a young lady in an evening gown! She smoothed the golden folds of her dress.

That's enough fussing, she scolded herself. Just listen.

Soon she had forgotten everything but the music. The story of Othello and Desdemona unfolded, and Holly was lost in the inexorable tide of the characters'

Let him see that she was not just a plain little shopgirl,
but a young lady in an evening gown!

fates, watching with fascinated horror as the heart of Othello was dismantled by Iago for the sport of it. So intent was Holly upon the tragedy before her that the intermission, when it came, seemed a rude interruption. She looked around hazily, and Hunter Hartman, whose interest in the proceedings onstage appeared to be limited, smiled at her confusion. "Do you care to take a turn in the lobby? Or shall I bring you an ice?"

"Oh no!" said Holly vehemently. "I don't want anything but for it to begin again! It's wonderful! Aren't the voices beautiful?"

"No. You are."

She ignored him and stared at the dropped curtain. "I never imagined it would be so exciting," she murmured. "It makes me shiver." She held up a trembling hand.

"Permit me," said Mr. Hartman, capturing her hand in his.

Holly slipped from his grasp. "Mr. Hartman, I believe I would like that ice you mentioned," she said. Something cool would be helpful; the enchanted snow that glittered on her dress struggled against the pressing heat of thirty-six hundred people in evening dress.

"At your service, Miss Claus." He paused at the

small, gilded door. "I hate to leave a young lady without protection. I do hope you won't mind if I avail myself of the key. Many confounded young fools have been known to walk into a box without an invitation." He did not wait for her reply but exited quickly. She heard the golden key turn in the lock.

He really is rather strange, Holly decided. Always staring with those eyes, but he can't be bothered to listen to me. Odd. Maybe all mortal men are that way. No, that's not true. Not Mr. Kleiner. Not Dr. Braunfels. They listen. And Mr. Carroll?

Shyly she stole a look at his box. He was leaning forward, scanning the seats below. He stood and peered up at the boxes above him. Frowning, he resettled himself in his seat and glared at the small program in his hands.

Whatever can he be about? Holly wondered, watching him shred the little paper book with an abstracted air. And why doesn't he look this way?

Click. The sound of the key turning in the lock brought her back to the present. Mr. Hartman delivered her ice with gallant inquiries as to her comfort and general well-being. Feeling somehow guilty, she rewarded him with a smile and consumed the delicious coolness in silence. She was relieved when the lights dimmed and the curtain rose again.

Her relief, however, was short-lived; from then on the terrible descent of Othello was almost more than she could stand. When the villain ground the fallen hero under his heel, Holly had to tear her eyes away. She glanced at her boxmate. He was more absorbed in this spectacle than in any other the opera had provided, and he seemed to know the music well, for he swayed in time to Iago's taunts. Unnerved, Holly looked toward Carroll's box. The lonely occupant sat still as a statue, his jaw set, his eyes lost in shadows.

The last mournful strains of song finished, and the house erupted into crashing applause. Holly, clapping fervently, stole another look at the nearby box. It was empty.

It was a small world, the one that glittered so brightly. The same elegant women and men who had occupied the boxes of the opera house now swept toward the cream and gold brocade seats of Delmonico's. They stopped to chat here and there, leaning confidentially down to receive or dispense gossip, laughing in low voices, extending a well-kept hand in greeting. Holly watched, but she found she was beginning to wish for somebody—anybody—who looked just a little bit different. She felt a sharp longing for Tundra, who cared nothing for any of this kind of show and thought humans should have fur. But while she was in the most famous restaurant in New York, he was outside, sitting uncomfortably in the snow. She sighed inwardly and tried to attend to Mr. Hartman. He was telling her stories of his cosmopolitan youth in Paris and London, and though she had always longed to travel to those grand cities, she found herself strangely unmoved by his tales of balls, royal receptions, yacht races, and fox hunts.

"—only to discover that it was the duke himself!" Mr. Hartman concluded a story she should have been listening to. Holly smiled noncommittally. He looked at her with a flash of impatience before his face relaxed into a warm smile. "Are you tired, Miss Claus?" he asked, moving his chair closer to hers.

"No, really, I'm not," she said, sitting up straighter than ever. "I'm still in a daze from that sad, sad story, I think."

"What, the opera?" He seemed to find this amusing. "Just a tale, child. Just a story. You shouldn't take it so to heart."

"How can you not?" Holly asked. "Didn't it stir your feelings?"

He shrugged. "The male animal is not so easily stirred as that, my dear. An opera, even one by your Maestro Verdi, cannot evoke in me even one fraction of the emotion that a moment's glimpse of you can, and does."

"A moment's glimpse of me?" she repeated. "I don't think I understand the things you say, Mr. Hartman."

In reply, his eyes wandered slowly over her, dropping from her eyes to her mouth to the escaped tendrils of hair that curled at her neck. Holly felt a flush of embarrassment rising in her cheeks, but Mr. Hartman continued his slow perusal of her face, and she lowered her eyes to the snowy tablecloth. He reached out and gently took her chin between two fingers. "Look at me," he demanded. She pulled away from his warm hand and met his eyes. "I think you understand me perfectly," he continued. "I think you know that I find you bewitching, that you have not left my mind for a moment since I saw you in the park two days ago, and that I have done everything in my power to put myself in your way, and that I will not rest until I make you mine." He drew his thumb along the edge of her jaw, watching, with a pleased smile, the bewildered alarm in her face.

"I—I know none of this!" said Holly quickly. "And I don't want to know it." She battled an urge to run from the table, for that would be rude. She shook her head. "Please, Mr. Hartman, take your hand away. I don't like it. And I never saw you in the park," she added.

"Mmm. But I saw you," he said. "And I followed you to that wretched shop."

"So the toys you bought today . . . they weren't for—anyone?"

"They were for me," he said. "They gave me a way to be with you. Wasn't I clever?" He pulled a thin blue box from his coat pocket and set it on the tablecloth. "Look, I bought you a toy too." He flicked the catch and the box sprang open. There, on a bed of velvet, lay a magnificent collar of diamonds and pearls.

"It's very beautiful," said Holly politely, "but I could never accept such a gift."

"Nonsense," he said, picking it up and looking closely at the diamonds. "It will look splendid on you. You really have quite an elegant neck, my dear. You will be an ornament to society, I guarantee it." He stood up and moved behind her chair. She felt his warm hands fumbling on her locket's chain. "How do you take this ridiculous thing off?" he muttered.

"There's no clasp."

"Sit down," said Holly tensely. "Sit down at once."

Mr. Hartman laughed and sat. "What is it, Holly? May I call you Holly, my dear?"

"No! No, you may not!"

Mr. Hartman's complacent smile faded. "I see," he said angrily. "You don't want to be won too easily. Come, my dear, don't be foolish. It's the life you want. I can give it to you. In return, all I ask is—you."

Holly stared at him, outraged. "How do you presume to know what sort of life I want? You know nothing about me. Nothing! But I will tell you one thing—I don't want the life you seem to be offering me."

Hunter Hartman shifted in his seat and looked sullenly at the untouched glass of champagne upon the table. "You want the necklace, don't you?" he said. "Go ahead and take it. It doesn't have to mean anything."

"What are you talking about?" asked Holly vehemently. "I don't want your necklace!" She stood, her cheeks pale now with anger. "Good night, Mr. Hartman."

"No!" he cried, seizing her hand. He stood, too, and his face was twisted with panic. "No, Miss Claus!

Please sit! It was my fault! I was too pressing! I ask nothing but to be in your presence!" He saw Holly's startled look. "Here, I'll throw the necklace away if it offends you. See?" He tossed it on the table. "Of course you wouldn't want to exchange your lovely locket for such a vulgar collar. I can understand that perfectly," he babbled, "perfectly. For your locket is charming, charming. Yes, charming." He swallowed, and she saw thin beads of perspiration crawl down his cheeks. He stammered on, "It is very like one my grandmother wore, may God rest her soul. Bless me, the similarity is remarkable. Would you be so kind as to permit me to inspect it?" Without waiting for an answer, he reached his hand out to touch the old gold.

But Holly was too quick for him. She leaped up and swiftly walked through the restaurant and out into the snowy night.

"It was Herrikhan," she concluded. Her voice was steady now.

The hansom cab rattled and squeaked. Finally Tundra said, "I knew that he would come here. I knew it and I dreaded it, but now that the thing has happened, I cannot think what to do. If you hide, he can find you. We cannot leave until Nicholas comes tomorrow. There is no safe place."

"I know."

Tundra considered. "Holly, remember this: the locket cannot be removed by force, but only by your consent. He has tried trickery and failed. Next he will try blackmail. You must not let him succeed. Promise me."

Holly's eyes were wide and frightened in the gloom. "No," she said. "I'm not going to promise that."

"Holly." Tundra sounded tired. "You must."

"No! I'm not going to let him—let him"—she couldn't bring herself to say the word—"hurt you if I have the power to stop him. Even without the locket, he can't take me away without my agreement. Remember? I'm not without power. I have to choose him. And I won't."

"Holly, you know it comes to the same thing," said Tundra. "Listen to me. If you lose this battle because of me, it will kill me. I've been your guardian for sixteen years; please, I beg you, don't become mine. I beg you."

"I'm not promising anything," said Holly, her mouth trembling.

Click. The little door in the roof of the carriage opened. "That's four times around the block, miss," said a beery voice. "Don't you want to go some- wheres?"

Tundra listened with surprise as Holly gave the address of the toy shop. The little door snapped shut. "Is that sensible?" he asked. "Perhaps the park would be safer."

"I don't want anything to happen to the children," said Holly. "And I've made a decision. Just now, I made it. It's no use hiding, we both know that. So I'll do what I hoped to do. I'm going to the store to find Empy and Lexy and Euphemia, just as I had planned. And then I'll go to the Kleiners' house. And tomor- row will be my last day in the Empire City, and I'll say good-bye to all my dear ones here"—her voice broke—"and then I'll go home. And I'll know that I helped Jeremy find his way, and Bat and Louise and Phoebe and Lissy and all the others. And if—if— something happens between now and then—well, then it will. I'm not going to give in." She felt stronger as she said the words and her fear began to ebb.

"That's right, Holly," said Tundra softly. "That's right. That's what bravery is—being afraid and going forward anyway."

She laid her hand on his head as the cab clattered on.

The key that Mr. Kleiner had given her turned smoothly in the lock, and they stepped inside the silent shop. The pale glow of the moon illuminated a small area near the window, but its weak light could not penetrate far, and the snow-dusted shelves and tables were just ghostly outlines in the shadowy dark. A few silvery snowflakes spiraled lazily to the floor, and the pungent spice of fir needles scented the room with Christmas. Holly strode purposefully to the storeroom with Tundra at her heels.

She lit a candle and saw the empty roll of silk laying where she had left it on the tall table.

"Boo!" shrieked three tinny voices. A tiny fox, owl, and penguin leaped out from behind a basket of teacups and saucers. "Fooled you!"

"It's not the time for child's play," began Tundra angrily. "Herrikhan is here!" As he explained, the three little creatures, now shamefaced and miserable, turned to Holly for forgiveness.

"Please, Holly, forgive us for being so silly!" began Alexia.

"Holly, dear, if only you could fly away," cried
Euphemia.

In silent despair, Empy butted his head against
Holly's hand until she petted him, a distracted look
upon her face.

"Where shall we go? What shall we do?" Alexia
was wailing when suddenly Holly interrupted her as
though she heard nothing.

"I'm going upstairs," she announced.

"What?" croaked everyone but Tundra.

"Upstairs. I'll be back." She slipped off the stool.

"But he's up there," hissed Lexy.

"I know," said Holly, her face unreadable.

"Go," said Tundra. "Go on. We'll wait."

The silk of her dress rustled over the carpet as she
ascended the darkened stairs. She was guided only by
the ticking of the clock above her, which grew louder
as she climbed. At the top of the gallery, she laid her
hand upon the balcony and edged her way toward the
velvet curtains she knew lay somewhere in the shadows. When the tips of her fingers brushed against the
yielding softness, she moved forward. This time she
felt protected inside the thick waves of velvet, and for
a childish moment she wanted to hide there forever.
She pushed aside the soft folds and found herself

standing in the wood-paneled hallway. Lighted candles
stood on a small table nearby, and they shed a glowing
light along the passage. As before, the dark doors that
lined the hall were closed. There—at the end—was
what she wanted. She moved forward cautiously,
trying to hush the whisper of her skirts, until she
stood again before the massive timepiece. It was
mysterious and haunting, its lovingly carved hands
halted at ten minutes before four. And there was something else. Something that Holly had not seen before.
Down below the clock's face was a carved wooden
scroll, unfurled, and written upon it, in capital letters,
were the words *Love Conquers Time*. Holly touched
the gleaming wood, tracing the carvings with her fingers. It was like a portal to another world, a magical
door that led to a unknown land, a beautiful place. It
was the world Mr. Carroll lived in. She wanted more
than anything to enter the room beyond, for it
seemed to hold the missing piece of her heart. She
rested her head against the shining wood. Then, with
golden silk spread around her like a pool of water, she
raised her head. There was no knob but, of course,
there wouldn't be. Slowly her slender white hand
crept across the smooth wood, searching for a tiny,
secret latch hidden within a scroll or festoon.

Absorbed in her quest, she did not hear the quiet footfalls behind her. She did not feel the dark eyes watching her. It was not until his hand reached around hers to lightly touch the number three that she realized he was there. With a gasp, she turned to face his wrath, and found him looking down at her. He said just one word. "Why?"

"I'm sorry," she began, breathlessly. "I had to see it one last time. The door, I mean. I know you don't like it. I'm sorry. It seems like magic to me—and you made it—and—I'll go now. I won't come again." Hurriedly she gathered up her skirts, not daring to look at him.

"Wait," he said in a low voice, his dark eyes shielded. "You were trying to find the latch, weren't you?"

"Yes," she whispered. "It seemed to me that the door would lead me into an enchanted world. I wanted to go there. I wanted to be safe."

His lips twisted into a smile. "I don't think you would find it safe. And it's not exactly an enchanted world. However, I have given you your wish—I've opened the door. You will be my first visitor. May you find more pleasure there than I." He extended his hand, and Holly felt the now-familiar current pass between their palms. Quickly he let go of her hand and pushed against the door. The face of time split in

Holly touched the gleaming wood, tracing the carvings
with her fingers.

half, and Holly stepped through.

Bursts of colored light met her eyes as she crossed the threshold. She drew in her breath sharply, for what she saw exceeded her wildest imaginings. The chamber was a carnival of light and movement, a whirling universe of toys that spun and danced across the floor, walls, and ceiling. Defying gravity and the known laws of physics were brilliantly painted galaxies and solar systems that revolved seemingly of their own accord. Winged chariots and tiny, wiggly creatures dove and plummeted among them, buzzing and whirring excitedly. A battalion of metallic beasts alternately flashed and honked across the floor. Lights twinkled and blazed from small boxes that spoke and sang in mechanical voices. Buttons gleamed upon bigger boxes that displayed moving images. Over and above the cheerful cacophony were fur-covered animals that marched, stood on their heads, and mooed, growled, or roared. Musical instruments played themselves, metal birds flew through the air, and above it all, a thousand electric stars shone radiantly.

Holly was amazed. It was all so bright and wild and—impossible. "But this is magic! How did you—? How could you—?" She did not even know where to begin.

He looked around him without much enthusiasm. "I'm an inventor." He shrugged. "I made them."

"But it's a whole world! Look at your stars! Look at all the lights—and how on Earth does that box talk?" she said, pointing.

"I could explain it if you had a year to listen. Would you be satisfied if I said they are the toys of the next century? These are the things that children will be playing with fifty years from now." He picked up a silver automaton that blazed blue light and then tossed it to the ground. "If they still play at all."

Holly stared at him. "Aren't you proud of it?" she asked tentatively. "You've invented all these marvelous, exciting toys, and yet, you seem—"

He looked into her eyes. "How do I seem? Rude? Impossible? Mad? All three have been suggested."

The weight of his gaze was almost unbearable, but Holly returned it as steadily as she could. "You seem to be in despair," she said finally.

Something melted in his face. He drew a long breath, never taking his eyes from her. "Who *are* you?" he asked incredulously, and then answered himself immediately, "No—don't answer—I don't want to hear that you're from Maine or whatever it was that you told Isaac. Just be what you are"—he looked

*"Would you be satisfied if I said they are the toys
of the next century?"*

apprehensive—"as long as you are real."

"I'm real," Holly said.

His eyes clung to hers. "How is it, then, how is it that you know me so well? But no—I'm afraid that if I try to find out, you'll leave. I don't know how to keep you here, and I want you to stay. No one sees. No one knows. But you stand in the middle of my secret prison and read my mind. For this is a prison, and the worst of it is that I made it myself." The words tumbled forth awkwardly, and Holly felt certain that he had not spoken so much in years. "Perhaps you know that already? You don't have to answer! Just come—come here, and I will show you the thing that has made me what I am." Pressing a single knob on the wall, he silenced the whizzing toys and led her to a simple black box that rested on a large table. It was approximately the size of a suitcase and, aside from a door on one side, it was plain and bare.

"What is it?" asked Holly curiously.

He looked at the box with loathing. "It doesn't have a name. It's a monster. I made it years ago, using Mr. Edison's telegraphic tubes and an incandescent screen. I thought I was creating a means of transferring photographic images over the telegraph, but what I got was something altogether different." He fell silent.

Holly waited.

"Altogether different," he repeated. "It doesn't show photographs that record past events. It shows the future. It tortures me." Holly glanced at him quickly. "Oh yes, you're quite right to think I've lost my mind. Even *I* thought I had lost my mind. And I may lose it yet. Because I can't really explain how it works, though I have some ideas. And I don't know if I can make another because I won't. But one thing I do know is that what I see when I look inside is the world to come—that much I know, because I have seen things come to pass—material things, events, even individual stories have played before my eyes and then happened in the real world." He smiled. "Isn't it funny? I still call this world the real one."

Holly leaned toward the box, thinking of her telescope. "Do you control it? I mean, can you make it show you a certain date or place?"

He almost laughed. "What an extraordinary person you are! You don't question my sanity at all! You simply ask, quite intelligently, whether I can direct it." His face grew serious again. "But no, I cannot. I don't know what year I'm looking at. Sometimes, from the dress and look of the people, I seem to be near our own time. Sometimes, it is altogether different than today." He shivered slightly. "It gets worse and worse."

"What do you mean?"

"That's the torture, don't you see? What's going to happen is the abyss. I see people stumbling about mindlessly, their faces petrified in horror, both hopeless and terrified. I see the world without love or charity, people striving only to force one another into submission." He paused, unable to meet her eyes. "The children, Miss Claus—the children are destroyed. They learn violence and teach it; there is no hope, or joy, or play, or laughter. They are stupefied with medicines or brutalized by harshness. The world that we know is gone. The dreams are gone. And I can only watch."

"Let me see it," said Holly.

"Miss Claus, I don't think you could bear it."

Her eyes darkened. "It's amazing what you can bear," she said. "Let me see."

He looked at her gravely, and then opened the door of the box and drew up a chair. Holly sat. Inside the dark cube was a sheet of glass, and upon this sheet a series of moving pictures jerked along. As she became accustomed to the darkness, Holly made out a shadowy street thronged with people and lined with buildings whose tops scraped the sky and blocked out the sunlight. The pedestrians stumbled along with uniform movements, their shoulders hunched. They slung themselves forward, each foot placed on the spot that the foot ahead had vacated. They watched the ground, except for some of the children, who looked fearfully to the dripping white sky. A boy darted ahead to pull something from the sludge at the end of the street. As he knelt, one of the bypassers kicked at him; he fell and lay where he had fallen. Figures trudged by him.

"You see their faces? Blank—blank and empty. Like doll faces."

"That's why you hate dolls," Holly murmured.

"I used to like them, but now they remind me of this."

Holly turned back to the black box. In a way, she thought, it's like a dark version of my telescope at home. It shows only the vicious things, the evil things, instead of the good things I witnessed. It has broken his heart. He cannot bear to think that it will all come to this. But will it? Something in her resisted the pictures she saw. She thought of her telescopic vision of the Empire City—how beautiful it had looked. The people smiled and the city gleamed with benevolence and prosperity. But the truth was otherwise. She remembered the children in the park, half-frozen and hungry, Jeremy's tears in the carriage, and the pink-faced young man who had nearly whipped Bat. Those were truths her spyglass had never told. She glanced at the screen again—and she thought, This is not the truth. Or at least, not the whole truth. Like an echo, she heard Sofya's wise voice in her ears. "There is not one certain future, that much I know. Each of our lives creates what is to come. . . ." Holly lifted her eyes from the black box. It had been up in the turret, that day that she had learned of the curse, the day that Sofya told her that she would learn what she must do to become an immortal. "Every time you make a choice, you make the future," she had said.

Holly looked up at Mr. Carroll with shining eyes. "No."

"No? No what?" he asked.

"This isn't the future. At least, it isn't the only future, because there isn't only one. A great and powerful woman once told me that the future doesn't move in one single direction; instead it's a maze, a puzzle that changes and grows each time one of the players chooses one path over another. Don't you see? This thing"—she waved at the box—"shows you what might happen. But it's a warning. It's meant to teach you how to live so that this will *not* be the future. You see?" She looked searchingly at him. "You were able to make this machine because you have the power to make the future different. Every time you make a choice, you make the future."

He looked skeptical. "How do you know you're right?"

She thought and then said slowly, "I don't know I'm right. We can't ever know, but why would the elders give us souls if we had no power to use them? Listen, I grew up, far away, among people who had done good in the world. Each of them had the power to change the course of the future, sometimes just a little, sometimes a great deal. And they did. Each of them made the world different; each created a new world. The future changes all the time—I know it does, even if I can't explain it!" Her mouth trembled. She wanted so much for him to believe her. His face remained closed as he listened, but she saw the trouble in his eyes lighten.

"On the contrary," he said haltingly. "You explain it very well. I could almost believe you. I have lived so many years without hoping for anything except a way out of the world. But perhaps you are right—" He broke off. "If I could only be certain that what you say is true."

"What else is faith for?" asked Holly.

His face softened further. "Yes. What else is faith for? Why should I have faith in you? You come from—from— Where is this place you come from?"

"Don't ask me, for I can't tell you. It's not Maine."

"All right," he said, almost cheerfully. "You come from a mysterious place and you turn my misery upside down. Why should I believe in you?"

Holly said gently, "Because it lessens your despair. Because what I say makes sense to your heart."

"When you say it, it does," he murmured. "Don't leave," he said abruptly.

"How did you know?" said Holly, flustered. And then, "I must."

"I heard you telling that vile man," he said savagely. "Why did you go to the opera with him, anyway? He's a scoundrel."

Holly looked at him demurely. "He *asked* me."

Mr. Carroll burst out laughing. "I should have asked you, shouldn't I?"

"Since you were going anyway," said Holly with a small smile.

"Did you see me? I looked for you everywhere."

"But you left before the end."

"Couldn't bear it."

Holly smiled luminously at him. He smiled back.

"Don't leave," he said softly, holding out his hand. She placed her palm in his, and they stared silently at their joined hands. "Strange," he murmured. He bent his head down to hers. "Why did you say that this afternoon?"

"What did I say?" she asked, knowing what he meant.

"You said, 'Why do you keep coming back?' What did you mean by that?"

"I feel—as though I know you," Holly said.

His lips were near her ear as he whispered, "I think you must."

I don't want to leave you, she thought. But what she said was, "Show me more of your toys." Far away, in another world, the clock chimed two.

Mr. Carroll seemed to be shedding years with each passing minute. He smiled and said, "Do you want to see the ones I like the best? They're much better than this silly stuff." He kicked a flying machine.

"Yes, please."

He approached a large cabinet and unlocked its door. "When I was a boy, I made my own toys, carvings mostly. Partly it was because my mother didn't have money to spend on such things, but also because

I loved to do it. The Christmas that I was ten, I made animals. The idea was that they would be our Christmas decorations, but there was something special about them. That was the Christmas after my father died, and—" He stopped and turned to look at Holly. "I don't know why I'm telling you this. Here they are." Tenderly, he placed four small wooden figures into her hands: a wolf, a fox, an owl, and a penguin. "Look, that one is rather like yours. That beast you call a dog."

Holly stared in disbelief. It was Tundra, down to his tail. Lexy, with her sharply pointed face. Euphemia, looking as though she had lost something. And Empy, his eyes wide and adoring. Each well-loved little animal was a perfect replica of its subject. Holly held her breath.

"There was another wolf," Carroll was saying. "But I lost her one day, not too long after I made her." He frowned.

"What's your name?" asked Holly urgently.

"Pardon me?"

"Your name, your given name?"

"Christopher. Christopher Winter Carroll. Why?" He smiled indulgently at her stunned face.

"How old are you?"

"You're full of impertinent questions, miss. Twenty-eight. Almost twenty-nine."

Holly's voice dropped to almost a whisper. "Was there anything else about that Christmas? The year you were ten? Did you write a letter to Santa Claus?"

An odd look came over Mr. Carroll's face. "Yes. My first. I didn't know how to do it, and in any case I didn't want anything. So I asked Santa Claus what he wished for Christmas." His laugh was slightly forced. "He wrote me back, too. I remember."

"He did?" Holly said breathlessly.

"Well, I'm sure it was my mother, really. The letter said that I had given him a gift he would treasure for eternity. And at the bottom of the letter, he wrote 'Love Conquers Time.' I remember thinking about that for—so long." He looked at Holly intently. "My dear mother died soon after that, you see, and I used to wish that love could really stop time, and she would come back to me. I was only a boy," he added to excuse himself.

"Do you still have it?"

"What—the letter?" Embarrassment tinged his voice. "Yes."

"May I see it?"

He looked at her quizzically. "I suppose so." He

Tenderly, he placed four small wooden figures into her hands.

reached into a small compartment within the cabinet and pulled forth a gold watch and a faded letter.

Time collapsed. The handwriting on the worn envelope was her father's. Holly could hear Nicholas's rich voice unfurling the old tale: "There was a boy. A boy named Christopher, who lived in the Empire City and sent me a letter. In that letter he asked me a question that I had never been asked before. He asked me if there was anything I wished for, anything I wanted and did not have. And do you know what I wished for? I wished for you, Holly. I wished for you."

"Are you all right? You look awfully pale."

"I'm all right," Holly said unsteadily. She gazed up into his gray eyes, her certainty growing with each moment. Her heart was pounding. That's why she had seemed to know him. That's why she had longed to see him. He was her beginning and he would be her eternity.

"Holly, come back." He put his hands on her shoulders, a little anxiously.

She lifted her head and smiled radiantly. "I'm here."

"Do you want to sit down? I have a chaise over here." He gestured to a long chair covered in boxes and books. "It's very comfortable. Or, well, it will be in just a minute." Hastily he swept the assemblage to the floor. "Please, sit. You must be dreadfully tired. Don't faint."

A wave of exhaustion swept over Holly. The chair looked temptingly soft and comfortable. *It will just be a minute. I'll just sit down for a minute.* "Thank you. I'll rest for a moment and then go."

With a sigh, she settled into the cool silk arms of the sofa. "Would you mind terribly opening a window?" she asked.

"Fresh air? Good idea." He strode to the window and opened it, and a blast of icy wind entered. "Is that better?"

There was no answer. He turned to find his guest asleep. Quietly he drew a chair to the center of the carpet and sat in it, watching Holly sleep.

Chapter Twenty-two

NEVER IN THE HISTORY of the Land of the Immortals had there been such a hush on the day before Christmas. For as long as anyone could remember—and some of them had memories that stretched many centuries—the day that led to Christmas Eve was a time of bustle and rush. Last-minute bows were tied, music swelled from every home, and kitchens began to hum and bubble with activity. This year, all was quiet. In the workshops, gylfyns and goblins efficiently packed toys for delivery, and Donner discussed flight patterns with Comet, but these were the only signs of the coming Christmas journey. The streets were deserted. No bells sounded from the towers. Delicious aromas did not curl from chimneys. Even the fairies sat soberly in their delicate, cobwebby palaces, waiting. They were all waiting.

Up in the castle, Nicholas, Viviana, and Sofya had spent nearly every moment of the last three days in Holly's room, taking turns peering through the enchanted telescope. Intently they had watched as Holly arrived in the Empire City and brought the compassion of her heart to the mortal world. At first there had been a few smiles, a little laughter, but now they simply watched, waiting for Herrikhan to finish the task he had begun so many years before. Sofya had known almost immediately that the genial Mr. Hartman was Herrikhan in disguise. There was something about the way he looked at Holly that wasn't quite human. She focused closely on his mouth, then his hair, where the little band of silver twinkled furtively; then she handed Nicholas the telescope, shaking her head.

Nicholas gazed into the glass for a long time. "It's him," he agreed. He walked to the window and stared without seeing at the snow outside. There was noth-ing he could do. There was nothing anyone could do until Christmas Eve.

Finally that day had dawned. Nicholas and Viviana sat stiffly on a sofa, their hands clasped, their eyes wide and dry. Sofya stood at the window, squinting into the white sky, trying to remember what was supposed to happen next. After a while, she gave up; there were simply too many different endings. They waited. The clock struck seven.

The clock struck seven, and Holly awoke with a gasp of terror. Frantically she brushed away the phantom fingers that coiled, dry and sinewy, around her neck and wound up through her hair. She sat up, tearing, clawing—at nothing. The only sound was that of her own panting breath. Weak sunlight streamed in through an open window, catching on a clutter of shining toys that lay on the floor. Holly stared at them fixedly, disentangling the threads of nightmare and reality that held her until memory returned in a flood. "Ohhh," she breathed, sitting up.

It was early yet, and all the world was quiet. Her eyes fell upon Christopher, fast asleep in an uncomfortable-looking chair in the center of the rug, and she smiled tenderly. He was wearing a heavy coat with a fur collar against the cold; she reflected that he must have put it on rather than close the window she had asked him to open, and this little mark of consideration brought a tightness to her throat. Everything will be decided today, she reflected. Then the unfathomable thought: This may be the last time I see him. Quietly she gathered up her rustling gown and tiptoed to his chair. She knelt beside him, learning his face. He looked much younger with his eyes closed, she decided. Less haunted, more like a boy. More like the boy who had written the letter to Santa Claus. She shook her head in wonderment. He stirred restlessly, and she caught her breath. Let him sleep.

She rose and walked from the room. Through the clock face she went again, feeling as though she was returning from a hundred-year voyage. On she walked, through the dark hall, the velvet curtains, and down into the toy shop, astonished to find that the walls and rugs and toys had remained the same while her universe had been changed entirely.

They would have been an odd sight, if there had been anyone but the pigeons to see them. Holly in her golden gown walked through the snowy streets talking absorbedly to the wolf at her side. Actually she was talking to all four of her friends, telling them of the wondrous inventions of the world behind the great door, of the malevolent black box that showed a dark future, and of the great discovery that Mr. Carroll was none other than the Christopher they had heard of so many, many times before. On and on she talked, but there was one thing she could not find a way to describe, and that was the new feeling that sang inside her. The little animals, listening from within the satchel, guessed that something was afoot, but Tundra, who could see her face, knew for certain that Holly was in love.

Finally Lexy, from inside the satchel, interrupted Holly to inquire sharply, "Why are we walking around in the freezing cold, Holly? Do you have any idea where you're going?"

Holly burst out laughing. "You're right, Lexy! I had forgotten! We're going to Mrs. Kleiner's so I can change my clothes and get back to the toy shop when it opens." And see him again, again, again, she added to herself.

And see him again, added Tundra to himself. Though he said nothing, Holly's happiness filled him with dread. It was one more obstacle between her and safety, one more reason she would be reluctant to leave this world. Over and over, like a charm against fear, he pictured her stepping into the sleigh next to Nicholas. That was all—one foot on the runner, the other lifting up out of the snow, her hands reaching out to clasp her father's. Just let that happen, he said to himself. Just let that come true.

The door of the boardinghouse creaked warningly as they entered, and Holly could smell the delicious scent of warm muffins and coffee wafting from the kitchen, but a sudden doubt about the propriety of appearing in her evening gown at seven-thirty in the morning assailed her. After an exchange of nods, Holly and Tundra and the satchel made their way up the carpeted stairs without a sound. Silently they proceeded down the hallway to Holly's room and slipped in the door.

"We did it!" whispered Holly exultantly to Tundra. "No one's the wiser!"

"I wouldn't be too certain, my dear," said a soft, whistling voice in the corner of the room. "I, for one, am distinctly wiser than I was last night."

Holly froze. Tundra, at her side, felt his heart begin to hammer against his chest. A dark figure rose from a chair and walked gracefully to the window. The curtain was pulled aside with a swift motion, and they stood, facing a smiling Hunter Hartman.

"Your rejected swain, in the flesh," sang the strange, whistling voice that seemed ill-matched to the bulk and height of the man. "Do I surprise you, my dear? Do forgive me"—he giggled a little—"but I wished to repay the surprise I endured last night with one of my own. I must have my little joke."

There was something silky and servile in the speech that filled Holly with contempt. "Get out," she said. "Get out or I'll call for help."

His laughter was more frightening than threats. "Get out? I don't think so. And," he added, his face suddenly growing cold, "I'll kill anyone who walks through that door, so be careful whom you call." He saw that she shivered. "Good. I'm glad you are so sensible. Now, dearest, let us discuss the events of last night before we proceed. I admit that I was wrong about you, I admit it handsomely. I was under the impression—which I now recognize as mistaken— that you were attracted to the glamour of mortal life. The telescope—my gift to you, for which I was never thanked, by the way—was designed to dwell on that very aspect of human exchange, and when I saw you peering through it night and day for all those years, I grew quite certain that you were bedazzled by the lives of the great and grand."

Hartman smiled, showing brilliant white teeth inside his dark mouth. "I thought that growing up in that musty old castle surrounded by those insipid, sugary little goblins and fairies, not to mention your insufferable father"—Holly put one hand warningly on Tundra's head—"that you would *welcome* a little light and life. But apparently, I was wrong." He glared at her with disgust. "You're even worse than they are. All that mucking about in the park with filthy urchins and distributing dollies to the mob should have told me. But perhaps I was infatuated." He snickered. "So I thought to tempt you with earthly delights—a brush with high society, a nod from Mrs. Astor and, as the final blow, a bauble that would serve the dual purpose of winning your heart and allowing me to remove that infernal locket." His narrow eyes rested on the necklace at Holly's throat. "My goals did not appear unreasonable, but I reckoned without your lamentable purity of spirit, and—well, you know the rest."

"And so now—?" Holly said, trying to keep her voice from shaking.

"Now, sweet, I will prove my generosity by offering you one more chance. Come with me, Holly, and I will give you anything in all the world that you desire."

Holly shifted nervously. She and Tundra exchanged glances. This was too easy. "No. I will not," she said.

He ran one finger around the inside of his collar. "These clothes drive me mad," he remarked conversationally. "You say no. Very well. I will ask you once more. Just once more. Holly, will you come with me and be my bride? Think carefully before you answer."

Holly shook her head silently.

He smiled. "Your answer does not surprise me. Nor does it displease me. This way will be much more thrilling for me, though, of course, less enjoyable for you. But that's not my fault. Always remember, I offered you a way out. Now, the first thing is to remove this disgusting flesh." Before Holly's terrified eyes, he raised his hands to his forehead and dug his nails into his skin. Then he pulled, grunting with effort, until the warm, pink skin hove up in rows. A little silver began to show through. He dug and tore at his face until it hung with ribbons of flesh. Trembling, Holly backed up until she was pressed against the door. Tundra placed himself in front of her, never taking his eyes off the being before him. Herrikhan was done with his face, though skin flapped around his neck, and had begun to work on his hands. The crabbed and shriveled fingers appeared, but the work apparently went too slowly for Herrikhan's satisfaction. With a hiss, he stopped his peeling and inserted his hands into his mouth. His jaw distended, and his mottled black and gray tongue jutted out, but he continued to pull and pull, until, with a light snapping like twigs breaking, he turned his mouth inside out. Holly and Tundra caught one glimpse of slippery gray tissue, and then it was done.

Herrikhan stood before them in his silver skin, lank gray hair against his scabbed scalp where the iron bit into the flesh, and yellowing robes. He scratched a remaining strand of pink with a long, dirty finger. "Not so comfortable, but faster," he said, "and time is of the essence." His eyes, thin and flat, like pewter discs, regarded Holly. "You see the trouble I went to for you. You should have taken Hartman while you had the chance. Well, no matter. Let us proceed. You did me a great favor last night, my dear. I shall be in your debt for eternity." He wheezed with laughter. "I'm not speaking of your treatment of me, of course, but of your interview with young Mr. Carroll."

Holly uttered an involuntary cry of dismay.

Herrikhan looked at her sharply. "Did you think I

wouldn't see you? Did you think you could keep a secret from me? You have no idea what I'm capable of."

"Tell me," said Holly. "Tell me what you're capable of."

"I was once a king, a king to rival your father," Herrikhan replied, almost dreamily. "They bowed to me, to *me*. Their foreheads in the mud, for *me*. They loved me. And then"—his voice went cold—"I was cast into a rotting pit for centuries. I was left alone in the sweat and steam for hundreds and hundreds of years. The elders thought they had buried me forever, but I outwitted them, didn't I? I grew stronger and stronger down there, for I had all the time I needed to plan my escape. I must have the stink of pure fear to venture outside my abode, and I made it happen, even in Forever. I found you, and I preserved your baby heart in snow, and I made you come here— where fear is more plentiful than air—and in the end, I will own you. And at that moment, this damnable, accursed ring that binds my head will shatter, and I will be able to breathe and prosper wherever I choose for as long as I see fit, instead of being forced to return to that sewer each day like a miserable worm in order to regain my strength." He glowered at the thought. "In answer to your question, my dear, there is nothing

I will not do to free myself. Nothing."

"What will you do then? When you are free?" asked Holly, watching him closely.

"What will I do? I will begin on Earth, with the mortal trash, and I will build an empire bigger than the one I had before. It's a simple task, but essential. After I've accomplished this, I shall begin my assault on your own land. Just think"—he smiled—"you will depose your own mother. For, of course, you will be my queen. Such an honor. Perhaps you will even preside over their departure. I'm picturing something of a ceremony: Nicholas will take up residence in my cell, and you and I will enter the Castle of Forever as its rulers." Tundra was making a sound in his throat that Holly had never heard before. Herrikhan flicked a look at him, and she held him with a shaking hand. "And then I will take all those adorable little fairies and sprites and goblins and heroes, and I—will— break—them!" His gray face shivered with rage.

"Why?" asked Holly simply.

The pewter eyes suddenly looked confused, but the moment passed swiftly. "Shut up! And shut up your wolf, too!" Holly felt Tundra tense to spring and prayed that he would not. "I've had my eye on you all along, dog. I thought I was going to be forced to use you as bait, though to my mind your value seemed rather limited. Thinking that two would be more compelling than one, I even regretted that I killed your mate in such a hasty manner—what was her name?—Terra the Terrible?" He smirked.

Tundra leaped for his neck but never reached his target. Smiling, Herrikhan extended his hand, and the wolf dropped limply on the floor. *"No!"* moaned Holly, hurling herself toward him. "Tundra! No! Please!" She gathered the body in her arms and rocked him gently. "Tundra, come back!" she pleaded. "Tundra, don't leave me. Don't leave me," she whispered into his ear. He lay still in the circle of her arms.

"Don't bother. He's dead," said Herrikhan.

Holly looked up, tears streaming down her face. "Why? Why did you do it?"

"You ask too many questions. You shall have to learn to please me better. However, making an exception just this once, I'll tell you why. He was of no use to me. I've found something better, thanks to you—Mr. Christopher Carroll. And rest assured, young lady, that what I'll do to him will make your Tundra's death look like paradise."

"Please, not Christopher. He's done nothing," whispered Holly, her hands clasping Tundra's fur convulsively.

"Of course he's done nothing!" hissed Herrikhan in exasperation. "That's why you'll want to save him. That and the fact that you're in love with him. Why else would I have chosen him? Christopher Carroll means nothing to me—I even rather like him—or I did until yesterday, when he showed up at the opera house to keep you from the filthy clutches of Mr. Hunter Hartman. Then he began to annoy me. But now I am fond of him again, for he is my best weapon. For his sake, you will remove that tiresome locket, and for his sake, you will give your heart to me."

"You were in the toy shop last night?" asked Holly, stunned.

"Of course. I arrived before you did."

"Where were you?"

He smiled mockingly. "Are you embarrassed to discover that your little romance had a spectator? Never fear, I only stayed long enough to learn what I needed. Your secrets, tedious as they are, are safe with me."

Holly didn't say anything. Instead she stroked Tundra's rough fur. What would he have advised her to do? Would he have wanted her to take the chance? Should she try it? Oh, Tundra, I need you now, she thought desperately. In answer, she seemed to hear his

Tundra leaped for his neck but never reached his target.

low voice saying 'You have nothing to lose.' That's right, she thought. She kept her eyes on the wolf. Then, after a moment, she said, "So, then you came here and waited all night?"

"Does my devotion charm you?"

"Not exactly," she said, bending to kiss Tundra one last time. Slowly she rose to her feet, and Herrikhan's silvery skin began to quiver with excitement.

"You are altogether more tractable than I expected, Holly," he said, holding out his hand for the locket.

"I think," she began, backing toward the door again. Her shoes met the satchel and she pushed it furtively behind her. "I think that you have miscalculated again. I've been calculating myself, as you talked. You've been here for twelve hours, probably more. You yourself said that you must return to your—your—place each day, and so I'm guessing that your magic is on the verge of failing; in fact, I'm guessing that you would find it nearly impossible to kill everyone out in the street right now if I were to—" Her hand on the brass knob turned quickly and, snatching the satchel up, she whisked around the edge of the open door and ran down the hallway. A long, furious hiss followed her.

Expecting any second to see Herrikhan before

her, and desperately hoping that Mr. and Mrs. Kleiner would not appear to become his victims, Holly stumbled down the stairs as fast as her feet could carry her.

"Is that you, Miss Claus?" called Mrs. Kleiner from the kitchen. "I was just going to come up and wake you!"

Without the breath to reply, Holly ran out the front door. Frantically she looked both ways and dove toward the most crowded streets. He had been on Earth for a long time; he must be weakening. He had said that he had to go back to Odyl every twenty-four hours, but what he hadn't told her was how long he had to stay. A glint of silver caught her eye, and she gasped in terror—but no, it was just a man pulling his watch out of his pocket. Holly fought to still the thundering of her heart and slow her steps. People were looking at her in amazement: still clad in her golden gown, with her hair tumbling down her back in a tangle of curls, she flew like a hunted bird through the slushy streets.

The streets were growing more and more crowded. Church bells were ringing out and carolers clustered at a few corners, singing the ancient songs. Holly saw cheerful children wiggling with excitement, vigorous old men marching out of the baker's with loaves under both arms, a sturdy cook with a goose in her basket, and a young mother with a baby in a perambulator. Their happiness seemed to exist in a world Holly no longer lived in.

"Hey! It's the doll girl!" Two dark-eyed girls balanced precariously on the edge of the curb, waving. "Where're you going, doll girl?"

She remembered them. She remembered their hands closing around their dream dolls the day before. They had looked at her with shining eyes, and she had known that their dreams—their futures—were her life's purpose. When they became immortals, they must be able to enter the land of Forever. She summoned up all her strength and replied, "I'm going to work. Merry Christmas!" Then she began to run again.

Her breath was ragged when she reached the shop. She could see Mr. Kleiner through the window, stepping back to admire a display of sailboats. Jeremy, at his side, was nodding approval. A few customers wandered through the aisles. She bowed her head and whispered, "Please, please, don't let them come to misery through me." And then she walked through the door.

"Miss Claus! In heaven's name!" Mr. Kleiner was exclaiming. "What has happened?"

Jeremy glanced behind her. "Holly? Where's Tundra at?" he asked quickly.

Holly looked from one to the other and shook her head. "Tundra's dead. Please don't make me explain. I have to see Christopher—Mr. Carroll—right away. Just let me go."

They stepped back to let her pass. As swiftly as her pounding heart would allow, she climbed the stairs and pushed through the velvet curtains. The sight of the clock on the door shook her; it had only been a few hours ago that she had passed through that portal in joy. Now her most precious friend was in peril. She felt utterly responsible for it all.

Gently touching the number three, she slipped inside Christopher's studio. Toys were buzzing and whizzing, and a brilliantly lighted galaxy spun from the ceiling, but their creator was not in sight. Someone began to whistle in the next room. She stared emptily at the window for a minute or two. Then she straightened. "Christopher?" she called softly.

The whistling stopped. His head peered around the edge of a door. "Holly!" he exclaimed, a smile flashing across his face. "I was thinking it might have been a dream!" He strode toward her and lifted her hands to his lips. "I'm so glad you came back," he said. "I can't get along without you now."

A wave of desolation broke over her. "You wouldn't say that if you knew," she said, trembling.

"Why, Holly, what's the matter? You're so pale, my love. Sit down here—I'll open the window." He flung open the casement and then returned to her side. "Now, sit down and tell me what's happened. Was there some sort of trouble at home?" he asked kindly, seating himself next to her.

Holly said bleakly, "Yes. There was. And part of it's about you. I don't know how to begin—" She faltered.

"Just begin at the beginning," he said.

Holly buried her face in her hands. "All right," she said slowly. "The beginning is you. When you were ten years old, you wrote to Santa Claus and asked him what he wished for Christmas. What he wished for was me. I am Santa's daughter." She looked up.

Christopher's face was fixed in a polite half smile, as if in response to a bad joke.

"I am Santa Claus's daughter," she repeated, "and I am the only child ever to be born in the Land of the Immortals. When a mortal soul sheds its body, it comes to my country if it has belonged to a human whose deeds and thoughts live beyond the span of mortal life. It's a magical place too, and all the enchanted creatures who have done good on Earth live there as well. I am the only one who did nothing to earn a place there. What I did, instead, was to bring a curse on my land and people."

"A curse," Christopher repeated in a blank voice.

"Yes. Because of my birth, seventeen years ago, a curse came to Forever—that's the other name of my country. There's a—a—warlock named Herrikhan, who was once very powerful. But he was proud and greedy and abused his power, and for his crimes he was imprisoned for many centuries. For a long time, he didn't know that he could earn his way to freedom by possessing a heart of pure compassion, and then, once he found out, he spent many centuries looking for the owner of this heart. But—" She broke off, not sure how to continue. "But," she repeated, taking a deep breath, "I was the one. He needs my heart to become free. One night when I was a baby, he set it in ice to keep it safe—that's why I must always have cold around me—and he cursed the Land of the Immortals. Ever since that night, no new souls have joined the immortal world and none of us have ventured out, except for my father, on Christmas

Eve. And now, me." She looked searchingly at Christopher's face.

"You. Indeed," he said stiffly.

She watched him for a sign of understanding, but she saw nothing in his eyes. Desperately she continued. "He's here. Or, rather, he's not here right now, but he'll be back. My heart must be given willingly— that's the rule—but there is nothing he will not do to force my hand. He killed Tundra. And he knows about you."

"About me?" said Christopher coldly. "What has this—this—*story* to do with me?"

Holly pressed her hands against her throbbing head. "He knows that I love you," she whispered.

Christopher's laugh was embarrassed. He stood abruptly and walked to the window. "Miss Claus," he said, not looking at her, "you honor me with your affection, but I'm sorry to say that I find all of this a trifle, well, implausible."

Holly's face grew white. "You don't believe me?"

"You must admit, it's somewhat outside the bounds of reason."

Her eyes rested on his unmoving back. "I never thought that you—" she began, and stopped. "I believed you," she said.

She heard his sharp intake of breath. He turned, his face defensive. "But Santa Claus! Warlocks! Curses! The Land of the Immortals! It's preposterous. There is no Santa Claus!"

"There is. He's my father. You believed in him once, and your belief brought my soul into this universe."

Christopher shook his head. "No. It's impossible."

Holly's green eyes slowly filled with tears. She had never felt so alone. Defeated, she sat upon the old sofa with her hands clasped together and tears streaming down her cheeks. Christopher looked away, his face rigid. Her teardrops fell on her hands and quivered there, turning into ice. Soon Holly's forlorn figure was seated in a swirl of dancing snowflakes.

Christopher watched the graceful crystals flutter about Holly's tumbled hair, and his heart twisted within him. Perhaps—? a tiny voice within him dared, but the whisper was crushed by the iron hand of logic: impossible. But the snow, the tiny voice persisted. Explain that.

It's all impossible. The snow is an optical illusion, and the girl is mad.

She's not. She's the sanest person you've ever met.

Santa Claus? Children's nonsense. "Nonsense!" he repeated aloud.

Holly looked up. "There's something I want to show you," she said. She reached into her bulging satchel, pulled forth the crystal music box, brought it to him. The thousand rainbows caught within it burst into color in the morning light and threw bright, gemlike sparkles on the sober ceiling and walls of Christopher's studio.

"Very pretty box," said Christopher, looking at her questioningly.

Holly didn't answer. She was listening to the first whispers of music that sang in her ears: the tune was like none she had ever heard before, wandering, beguiling, bending, and swaying. It was like flying. It was like a secret. She lifted her eyes, wide with listening, to Christopher. "Do you hear it?" she asked.

He pitied her. "I don't hear anything," he said gently. "It's a very pretty box." Quite mad, he thought, wondering why it hurt him so.

Holly's face became still again. The music faded. She looked miserably at Christopher. "I'm sorry. I'm sorry I troubled you, Mr. Carroll. What time is it?" she asked quickly.

"I don't know. Eleven," he said, unable to take his

eyes from her face.

"He'll be back soon," she murmured, more to her-self than to him. "I must go. Is it warm?"

"Warm? I don't know." He roused himself. "Yes. It does seem as though it's become rather warm. Perhaps our cold spell is over." He tried to speak normally.

"Our cold spell is over," she repeated. "Then I haven't much time. Mr. Carroll, I have one last favor to ask you—don't say no—" She placed her fingers gently on his mouth to stop his words. "Take this locket. It will protect you from harm. I know you don't believe in what I've said, but please." She lifted her fingers to the slim gold chain around her neck and the metal dissolved as if it were water. "Please. Will you put it in your pocket near your heart?"

He nodded once and held out his hand. She placed the locket in his palm and then closed his hand around it.

They looked at each other without saying a word. "Put it in your pocket," she said finally, and he tucked it into his waistcoat. She nodded. "Don't give it to him. No matter what he says or does, keep the locket. Promise me."

"I promise."

"Good-bye," she said simply, and turned away.

"Holly!" he burst out. She shook her head without looking back and slipped through the door. "Don't go," he said quietly.

With her satchel in her hand, Holly trailed down the dark staircase for the last time. Before she could stop herself, she looked to the corner where Tundra had always sat, and its emptiness was like broken glass in her throat. She stopped, dizzy with sorrow. Jeremy and Mr. Kleiner stopped their dealings with customers to hurry to her side.

"Holly," said Jeremy anxiously, "you look terrible."

"Not terrible," assured the kind Mr. Kleiner, "but distraught and tired. Do sit down, Miss Claus." Hastily he brought a stool forward and gestured to it invitingly.

"Dear Mr. Kleiner," said Holly gratefully, "I shall never forget your good heart. It's time for me to go now, my friend. I wish—oh, how I wish—that I could stay, but I can't."

"Miss Claus? Are you all right?" asked Mr. Kleiner. "You don't look well enough to travel."

Despite her pain, Holly almost laughed at that.

"Bless you, Mr. Kleiner, and"—she hesitated—"watch over Mr. Carroll, will you?"

He nodded seriously, and she knew that he took her request to heart. "Miss Claus, thank you for what you've done for the shop. And for all of us. And for me." He reached out to shake her hand, then thought better of it and kissed her forehead instead. "Thank you."

Holly turned to Jeremy. He backed away, his mouth straightening into a stubborn line. "Don't you say it, Holly. Don't say good-bye to me. I'm coming with you."

"Oh, Jeremy, my dear, don't come. It might be dangerous."

"Nuh-huh." He shook his head firmly. "I don't care. You ain't got Tundra, and I'm coming with you. To see you off."

Her eyes shone. "You are a loyal friend, Jeremy. Thank you. Is it all right, Mr. Kleiner?"

"Yes, of course. Go, my boy," said Mr. Kleiner, wisely stifling his curiosity as to what could possibly be so dangerous about a train station.

Wearily Holly picked up her satchel and turned to go. Without a word, Jeremy pulled the bag from her hand and placed himself at her side. As they walked through the door, a blast of warm, moist air greeted them, and Holly staggered. "Just hang on to me, Holly, and we'll get there," urged Jeremy.

She put her hand on his shoulder and took a deep gulp of tepid air. "This is Herrikhan's doing," she murmured. She could not be sure. But indeed Herrikhan's force of evil had caused this supernatural heat storm. So even Holly's magical snowflakes were unable to protect her.

Jeremy, who had not the slightest idea what she was talking about, nodded sympathetically. "Tell me who's Herrikhan," he said, hoping to distract her.

"He's a being who will try to stop me from going home," Holly said. "I think he'll be at the park when we get there." She tried to hurry, but the close air seemed to grow thicker by the minute. "Does it look like all the snow has melted?" Her eyes didn't seem to be working properly.

Jeremy looked at the ground. "Yup. Turning to slush. And look over there." He pointed. "It's sort of steaming."

It was true. The summer heat that beat down on New York on that winter's day not only melted the snow, but sizzled it into steam. All up and down the street, shopkeepers and bypassers were looking up into the sky with puzzled, worried faces. "All of a sudden, it just turned hot," they were saying. "I never seen anything like it." "On Christmas Eve, too." "Feels like devil's work." "Must be eighty degrees." "Maybe more." "Sure doesn't seem like Christmas."

Children turned their eyes away from the sweltering sky, disappointed. Children who had whooped into the street with their sleds at eight o'clock that morning now stood in disconsolate clusters, watching their snow dribble into puddles.

"Hey, there's the doll lady!" shouted a little girl outside the bakery.

Summoning up her strength, Holly smiled toward the call, for her vision was blurred and things gleamed strangely. On Jeremy's shoulder, her hand grew heavy.

"Why, it's the girl with the dream dolls! Miss! Thank you!" called a voice from a carriage. Holly nodded her head blindly as Jeremy guided her against the scudding waves of heat that billowed from the very bricks around her. She grew paler and paler, and the cheerful greetings that met the little procession were more and more replaced by looks of concern.

✳ ✳ ✳

Far away, Nicholas thrust the telescope aside and began to pace around Holly's room like a caged animal. Viviana and Sofya watched him in silence. He stopped and chewed his knuckle. Then he paced. "I'm leaving now," he said, finally. "Christmas Eve will come early this year."

"Nicholas, you can't stop this from happening," Sofya reminded him.

Nicholas stopped chewing his knuckle for a moment. "I know," he said. "I know that. I just can't stand to watch anymore."

"Well. Yes. Go in peace, then."

The distraught king hurried from the room.

Across the city of New York, strange things were happening. The crisp blue sky of winter had now faded to the color of a bruise. Thick yellow clouds hovered over the towers of the metropolis, and the air was filled with a greasy softness. The streets with their sweating brown bricks now seemed like tunnels, and the pungent, spicy smells of Christmas were foiled by a putrid stench that rose from the darkest corners of the city.

There was a faint buzzing, too, as if angry, stinging insects were penned somewhere underneath the granite streets, waiting for release. This thin sound invaded the minds of the citizens and stretched their nerves. People jumped guiltily when they were spoken to and twisted their heads around to get a better look at a dark shape they had seen from the corners of their eyes. Big-bellied, complacent businessmen rushed down Wall Street as if pursued. Little children sat quietly in corners, hiding their eyes. Horses shied and whinnied. Kindly old dogs growled at their masters. Aged spinsters began to rip their petticoats into bandages as though a war had begun. Out in the harbor, the captain of a little tugboat looked at a green shape floating just beneath the surface of the water and gave swift orders to return to dock.

But suddenly, another sound was heard. The children heard it first. In crowded, airless tenement rooms and prosperous stone mansions, children uncovered their eyes and listened in wonder.

The dream-dolls were speaking: "Go," they said, "go now. Holly needs you. Remember, love conquers time. You must go now."

The children took up their dolls—in grubby hands and tidy ones—and began to walk toward Central Park.

Grown-ups are hard of hearing, or perhaps just

hard of believing. Some pretended they didn't notice the dolls speaking. Some even tried to hold the children back with scoldings. But the weird, lowering clouds had unsettled them, and the buzz seeping up from the pavement had frightened them. The light, chiming voices of the dolls and children were soothing, and, despite themselves, the adults began to listen. They began to believe. Without really noticing what they were doing, the grown-ups drifted out onto the stone sidewalks and began to walk toward Central Park.

Far ahead, Jeremy and Holly rounded the corner into the plaza and entered the park. They were walking very slowly now, for Holly had grown so weak that it was only her will that was keeping her upright at all. All the color had drained away from her face, and she looked somehow transparent. Jeremy, sick with fear, could not speak, but Holly was talking about Tundra, to keep herself from falling. "One time, when I was a very little girl, I hid from him in the garden. It was freezing that day, and we were the only ones out, he and I"—she gasped for air and then continued—"and it was beautiful. Do you know, Jeremy dear, that you cannot hide from a wolf? Not really, anyway." Holly stumbled, but Jeremy caught her.

"Thank you. Because, you see, they have the most acute sense of smell, the most—" She paused, dazedly. "Where was I?"

"You was hiding."

"Yes, I was. And Tundra, he loved me so, he pretended that he could not find me. I watched him hunt for me behind the bushes and trees. He was pretending, but you see, I didn't understand that, and suddenly I was so frightened I began to cry. Because"—she took a great, hollow gulp of air—"I had realized for the first time that we were two instead of one. I had never known that we could be separated." She staggered and then straightened. "And when he heard me crying, he jumped to my side. Like flying, he was so fast. He was so fast." She stopped. "And now we're two again. I can't go any farther."

Jeremy looked around. It was a particularly empty stretch of the park. Before them was the Sheep Meadow, which had lain under a blanket of snow that morning. Now it had turned into a sea of mud, held together with bits of grass and the odd pile of rapidly melting slush. There was a thin iron bench overlooking the swampy expanse, and there Jeremy led Holly. She sat with a sigh. After a moment she reached her hand into the lumpy satchel and began to feel for the silken scarf that contained her tiny friends. She patted and rustled and finally peered into the bag. "Oh no. No," she whispered. "They're lost again."

They were not lost. A few minutes after Holly's departure, Alexia, Euphemia, and Empy had wiggled and shrugged and pushed their way out of the folds of green silk that seemed determined to baffle them. Finally Euphemia worked her wings free and spread them wide. "Scadoddle, Scadaddle, Scadee!" she said breathlessly and, with a quiet *pop,* she, Lexy, and Empy regained their rightful sizes. They looked around cautiously, but Christopher Carroll was not in sight.

"Well, where is he?" hissed Lexy.

"My goodness, look at that shining doll. Ugh, it walks!" exclaimed Euphemia, hopping backward to avoid a robot.

Empy, quiet Empy, spoke up. "Stop fussing about dolls. Holly's in trouble," he said firmly. "First we have to find Mr. Carroll and then somehow make him go to the park with the locket."

Impressed, Lexy and Euphemia nodded. There was a silence. "Well, where do we find him?" Euphemia asked the penguin.

As if in answer to her question, Christopher Carroll

entered his workroom and walked restlessly to the window. He did not notice the three new additions to his menagerie of toys; he did not notice anything. He stood gazing at the purple-yellow sky and the sodden squash of mud that lay in the street below. "Not like Christmas at all," he murmured.

The animals watched him and exchanged anxious glances. How could they begin to persuade him to believe Holly? What would he do if they began to talk? Tundra had said that humans were terrified of talking animals. Would he think that he had gone mad? Empy, driven by his heart's devotion, became brave. He looked around the buzzing, glinting room, and something caught his eye. On Christopher's worktable, four little wooden animals rested where Holly had placed them with shaking hands the night before. Inside the satchel, bouncing along in a bed of green silk, Empy had heard Holly describe the animals to Tundra that morning. "They were identical to you and Lexy and Euphemia and Empy. It was as though you had all been destined to play a part in my life. And his, perhaps," she had added musingly. Empy squinted; there were the figures. He knew what to do. Gesturing to the other two to follow him, he waddled over to the table and climbed laboriously up

Christopher's chair. Much more gracefully, Lexy and Euphemia ascended the table and, as he turned, startled by the rustle and creak, Christopher Carroll was greeted by the sight of a small red fox and a great white owl perched behind his own wooden figures of the same beasts. With a grunt and a heave, a penguin rolled onto the table and joined his own model. The three—or rather, the six—of them stood there in a line, facing him.

Christopher's eyes moved slowly from one to the other. Even their expressions were the same as their wooden counterparts, he observed. He picked up the single wooden wolf and looked at it closely. It was identical to the animal that had guarded Holly, he saw now, even down to the wise and watchful eyes. He looked gravely into Lexy's face, then Euphemia's, and finally Empy's. "You belong to her?" he asked.

They nodded.

He sat back in the chair. Somehow, now, it didn't surprise him that they understood him. It was strange how easily a world constructed of logic could shatter when it faced the secret universe beyond logic. The destruction of Christopher Carroll's carefully created lonely life took only a moment and, he reflected, it hurt a great deal less than his refusal to believe Holly had. Something closed and cold within him began to unfurl and grow; it had been so many years since he had last encountered it that he did not recognize the feeling as hope. Quietly he asked, "You are from her land? What did she call it—the Land of the Immortals?"

"Yes," said Empy in a low voice.

"You talk, too?" Christopher said without alarm.

"Yes."

"Have I become insane?"

"Look at us, Mr. Carroll. Isn't it easier to believe that we are real than to try to explain our presence by any other means?" Euphemia and Lexy stared. It was the longest speech they had ever heard from Empy's mouth. "Think, Mr. Carroll. Years ago you made these little creatures that look just like us. It shows, don't you see, that even then you were part of Holly's life."

"And the letter I wrote to Santa Claus?"

"Your letter was the beginning of her existence," said Empy.

Christopher closed his eyes. "And it's all just as she said?"

"Everything she said is true," avowed Empy.

"Everything," Lexy added. "Including the part about Herrikhan. It's happening right now."

Christopher's eyes clicked open. "What will he do?"

"He will try to force her to give her heart to him, to become his possession," said Lexy.

"Then he's going to kill her," said Euphemia. She turned her huge black eyes on Christopher's face. "The locket's the only thing that can save her, and you've got it, and he's going to kill her."

Christopher stared at her. Wordlessly he reached into his waistcoat and brought forth the locket. It shone more brightly than ever. He seemed to see her face, warm and trusting, before him. There she was, her fingers grasping his as he pulled her from the swath of velvet. "Why do you keep coming back?" she had said. Because we belong to each other, he thought. A faint whisper of music reached him. The tune was like none he had ever heard before, wandering, beguiling, bending. He looked around distractedly—who was playing music?—and found himself staring at the music box Holly had left behind. Now he heard the music. It was like flying. It was like a secret. He heard her saying, "Every time you make a choice, you make the future," and he knew now that there was only one future he wanted. I believe you. I believe you, he thought.

It might be too late, something inside him warned. Go. Now. Run.

"Where is she?" he said, rising to his feet.

"The park," said Empy. "She went to the park to meet her father."

"Come on," he said, scooping up Empy. "Let's go find her."

Then, with a penguin under one arm, a fox at his heels, and an owl flying overhead, Christopher Carroll strode from his lonely, bitter past into his future.

Chapter Twenty-three

I T WAS VERY QUIET. The birds had stopped singing, and the clatter of faraway carts and carriages had faded into eerie silence. There was not a single breath of air stirring the black branches or ruffling the bushes; the sky seemed to press down instead, muzzling the tiny sounds of the park with its thick yellow hands. Alone on her bench, Holly gazed out at the swamp of mud before her and tried to remember all the wonderful things that had happened in the past three days. It was growing more and more difficult, remembering, for her heart fluttered and knocked against her ribs like a trapped bird.

If only I could breathe—no, can't think like that, it will make me desperate. Got to save up, he's coming, Herrikhan is coming—no, don't think that, no, think how lucky it is—what?—I forgot—oh yes, now I remember—that Jeremy agreed to go back for Lexy, Euphemia, and Empy. Papa will get them home. And Jeremy won't be here when the worst of it happens. Mustn't give in. No matter what. Don't be silly. Not much longer now. Christopher's safe. It will just be me. Just me. No one else in danger. If only I could breathe.

She wavered and collapsed into blissful darkness, velvet smooth. No, must wake up, she told herself, and opened her eyes. She could see perfectly clearly now. There was something moving down in the swampy meadow, something underneath the earth. The grass-clotted mud was heaving up, buckling and lurching, and then, before her horrified eyes, it spewed forth a shrunken, yellowed creature who seemed to ooze a vile white syrup from its pores. The thing swiveled its head, casting about for what it desired, and then it saw her. Its face split into a grin and it beckoned, extending a long, limp finger in her direction.

Holly struggled to rise to her feet, but her panic could not surmount her weakness, and she fell back.

Again she begged her feet to carry her, but they could not. The long, rubbery finger seemed to grow—it was almost reaching her, and Holly recoiled, shutting her eyes against the horror of its touch.

"Déjà vu, Holly?" It was Herrikhan's voice.

The shriveled creature was gone, and the warlock stood before her in his familiar guise, grinning. Holly said wearily, "That was cruel."

"That was nothing. I've had ample time to think about every detail of this day, my darling. You wouldn't begrudge me a moment's fun, would you? I've been planning that one for ten years."

"I'm sure, but—"

"You look unwell, Holly. Do you find the weather unseasonable?"

Holly gazed at him unsteadily and took a deep breath. "Why are you bothering with all this talk? It's over. Christopher's safe," she said with a gasp. "He's got the locket. Tundra's dead. I'm all alone. I'll never be yours. You know that—I'll never give you my heart. I'm not afraid to die."

Herrikhan opened his mouth—Holly looked away—and snapped it shut. "Oh, you'll die soon enough," he said bitterly. "But I have an idea—a hope—it's really quite possible—though I'm not certain.

However, I can wait. You'll find me a very patient husband, darling." He ran a long, ragged finger along her arm, and Holly recoiled. "At the very least I'll have the pleasure of watching Nicholas come too late to save you. You're looking worse and worse, Holly, did you know that? Your heart is melting. Look at your hands—they're transparent."

Holly glanced down and saw that he told the truth. Her skin was becoming clear and brittle, like glass. As her blood faded and gave way, her breath became more labored; she felt as if her lungs were hardening into something sharp and fragile too. Each breath was piercing.

"Holly. Give up." Herrikhan's flat eyes looked almost human. "You aren't meant for a painful death. Say the word—just one little yes, and I'll save you. I'll reach into your heart and make you whole again. You'll feel neither pain nor sorrow ever again, for all eternity."

Holly, scarcely able to speak now, whispered, "No. Never. I choose this."

At that moment, as Herrikhan's claw wavered in the thick air, a voice shouted across the empty landscape, "Holly!" Herrikhan faded from Holly's side.

It was Christopher. She couldn't see any longer,

but he saw her, and the sight froze his soul. Holly had turned to glass; she lay before him still as death, and his first thought was that she had never been any more than an illusion. He felt his heart breaking. "No!" he cried, falling to his knees at her side, willing her to be alive. "Take it!" he commanded, pressing the golden locket into her icy hands. He could see it glimmer through her palms.

"Christopher, don't do this," begged Holly. "You promised me."

"Thank God you're alive," he said, bending close to her. "I can bear anything if you're alive."

"Take it back," she pleaded. Already, the locket was working its magic; her breath did not feel like knives now, and her glass skin was less fragile. But she dreaded the feeling of her returning life, because she knew what the price would be. "You promised that you wouldn't give it up."

"I promised I wouldn't give it up to him. I didn't say anything about you."

Holly was able to lift her head now. She looked about, but Herrikhan had disappeared. "He's here, even if we can't see him. Please, Christopher. He'll kill you." She held out the locket with shaking hands.

"No, Holly," he said, looking at her tenderly. "If

this saves you, it saves me as well, even if I die."

Suddenly a scabbed silver figure appeared. Wordlessly the creature stared at Christopher with his yellowed eyes, and then he raised his hand.

Christopher glanced at the creature, and his face registered no fear. "Good-bye, my Holly," he said. As though he counted time in years instead of minutes, he raised her soft hand to his lips and kissed it lingeringly. "I believe you."

He rose and turned to Herrikhan. His face hardened. "I'll not make it easy for you," he said, stepping toward the shrunken warlock.

In all the centuries of his immortal life, no human had ever moved toward Herrikhan, but only away. He was shaken, Holly saw, by Christopher's steady advance. He wavered, took a step back—and then rallied. "You won't make it easy for me?" Herrikhan sneered. "Well. How courageous. This promises to be more amusing than I expected. Do tell me how you intend to make it difficult."

Christopher lunged for him, wrapping his strong hands around the warlock's throat. Herrikhan let out a surprised grunt and stumbled back, and for a moment he seemed unable to speak. Then he gathered together his forces and let forth a roar. "You dare to lay hands on me, you worm?" he screamed. "You. Will. Die!" He raised his arms and there came a mighty, grinding roar, and the lowering purple clouds suddenly met in a murderous crash. The silence that had lain over the land so threateningly erupted into a heaving, tossing storm, and the trees thrashed together as if they were sticks held by giants. The meadow's smooth curves buckled and furrowed as though something boiled beneath the ground.

Holly closed her eyes. She could not bear to see the end.

But then, though the wind wailed and seethed, though the trees lurched from the muddy ground as if bent on their own destruction, though the mad buzzing of the insects underground droned louder than ever, a soft, even sound suddenly made itself heard. It was rhythmic, it was moving closer and closer—it was the sound of hundreds of people, children and grown-ups both, summoned by the dream dolls they held in their hands. Gracefully, drawn by some force that made them as light as air and as strong as love, they moved toward the meadow in a great arc. In the thick glow of the heat, they seemed to shimmer, and she rubbed her eyes. But they were still there when she looked again. There was Jeremy, at the front, with Empy under his arm and Sidewalk at his feet. Phoebe and her brothers. Louise and her grandfather. Mr. Kleiner, with his hand in Mrs. Kleiner's. The roly-poly twins, the girls from the street, the sliding shop-girls, the pudgy babies and flyaway mothers, the nurses, the coachmen, the urchins, and all the dreamy, serious, and silly children who had taken their dolls from her hands and suddenly seen their dreams take shape. There were Bat, Marty, Grub, Joan, and all the children from the Place. Mr. McElhenny and his wife. Euphemia flapped overhead, and Lexy sat solemnly with her tail wrapped around her legs. And there were Charles and Dr. Braunfels, slightly out of breath, and Miss Bellows leading Jerome and Harrison by either hand. And Evelyn and Alice, supporting Lissy between them. They had all come for Holly, as she had come for them.

She took a deep breath and opened her eyes. "Love conquers time," she whispered. But how? How could she stop time for Christopher, who now stood alone in the meadow that roiled with Herrikhan's evil force? Already, she saw with a racing heart, thin silver coils erupted from the mud and crept toward him. Christopher watched them, his eyes narrowed, and when the first slithering strand slid over his feet, he wrenched it away furiously. The eyeless reptile quivered and drew back, but it was replaced by a seething cluster of its fellows. The fleshy strands choked and grappled him, ever closer, ever tighter, and Holly watched helplessly as Christopher's hands were bound by two thick coils. A rope circled his throat.

Herrikhan's scabbed face bent toward hers, and she felt his fetid breath on her neck as he whispered, "You could save him."

Holly made no reply.

The yellow sky sucked in its breath, and the trees stood still. All was quiet, save for the smooth slipping of the silver coils.

"He doesn't have to die," Herrikhan's mossy mouth muttered in her ear. "Give me your heart."

Holly looked up to the sky. In a blinding instant, she knew. The truth rang like golden bells in her heart. "Herrikhan," she said, her voice strong and sure, "if you will set Christopher free, I will not only give you my heart. I will love you."

Herrikhan drew back. His pewter eyes thinned. "What?" he said.

"If you let him live, I will go with you willingly, and I will love you," said Holly. Fear had vanished from her, and she looked at Herrikhan with clear eyes.

"Love?" His voice sounded uncertain.

"Yes. I will love you," said Holly.

It was the one thing he had never planned for. He shivered at the weakness that he felt moving through his hollow veins. "M-me?" he stuttered. "You would love me? After what I've done to bring misery to you and everyone you care about, you would *love* me?"

"I forgive you," said Holly. She looked at him with the strength that comes from truth.

He felt a tiny jolt, the stab of a needle, somewhere in the region where his heart once resided. Oh, he thought. No. Not this. He remembered, so many centuries before, the same stab. It had been love then and it was love now. Not this, he thought once more, before his silver skin began to collapse into dust. Desperately he fought to regain his power, but like an ancient skeleton brought from its coffin to the breathing air, the material that gave him form dissolved in the light of love. "Holly Claus, you have conquered me. You have conquered evil," he said, his voice as dry and weightless as leaves flying in the wind. His face cracked open as he spoke and, like sand, the scales of his skin blew into the air bit by bit. In a minute only his robe was left, the stained yellow shape sustained by the memory of its inhabitant. Then it, too, shredded

*"He doesn't have to die," Herrikhan's mossy mouth muttered
in her ear. "Give me your heart."*

and fluttered into dust. He was gone.

Snow began to fall quietly. Holly drew her fingers through the thin, gray powder that was scattered on the bench. Then she blew it away and stood up to meet Christopher. He limped toward her, mud spattered but alive, and she stretched out her hand with the locket in it. His fingers met hers and they twined together, and the necklace began to shine with the radiance of a star.

"Hello," Holly whispered.

"Hello," he said softly. "Thank you for my life."

Their eyes locked together and spoke all the words they could not say, until suddenly Holly shivered. She looked up to the falling snow and smiled. "I'm not certain, but I think I'm cold." Christopher pulled off his coat and wrapped it around her shoulders. And then, together, they approached the watching crowd.

There was a soft sound above. Christopher, Holly,

and Jeremy looked up to see the gilded angel of the park, who for years had been standing so stiffly atop her fountain, flying in lazy circles above their heads. They looked in silent wonder at the golden creature against the snow. They were rewarded with golden feathers that drifted into their fingers as lightly as clouds; the angel smiled down at them and called, "The curse is broken. New souls are streaming into the immortal world and magical creatures are going home to the mortals who need them. Love has prevailed and Christmas is come!"

There was a faint ringing in the air. Holly, to whom the sound was as familiar as the tick of a clock, called to the children, "It's Santa Claus!" She pointed—and suddenly, soaring through the sky came the Christmas sleigh, replete with reindeer, jingling bells, and Santa Claus himself. Nicholas guided the craft to an open field nearby and stood up in the sleigh.

Holly ran as lightly as a deer, and Nicholas gathered her up in a mighty hug. "Oh, my daughter! You have done it! You have made all of our dreams come true. And you have begun to make the dreams of many mortals come true as well." He smiled his welcome to Christopher, who followed Holly. "Bless you,

Christopher. I'm glad to see you again."

"Thank you, sir. I am truly glad to meet you." Their eyes met and they understood each other.

"As I always said, Nicholas, love will prevail." Sofya stood beside the gleaming sleigh, her white robes covered with a lace of snow. Her eyes were filled with tears, but her smile was filled with joy. "My dearest child, you have succeeded where I could not, and in doing so you take your place among the immortals. I honor you and I love you." Gracefully she bowed to Holly.

"No! Don't bow to me, Sofya," said Holly, seizing her godmother's hand and lifting her. "There is no need. I could not be who I am without you. Your love and your wisdom have taught me everything."

Sofya turned now to Christopher. "I have known you for many years," she said gently. "Welcome."

"You know me?" Christopher said, mystified.

"Of course," she answered. "For it was your heart that called Holly's into the universe. You were more willing to give than to receive. And now you and your message are immortalized. You are one of us—you are immortal, Christopher."

Holly turned to him. "Don't you see? Don't you see, Christopher? The story began with you."

Holly turned to Jeremy. "My dear, I must return to my home now. But I will return to you in your dreams. Remember," she said urgently, "remember your dreams. Don't give them up. You will become what you choose to dream. Believe in yourself. Good-bye, Jeremy. I'll see you again," she said. "I know I will."

He rubbed his nose violently. "Okay. I'll be okay."

"I know. Thank you for all you taught me."

Jeremy did not answer, but he straightened and smiled proudly.

One by one, Holly took her leave of her friends with a few special words. Some cried and some clung to her, but most were smiling as she turned away. Finally, she was finished. Christopher took her hand protectively as they returned to the sleigh.

"Well, shall we?" said Nicholas, gesturing them in.

Holly began to step forward and then stopped. "No," she said thoughtfully. "No thank you, Papa."

"What? Why?" asked Nicholas, bewildered.

Again, the faint ringing of bells sounded in the drifting snow, far away but coming closer and closer. Again hundreds of eyes scanned the sky. A gilded sleigh, drawn by nine magical rainbow deer, swooped among the clouds and came to a rest near the Christmas sleigh.

"Nice shade of purple," offered Donner.

"Thanks," said Meteor, hiding a grin. "Did you want us, Holly?"

"Yes, please, Meteor," replied Holly with a luminous smile. She turned to her father. "You understand, don't you, Papa? Christopher and I will go together."

Nicholas nodded. "I understand, my love." He was suddenly very absorbed in adjusting Blitzen's bridle. Now stop it, he said sternly to himself, just as he heard Holly give a wild gasp. He turned in alarm to see her running madly through the deepening snow. "What's she doing?"

"I don't know," said Christopher, looking after Holly in confusion. "What on Earth? What is that thing?"

It was a streak of white, barely visible against the snow, and it was racing toward Holly the way fire races across paper. The two figures collided, and Holly was on her knees in the snow, her face buried in Tundra's fur, laughing and crying at the same time. "Oh, my dearest friend, I thought my heart would break! I thought you were dead!"

"I thought I was, too," Tundra admitted, "and then

I began to feel again. It was as though something was burning away the coldness, as though his curse was peeling away." The wolf shook his head wonderingly. "A most peculiar sensation."

Weeping, Holly embraced him again. "You know what it means, don't you? It means that he's undone. The curse is undone. And now I'm whole again. And Tundra, I'm free! You won't believe what happened. Oh, my precious friend—Tundra, wait till you hear— I tried to think what you would do—and I ran—oh, I'll have to begin at the beginning—"

For a few minutes, Tundra's heart was too full for speech, and he let Holly babble on. Then he bumped her head with his nose and sat back. "I can tell that it's all right. I know that somehow you've broken the curse and Herrikhan is gone and you are safe. That's all I need to know now."

Lexy, leaping through the snow, joined them, and Euphemia flapped down too. Empy, waddling, was slower, but they waited for him. "I didn't think we'd see you again, Tundra," said Lexy. "I thought we were all goners."

"An adventure, to be sure," said Euphemia.

"I'm glad it's over," said Empy. "Everything will be back together again."

"Everything will be back together again," repeated Holly, stroking Tundra and Empy.

The five friends plodded through the soggy snow, back to the waiting sleighs. Christopher watched Holly approach, and Tundra, catching sight of his eyes, stole a glance at Holly's answering gaze. Together again, but not the same, he thought. He turned toward Nicholas and the Christmas sleigh.

"Tundra," said Nicholas simply, "I am glad to have you back."

"Thank you, sire. I see that you are in the midst of your duties. May I accompany you?"

"Ah, Tundra. You would be only too welcome, but Holly will now embark on another journey, and I know that she will want her friends at her side," said Nicholas. "You cannot be parted from her now."

Holly smiled from Christopher's side. "Yes, Tundra. There is one last step to our mortal journey. We have dolls to deliver."

Tundra understood. "Dream dolls?"

"Of course! We've only just begun to make dreams come true."

"Can we come too?" said Lexy. She jumped into the gilded sleigh without waiting for an answer.

"Of course!" Holly laughed. "Didn't we find out

today that we can't manage without one another?"

Following the fox, Euphemia settled herself upon the scrolled back of the sleigh, and Empy managed to lurch onto the floor, where he fell into an instant slumber. Christopher and Holly settled themselves with blankets snug around them, and Holly leaned forward, gathering the reins into her hands, and exclaimed, "It's time to begin."

Meteor lifted the sleigh into the darkening sky.

"Merry Christmas!" Holly called. She leaned over the edge of the sleigh and two tears dropped into the air. The two drops quivered slightly and turned to snow. They hung in the air for a moment and then they spiraled down to the waiting earth.

"We've only just begun to make dreams come true."

Epilogue

From *The Book of Forever*

THESE PAGES MAY grow more numerous than the stars, and yet none will exceed in beauty and blessings those upon which is written the legend of Holly Claus, princess royal and cherished daughter of Nicholas and Viviana, our king and queen.

With bravery and faith, she has brought to an end the curse of exile that darkened our land for years upon years. Through the gates that she opened, immortal souls shall enter Forevermore.

With love and compassion, she has fired the flame of hope in the mortal world, and awakened dreams that *slept in the souls of the mortals who dwelled there.*

With a pure heart, she has vanquished the evil named Herrikhan that lay so heavily upon our land.

And, by her example and in her path, the inhabitants of our universe have learned that immortality is earned when Love Conquers Time.

The Characters and Places of Forever

Albigenes: A philosopher and academician who, with Sebastian Brax, persecuted magicians in Paris in the sixteenth century. Rumors persist that Albigenes was himself magical.

Alexia: Nicknamed Lexy, a highly opinionated fox and dear friend to Holly Claus.

Amaranthine Gates: The towering golden gates that mark the entrance to Forever, the Land of the Immortals. Each immortal soul that passes through them sets a diamond into the gates' bars.

apHoug: A centaur.

Bach: A prodigious and prolific family of German composers and musicians in the seventeenth and eighteenth centuries.

Beatrice: The woman whose radiant beauty and virtue inspired Dante Alighieri, the celebrated Italian poet.

Befana: A good-hearted witch of Italy who brings treats to children on Twelfth Night.

Berchta: A hideous yet essentially kindhearted witch, native to southern Germany, who assigns punishment for slovenliness and unkindness to children.

Beyschlag: The servant of Herrikhan. Resident of Odyl, a place of misery and fear.

Boucane sisters: Twelve fairy sisters who reside in the Castle of Forever. *See also* Emmalylis; Io and Pialana; Makena; Nemekele.

Cadmus: King of Thebes and founder of the Greek alphabet. After death, he was transformed into a snake and advised mortal rulers for several thousand years.

Callistus: An immortal owl.

Centaurs: Powerful magical creatures, half horse, half human, native to Crete but now primarily living in the Land of the Immortals. Noted for their excellent athletic skills and short tempers. *See also* apHoug; Leneth; Lysinias; Zenwyler.

Chaldean witches: A group of witches renowned as the founders of astrology.

Claus, Holly: First child born in the Land of the Immortals. Daughter of Nicholas and Viviana; Princess of Forever, the Land of the Immortals.

Claus, Nicholas: King of Forever, the Land of the Immortals, familiar to the mortal world as Saint Nicholas, Sinter Klaas, and Santa Claus. Bishop of Myra during his mortal life, Nicholas is known as a protector and benefactor of children and captives.

Claus, Viviana: Queen of Forever, the Land of the Immortals.

Comet: One of the eight reindeer in charge of pulling the

Christmas sleigh. Also head instructor, with Donner, of flying lessons at the Castle of Forever.

Dappertutto, Edgardo: A nineteenth-century folklorist.

Darwin, Erasmus: Botanist and formulator of a preliminary theory of evolution.

Demeter: Goddess of the harvest. In thanks to the mortal who helped her find her daughter, Persephone, who had been kidnapped by Hades, Demeter taught humans how to sow seeds and reap the fruits of the earth.

Deucalion: The son of Prometheus and founder of Greek civilization.

Donner: One of the eight reindeer in charge of pulling the Christmas sleigh. Also head instructor, with Comet, of flying lessons at the Castle of Forever.

Dragons: Fire-breathing flying creatures, guardians and mail carriers to the Castle of Forever.

Dwarves: Earth-dwelling gnomes of large stature, proficient in mining.

Edison, Thomas A.: American creator of over a thousand inventions, including the incandescent electric lamp, the microphone, the phonograph, and talking motion pictures.

Elitrion: Also known as Fritz, goblin referee for immortal pelote games.

Elves: Earth-dwelling cousins and rivals of goblins, known for their cheery dispositions.

Emmalylis: The youngest and smallest of the twelve fairy sisters who reside in the Castle of Forever.

Emmanuel Philibert, Duke of Savoy: Also known as Ironhead, he unified a number of territories into the Duchy of Savoy.

Empire: A penguin, commonly known as Empy. Dear friend to Holly Claus.

Erasmus, Desiderius: Philosopher and opponent of extremism who worked to find the moral basis shared by various religious traditions in the sixteenth century.

Erst, Helvetius: Explorer and cartographer, one of five mortals known to have seen the Land of the Immortals before death.

Euphemia: A snowy owl with a dubious memory. Dear friend to Holly Claus.

Fairies: Various species of magical winged creatures inhabiting the Land of the Immortals and the mortal world. Though all fairies speak the same language, Earth fairies are substantially larger than their immortal counterparts, and the immortal will-o'-the-wisps are so tiny as to be invisible to the human eye. *See also* Boucane sisters; Will-o'-the-wisps.

Farmer, Horatio Thaddeus: Prescient meteorologist of the Land of the Immortals.

Faucemberg, Henry de: Otherwise known as the Sheriff of Nottingham, Robin Hood's mortal enemy.

Fauns: Woodland beings, half human, half goat. Though they lack major magical powers, they are noted for their tact and refined manners. *See also* Macsu; Romulus; Silenux.

Finta: Assistant to Mother Selting. Though not herself a witch, Finta regarded the persecution of witches as a sin and helped countless witches and those falsely accused of witchery elude their captors. Finta's mortal life ended in 1699.

Fortinbras: Noble carillonneur of the Land of the Immortals.

Gaia: Goddess of Earth and its abundance.

Galen: Second-century Greek physician and philosopher, and founder of the concept of medicine as a science rather than a collection of superstitions.

Gawaine: Knight of King Arthur's Round Table, noted for his bravery, chivalry, honor, and temper. His mortal life was brought to an end by Sir Lancelot.

Gnomes: Magical creatures who live in vast tribes inside mountains. Most are extremely hardworking and devoted to mining or forging metal. A few northerly tribes, the largest of the gnome species, practice dark enchantments and are much feared by their law-abiding relatives. *See also* Valkonyd gnomes.

Goblins: A family of blue-skinned magical beings famed for their administrative skills. They are loyal, hardworking, and somber. *See also* Elitrion; Lotho; Melchior; Mraka.

Great Prospect: A vast open meadow on the banks of the Veridian River, ringed by whispering aspens on one end and often used as a ceremonial gathering place for the citizens of the immortal world.

Griffin: Possibly the fiercest of all magical creatures, the griffin combines the head and wings of the eagle with the body of a lion and the tail of a snake. Unlike most melded creatures, he embodies the whole nature of the three animals he comprises. Thus he is brave, clever, strong, and elusive.

Guillée, Gilbert: Magical couturier to the royal house of Forever, widely known for his use of unusual materials, such as snowflakes, in his creations.

Gylfyns: Six-armed magical beings, variously hued and ranging in height from four to eight feet. Noted for their coordination. *See also* Thelejima.

Herrikhan: The monstrous warlock whose intention is to rule the universe. Resident of Odyl.

Io and Pialana: Inseparable fairy twins, the sixth and seventh of the Boucane sisters.

Lamellicorns: Distant, rare cousins of the unicorn, these slender, horselike creatures have a hard, golden hide rather than hair. The lamellicorn's horn is nearly transparent.

Lavalier, Gaston: French physician and pioneer in the field of neurology on Earth and physician to the royal family in the Land of the Immortals.

Leneth: A centaur.

Leprechauns: Mischievous pixies of Ireland, known for their green skin and tricky ways.

Lotho: A goblin servant in the Castle of Forever.

Lusus, Juan de: Magician of the court of Ferdinand III, famous for his claim to have found the treasure beneath Carn Gafall. He was found to be a liar in 1652, at which time de Lusus fled to the Netherlands, where he was rumored to live until 1803.

Lysinias: A centaur.

Macsu: A faun.

Makena: A fairy, eldest of the Boucane sisters and mistress of all fairy revels in the Land of the Immortals.

Malibran, Maria: A famous contralto during her mortal life and singing mistress at the Castle of Forever thereafter.

Melchior: A goblin, steward of the Castle of Forever and head of its goblin staff.

Melisande: The most famous mermaid in French history, who married a count and successfully kept her mermish nature a secret for twenty years. When discovered, she was banished from his realm and died of a broken heart.

Merlin: Possibly the greatest wizard who ever lived on Earth, responsible for the education of King Arthur.

Mermaids: Young female merpeople, uniting fish tails and human torsos. Mermaids are the least hostile of all mermish to humans. *See also* Melisande.

Meteor: An amethyst, wall-eyed member of the reindeer cadre of Forever.

Mozart, Wolfgang Amadeus: Austrian composer of the eighteenth century. Composed over six hundred works. Mozart died at the age of thirty-five, impecunious.

Mraka: A goblin employed in toy manufacture and distribution in the Land of the Immortals.

Muses: The nine Muses are the goddesses of the arts.

Mylius, Johann Daniel: Alchemist and author of *Opus medico-chymicum*.

Naiads: Water goddesses dedicated to specific bodies of water.

Nemekele: A fairy, third of the Boucane sisters.

Nicholls, Mrs. Arthur Bell: The married name of Charlotte Brontë, who wrote one of the most successful novels of the nineteenth century, *Jane Eyre*.

Nymphs: A general term for spirits that occupy natural forms. Water nymphs, more elegant cousins of water sprites, live in rivers and oceans; tree nymphs live in large, old trees, especially oaks; and the rarest form of nymph resides within mountains and large standing stones.

Pan: The king of the fauns and satyrs and god of the countryside.

Parian Field: The wide meadow, named for its marble smoothness, where immortal pelote is played.

Parian Pond: A small body of water on the Castle of Forever's grounds, named for the marblelike luster of the water it contains.

Pegasus: A winged horse of pure white, released by Perseus from its imprisonment within Medusa's body, whereupon it flew to Greece and was tended by the Muses.

Persephone: Daughter of Demeter and maiden of the spring. She spends six months each year in the underworld, where she is queen. Her return to Earth marks the arrival of spring.

Phoenix: A great and beautiful flame-colored bird who flies to the magical land of Heliopolis at the end of his five-hundred-year life span. There he is immolated and reborn of his own ashes. As he eats only dew and brings harm to no living thing, the phoenix is said to be free of sin. Some say that there is only one phoenix that is reborn continually; others believe that four separate phoenixes exist.

Pixies: A huge family of Earth-dwelling and immortal creatures who generally exercise their limited magical powers for the benefit of humankind, though they are sometimes tempted to mischief and trickery.

Prometheus: The fabricator of the human race who brought fire to humankind, for which he was punished by the gods.

Reszke, Jean de: Singer famed for his glowing voice and charisma; the leading tenor at the Metropolitan Opera in the 1890s.

Robin Hood: English outlaw and forest dweller. Popular for his generosity to the poor and daring plots against the rich, Robin Hood is the hero of a number of medieval poems and plays.

Roc: A gigantic bird, native of Arabia, who relished elephants during his life on Earth.

Romulus: A faun, expert on the flora of Forever.

Rusalki: Slavic water spirits, said to embody the spirits of young girls who have died. Northern rusalki are a demonic race, while those of the south are benevolent.

Samander: Leader of the Valkonyd gnomes.

Satyrs: Like their cousins the fauns, satyrs are half human, half goat. Satyrs are a bit larger than fauns and are uninterested in diplomacy and devoted to festivities. They are expert charm casters.

Savoy, Duke of: *See* Emmanuel Philibert, Duke of Savoy.

Selting, Mother: A witch noted for protecting those accused of witchcraft and assisting them in eluding the authorities. Finally captured herself, Mother Selting was burned at the stake in 1733 but has since appeared on Earth to offer her services to witches in need.

Sendivogius, Michael: Polish nobleman and liberator of the great alchemist Alexander Seton from the dungeons of Saxony. Also heir to the Red Stone, he died brokenhearted when the philosopher's stone was destroyed by the thief Mullenfels.

Sileni: A species of woodland faun with horse ears and a jovial, fun-loving nature.

Silenux: A faun.

Sofya: Wise and ancient patroness of Russia. Born in Ukraine, Sofya was discovered to have magical powers at an early age. Though her mortal life came to an end in the fifth century, she continued to reside in Russia, offering her protection and wisdom to the Russian people for centuries.

Sphinx: An ancient Earth-dwelling creature of immense power and mystery. She combines the head of a woman with the body of a cat and is known for both the riddles she poses to challengers and for the swift retribution she takes upon those who fail to divine the correct answer.

Square of the Sybils: The large square in the center of the village of Forever. At its east end stands the sapphire Cathedral of the Wise.

Strigigormese: The ancient language of owls, used in modern times primarily for incantations.

Terra Immortalium: "Land of the Immortals" in the Latin language.

Thelejima: A lavender gylfyn.

Thucydides: Athenian general and founder of the discipline of history during his mortal life, which ended in 400 B.C.

Tintoretto: Italian painter, known as *Il Furioso* for his rapid method of working.

Trojan heroes: The leaders and champions who fought on both sides of the Trojan War and reside in the Land of the Immortals in perfect harmony.

Trolls: Earth-dwelling creatures with minor, primarily malevolent magical powers and a propensity for stealing. Only six trolls have attained entrance to the Land of the Immortals.

Tundra: A wolf who serves as Lord High Chamberlain of the King's Household and unofficial guardian of Holly Claus. Old and trusted friend of both Nicholas and Holly Claus.

Unicorns: Magical horned horses, the most innocent of all creatures.

Valkonyd gnomes: A tribe of gnomes renowned for their taciturnity and metalwork. They are reputed to possess the largest store of silver in the world. *See also* Samander.

Verdi, Giuseppe: The most famous Italian composer of the nineteenth century; creator of such operatic masterpieces as *Rigoletto*, *La Traviata*, and *Aida*.

Veridian River: The large river that winds through the Land of the Immortals, named for its brilliant green water.

Vobis: The fastest of the magical horses in the stable of the Castle of Forever.

Warlocks: Extremely powerful wizards. Usually, though not exclusively, practitioners of dark magic.

Water sprites: Water-dwelling creatures of fairy extraction, less august and more playful than naiads, but quick to take offense and prone to punishing trespassers with drenchings.

Will-o'-the-wisps: The smallest of all fairies, virtually invisible to adult humans, who often confuse them with dust motes. Despite their reserved nature, will-o'-the-wisps are fond of babies, who can see and delight in them.

Wizards: Male practitioners of witchcraft.

Zenwyler: A centaur renowned for his strength and speed.

From the Desk of Holly Claus

My story does not end here . . . the magic continues.
I live in the Land of the Immortals, in the City of Forever.
I would love to hear from you, so please send me a letter
at the following address:

       Holly Claus
       The Royal Palace
       The City of Forever
       The Land of the Immortals 90209-1225

                  Yours in Enchantment,

                  Holly Claus™

P. S. Please visit us at: www.hollyclaus.com

McLEAN MERCER
REGIONAL LIBRARY
BOX 505
RIVERDALE, ND 58565

ADDED